Sisters

DeJay

LESBIANFICTIONPRESS

Sisters

ISBN 978-0-9889453-5-7

This Trade Paperback Original Is Published By
Lesbian Fiction Press
PO Box 457
Newfoundland, PA, USA

Credits

Editor: Linda "Proofrdr" Lorenzo
Cover Design: Lilien Hoffman, lilien.hoffman@gmail.com

Acknowledgements

Thank you to Elaine Burnes, and Lily Hoffman for their due diligence and care in beta reading this book. Yes, Lily I will never be as techy as you. And Elaine, your insights make this a much better book. No words can ever express my gratitude. Thank you both for your hard work.

A special thank-you to Lilien Hoffman for creating such an outstanding cover, I'm thrilled with it. You talent knows no bounds and you prove that every day

Thank you to Linda "Proofrdr" Lorenzo the editor on this book. Editing is a tough job, especially when dealing with someone who doesn't get it. I'm trying though. I bet there's a lot more grey hairs after dealing with me.

Lastly many, many people helped me along the way to make this story what it is. If you enjoy the book they should all get the credit; however, if there are any mistakes they are mine and mine alone.

Dedication

To Lee, I love you more every day that passes. Thank you for everything. You've given my life meaning these last 36 years and I look forward to the next 36. *Always and forever.*

Prologue

"JESUS! SLOW THE fuck down, Anna, you're gonna kill us!"

I gripped the armrest as she took the turn onto Montgomery, tires squealing, siren screaming, engine straining to keep up under the pressure of acceleration. The dispatcher had advised there was a 2-7-3 on Hollingsworth, and the officer on site called for immediate backup. I told Sergeant Wolber we were ten blocks out and advised we would respond pronto. Anna gripped the steering wheel with both hands, her focus intent on our destination. She swerved onto Caldwell, followed it for two blocks, then took a hard right onto Waterford.

"Watch out!" Two kids were playing ball on the side of the street. They stopped to watch as we drove past.

Anna sped on by them. "Relax. I got this one . . . you old fart."

"Yeah, yeah."

"You getting soft on me, Lieutenant?"

"No, Delgado, but we're not gonna be any help to anyone if we're dead."

"Chill, we're almost there."

"Just don't friggin' crash into the damned house. That might be regarded as extreme by the jokers in IAB."

As Anna pulled the wheel hard to the left, the car skidded into the final turn.

"There"—I pointed—"middle of the block."

"I see it."

She slowed the vehicle halfway to our destination, and cut off the siren.

"I don't like this," I said. "It's deserted."

She parked behind the black and white while I scanned the area.

"I don't see anyone. I mean no one. That can't be good."

1

"Probably all at soccer practice," Anna quipped.

"Call in, let them know we're on scene."

Anna radioed dispatch, advised the sergeant there was no visual on the patrolman, and that we would report as soon as we knew something.

We left the car and approached the hovel where the disturbance was said to be taking place. The windows were either boarded up or heavy drapes blocked any view inside. The single-family dwelling was run down, the paint peeling, the front porch sagging in places. A screen door hung from one hinge, the glass long ago broken out and the lock non-existent. A chain link fence once stood guardian of the perimeter, but now was mostly in disrepair. Sections of the fence were torn or bent, metal poles leaned precariously or were missing altogether. An attempt had once been made to electrify the metal; those connections now hung loosely, flapping in the breeze.

It was hot, ninety-seven degrees in the sun that shone, thankfully at our backs. I signaled Anna to go wide, while I moved closer toward the front door. Something was off. The hair on the back of my neck told me so, and it's rarely been wrong. No neighbors on the street, no busybodies trying to tell us how to do our job. That was a tell, a big one. As I neared the front path, I unclipped the safety on my gun, loosely gripping the holster. Then I climbed the three steps and called out, "Police, anybody there? Show yourself."

I saw the glint of steel and jerked as the bullets rang out. The first struck an inch above my left knee; my body twisted from the jolt. The second hit the back of my thigh and took me down. The fall rolled me off the steps where I landed with a thud on the walkway. Blood poured from the wounds.

"Maddison!" Anna started toward me.

"Don't!" I hissed. "Stay back."

"Get atta here pig, or I'll kill 'em all." The voice inside the building shattered the otherwise quiet of the street. He demanded we leave his property. Demanded he had rights.

I pulled myself to the edge of the porch for some protection while Anna used her cell phone to direct-connect to the desk sergeant.

"Can we talk about this?" I hollered out.

"Don't test me, you asshole. I'm not kidding, I'll kill 'em."

I believed him. "We just want to know what's going on inside there," I said. "Does anyone need medical assistance?"

"Did you hear me? Get off my property. Now." He fired haphazardly through the door to clarify his intentions.

As soon as Anna finished the call for more support, she eased along the porch, toward the door. I motioned for her to stop. To go around back. She nodded and reversed direction. Crouched low and backing up slowly, she had already passed the double window and was almost at the corner of the porch when the assailant exploded through the entrance, his gun in one hand, a bottle of beer in the other. He grinned as he pointed the automatic weapon at me and pulled the trigger. A bullet caught me in the shoulder, temporarily flattening me to the ground. My vision blurred as my mind dealt with the added pain.

"I'm gonna kill me some pigs today." The man held his gun out, a maniacal look on his face.

Anna stood up, she took aim, holding her firearm with two hands, her target clear. The reciprocating shots rang out simultaneously. The ass-wipe staggered as Anna's bullet impacted his chest. I watched as the crimson stain spread across his dirty T-shirt. He dropped the bottle and fell against the door frame.

A grizzly moan from the opposite direction stunned me. I turned my head to discover that Anna, too, was hit. Her hand clutched her throat as blood oozed between her fingers. She began to fall backward in slow motion, her arms flailing, a resigned look in her eyes. I watched horrified as blood spurted from her neck in an arcing display of red splatter.

"Nooooo." I grasped my gun with my left hand, squinted through my blurred vision, and pulled the trigger. The unsub fell to the wooden floor and rolled off the edge onto my feet.

Everything dimmed after that.

Chapter One

October 18, 2008

BEEP BEEP BEEP. Fiona reached for the annoying alarm and slammed down the button. She rubbed her face with two hands and opened her eyes. The room was dark, but that was to be expected at four in the morning. She hopped in the shower, brushed her teeth, dressed and, twenty minutes later, was sitting in the rental car waiting for it to warm up.

She had picked up the rental at Missoula's International Airport the night before. She got a room at the first hotel she spotted on the interstate and set her alarm for four. With lots of ground to cover and little time left on her leave of absence, she needed to work quickly to find the truth.

She anticipated the trip to Libby taking three or more hours. Especially since she had been warned by the hotel clerk to avoid Route 200 as it was closed for construction in both directions. She had printed out the new directions and set them on the passenger seat.

While getting gas a mile up the road, her phone beeped. There was a message from Addison's publishing house. She immediately tried retrieving the message. Her bars were down to one; the call failed. Twice. She tossed the phone onto the dashboard in frustration.

The long drive was monotonous for the most part. Though the landscape was beautiful, Fiona was unable to truly appreciate it. She kept worrying. She needed to get answers regarding her sister, Kari, and discover what happened to her. Most importantly she needed to give their aging mother closure.

EVER SINCE KARILEAH left their small-town life, hopeful of stardom in Hollywood, she had been diligent about writing home. It started with long, hand-written letters. Once she was settled and had familiarized herself with the library, she'd throw in an e-mail. If she was feeling flush, she'd phone home and gossip with her mother for hours. No matter her circumstances, she *always* kept in touch.

Like many others before her who tried to become stars, Kari worked full time at various menial jobs to support herself while going on auditions. Two years ago she was hired by Procare full time and had soon become their senior therapist. Then she got the gig working for L. M. Addison, crime novelist. Shortly after that, the bit parts started coming—a waitress on a crime show, a meter maid on the Monday night comedy. Soon she was popping up regularly on a variety of shows. Their mother devotedly taped every one of them to view over and over again. Kari eventually was signed

4

for a new crime show, a thirteen-week drama. If the ratings were good, they'd be re-signed. Everything was going her way.

Abruptly, it became evident something was wrong. Mom wrote and asked questions; Kari just ignored her. There was no more talk of auditions, casting calls, or anything to do with Hollywood. *When* she wrote, which wasn't often, it was about trips she and author Addison had taken, places they went, sights they saw. The last year or so, her correspondence became even less frequent. Exciting adventures no longer filled the pages. Instead, mundane items took their place, fewer each time and with longer spans between each letter.

What happened, Kari? Fiona blew out a breath in frustration. She checked the gas gauge and pulled into the next station to fill up. According to the map she was outside Kalispell. Only another hour or so to go. Then the real work would begin—finding Addison. Holding out any hope that Kari was with him was foolish and Fiona knew it. She checked her phone; she still had no bars. After paying for the gas, she stopped at the soda machine out front and bought a cola, then climbed in the car and headed out.

Two months after Kari's last letter, Addison's newest book had hit the stands. Fiona raced out to get a copy, hoping to see Kari's name on the acknowledgement page. That would have meant all was well. Over the years, Addison had thanked Kari for her assistance. "What a great friend." "The best beta reader ever." "An insightful ingénue." "Without Kari's help, the books would not have been as well received."

Fiona paid the cashier then went to sit in her car. She prayed there'd be some indication of Kari's well-being. She opened to the dedication page. It began, "In loving memory." Her vision blurred as she repeated the words. A small sob escaped her. Tears filled her eyes, and she swiped them away to read it again. "In loving memory of and dedicated to my wife and best friend." Tear drops dampened the page as Fiona sobbed. A cold grip of terror engulfed her. She read and reread the page, but still the words never changed.

TWO AND A half hours later, Fiona was stiff, angry, verging on exhaustion and nearly frozen. She banged on the dashboard with her hand, trying to get the heater to emit something other than the sickly whining noise it had been making for the last hour. The car's heater evidently was no match for the bitter cold of Montana. She should have stipulated a car with heat.

Another miscalculation. Fiona hadn't thought about her wardrobe. It would have been fine if she had found Kari in Los Angeles as expected. Having packed light sweaters, T-shirts, jeans, and sneakers for the trip, she

5

was not prepared for this bone-chilling cold. According to the radio, there was an arctic blast invading the Northwest for the third day in a row. She believed it.

The engine coughed and sputtered. It had been doing that for the last mile or so, causing her to question its roadworthiness. The rental agent had assured her it was the best vehicle they offered. Fiona very much doubted the validity of that statement. Factored in with the engine's misfiring was the red line on the gas gauge. The fuel light came on shortly after she negotiated the last turn. It was supposed to be less than five miles to her destination. "Dammit."

No town in site and no homes to speak of. She was headed for the ass-end of nowhere. To top off her anxiety, there were angry dark skies in every direction promising a storm forthwith. She hadn't seen anything resembling civilization for the last twenty or so miles. Pushing her bangs out of her eyes, Fiona scrubbed her hand over her face. "What the hell am I going to do now?"

She frowned and shook her head. *Come on, you can do this. Concentrate.* She needed to stop letting her mind wander and start figuring out where she was and how to find a gas station. She glanced at the map lying in the passenger seat. She had turned onto Mountain Road 37, per the instructions. At the fork in the road she bore right, just as the map indicated. That was an hour ago. Other than an old church back a ways, nothing else appeared on the horizon. She picked up the map and studied it. She was tired, her eyes blurry and, right now, it just looked like a lot of green mountains with sparse squiggly lines indicating roads or highways. After the last turn off, she was supposed to have been within a few miles of Libby, a town of twelve hundred people. There was no town. No homes. Nothing. She needed to figure out where she had gone wrong and how to get back.

Turning her attention back to the roadway, she screamed as a family of deer darted across in front of the car. "Oh shit!" She yanked the wheel and swerved off the side of the road.

The drop-off was steep. The vehicle flipped on its side and slid into a downed tree at the bottom of the ten foot chasm.

Oh . . . Kari, I'm so sorry.

Sisters

Chapter Two

IN AN ATTEMPT to get the kinks out of my aching back, I tossed the three pieces of wood onto the growing woodpile, then straightened, raised my hands over my head and twisted from side to side. The day was gray, damp, and blustery. A normal late autumn offering here in the mountains. Worse, I suspected it was but an omen of things to come. Off to the west was a darkening sky. An early storm had been predicted; I feared it might already be moving in. I knew once it did, it would be just the beginning of upwards of three-hundred-inches of snow. Very likely, Mother Nature would not release her grip on the area until late spring or early summer, depending on her mood. In my present state of mind that fit perfectly with my plans of seclusion and time needed to work. The last thing I needed was phony sympathetic visitors with nosy, insensitive questions or interruptions to our daily schedule. The healing process was a long, tedious progression of baby steps that was being made more difficult by Anastasia's constant questions of why. How to explain death to a four-year old was proving to be beyond the realm of my capabilities.

I turned my attention back to the wood still waiting to be stacked. I'd been splitting and stacking it for the past seven hours, anything to avoid staring at the blank screen of my laptop.

"Hellooo."

I jerked at the sound and spun around, but nothing and no one came into view. Chance, my German Shepherd, lounged in the brown hibernating grass, napping. A sure sign I was imagining things. I shook my head and returned to the task at hand. Up until last night, when Sophia came to fetch Anastasia for a weekend visit, the three of us had been holed up alone for two weeks. With the prospects of a long hard winter ahead of us, the last thing I needed was to start hearing voices this early in the season. Assuredly, it wouldn't be the voice I wanted to hear, or that Anya *needed* to hear. I shook my head in disgust and gripped two pieces of wood and added them to the pile.

"Hellooo. Is anybody there?" A slight pause. "Can you help me?"

This time Chance jumped to her feet and took off down the path barking like a banshee. I caught up with her after a difficult trip to the end of the driveway, some fifteen hundred feet down a steep, twisted incline. The person behind the plea for help sat on a tree stump that had been fashioned earlier this year, the result of a late spring storm. The mighty lodgepole pine had toppled during the snow-driven, gale-force winds and blocked the driveway for weeks. Its demise provided the wood I was currently splitting and stacking. The impediment of having the driveway

7

blocked and being trapped hadn't mattered. Anastasia, Chance, and I weren't going anywhere, and outsiders rarely ventured here. Clearly that was about to change. *Dang.*

The stranger was in her thirties at my guess, attractive in her own way. Height was impossible to calculate from her current position, but it looked like she was of medium build. It also appeared she had taken a fall. There were dead leaves on her clothes, scratches on her face, twigs in her hair and dirt on her hands. Upon closer scrutiny, I discovered a make-shift splint and bloody rags that held it together on her lower right leg.

"Where the heck did you come from?" *I was more than wary. At this point in our daily life, we didn't need interruptions. And definitely not outsiders! I had to protect Anya.* She brushed her wild raven-black hair back behind her ear with one hand and with the other continued to pet my ferocious attack dog currently sitting at her feet.

"My rental car skidded off the road and ended up in a ditch maybe a mile further up that way. It happened when I swerved to avoid a family of deer."

The more I observed, the clearer it was she was attractive by most people's standards. Once she was cleaned up, she'd likely verge on beautiful. The sultry speech was what did it for me. The gravelly voice added a sex appeal that had no business in my immediate realm. *Crap.* I watched as she hooked her thumb towards the left. That road is a private one used only by the park rangers and me. She had no business being on it.

"Are you the caretaker?" she asked.

"Huh?" I couldn't shake the feeling I knew her. I felt uneasy.

"The caretaker . . . for the church?"

I shook my head. "No."

"Well you sure don't look like any minister I've ever known."

"What exactly does a minister look like?" I crossed my arms over my chest and glared at her. This woman was going to be trouble, I could feel it in my gut and my gut has never failed me.

"Sorry"—she quickly continued—"I slipped climbing out of the car and that's how this happened." She indicated her ankle. "I remembered passing the church, so I came back. May I use your phone? I can't get reception on my cell."

I stared at her—feeling numb inside, dreading the inevitable. That voice could melt an iceberg. But it wasn't going to melt me.

Meanwhile my traitorous pet lapped up the attention from this stranger and returned it tenfold. "I don't . . .I . . .don't have a landline."

"Do you have a cell that I can use?" She gestured with her dead phone in her hand.

"Cells don't work out here; only a satellite phone will."

"Then do you have a satellite phone, please!" Her voice dropped an octave.

8

"Yup."

She smiled and it transformed her entire face. "Great. I'll pay for the call or reverse the charges if you like."

I looked up at the cloud-covered sky to the west, then back to her. "You won't get reception . . . not today anymore."

"I see." She grasped the sturdy tree branch at her side and pulled herself upright with it. "Can you tell me where I might find a phone that will accommodate my needs?"

I sighed. *City folk.* "Not for about twenty miles back down that road, then another fifteen or so on the highway south, and not tonight, that's for sure." I shoved my hands in my pockets and hunkered down into my heavy fleece. The perspiration of my labors now chilled my skin.

"Storm's coming in. We're gonna get snow"—I looked back at the swirling skies—"a lot would be my guess." I rubbed my thigh where it ached, always a good indicator of foul weather.

She followed my gaze, and I noticed her shiver as well. Her leather coat and gloves might be all the fashion, but they did little to keep the bitter north winds from penetrating the skin beneath.

I turned and started up the drive, calling for Chance. "Come on, lil' doggie."

"And what am I supposed to do?"

I stopped after a moment and turned back to the pushy woman. "You're on a private road and trespassing. You had to have seen the signs. They're posted every mile." I pulled my thumb up to my chest. "I know, because I posted them. So you passed twenty of them to get to this point. I suggest you head back where you came from." She was not my problem and I didn't need her to be.

"Are you crazy?" She leaned on her makeshift crutch with her hand on her hip. "How am I supposed to do that? You've already stated the obvious—it's getting late. As you can see, I'm injured, and now you tell me it's going to snow. You can't leave me out in the elements like this. I'll die!"

Her gravelly voice suited her. *Fuck! Double fuck! And crap. That's two dollars now and I was doing so good.* I motioned to her. "Fine, come on, then." I took another step.

"Waitaminute. Could you . . . would it be possible?" She held her hand out. "Do you think you could help me up the path? I'm sorry, but I have a badly sprained ankle. I barely made it this far and that was level ground."

I stared at her testily, then stomped down to where she stood leaning on the broken tree limb. The dog had followed me and was once again enjoying the stranger's attentions.

The woman's ankle *was* swollen, even I could see that. Thin strips of material secured three pieces of wood that she'd formed into a splint. It appeared to be tied much too tight which was adding to the edema. *This*

9

was gonna be fun. Not! An old injury limited my own mobility and left me few options.

"Okay." Taking a deep breath, I put her arm around my neck and held it in place with my left hand. Then I secured her waist with my right arm, taking her weight on my good leg. "Come on Chance, time for dinner."

The dog ran ahead of us while I tried to brace the woman without having to actually touch her more than was necessary.

"I didn't mean you had to carry me. I just need some support." Her words were said through gritted teeth.

"I'm not carrying you. Do I look like I'm carrying you?"

"I think I can put some weight on the leg. It would be less stressful for you."

I paused and loosened my hold to let her try. Her grimace was all the evidence I needed.

"Now we'll do this my way." I pulled her against me and began again. A shudder ran up my spine. Priss had been the nice one, the person people sought when in trouble. I didn't have those skills and, honestly, I was glad.

"I'm sorry."

"It's fine." We moved slowly, one foot in front of the other. The incline, difficult on a normal day, was made more so by the woman's injury. I started making a mental list of what needed to be done and in what order.

"I hate to be such a bother to you, I—"

"Yup." I just kept walking, concentrating on the ground below me, struggling to get her to the house and not strain my own damaged and weakened leg. Priss would say make a plan. List the things you need to do to reach your goal. My brain felt numb. The only goal I had was getting Anya and myself through our grief. This woman was an intrusion. A much unwanted one. Any discussion on my part was out of the question as I struggled with my burden and the slope of the driveway up to the house. Sweat began to form on my upper lip and the base of my neck. The list, think about the list. The fire would need stoking. Chance needed to be fed. This woman needed medical care. Hopefully it would be within my limited knowledge. Then dinner. I'd have to feed her. Anya? She wouldn't be back till tomorrow, with luck—"

Snow begun to fall, and the ground was quickly getting slick beneath our feet. *Crap.* After an indeterminate amount of time, I slowly and carefully climbed the steps to the entrance, using my arms to pull myself and the injured woman up the stairs to the landing.

"Get the door." My words spilled out through ragged breath, my leg was throbbing, and I was sweating.

She reached out, turned the knob, and gave the door a shove all in the same movement. We staggered in and I deposited her none too gently on the couch. After a siege of gasping for air, I was able to breathe normally again.

She sat quietly as she caught her own breath. I watched her take in her surroundings. "You live in a church?"

"Clearly it's not a church any longer."

"This is incredible."

"Yup." I looked around a moment, trying to see what she saw. All I saw was who was missing.

"Look, the fire needs tending, I'll feed Chance, then we'll see about your leg. Once we get your injuries squared away, I'll fix some dinner. Sound all right?"

"Yes, whatever you need to do."

Okay so far, so good, I was communicating and she seemed to understand.

"Thank you, I'm really sorry to intrude on you." She was getting kisses from Chance, who had jumped up on the couch beside her.

"Uh-huh."

I bent within the eight-foot-high, six-foot-wide river rock fireplace and poked the glowing embers, then laid three logs onto the grate.

"Chance, get down. Leave her alone." The dog ignored me.

"I can't believe the size of that fireplace, I didn't even see a chimney on the outside."

A small smile tweaked my lips. "I hid it within the steeple."

Her eyes followed the rock formation up through the roof. "Amazing."

"Chance!"

"It's okay. Really. She's a sweetie. Aren't you, baby? Yes, you are. Yes, you are." After divesting herself of her coat and gloves, she scratched Chance's back with two hands and returned her enthusiastic kisses.

Within seconds flames licked up the sides of the dry wood and warmth quickly began to fill the room. I turned back to the woman. She was watching me closely.

"Here." I handed her the afghan from the side chair. "That'll help warm you up till the fire does its job." Her coat and gloves lay at her side; I took them and hung her cloak and mine on the rack by the front door and stuck the gloves in her pocket.

"Chance, dinner."

The dog jumped down and followed me as I limped into the open kitchen. She danced at my feet while I prepared her meal, then jumped as I lowered her dish. She was always eager to eat after a hard day of lolling in the grass while I tended our chores. I emptied her water bowl, refilled it with fresh, and put that down beside her.

At the sink, I washed my hands thoroughly with the antiseptic soap. It was time. I had procrastinated long enough. I needed to help the woman and get her settled for the night. I hobbled toward the couch, "Do you think the ankle is broken?" The woman had torn the leg of her pants up the seam past her knee and was attempting to untie the knots of her splint.

11

"No"—she looked up—"it's just a very bad sprain. My foot slipped and my ankle rolled over on a rock. I shouldn't have walked on it, but I had no choice. The real issue is the gash here." She pointed to where a bloody rag covered her calf. "A piece of metal from the car ripped my skin. It tore down almost to the dermis which is why there's so much blood. I need to clean it and stitch it closed, then hope it doesn't get infected." Perspiration glistened on her brow as she spoke.

"Tetanus shot should help with that." I hobbled toward the bathroom to gather the necessary supplies.

"Yes, it would. I don't suppose you have any lying around here?" She called after me.

"You thought wrong." I continued through the doorway and started pulling the cabinets open, collecting gauze, tape, a partial bottle of Betadine, a bottle of antibacterial cleanser, surgical gloves, and my trusty needle and thread. I knew I needed to attend her medical issues quickly, then the woman would heal and hopefully go away.

Back in the nave, I placed the articles on the coffee table and sat on the edge of the ottoman to look at the woman's injury. She had removed the splint and dirty rags which she now used as a compress on the wound. "It's pretty swollen."

She looked up. "It's like I said, I shouldn't have walked on it."

"Here." I handed her some hand sanitizer and a clean hand towel, then used the liquid soap myself. Unfortunately, I knew all about the dangers of infections and what could happen.

"Thank you."

Next I picked up the cotton balls and the bottle of antiseptic. "You better let me, it's at an awkward angle for you."

She grimaced. "True, but I'm a doctor." She twisted her upper body and attempted to adjust her leg to get a better grip on the injury as she spoke.

"Ahh trumped me." I looked on with interest. "Here."

She took the cleanser and dabbed some on the cotton ball. "I wasn't trying to outmaneuver you. I just thought I should mention it."

"That's fine."

"Fiona."

I stared at her blankly, not understanding.

"My name—it's Fiona." She talked as she worked. The wound was deep and I was right, she could barely reach it. However much she turned or twisted her body, it was just out of her reach.

"Well, Doc, I'm thinking you're not doing a very good job there. Better let me handle it. You can supervise, if you like."

She nodded and handed the bottle back to me. I pulled a clean cotton ball from the pile and doused it with the antiseptic, then poured a little directly into the wound. To her credit, she merely hissed.

"We're making a mess of your couch."

"It's leather. It'll clean."

Once we were both satisfied the deep laceration was sterile, it was time to close it. "You have a preference on thread?"

"I'm afraid to ask."

She looked stressed and it appeared the pain was getting to her. Her skin was cold and damp at the same time.

"I usually use nylon fishing line. It's strong, doesn't break easily, and it saves me having to sew things twice."

"It's unused, right?"

I chuckled softly. "Spanking new."

She leaned back, as a sheen of sweat appeared on her forehead. "That's fine, then."

"Before you pass out, here." I handed her a thirty gauge syringe and the vial of tetanus vaccine. "Give yourself a shot. It's better for you if I don't guess at the dosage."

She took the tiny bottle and read the label. "This is antitoxin for a dog."

"Yup."

"You want me to use this on myself?"

"We both know the medicine is the same. It's the dosage that changes between humans and animals."

She read the label a second time. I could see the hesitation in her eyes.

"Your call, Doc."

"You wouldn't have any pain killers hidden around here would you?" She started to unbutton her blouse and slip it off her shoulders.

"Yo, whoa." I quickly turned my back.

"I get the distinct impression you've seen a woman's body before. I certainly don't have anything unique"—she snickered— "besides I have something on underneath."

Even as she giggled, I could feel the blood rushing to my face and ears. "About the pain killers . . . I don't . . . sorry." I turned back in time to watch her puncture the vial with the needle, then draw the liquid into the syringe. "I've got Advil, Tylenol, or nighttime Bayer. Your choice. And some whiskey or brandy."

"I'll take the Tylenol and some water— Please." She swiped a spot on her upper arm with the antiseptic, then jabbed the needle in and pushed the plunger till the hypodermic was empty. The needle dangled from her grip as she leaned back against the couch.

I recovered the needle and syringe. "I'll get those pills and drink for you." In the kitchen, I reached for a glass then searched the back of the cabinet for the brandy and poured till the juice glass was half filled. The pills were on the counter, handy for my own use. "Here, you're gonna need it when I start to sew you up." I handed her the brandy and pill bottle.

"I can't drink that. Just water, please."

"Look Doc, it's likely going to hurt like hell. The brandy might dull the pain."

She vehemently shook her head. "I can't."

I shrugged. "Suit yourself."

"Have you . . . ahh . . . ever . . . closed an open wound?" Her apprehension was obvious.

"Well, the alternative is a sure fire way to get an infection, so you're about to find out." I nodded toward the glass of water I had retrieved. "Drink up, Doc." Minutes later, with the needle threaded and a few deep breaths, I peeked at the patient. "Ready?"

"As I'll ever be." Her voice trembled.

I sat on the edge of the ottoman and cleaned the area one more time, then dipped the needle into the antiseptic before sticking it into the skin. Gritting my teeth, I pinched the two sides of the wound and pushed the needle in. The nylon thread trailed the needle through, around and down, again and again until the wound was closed and the seeping blood had stopped. I released the breath I had been holding, grateful it seemed to have gone well. The unsightly gash took seventeen sutures in all. I sterilized it one more time then placed a bandage over my handiwork. The lady doctor appeared unconscious by the time I was done. I gently lifted her eyelid to check her pupils.

"I'm fine. Just resting."

"I need to clean the scratches on your face and hands."

"I can do it."

"Relax, Doc, I haven't killed you yet." I poured antiseptic on a clean cotton ball and gently applied it to her cheek, forehead and chin. The scratches were minor, but I still felt they should be tended to. If there was one thing I had learned, it was to be thorough when it came to germs.

"Did you hit your mouth in the accident?"

Fiona opened her eyes. "No. Why?"

"Your lip looks swollen."

She touched her hand to her mouth then shook her head. "You mean my bottom lip?"

"Yeah, pretty much."

"No, it's always been full. Mom used to think I had been in a tussle."

"Did you do that, fight a lot?" She didn't seem the type somehow.

"No. Well, once, actually."

I nodded. "So you think it's okay?"

"Without a mirror, yeah. I don't have any pain and there's no cut, right?"

"No, they're perfect . . . I mean . . . I'm just saying—" Staring down at her mouth, I wondered what it would be like to kiss such perfect lips. I shook my head to block the thought. Trouble, I knew it.

"Relax, I'm teasing you."

14

I finished examining her face, then moved to her hands. One wrist had a small mark, but the skin had not been broken. "All done, Ma'am." I leaned over to gather my debris.

"Thank you."

"Yup." I tried to avert my eyes; it was no good and I couldn't figure out why. "Look, I've got an aircast walker if you think it will help with the ankle."

"Quite the little medical supply house, aren't you?" She opened one eye to gaze at me.

"We live alone. One's gotta be prepared." I shrugged. "Need to be able handle things. Chance, there, isn't much in the help department. Know what I mean?"

"Do you have ice? I should try to reduce the swelling some. I appreciate the offer though and my foot will welcome any and all support."

I walked back to the bathroom with my supplies, then found the aircast on the shelf of the linen closet. "Here you go. I'll get the ice for ya."

In the kitchen, I filled a gallon-size Baggie with ice, then wrapped it in a kitchen towel. "Here ya are."

I elevated her leg on a throw pillow, put the brace on the floor and settled the ice pack in its place. Fiona lay back watching.

"Rest. I'll wake you when dinner's ready."

She adjusted a throw pillow under her head and closed her eyes. "Can I ask you something?"

"If you feel the need." I braced for the unknown.

"Have you ever had to sew someone up before?"

"Yup."

"I thought so. It explains the well-placed sutures. I doubt the scar will even show after a while. You might have missed your true calling."

After throwing the broken pieces of wood into the fire and rolling up the bloody rags, I bent to gather the remaining garbage,

"What's your name?" she asked.

A frown formed before I could stop it. It was inevitable. People expect conversation. It was moments like this when I felt Priss's absence the most. "Maddison."

"Way too formal. What do people call you?"

"Maddison."

She sighed. "For now it's Maddison. I'll come up with something better, I'm sure. After all, I don't let just anyone perform medical procedures on me." She petted Chance on the head. "Thank you. For everything."

A talker too. Of course she is. "Rest." I laid the afghan over her and took the empty water glass from the table. Lastly, I motioned for Chance to stay. The dog would alert me if need be.

Chapter Three

FIONA CAME ALERT as the aromas of food filled her senses. She opened her eyes, turned her head, looked down and smiled. Chance's head rested next to her hand on the couch, the dog's breath wafting ever so lightly over her fingers. Her willing companion patiently lay on the floor beside her. She took a moment to look around the spacious room and at the intricate cedar ceiling. What was once a church had been transformed with extraordinary results into a cozy home. When in truth, the room was probably small by today's standards, the open post-and-beam structure provided a spacious concept making it feel larger than it actually was. The fireplace undoubtedly was meant to be the focal point as it ran from floor to ceiling and beyond through the bell tower. The hearth easily took up one-third of the entire west wall. Clearly it generated the main heat for the building, though Fiona did note air ducts on the floor at various junctures, so another source was available. There were four doors leading to who knew where, two on each side of the centered staircase that led to the loft area. Baby gates blocked the steps and two of the doorways. The east wall was made up of full-length, stained-glass windows, their pale mosaic colors illuminated by the flickering fire. The kitchen was off to her left completing the west wall, that's where Maddison currently stood cooking. Soup, or stew if Fiona's nose was working, and fresh-baked bread. The smell reminded her how hungry she was and that she hadn't eaten since early morning when she set off on this part of her journey. Suddenly the fears rose up as she remembered what brought her here.

A SECOND MONTH had passed without word from Kari. Fiona had had enough. The not knowing was affecting her job performance and her health. Worst, she could see the effect it was having on their elderly mother. Fiona put in for, and was granted, a personal leave of absence. She made reservations for a flight to Los Angeles. Departure would be early the following morning. During the flight she jotted down questions and noted facts she knew to be true. As soon as she was settled at the hotel she would begin her search for answers.

Impatient as ever, Fiona had driven the rental car directly to Kari's last known address instead of checking-in at the hotel first. The house stood empty. A weathered sold sign stood sentry on the front lawn. How did the investigator fucking miss this? The grass was unkempt, newspapers lay strewn across the sidewalk. She stopped and queried neighbors, but none could tell her anything substantive. Fiona drove back to the hotel to check in with her mom and regroup.

She recalled a reference in Addison's second book. It was a thank you to an officer at the West Los Angeles precinct downtown. She phoned home and had her mother read the sergeant's name, and provide the spelling. She jotted it down, Juan Delgado. A call to the precinct confirmed he was an actual person. The operator advised her, "Yes, Sergeant Delgado worked here in 1999 through 2003." Fiona asked where she might find him and was transferred to an information desk. Captain John Carter's secretary, Sharon, listened politely to Fiona's tale of woe and promised to get back to her. An hour later the call came. "I'm sorry, ma'am, Officer Delgado committed suicide in December of 2003."

FIONA SHOOK HER head, willing those disturbing thoughts away, at least for now. She continued her examination of the room. She felt sure that in daylight the windows surrounding the massive French doors at the entry would afford a gorgeous view of the valley below and the mountain range off to the west. In the dark all Fiona could see was the snow piling up on the landing, ominously reflected by a single outside light fixture next to the door. She could hear sleet at times pinging against the thermal glass panes. Another delay. Another obstacle. When was her luck going to change?

Kari, what the hell happened? Why didn't you tell us you were in trouble? Why am I even looking?

Fiona looked fleetingly at the solemn woman preparing a tray. Her gaydar was tolling hard with regards to the gruff, mannish specimen before her. A lady lumberjack if there ever was one. Even without the stereotypical flannel shirt and work boots, her host could only be described as a dyke. Fiona preferred women with soft feminine qualities. A lady who oozed female pheromones and liked to flaunt them. Someone who enjoyed getting dressed up, wearing make-up, jewelry and heels. Someone to take in a concert with, a Broadway show, or go dancing with, or even visit a museum with. Someone who knew how to treat a partner. An equal who would share the household duties. A person who could commit. This stranger had history. Commitment didn't appear to be in her vocabulary. There was something about her, a damaged facet, or maybe *distressed* described it better, that Fiona found curious. She attempted to sit up and laughed out loud as the dog immediately jumped up on the couch next to her.

"Chance, leave her be."

The dog turned sad eyes toward her owner, but jumped down all the same.

"I don't mind really. She's beautiful."

"Dinner's almost ready."

"It smells wonderful. Would I be able to clean up a bit first?"

17

Maddison turned around and appeared to study her, then nodded once. "There's a set of crutches next to you, bathroom's on the right of the stairs behind you. The one with the baby gate." She indicated the door approximately ten feet away from the couch. "Can you make it by yourself?"

"I can't believe you have crutches too?"

"They're mine." Maddison pivoted back to the counter. "Old injury."

Fiona noted the tension in her host's shoulders and regretted her comment. "I won't be long." She gripped the crutches and realized they were already adjusted for her height. Maddison was clearly three or four inches taller than her own five-feet-four-inch stature. She took a tentative step, then another. They fit well and she needn't put any pressure on her injured ankle. She thumped across the room and entered the bathroom. The building was deceiving, the bathroom immense. There was a separate shower stall that sported ten jets with a programmable faucet which would deliver hot water to all of a person's aching parts. *Oh my god.* Fiona was almost giddy at the thought of a steaming hot shower. An enormous spa soaking tub with multiple jets sat directly ahead of her. She stepped back out of the bathroom. "Is there time for me to take a shower?"

Maddison turned around to look at her. "If you like, I'll get some warmer clothes for you."

"Do you have any plastic wrap I could cover my leg with?"

Maddison turned to the cabinet and pulled out a roll. "Ya want tape for it?"

"No thanks. The wrap will work fine."

"I'll get those clothes and some towels."

"That would be wonderful, thank you." Fiona turned and entered the bathroom again. She sat on the throne and struggled out of her slacks and panties. She was unbuttoning her blouse when there was a knock at the door. "Yes."

The door opened and an arm emerged. "I have the clothes and a stool you can use in the shower if you want."

"Could you bring them in, I can't hold the crutches and collect them too."

Fiona watched as the hand retreated. A minute, maybe two passed before the door opened further and Maddison stepped in backwards. She put the stool in the shower, placed the clean clothes on the edge of the sink, and draped two towels over the electric warming rack, then flipped the switch to turn it on. She kept her head down, her eyes averted the entire time. And she left without a word.

What a strange woman you are. Fiona shook her head, continued disrobing and slipped onto the stool. She dropped the crutches at her feet, removed the air brace and stared at the blood-free bandage. Pleased, she picked up the plastic wrap and covered the entire length of her calf. Once complete, Fiona dangled her injured leg outside the stall where she had pushed the crutches and brace. She turned the temperature dial on the faucet, immediately hot water blasted out of the varying spigots. She added more hot and quickly began to feel better. The soap was a utilitarian brown variety. Her mother often used it on stubborn stains and after working in her yard pulling weeds. Nonetheless it felt wonderful to be washing away the grit and grime of the road. She looked for shampoo, didn't find any and elected to use the same soap on her hair.

Once out of the shower, she pulled the towel from the rack and wrapped the luxuriously warm cloth around herself. She hugged it close, enjoying the heat on her skin. She opened the first drawer on the side of the sink cabinet, found a hairbrush, and used it to brush the knots out of her locks. Her mouth tasted like week-old socks. She continued her search. The middle drawer contained a stockpile of rubber toys for the tub. Fiona opted not to dwell on them or why they were there. In the bottom drawer she discovered a couple of toothbrushes still in the wrapping. Voilà. Ten minutes later she clomped out of the bathroom and across the space. "Thank you. I feel almost human again."

Maddison turned to watch her approach.

"I hope you don't mind. I helped myself to one of the extra toothbrushes."

Maddison could only stare. The sweats she had provided were clearly two sizes too big and yet they showed all the Doc's curves and assets. Fiona had folded up the cuffs of the sleeves and tucked one pant leg into a sock. The aircast worked to secure the other leg.

"Did I take too long?" Fiona watched as Maddison stood mutely staring at her.

Maddison gulped audibly. "No . . . No, ahhh, not at all. You up to eating at the table or would you prefer the couch?"

"The table's fine, thank you."

Maddison held the chair as Fiona sat down, She wanted to make sure not to bang Fiona's limb on the legs of the table.

"Thank you."

"Better put your leg up on this." Maddison placed the foot stool under the table and helped Fiona raise her foot.

"Thank you again."

"Uh-huh." She served the black bean, onion, and garlic soup in large bowls with shredded cheese melted on top. A platter of hot sliced bread sat between them with butter in a separate bowl.

"You're a police officer?"

"Huh?"

"The kiss a cop sweatshirt—I'm guessing it's you." Fiona ran her hand over the faded worn imprint on her chest.

"Not anymore." Maddison took a piece of bread and dipped it in the soup, then took a bite.

Fiona tasted the broth then slathered butter on a piece of the bread. "Everything looks delicious." She took a bite of the bread and hummed in gratification. "Oh my god, this is amazing."

Maddison ignored the complement and kept eating. They consumed the rest of the meal in silence, each emptying their bowls and finishing nearly all the bread. She took the dirty dishes to the sink and started cleaning up.

Fiona reached for one more slice of bread, tore a piece off ready to feed it to Chance, then stopped. "Can the baby have a little of the bread?"

Maddison turned to see the piece already in Fiona's hand and the dog sitting in front of her, her tail sweeping back and forth across the floor, her tongue lolling in eager anticipation. "Yup."

Fiona dropped the bread for Chance then hobbled over to the counter. "I can dry if you like?"

"You better rest that ankle, it's still pretty swollen." She didn't bother to turn around.

Glancing down, Fiona had to agree. She moved back to the couch and lifted her leg onto the pillow. She picked up the almost melted ice pack and rested it on her ankle. "How long do you think the snow will last?"

Maddison looked out the window. "Likely a blizzard, could last until late tomorrow, or longer."

Fiona groaned loudly.

TWENTY MINUTES LATER, after I had cleaned up the kitchen and put the leftovers away. I brought Doc more aspirin, a cup of hot chocolate and a new ice pack. "Time for more pain meds and some fresh ice."

"Thank you. I'm sorry to be such a bother."

If that were true you wouldn't have trespassed lady. I took a deep breath, counted to ten. "So how did you end up on a private road?"

"I must have taken a wrong turn." Fiona said.

"Clearly. And you didn't notice the twenty no trespassing signs either."

"I'm happy to pay you for the supplies and my meals."

"Don't want your money, I just need you gone." I ran my hands through my hair frustrated.

"Do you *not* have any social skills at all, or do you get off on being a friggin' bully?"

I walked to the window and stared out into the stormy night. The yard stick on the stair post was already showing the snow as six inches deep. It would probably reach two feet before it was over. That meant two days to clear the driveway and road out to the highway. Another day to pull the car out of the ditch and get it running, that is, if I could. Three more days of this enchanting stranger in the house with me. Three days of questions and forced conversation. Three days of my body reminding me I'm all alone and fucking lonely. I shook my head in disgust.

"Apparently not, Doc. Sorry." I moved to the counter and opened my laptop then clicked on my work in progress, typed in that password and opened the manuscript for 'Vigilante'.

"What are you doing?"

"I've got work to do."

"Do you have Wi-Fi?"

"Yup." I started to re-read the last chapter.

"May I send a quick message to my family? I need to let them know where I am and give them a status update." Fiona leaned forward.

"Nope."

"Nope?"

I watched out of the corner of my eye as she carefully swung her legs down and pulled herself up onto the crutches.

"Could you possibly say more than yup or nope?" She approached slowly. "I'll pay you for the damned air-time, but I need to let my family know I'm okay."

I faced my uninvited houseguest. "I said nope, because the Wi-Fi is down. It's sketchy at best, but during storms it's non-existent." I turned back to my computer.

"What are you doing then?"

"I told you. Working."

"On what?"

"On none of your damned business." I dropped my head to my chest. Priss would be so angry at me about now.

"I'm only asking because my family will worry if they don't hear from me. I need to let them know I'm okay."

"You should have discussed this trip with your husband *before* you came west. Maybe he could have talked some sense into you. The Wi-Fi is not working and won't be until the weather clears, and I told you the satellite phone won't work during the storm."

"I don't have a husband."

"*Whoever.* I don't give a hoot."

"How can you stand living like this?"

I turned around, the strain of the last five months bubbling to the edge. "How I live is no concern of yours. You concentrate on getting better so you can get the hell out of my house and off my property."

"You pious son-of-a-bitch. I'm sorry, okay. Sorry, I trespassed on your precious property, sorry I got lost. It happens. Get over it. Apparently I took a wrong turn. I'm sure I'm not the first one to do that and I doubt I'll be the last. I'm trying to find my damned sister."

"Why? She get lost too?" I kept my eyes on the computer screen.

"Oh—you—" Fiona sputtered, words presumably failing her. She thumped back to the couch. She pulled the blanket off the back and threw it over herself and turned her head away from me. "I'm going to sleep."

"Good." I mumbled the word, thankful to be getting some peace and quiet back. I had work to do and didn't need the annoying woman interrupting me every five minutes with questions or inane conversation. Times like this I missed Priss the most. She was the people person. She knew how to make nice, be sociable. I'd never mastered that skill and at this point didn't expect to. More importantly this intruder was awakening feelings I had thought long dead. The more we talked, the more I'd become involved. That would end in nothing good. I rose and turned the overhead lights out, loaded the fire grate one more time, then returned to my laptop.

I WORKED NON-STOP for the next four hours. *Vigilante* would be my final tribute to Priss and I needed to make it perfect for her and for Anastasia once she was old enough to read and understand. Priss had saved my life and given me back my dignity. I needed to do the same for her posthumously. Though our relationship was not typical, she had taught me about love, selflessness, and devotion. I needed to be worthy of her and all she bequeathed me.

I started by re-reading the last scene, deleted it, then used my irritation at the interloper to rewrite the entire chapter. The turmoil proved the very motivation I needed to reach deep inside to expose my true angst. My emotions were raw and I was thankful Doc appeared to be asleep. Tears ran down my cheeks as I wrote the hospice scene and the conversation between my victim and the private eye.

Marni, my editor, had been right—this book demanded that I show the hatred my detective felt, and that this case could not resolve itself simply but would redefine my character for all the books to come. Love, anger, heartache, and pain all merged together at once, and the words flowed from my fingertips.

I went to get a glass of water from the tap. My left shoulder was stiff, so I stretched and rolled it trying to work out the soreness. After re-reading the new chapter, I sat back pleased with the results. There was more work to be done, for sure, but at least I was writing again. The blank screen no longer intimidated me.

I turned to discover Chance lying on the couch beside the woman and snoring in unison with her. *Damned dog.* I walked to the door and whistled softly. She lifted her head, jumped down, and shook herself once. "Wanna go out?" She skittered across the floor and met me at the door. I quickly snatched my coat.

While Chance ran and found the perfect spot to relieve herself, I shoveled the snow off the landing. Another five inches had fallen, and it was still coming down hard. I gazed at the meadow further up the mountain behind the house and whispered, "Good night, Ms. Priss. I'll see you soon."

Chapter Four

Seven Years Earlier (September 2001)

MARNI ROBERTS SAT on the wooden chair listening to the various machines positioned over Maddison's head and watching the readouts. Though she had been assured they were merely monitors and not life-saving equipment, she kept staring at them. Terry, the morning nurse, was injecting medicine into the IV already hooked up to the patient's arm.

"Is there any improvement?" Marni chewed her lip nervously.

Terry looked up. "Hard to tell, but the good news is she's still with us. That shows how tough her will is." She grinned at Marni and returned to her task.

Marni checked her PDA for messages. She had sent out inquiries to various friends in the medical field and was eagerly awaiting answers. One of the perks of being with a publishing house was having contacts in all walks of life. She was still listening to some of the responses when Maddison's doctor walked in.

"Morning, Ms. Roberts."

"Morning, Doctor Franco, how are you today?"

He didn't answer right away. Instead, he read the notes left by the night staff and checked Maddison's pulse and eye response. After making notes on the chart, he turned to Marni.

"May I?" He indicated the chair next to her.

"Of course."

"As Maddison has no family to speak of, and you're listed on her DNR and Living Will, I'm obliged to confer with you and get your input for the next phase of her recovery."

Marni leaned back, her stomach clenching. "Go ahead."

"Don't look so frightened." He patted Marni's hand. "I believe she's going to recover. She's young and strong, so there's no reason to assume she won't. I believe this coma is an anomaly, a coping mechanism if you will. She sustained no injury to her head. All her scans show strong brain activity. My concern is the rehabilitation of her arm and leg. As I've explained, there's extensive damage to her leg, she'll need months of therapy and, even then, I can't be sure she'll ever walk on her own. Adding to the difficulty of her leg's recovery is the damage to her shoulder. Normally, a patient who's sustained wounds like this is able to get around on crutches. That's not an option for Maddison."

"What do you propose?"

24

"I suggest we move her to a rehabilitation center where she'll get intensive treatment for her injured limbs whether she's able to participate or not."

Marni huffed. "Are you saying she'll remain in this coma indefinitely?"

"No, but the longer we wait on starting a regimen of exercises, the less likely she will be to regain use of her leg." He tipped his head toward the bed. "I've known Maddison a long time . . . she'd hate that, *almost* as much as she's going to hate not being a cop. We need to salvage what we can for her. So I'm asking you to sign off on this."

Marni took a deep breath. "Do you have a facility in mind?"

"I do." He pulled a card from his pocket and handed it to Marni. "It's not cheap, but I believe if she's going to regain use of her leg, this is the center that can make it happen. They assign round-the-clock therapists to their patients. They use hydrotherapy, deep massage, and all the latest technology and treatments to ensure recovery. It's intense and difficult. And it's exactly what she needs."

Marni took the card: Stephens, Michael, Burnwall Physical Therapy, North Hollywood. "I'll call and see about making the arrangements."

"They're already made. I just need you to approve them." The doctor picked up the medical binder and pulled out a sheet of paper. "If you sign here and initial there we can have her transferred later today."

Marni studied her friend lying unconscious in the bed. "Do you have a pen?"

THREE O'CLOCK THAT afternoon, Marni nervously followed the ambulance that transported Maddison to the rehabilitation center. An hour later, after filling out extensive paperwork and personally guaranteeing the expense if the police insurance provider balked, she was shown into Maddison's room and introduced to Karileah Gallagher, senior therapist assigned to her case.

"Can you tell me what her treatment will entail?"

"Certainly. Why don't I give you a quick tour of our facility, so you can see what we do here and the kind of one-on-one treatment Ms. Delanie will receive."

While two aides and a nurse worked to settle Maddison and check her vitals, Karileah led the way down the hall.

"Based on the patient's needs, we offer various degrees of rehabilitation. Ms. Delanie will receive the most intensive program we offer."

They walked into a large room where several forms of treatment were taking place. A woman walked on steps with a harness attached to the ceiling to keep her upright. An older man received electro-heat therapy on his shoulder. With a therapist following her from behind, a young girl held onto parallel bars as she attempted to walk with leg braces.

"Does Ms. Delanie have any issues I should know about?"

"Excuse me?" Marni almost choked in disbelief.

Karileah repeated her question. "Does she have any issues I should know about?"

"You mean other than getting shot and being unconscious at the moment?"

The young woman started to stutter then regained her composure. "Shot?"

"Yes. Didn't you know?" A frown formed on Marni's brow. Dr. Franco had made the arrangements, how could he have not mentioned the damage to Maddison's leg. Or the bullets that ripped through her body and the resulting carnage to both life and limb.

"No." Karileah pushed against the door marked *Waiting Room*, and Marni followed her inside.

"I'm so sorry. I didn't know. You must understand, I received a call from Doctor Stephens late this morning asking that I come in to meet with a new patient. I haven't had time to be briefed on the details of her injuries as yet."

"I see."

"Please, don't be upset. I was supposed to be off for a week, but when Doctor Stephens explained the patient was comatose with extensive damage, I knew I was needed back here."

"Were you on vacation?"

Karileah shook her head. "No, nothing like that."

"Have you experience with gunshot wounds then?"

"Unfortunately, yes. Being close to the Central District, it's hard not to be in this job."

"But not all victims can afford these services, I'm sure— Oh, I apologize. I did not mean that the way it came out."

Karileah's face remained impassive. "No, you're right. Our services come at a stiff price, but we almost always get the desired results." She placed her hand over Marni's. "How did it happen?"

A shudder visibly shook Marni. "Her captain told me she went out on a routine back-up call with her partner. It was a domestic violence incident. The officer on site had asked for assistance. It was reported that Maddison was shot in the leg almost immediately upon arrival. That's when her partner called for even more back-up. The details are hazy from there. When the three responding units arrived, minutes later, everyone was dead except Maddison."

A gasp escaped Karileah's lips. "How awful."

"Awful. Yes. Seven people lost their lives including the suspect. What ticks me off is it could have been avoided, but a judge had given the bastard early release from prison because of overcrowding in the jails."

Karileah paled. "Seven . . . people?"

"The idiot's ex-girlfriend, her three children all under age ten, the original responding officer, and Anna Delgado, Maddison's partner."

"That's outrageous."

"I'm just thankful the son-of-a-bitch is dead, or I'd kill him myself."

Silence fell between them. Finally Karileah said, "We should be getting back. It appears Ms. Delanie needs to start her therapy as soon as possible. We need to get her leg functioning again."

THAT EVENING, KARILEAH sat on her bed and composed a response to her mother's latest letter. Since relocating to California, she had tried to be diligent about writing home, letting her mother know where she was living and how she was doing. Her mother had been against the move from the start, but Kari insisted she needed to follow her dream.

```
Karileah,
     I don't understand you, child. Why do
you need to be so far from home? I miss you,
miss being part of your life. Why can't you
be more like Fiona? Use that degree you
worked   so   hard   to   earn   instead   of
daydreaming about stardom. Did I tell you
Fiona finished school? She's interning now.
She has a good future ahead of her. Why are
you willing to settle for bit parts and
irregular paychecks?
     You haven't mentioned Church of late,
are you not going? Father Francis asks
about you all the time. He asked what
church you belong to out there, I was
embarrassed to tell him I didn't know. I
wish you'd come home and settle down,
forget this foolishness. Get married have
some children. Father Francis says Hi. I
love you, you can always come home.
Love Mom
```

Karileah reread her mother's letter. It was always the same. Why can't you be more like your sister? Why can't you be successful like Nonie. Karileah didn't want to hate Nonie, but she was tired of being compared to her older sister and her accomplishments.

```
Dear Momma
     Things have turned around for me here.
I'm working full time as a therapist, so I
```

27

am using my degree. The new apartment is tiny, but my roommate is very nice and it's close to everything. I'm going on auditions weekly. I just know I'm going to be picked one of these times and then you'll get to see me on TV.

Hope all is well there, I miss you both. I'll write soon.
Love Karileah

Chapter Five

October 19, 2008

I WOKE TO the sound of Chance's tail thumping against the floor at my feet. I automatically dropped my arm and buried my hand in her soft fur before getting up to start the day. I had slept in the chair next to our patient so I could listen for her and maintain the fire during the night. I emptied some embers and loaded up the grate with more logs. Dancing upward and over, the flames greedily fed off the dry wood. I stood mesmerized by the sizzle and crack of the bark as it burned and fell from the timber. I watched the wood blacken as the fire scorched it.

The beating of Chance's tail finally roused the woman on the couch.

"Owww." She lay on her back, her eyes weary as she reached to pet Chance.

"How are you feeling?" I asked.

"Not so hot, or good . . . I should say. In fact, I *am* hot. I think I might have a fever." Her voice was even more raspy than yesterday, and her eyes looked glassy and red. She flattened her palm to her forehead.

I approached slowly, laid my hand against her cheek. She was burning up. I checked her pulse. My own was racing in comparison. "I'll get you more aspirin. Is your throat sore?"

"Everything's sore today. I can't tell what's due to the accident and what's not." She tried to sit up, but fell backward.

"Stay." Seeming to understand, Chance watched for a moment then lay back down beside the patient, her head nuzzling the woman's hand.

I went to the kitchen and put the kettle on. Some hot tea and the pills would hopefully help.

"I really need to pee." Fiona said. She was trying to stand, but without much success.

I went back to her. "Give me your hand and push with your good leg." I got her up and handed her the crutches, then walked behind to steady her.

At the doorway she turned. "I've got this, thanks."

I nodded. "Call when you're ready to come out." I waited for her to enter then closed the door. Meanwhile the kettle started to whistle. I took out two tea bags and a thermal soup cup. The hot liquid would go far to help with her throat and fever. I added a generous squirt of honey, then left it to steep while I added more logs to the fire.

When the door to the bath opened, I rushed to her side as she maneuvered through the doorway. "I feel like crap."

"You look it too."

She turned and glared at me. "You don't date much, do you?" She shook her head.

Clearly not the right response. Why does this woman make me feel like a damned teenager with a crush?

"I'm just gonna lie down, if that's all right?"

"I made you tea. Take some more Tylenol and sip the brew. I put honey in it. Between the two, you might feel better after a nap." I walked alongside her then helped her sit and raised her leg up on the pillow.

Fiona nodded, took the offered bottle from my hand and metered out four pills. She swallowed them with water I handed her.

"Isn't four a lot?"

"I'll pay you for them, okay?"

"Fuck you." *Another dollar.* I snatched the empty glass out of her hand, but placed the pills on the end table. "You're a pain-in-the-butt, Doc." I returned with the tea. "It's hot." Though it was obvious from the steam rising out of the cup, I still felt the need to warn her.

Fiona looked up. "I'm sorry. Four pills is safe at the over-the-counter dosage as long as it's not abused long term." She gripped the mug with two hands as she took it from me.

"So I don't have to worry about side-effects if you fall asleep?"

She surprised me with a smile. "Worried I might die?"

I pointed to the front windows. "Well, it's too cold for burial right now. If you're not opposed to the notion of cremation, I can handle that." I turned and walked to the door.

"Don't leave on my account."

"I need to shovel the snow off the stoop and the roof. I'll be back to check on you and keep the fire going." I put on my coat and boots. "I'll make breakfast when I get done outside. In the meantime, rest." Chance danced at my feet, spinning in circles, eager to get out and play in the snow.

"Okay."

I left Fiona sipping her tea and staring into the fire.

THE SNOW ON the landing was sixteen inches deep, more in some places where the wind blew. I spent an hour clearing the wraparound walkway, then secured the ladder to the hooks at each corner of the roofline so I could clear that as well. Unfortunately I couldn't clear the vision of Doc sitting on my sofa, or sleeping there. The woman made me jittery. There was something familiar about her, and yet I had never met her. I was sure of it.

The gabled peak has an eighteen-twelve pitch with a new metal roof; still, it's never a good thing to let snow accumulate. I had witnessed two structural failures and was determined it wouldn't happen with the church's ancient framing. Thankfully this storm left fluffy stuff and a broom sent the snow rumbling down each side without much effort.

I redid the stoop where some of the cleared snow had fallen, then swept the stairs so Chance and I would have easy access to the ground level. Lastly, I went around to the back of the building to clear the snow off the two lower shed roofs. One covered the main floor bath and the other covered the newly built addition, a master bedroom at the back of the building.

Chance was off hunting a rabbit caught out in the storm. I didn't worry. if she managed to capture it, she would bring it home to me—she always did.

The view to the west showed clearing skies over the mountains. The snow should stop within a couple of hours. If all went well, I might even get the driveway started later on today. First, I wanted to retrieve Anastasia. But, I couldn't do that until I knew how my visitor was. I would not subject Anastasia to germs or infections, and there was no feasible way to evict Doc.

At the base of the stairs off to the right of the drive was the woodpile. It would provide enough fuel for the entire season and most of the next. Meanwhile the three rings by the front doors needed to be restocked as well as the one by the hearth. Forty minutes later and seven trips up and down the stairs had the rings full plus an overflowing carpetbag of wood for the grate by the hearth. With one last survey around to confirm all was in its proper place, it was time to check on the fire and my patient.

THE HOUSE WAS toasty warm as I entered. I removed my hat, coat and boots then walked in stocking feet to the fireplace to check if I needed to add wood. Flames flickered low. The wood was mostly tinder. I used the poker to knock down what remained of the wood, then placed three logs back in the metal grate, above the hot coals. Flames immediately sought the new combustible and greedily engulfed the wood.

Fiona appeared to be asleep. At first glance, she looked troubled. Her eyelids constantly shifted under a furrowed brow. She moaned softly. It sounded like she was in pain. Much as I resented her invasion, I didn't wish her ill. I leaned over and whispered. "Shhhh, it's okay, Doc. You're safe. Nothing's going to hurt you." I touched her forehead—the skin was hot. She clutched the blanket around her and still she shivered, all while within five feet of the massive fireplace that radiated heat clear across the room. I walked to the linen closet and pulled another blanket off the shelf to cover her with. A bad feeling settled in the pit of my stomach. What if she's really sick? What if her leg's infected?

In the kitchen I worked quietly, making toast and oatmeal. I diced an apple into small squares and mixed it in with the hot cereal. Then I sprinkled it with cinnamon and added a wee amount of milk. I fixed a tray and set it on the coffee table. "Hey, Doc. I made 'ya breakfast."

"Mmmmm." The moan was barely audible.

"Come on, Doc, wake up." I shook her shoulder gently but she remained fast asleep. I touched her head again, it was hotter than before, and still she appeared to shiver. I reached to place her arm back under the blanket only to discover the sweats I had given her were damp with perspiration. I knew that couldn't be good.

In the kitchen, I stared out the window. There were breaks in the clouds and patches of blue shown through. Maybe we had a satellite connection. I picked up the handset and listened. There was a dial tone, so I hit the speed dial.

"Hi, Sophia, how you and Anya getting along?" After I heard a short recitation of their activities since Friday evening, I explained the situation. "A woman went off the road here. She only had minor injuries, but now she's got a fever."

I rubbed my forehead as Sophia responded.

"I know. That's why I'm calling. Think you can keep Anastasia a couple more days?"

Sophia assured me they would be fine. I hoped I would be too.

"Okay, I'll let you know when I can get there. Thanks and give her a kiss for me."

I climbed the steps to the second-floor bedroom and got another set of sweats and a sock for Fiona's uninjured foot. Back downstairs I stopped for a clean bath towel then turned toward the couch. *I don't need this crap. Really I don't.* I pulled the blankets away and discovered the borrowed clothes were perspiration soaked, top and bottom. *Blast!* I gently pulled her upright into a sitting position, even though she moaned in protest. With a tight grip on the hem of the shirt, I gradually pulled it up and over her head. She was naked beneath the damp top. I used the towel to dry her clammy skin, then quickly placed a clean garment over her head. I fought to get her arms into the correct openings, then I pulled it down, trying desperately not to notice the perfect lush roundness of her breasts. Or the taupe color of her ripe erect nipples. Or the fact that my heartbeat had jumped into overdrive. I laid her back down, then tugged on the waistband of her pants, they slid lower then caught. I slipped a hand under her back and lifted till I could push them past her butt. Again she was nude underneath. *Why me?* I'm not by nature a lech, but this endeavor was seriously testing my moral compass. I used the towel to dry the remaining parts of her body, finally able to pull up the clean pants, put the sock on her foot, and cover her with the two blankets. By the time the task was done, I was overheated myself and knew neither the temperature of the room nor my exertions had anything to do with it. I picked up the tray of food and took it back to the kitchen.

Sisters

Fiona and I ended up repeating the process five more times over the next forty-eight-hour-period. Time got away from me; chores went untended. My laptop remained closed. My mind was jumbled with what ifs and various remedies I had heard of or read about over the years.

I stayed at her side spooning sips of water through dry cracked lips, feeding her ice chips, keeping her warm and dry and checking her leg repeatedly for signs of infection. As far as I could tell there was none. I had no hint of what was causing her temperature. The longer it went on, the more concerned I got. The woman might not have been an invited guest, but I never meant her any harm.

Chapter Six

October 22, 2008

MIDMORNING ON THE third day, I stirred from a catnap. Fiona still slept, but appeared more at rest than agitated. Chance sat at the door begging to be let out. I complied quickly. After cleaning and filling the hearth, I stepped to Fiona's side. The skin of her forehead was warm to the touch, but she didn't appear to be perspiring.

"What—are you doing?" She swatted at my hand. Her words were low and forced.

"I'm trying to see if your fever broke yet or not." I looked into her eyes. They appeared clearer, less red.

"I ache all over."

"Here, take these." I handed her four more aspirin along with a glass of water. "You need to fight this, Doc. I don't have anything stronger, and we can't get out for help just yet." I didn't add that she was scaring the crap out of me, but she didn't need to know that.

She took the pills with half the water and my help, then fell back against the pillow and went right to sleep. I pulled the covers up to her chin.

A MEDICAL REFERENCE book generally sits on the shelf in the closet for times like these when I feel totally useless. I had pulled it down on Sunday afternoon and struggled to read about high temperatures. The book was not meant for the lay person, that was clear. It stated that fevers are normally caused by infections. Symptoms could include anything from aching joints, sore throat to vomiting. So far Fiona had two of them. It strongly warned of possible dehydration, and stressed that liquids had to be consumed to help fight the illness. And it said if the fever persisted longer than three days to see a doctor. This was the third day! *Crap.* I stared out the window. Unless a miracle took place, she wasn't going anywhere for help.

In the kitchen, I opened the fridge and found a whole chicken fully defrosted. It was supposed to have been roasted with little potatoes; instead, I'd use it for soup. I peeled two onions, and a clove of garlic, diced them and set them in the large kettle to cook. I looked up from my task and stared at Fiona. She appeared to be resting, finally. I took a deep breath and then another. I hoped she would continue to improve. Our options were few and my knowledge even more miniscule. Gashes or stomach upsets I could deal with; this was more serious and I felt useless.

Next I cut up three carrots, two celery stalks, and two medium potatoes, dumping them all in the same pot. Lastly I cut the chicken into pieces, placed that into the kettle and added salt, pepper, a bay leaf along with two-and-a-half quarts of water before covering it. I set it to simmer. Hopefully, in three hours, Doc would feel up to having some. She needed to eat and, as long as she was here, I needed to help her get better. She might unnerve me, but that's on me, not her.

As I turned to head into the shower, Chance arrived on the stoop wanting to be let in. I opened the door and snagged her collar before she could run past me for Fiona's attention. "Stay." I ordered. I got her towel from the cabinet under the coat rack and rubbed her down to dry her fur of the cold and wetness. Then I pointed to the kitchen where I had placed her dish on the floor along with fresh water. "You stay here." Her ears were flat back. Clearly I had insulted her, but most likely she would obey.

I went to the bathroom for a shower. Hot water sprayed across my neck, back and shoulders. I kept my head bent forward to let the water do its thing. Every muscle ached, and I was exhausted. Three nights of listening to Fiona breath, worrying about her welfare, and caring for her every need had wiped me out. The shower would go a long way to reviving me.

I still had edits to do, and the final three chapters to write before I could resubmit the manuscript.

As I used the soap to wash my arms, stomach and chest, I thought back to my body's shameless response to Fiona's nakedness. I'm not a saint, that's for sure, but I'd never ogled a woman in my life. Yet that's how it felt when I was undressing and re-dressing the sickly doctor. *What the heck was that about?* Who gets turned on when someone's vulnerable? The more I thought on it, the more aroused I became. I lathered my hair, rinsed off, and quickly stepped out of the shower before I let my memories cause a physical release. No sense fantasizing about what will never happen.

BY LATE AFTERNOON, I had drained the soup broth into a large bowl, added fresh sautéed vegetables and deboned the chicken before returning the meat to the rest of the fixings. I had mixed the ingredients in the bread machine and put it in the oven. By the smell of it, the fresh bread was coming along.

My laptop sat open on the counter, its screen dark and time fast becoming my enemy. Though the deadline was lurking, I couldn't stop worrying about Fiona. I stood next to the couch watching her breathe. It didn't appear labored. Unfortunately for me, even in sleep she was damned attractive. Black hair cut in a modern shoulder-length style, full eyebrows that arched when she frowned, and thick lashes that fluttered in her sleep. Her pale complexion could be caused by her physical state, but I didn't think so. The skin on her arms and legs was just as pale. No, this woman rarely spent time in the sun and it showed. I leaned over and gently touched her cheek.

"Wha—"

"It's okay, I'm just checking to see if you still have a fever."

She lifted her hand to her face before opening her eyes. "Not as bad, I don't think."

"Let me check, okay?"

She nodded and I placed my hand on her forehead. "I'm not sure, but I think you're better. " I sat on the coffee table and leaned toward her. "You've been pretty sick. I couldn't wake you."

She tried to sit up, concern on her face. "Is my leg infected?"

"No, I checked that first thing."

"My ankle?"

"I've been icing it, and it's looking good. I checked the pulse in your ankle multiple times; it's strong."

Fiona fell back and nodded. "Likely fatigue then."

I nodded. "Think you could eat some soup? You're supposed to keep hydrated and you probably should take more aspirin."

She pushed the blankets aside, then attempted to sit up. She failed. "These are green?"

I stared at her blankly, confused.

"The sweats. The ones I had on this morning were navy."

I shook my head. "That was three days ago, Doc." I felt the color rush to my face. "You've been sweating real bad. Your clothes soaked through a couple times, and you were shivering. I swapped them out for dry ones and gave you a second blanket to keep warm."

"Days ago? How many times, exactly?"

"Look, I can show you the dirty sweats. The pile's in the kitchen waiting to be washed."

She put her hand up. "I believe you. Why are you blushing."

I stood and went to the fireplace, knocked down the embers, and placed two logs on the grate. "I told you the other day—it's too cold for burial, and frankly, I'm not sure I could separate your ashes from the wood's during cremation. I assume you're family might want them."

"Damn it! I haven't called home." She pushed her hands through her hair. "Can I use your phone? I forgot about calling home. Is it still snowing? Are the roads clear yet? When can I get out of here?"

I went to the counter to get the satellite phone. Expecting she'd want to make a call, I'd had it charging for the last three days. "The snow stopped Tuesday and started again about an hour ago. The highways aren't cleared. I haven't gone out to work on this road because of you, and it's too late in the day now. That's likely to take a day or more, in and of itself. The earliest I see you being able to leave, *if* I can get your car working, is three days from now." I returned and handed her the phone. "This isn't like a cell phone. It's got to bounce off two satellites and back to earth before a connection is made, so there's a delay and echo in between. Be patient."

"Thank you." She took the phone from my hand.

I returned to the kitchen to give her as much privacy as possible in one room. The bread was done, so I took it out of the oven to cool. Then I set out a tray with a bowl and spoon for the soup and a plate and knife for the bread and butter

"MOM? CAN YOU hear me?" Fiona yelled into the handset.

"Of course I can hear you, I'm not deaf." Her mother's voice came through the handset strong and clear. It was delayed as Maddison had warned.

Fiona laughed, tears filling her eyes. "Sorry, I'm on a borrowed phone and it works differently than what I'm used to."

"What's wrong with your phone and where are you? I've been worried sick. It's been four days since I heard from you." Mary Margaret Gallagher stated the obvious. But then the woman was known for her bluntness. A devout Catholic, she raised her girls to believe in God and to obey without question.

"It's a long story. The car I rented went off the road when a deer ran in front of me. I had to walk to find help. Then it started snowing, and Maddison, that's the woman who took me in, well her phone doesn't work in bad weather and mine isn't getting a signal at all."

"Did you find out anything about your sister?"

Fiona took a long, deep breath. "No, Mom, and I guess that means you haven't heard anything either?"

"I think you should come home," Mary said.

"You wanted answers, I'm trying to get them for you." Fiona swiped at the tear that ran down her cheek.

"Humph. What's next then?"

"That depends on the weather, the car getting pulled out of the ditch, if it works, and how soon the roads will be cleared."

"Well, keep me posted and be careful. I don't need to be worrying about you too."

"I will be, and you take your medicine. I'll keep in touch. Bye."

"I love you, Fiona." Her mother's voice was gruff.

"Love you too, Mom."

WHEN I HEARD Fiona put the phone down, I turned and was surprised to see tears in her eyes. "Everything okay?" I hated when a woman cried. I never knew how to help, and this time was no different.

She nodded but didn't speak.

"I made soup while you slept and there's hot bread. How about a bowl?" I waited for her response.

"I need to use the bathroom first and, I'm sorry, but I think I need dry clothes again too."

I walked closer. There was a sheen of perspiration on her upper lip, and goose bumps on her arms where she had pushed up the sleeves of her shirt. "Wanna take a hot shower or soak in the tub while you're in there?"

"I'm not sure I have the energy to stay upright. I feel so weak."

I quickly averted my gaze. "I could . . . if you . . . what I mean is . . . I—"

"Are you asking if I need your help?"

I looked back to see if she was mocking me; she wasn't. "Yeah . . . that is . . . I mean if you want—" I could feel the blood rushing to my face and spreading across my cheeks.

She stared at me before answering. "Do you think you can keep from passing out if you see me nekkid again." She chuckled as she spoke.

"I only—"

She put her hand up, "I know what you were doing, and believe me I appreciate it. Clearly you're uncomfortable though, and I'm not sure I could help you if you fainted."

I squared my shoulders. "I can do it."

"Then I would love a hot shower, some warm, dry clothes, and some of that soup . . . if it's not too much trouble?"

"I'll go get . . . upstairs . . . ahh sweats . . . I'll be . . . wait." *Fuck! I'm like a blithering idiot. What's wrong with me?* I hurried upstairs, pulled two sets of sweats from my bureau and then stopped at the linen closet for more towels.

"I'm ready, if you are."

She giggled and a small sparkle lit her eyes. "Ohh, I'm ready, the question is are you *sure* you are?"

I gulped. "I am."

I helped her up, and held the back of her shirt as she maneuvered toward the bathroom. Once inside, she went to the toilet and dropped her pants. "I just need to pee first."

I quickly turned my back, set the towels on the warming rack behind the door, and placed the dry clothes on the side of the sink.

"You didn't have to turn away. You're about to see me nekkid anyway." She chuckled softly. "Exactly how many times is this now?"

I started to turn my head, but realized she was finishing business and quickly turned away. "I just thought you'd want privacy . . . for that."

"Didn't have siblings did you?"

"How did you know that?"

"You're shy about the human form, not something someone with sisters usually is. Odd for a cop, I would think."

38

I turned to discover her removing her top and quickly turned back again. "How hot do you want this?"

"As hot as it will go, please."

She removed the aircast, then the bandage on her leg. "Well at least this looks good."

I turned to see what she meant. The skin around the stitches was pink, but there was no pus or swelling, a good sign. "It does, doesn't it?"

"You did a good job."

"When your temperature was raging and I couldn't wake you, I checked it every couple hours, but it looked fine. I even researched our medical book, but nothing indicated what was happening."

Fiona brought her hand up to her heart. "Thank you for taking care of me. And for worrying. I'm feeling better . . . just a little weak at the moment." She gripped the towel bar and stood up in all her nakedness before stepping toward the shower.

I struggled to keep my eyes averted while still watching to be sure she was safe. Seeing her upright and nude sent my inner compass spinning. If I felt tortured by glimpses of her body while tending her during the fever, this was likely to kill me. Her body was magnificent. She curved in all the right places, with a roundedness that screamed femininity. I felt as if my breath had been stolen.

"You might as well strip too."

"What?" I was sure I misunderstood. "Why?"

"Because if I need help, you're going to get wet." She sat on the stool and smirked. "Why get your clothes soaked?"

I repeated her words in my mind. Logically they made sense, but putting action to them sent shivers up my spine. If I stripped, we'd both be naked. Together. In a small space. Hot water sluicing over our bodies. That thought alone conjured up images that had nothing to do with helping a sick woman and everything to do with raging hormones. *Mine.*

"I don't bite." She watched me intently, waiting. "Unless you ask nicely." She giggled when I frowned.

"Okay." I turned my back and lifted the fleece over my head then let it drop to the floor. I took a cleansing breath. My stomach was churning as I undid my belt, opened the button to my jeans and slid the zipper down. Each sound echoed in my brain, seeming to bounce off the walls of the room. I gripped the waistband and lowered my pants, kicked them aside, and turned back around. "All ready." Perspiration formed on my upper lip and under my arms. I hoped I looked steadier than I felt.

As I peered at her, her eyes roamed over my torso like a warm caress. She let out a soft puff, her hand reaching out half way. "That looks pretty nasty." She was gazing at the mutilation visible below the leg of my boxers.

Though not entirely visible, the scar ran the length of my left thigh. "You should see the other guy."

Her eyes took in the damage. "What kind of injury?"

"Gunshot."

"What'd they do to fix it?"

"There's two metal rods with sixty screws holding it together."

She looked at me with compassion, not the aversion I expected. "It's a miracle you can walk, never mind manage this place."

"I had an angel who worked her magic. The therapy was intense, but as you can see, she got it right."

She nodded her head. "You're not going to shower in your underwear, are you?"

"Yeah."

"Why?"

"Well . . . I didn't . . . it just seemed . . . look, let's just get this done, okay?" I stepped into the hot spray, and handed her a facecloth and the soap.

FORTY-FIVE MINUTES later, when I brought her dinner, Fiona was back on the couch with Chance lying next to her and a blanket covering both of them.

"How are you feeling?"

She lay there, her arm resting across her eyes. "Tired."

"Chance, get down." I put the tray of food on the coffee table and helped Fiona sit up. "Take some more aspirin, drink all the water, and then eat. Hopefully you'll feel better tomorrow."

"I thought I was the doctor here?"

"You are. And let me just say, you're a lousy patient. You'd rather sleep than fight whatever it is you're dealing with, and that's not rational."

When I came back from the kitchen with my own tray, she was finishing the water. "I'll get you more, or would you like some juice?"

She nodded and smiled. "I'd love juice for a change."

As I turned to go to the kitchen, I looked out the window. "Crap."

Fiona followed my gaze. "Please tell me that's not another storm coming in?"

I went to the door for a better look. Dark clouds moved swiftly through the valley below. Not a good sign. "Could be"—I shrugged—"or it might just be a blow."

"A blow?"

"Just the snow already on the ground blowing around, doesn't mean it's fresh."

I poured the juice and brought it to her. "Eat, you need to keep hydrated."

She shook her head but picked up the spoon. Chance lay at her feet, waiting.

"Chance, out. Go do business, now." I went to the door and waited. The dog jumped up and ran through as I opened it.

"She wasn't bothering me."

I watched Chance for a moment before turning around. "She knows better than to beg, but she seems to think she can wrap you around her damned paw."

Fiona guffawed at that. "She's right, I'm a pushover for animals." She gripped her spoon and blew on the soup to cool it. "You seriously searched a medical book? What for?"

I balanced my bowl of soup on my thigh and dipped the spoon in. "It's not like it did me any good. The friggin' thing is meant for a professional, not a lay person."

Fiona nodded as she swallowed.

"Basically, I couldn't wake you. You were sweating through the clothes and even with two blankets and this fire going, you kept shivering. You scared the hell out of me. The only thing I fully understood was that it could be life threatening."

I dipped the bread in the soup and kept my eyes averted, the memory sending a shiver down my spine. "Even I know that simple infections or fevers can cause death in some cases. The book emphasized the need to drink lots of fluids."

Fiona looked up. "I'm sorry you were frightened, and I really do appreciate the care you gave me. Trust me, I know how unsettling it can be when you don't know what's happening. Thank you."

"Eat. You need your strength."

Chapter Seven

OCTOBER 2001

KARILEAH WORKED THE patient's leg for thirty minutes, then iced it for ten, finally massaging it for another fifteen. She had been working with the unconscious officer for two days, overseeing her around-the-clock care. She understood Ms. Roberts concern regarding the coma-like state. She felt sure the patient was merely resting her mind because of the trauma she had experienced.

Kari had worked with other gunshot victims in the past. She knew the brain and God only forced you to deal with what you could handle. Obviously the officer needed time to process what she had experienced. Eventually, she would heal, but in the meantime, her body was Karileah's responsibility and she took it very seriously.

"Good morning, Karileah," Marni said as she swept into the room. "How's our patient?"

A smiling Karileah was slowly rotating Maddison's arm at the shoulder, stretching the damaged tendons and muscles in increments, forcing the mobility back into the stiff limb. "I think she's doing better, Ms. Roberts."

"Call me Marni." Marni walked toward the bottom of the bed and squeezed Maddison's foot. "Do you really think she's better?"

Karileah looked up and smiled. "I do. She's starting to moan during certain techniques and that's—"

As if to prove her right, Maddison let out a groan, and her face twisted in a grimace.

"Oh my god, she's waking up!" Marni clapped her hands together. "She's really waking up? You did it. She's—"

"Not yet, but soon. I'm sure of it." Karileah continued the tight circular movement of the shoulder. It was where she got the most response from the patient and felt sure it would be key to stimulating wakefulness.

Karileah supported the patient's injured arm and adjusted it in augmentations, meticulously noting the range of movement in the medical chart each time, then reversing the process slowly. "I just have to massage the muscles and then you can spend some time alone with her."

"You keep doing what you're doing. That's more important. She needs your ministrations more than she needs me nagging her."

Karileah looked on quizzically. "Nagging?"

Marni sidled to the chair, dropped her purse and briefcase on the floor next to it and sat. "Besides being a detective, Maddison is a crime novelist. We recently finished prepping her first book. Now there's interest in

42

turning it into a weekly crime drama, but I need her to wake up before that can happen."

"Wow, I didn't know she was famous."

Marni laughed out loud. "She's not, and don't ever ask for her autograph or she'll go running in the opposite direction."

"Why ever would she run away?"

"I'm not sure. Shyness, no confidence, you name it."

Karileah lowered Maddison's arm and placed the hot wrap on the joint, tucking it around the shoulder. "I would love to be famous. That's why I'm here . . . in California, I mean." Her hand flew up and covered her mouth, her eyes wide. "I'm so sorry, I didn't mean to—"

Marni waved her off. "Nothing to be sorry about. You're entitled to your dreams." She smiled. "Do you have an agent?"

Karileah nodded. "I don't expect to be a big star, but I'd love to be a sidekick for someone famous."

"Character actors can have long and fulfilling careers. There's nothing wrong with dreaming. Have you taken any classes?"

Karileah nodded.

"Good, then I'd say you covered all the bases. Now you just need a little luck."

"Thank you, I didn't mean to dump my problems on you. Ms. Delanie is doing better. I can see a big difference just since she arrived. She's resisting, which means she's feeling discomfort. In this case that's a good thing. She has a long, hard road ahead of her, but it will go faster and easier if she's participating. I think she'll be doing that any day now." Karileah pulled the blanket up to cover Maddison. "I'm going to get a cup of coffee, I'll be back in thirty minutes.

Marni stood. "Thank you for all you're doing and for keeping me posted."

LATE THAT NIGHT, Karileah sat at the kitchen table and read the latest letter from home.

> Karileah,
> Things here are good, your sister just got a full time position with a medical group affiliated with Wilkes-Barre General. She's doing so well, and now her career is set. I wish you would come home and forget about being an actress. What kind of life is that? The work isn't steady, you don't know from week to week if you'll even have a job. Don't you want to settle down and have a family? I worry so about you, I want

you to be happy, but being an actress is
thankless work unless you're a star.

Father Francis asks about you all the
time. He's praying for your soul. The
ladies of the Rosary are also praying for
you. God meant families to stick together.

Have you been to confession of late? I
worry about you, it's time to grow up and
take responsibility for yourself.

Write soon. I love you.
Mom

Kari reread her mother's words and a deep sense of sadness filled her.
Why can't she understand I'm not Fiona. Why can't she be proud of what
I'm doing?

Dear Momma,

I went on a casting call last week,
they've called me back, I can't believe it,
I'm so excited. I got a part on Diagnosis
Murder, starring Dick Van Dyke. See, I am
getting parts. I'm going to serve him and a
co-star coffee. I even get to say, "Have a
nice day."

This is it, Mom, I just know I'm going
to get more parts now, maybe a sitcom
someday, wouldn't that be wonderful?
Wouldn't you like to brag to your friends
about your daughter the actress?

I'll try to call Sunday, but my full-
time job has gotten really busy and I'm not
sure what my hours will be.

Take care and love to you both, write
soon.
Love Karileah

Chapter Eight

OCTOBER 23, 2008

"**MORNING DOC.**" **DAWN** had not yet lit the skies but I was already feeding the fire when Fiona started to stir. She mumbled an incoherent response, sat up, and began folding the blanket she'd slept under. It appeared neither of us slept well last night. For me it was worry and frustration and the incessant need to use the toilet every hour that kept sleep at bay. Evidently she was dealing with similar issues this morning.

Upon her return from the bathroom, she finally spoke. "Morning."

"How you feeling today?"

"Better, thank you." She sat up straight and lifted her leg onto the coffee table. "Between the hot shower and that dinner last night, the fever is gone and I'm actually feeling pretty good."

"Excellent."

"How about you?"

"Whadda ya mean?"

"You were restless." She put her hand up to stop any retort. "Which I can more than understand. That chair can't be comfortable enough for more than a nap. But you were fidgety all night."

"Lots of things on my mind. You. The weather—"

Fiona nodded. "I was afraid of that, I'm sorry."

"Not a problem, but we need to get you better, okay?"

She laughed. "I am better, promise."

"Are you sure?"

"I'm not saying I can run the Boston Marathon, but I'm definitely on the mend."

"Do you think you have an infection of some kind?"

"No, why?"

"Are you sure?"

"Yes. Absolutely. The fever's gone, and I have no symptoms other than a little weakness. That's normal after what I've been through."

"Good." I walked into the kitchen and reached for the phone. It was picked up on the second ring. "Morning, baby." My heart surged with joy at the sound of her voice.

"Mam! Are you coming to get me today?" Anya asked.

"Yes, I promise. Let me talk to Nana Sophia, okay?" After a mild tussle, Sophia's voice came through the phone.

"Morning, what's up?"

"Hey, my patient's doing better today. I'll come get Anya—"

"I'll bring her home, no sense leaving a stranger alone in the house."

"Are you sure?"

"I got nothing else to do. Me and the Munchkin can race up the mountain together." Sophia chuckled.

"Okay, but let me know when you're leaving so I can judge your arrival. And drive slow . . . you're carrying precious cargo." I hung the phone up to find Fiona staring at me. "My daughter's grandmother is bringing her home later this morning." I walked to the coffee pot and hit the start button.

"The roads are clear?" The hope in Doc's voice made me cringe.

"No." I walked back toward her. "We mostly travel by snowmobile around here during the winter months."

"Could you get me to an airport on one?"

"I'm sorry. The nearest city with that kind of transportation would be Kalispell. It's too far to travel by snowmobile and the variables make it too dangerous to even try."

"I see."

"I am sorry, Doc. I'd attempt it if it wasn't so dicey." I felt bad, and she clearly was upset.

She nodded her head. "I understand."

"But?"

She looked up, her brow furrowed. "Did I hear correctly? You said you have a daughter?"

I felt the grin split my face in two. "Yup. Her name is Anastasia. She's four going on forty and spoiled rotten, but I love her more than life."

"You were married?"

I could see the wheels turning in her head. "Yes. My partner gave birth to Anya, but I'm on the birth certificate as a parent."

"Your partner?"

"That's right." I walked into the kitchen to pour the coffee and avoid any nasty exchanges. If she has a problem with two women together, I didn't want to know about it.

Silence filled the space while I retrieved two mugs, set the milk and sugar on the counter and got a spoon out. Fiona rose and approached slowly.

"Now I understand why my being here is such an imposition."

I wanted to say yes, but what were her options? "It can't be helped."

"I'm sorry, truly I am."

"It'll work out."

"I didn't notice a ring . . . I never thought." Fiona shook her head.

I pulled the chain that hung around my neck out from under my shirt. Two wedding bands dangled from it.

"You . . . you wear . . . both rings?"

"Priss, my partner . . . is dead."

"Oh, I'm so sorry. I just keep making this worse."

I pushed the mug to her side of the counter. "It won't be a problem, as long as you don't make Anya uncomfortable."

"Why would I do that?"

I stared at her incredulously.

She gazed back at me interminably. "Oh, no. I'm not . . . I don't . . . I'm not homophobic." She laughed heartily. "Actually, I'm a lesbian. You just surprised me about having a daughter. I never imagined."

It was my turn to stare. A lesbian? What are the freaking chances of that happening out here in the middle of nowhere? *Crap.* "Look, I have some chores to take care of, and I need a shower badly. Will you be okay?"

"Uh, of course. Whatever you need to do, I'm fine."

I put my empty mug in the sink.

When Fiona thumped back to the couch to sit, I brought her mug and placed it on the table in front of her.

"You sure you'll be okay?"

"I'm feeling better, truly."

"In that case, if *you're* interested, and feel strong enough to maneuver the stairs, there's a bedroom in the loft with a full bath. The sheets are clean and the down comforter very warm and cozy. The bed will surely provide a better night's rest than the couch."

The second floor of the church was originally used by the choir. The renovated space took advantage of the open area below and the floor-to-ceiling windows from the front doors, offering the same spectacular view of the Rockies as the first floor.

Fiona peered up toward the open area. "Where would you sleep then?"

I felt the flush and knew it was useless to try to hide it. "Chance and I normally sleep on the couch."

Fiona seemed to mull that information over. "Is there only one bedroom up there?"

"There's two rooms, but I converted one into an office."

"An office you apparently don't employ any more than you do the bedroom." She smirked as she indicated my laptop on the counter.

I dropped the poker into its stand. "How I live, why I choose to do the things I do and where I choose to work is really none of your concern." I stepped closer to the front of the coffee table. "I'm not trying to be rude. I do things the way I do because it works for me and my daughter, and honestly you have no right to judge that, when right now it's the only thing keeping you alive."

"I'm sorry. I didn't mean to upset you or to insult the accommodations." She picked up her cup and took a sip. "Where does Anastasia sleep?"

I gestured with a tilt of my head to the left. "The closed door on the left is her room."

"Ah, so that's why you have so many baby gates. I thought they were for Chance."

"No, they're to keep Anya safe." I walked away, still a bit ticked off.

"I *am* sorry I upset you. Honestly. I'm just frustrated. I hate being needy and I really resent the fact that I require your assistance for more than the simplest things. I'm already late getting back to my job. I only had a ten-day leave."

She ran her hands through her hair. "I appreciate everything you've done." She held her hands out, her eyes reflecting the truth of her words. "I'm going stir crazy. When I couldn't sleep last night, my mind just raced and raced. Normally I'd get up and read, maybe watch TV. I'm worried about my mother back home, and I'm angry at my stupid sister, and—"

Tears had formed and I could see her struggle to blink them away. Guilt flooded me as I recalled my rather volatile reaction. I knew I had been hard and distant, but I had my own issues and was trying to deal with them the best I could. Now I realized this was not a flight of fancy, but a purposeful trip that apparently turned out badly. I picked up the satellite phone off the charger and brought it to her. "Why don't you call home, check in with your mom." I stepped back against the counter and crossed my arms over my chest. "As for the boredom, my office houses a mini library. Since you like to read, you're welcome to take a look. There's a lot of books up there, I'm sure you can find something you'd—"

"I *knew* you had to have something here to entertain yourself with!"

"You mean besides my daughter?" I chuckled. "There's a TV in there too, with a large selection of movies. I'm afraid that's it though. I don't subscribe to a service provider."

"Oh my god." A smile lit up her face. "Why didn't you tell me?"

"I honestly didn't consider it a priority, what with your injuries, and then the fever you've been running."

"You're right. I'm not thinking." She closed her eyes and nodded. "Sorry, again."

I shrugged. "On the desk there's a tablet. It's an e-Reader and it will need charging, but there's a bunch of books on that as well."

"Thank you, I promise to stop being so needy."

"Can I ask you something?"

She searched my face. "Of course."

"You don't have to answer, but you've mentioned your sister twice now . . . cryptically. What's the story behind that?"

"My sister is a screw-up, and there aren't enough hours in the day to explain it all. Suffice it to say, she's got our elderly mother worried sick." Fiona reached for the crutches, and placed the phone in the pocket of her pants. "I'm going to need these stitches taken out soon. Are you up to it?"

An interesting comeback. If this were a criminal investigation, my mind would be running with possibilities, my powers of deduction running rampant, but there is no crime and I'm no longer a cop. I shook my head. "You're the doctor, let me know when it's time."

Fiona beamed. She used the crutches and pulled herself up. "I will. But for now I'm going upstairs to find something to read, then I'm going to call home and check in with my mother. Let her know I'm still alive." She stopped at the bottom of the stairs. "I'm really looking forward to meeting your daughter. Thank you, Maddison. I mean it."

"Make sure you have Chance go up ahead of you and down before you."

"I will." She nodded as she maneuvered to open the gate. Immediately, Chance ran ahead, and I could hear her jumping onto the bed.

Midway up the stairs Fiona paused. "Maddison," she called, "let the hot water run on that leg for a while."

"Hey, Doc, anyone ever tell you, you're a damn nag."

"As a matter of fact, my sister used to tell me that all the time."

Fiona grinned and I decided that was her best look. Just my luck she had a beautiful smile. I felt my heart lurch. "Your sister was right."

FIONA SCANNED THE room, letting her eyes travel over all the books. The collection was interesting and eclectic. Mostly women authors, mostly mysteries and some romances. But then there'd be a history of some obscure subject, or a how-to book interspersed. None of the popular science fiction or vampire stuff here. It amused her that all the books were lined up exactly, shelved alphabetically by author, and then title. Talk about OCD. She shook her head in amusement.

She walked back to the top of the staircase. "Maddison, thank you. That is truly an amazing room. I can see myself spending hours in there."

Maddison looked up. "Good, I'm glad."

Fiona returned to the office and sat in the recliner for a long time pondering the unusual circumstances that brought her here in the first place. Karileah's continued silence and now disappearance, her mother's persistent health issues, and the reclusive author L.M. Addison's dedication in his latest book.

Most importantly, she owed it to her host to reassess her initial opinion made in a moment of haste. A daughter? She never would have guessed. She looked around the room again, feeling at home in an odd way. Warmth filled the space. Fiona pulled a couple of books from the shelves, their spines like new, no corners of the pages bent or torn. The office was so like the owner, dark, austere, just the essentials, but wonderfully efficient. *She probably makes love the same way. Where the hell did that come from?*

THE HOT SHOWER had done a lot to loosen the muscles in my arms and clear my tired brain. It didn't explain my outburst earlier. Why was this woman causing such extreme responses from me? What was it

49

about Doc that made me want to run away before I did something really stupid? I walked over to the hearth to add wood.

The sound of the crutches thumping across the hardwood floor overhead caught my attention. Fiona started down the stairs.

"Wait!" I hadn't meant to startle her, but saw the danger she had ignored. "Let me call her down first, otherwise she's apt to bump you. Chance, come." The dog barreled down the steps, oblivious to any peril and ran to my side.

"Thank you, I didn't think. I should know better. My own brat, Abby, is just like her."

"It's okay. She gets too excited. We can't afford your other ankle being sprained or worse."

She settled herself on the couch. Chance jumped up next to her, her head resting in Fiona's lap. Fiona's hand scratched her gently. A moment of jealousy sped through me. I thought about that for a second. Was I really jealous of Chance? Of the attention this stranger was giving her? I shook my head in disgust. I was.

"Find something you like?"

"Yes, thank you."

I turned back to the hearth to poke the fire before starting my daily chores. Fiona had settled on the couch, her leg extended to the coffee table, Chance at her side, and the book opened. "You do realize most of the books up there are by lesbian authors, right?"

Fiona looked over the top of the book. "Yes."

"Just checking."

She laughed heartily. "I've read everything by this author, besides I already told you, so am I."

"So are you?"

"A lesbian."

I nodded mutely. *She said it again.* I turned back to the fire and put two more logs on the grate. *What the hell happened to my gaydar? How did I miss that?*

I walked to the door, pulled my coat off the hook. "A fresh pot's brewing. I'm taking her highness out. The deck needs shoveling and then we'll go for her morning walk. Should be back in an hour or so."

"Coffee sounds divine right now, thank you." Fiona was sitting safely on the couch. "When's Anastasia arriving?"

I glanced at the clock on the microwave. Sophia had said around one; it was barely seven. "Early afternoon. We'll be back in time." I opened the door and a blast of arctic air blew in along with pelting snow. "There's a fleece top on the back of the chair if you get chilled."

I pulled the door closed before she could respond.

50

Chapter Nine

December 2001

"MORNING MADDISON, HOW are you feeling today?"

"With my hands, Miss Priss, with my hands." I chuckled as I watched her face turn beet red. "Want me to demonstrate for ya?"

Karileah blushed even harder and pointed to the jar on the nightstand.

"Uh-uh." I wagged my finger at the therapist. "I didn't swear."

"Hitting on me is just as bad. You know I'm straight and you know it embarrasses me." She handed the five-pound weights to me. "Ten reps each."

"Shit," I said. "Sorry, but seriously, ten reps? You trying to kill me?"

"That's two dollars you owe the jar. Now get to it." Karileah stood at the end of the bed, her arms crossed over her ample chest and started the count.

I lifted my left arm and began the annoying repetitions. I knew better than to cross the slave driver glaring at me. Miss Priss might be petite but she was demanding and so far had won every round we fought. That thought had me remembering our first skirmish.

I had first come back to consciousness almost six weeks ago during an intensive therapy session on my shoulder. I let fly with an explosion of expletives as pain shot through my arm.

Ms. Priss was shocked into stillness. She later told me she felt sure she'd need to attend confession for having heard such blasphemy. She quickly set the ground rules: "No more cursing, or she'd quit."

Marni had walked in to find the two of us arguing. "Maddison! You're awake."

"Of course, I'm awake, what the fuck did you expect?"

"I'm warning you, Ms. Delanie." The physical therapist stood with hands on hips, glaring at me.

"It's been three weeks my friend, so yeah, I'm very happy to see you conscious." Marni had rushed over and hugged her tight. "Those baby blues have never looked so good. Wait till I call your captain."

"Three weeks?"

Marni glanced at Karileah. "Does she remember anything?"

"No chance to find out, she's been spewing obscenities at me since she woke up."

Marni shook her finger at me. "Kari, did you inform the doctor?"

"He's on his way. I barely managed to call between the profanities and the incessant wrestling."

Marni scowled at me, I knew that look too well.

"Could we have a minute, please, Kari."

Karileah nodded and walked out of the room.

Marni turned to me. "Do you remember how you got here?"

I tried to recall. I had been on patrol with Anna. There was a call, a black and white needed back-up. I was shot in the leg. My eyes slammed shut as the rest of the flashbacks flooded my brain. "Anna's dead . . . isn't she."

Marni held my hand. "Yes," she whispered.

"Where am I?"

"The Stephens, Michael, Burnwall Physical Therapy Center in North Hollywood."

Silence filled the room as the gruesome events played over and over in my head. I looked down at my leg. It was in a metal contraption suspended on an angle. "How bad is it?"

Marni shrugged. "It wasn't life threatening, but you sustained extensive damage and a wound to your arm."

"That's why that little bitch is trying to kill me."

Marni pulled the chair closer and sat. "Listen to me. You needed and will continue to need intensive therapy to get the use of your leg back. Karileah's in charge of your care, so don't piss her off. I'm told she's the best there is."

"It hurt, for fuck sake." I peeked sideways at Marni. "What she did to my arm. It hurt like a mother. Cursing helps."

Karileah walked back into the room with a large glass jar. The label taped to it read, "Blankety-Blank" and underneath that was printed, "One dollar per curse word" in magic marker. She placed the container on the tray. "Do we have a deal?"

I glared at the witch, stubbornly refusing to give in.

Marni pinched my arm . . . hard. "Yes, you do."

I WAS SWEATING by the time I completed the ten repetitions, but my shoulder no longer screamed like it had when I first started therapy on it. "Done."

Priss nodded. "Keep that up and I might let you slide on the blaspheming."

"What about hitting on you?" I wagged my eyebrows.

"You enjoy being naughty." She took the weights and placed them on the tray. "My mother warned me about types like you."

"Really!"

The doctor walked in at that point, so I chose not to say more. My teasing of the therapist was between us. I would never embarrass her in front of her colleagues or superiors.

"How goes it, Lieutenant?"

Sisters

"Good, Doc. Real good."

"I agree. How would you like to go home?"

I sat up straighter. "Do you mean it?"

"You'll need help full time. I anticipate it being long term to start with. You've made remarkable strides. I see no reason it won't continue. With an in-home aide and daily therapy, you should do fine."

"Great, when?" I hated hospitals and I knew I'd heal faster at home.

"As soon as you can make caregiver arrangements. How's that?"

I HAD BEEN mulling over the doctor's announcement and conditions for my release all afternoon. I had a number of options, but knew which one was essential to my complete recovery.

"Hey, I just wanted to stop by and say goodnight." Karileah leaned in the doorway.

"What's this, Miss Priss, a half day for you." In fact it was after six, and an hour beyond the girl's usual quitting time.

"I have an audition tonight. I'll see you in the morning. Try to behave yourself, and don't be grabbing at the nurses!"

"Break a leg," I said.

Karileah waved and left.

THE NEXT MORNING, at six, Karileah arrived for our first therapy session of the day.

"So should I beg for an autograph before you become famous and forget us little people?"

The therapist's ever-present smile collapsed, she shook her head. "No, they had already hired someone by the time I got there."

"I'm sorry, Miss Priss."

Karileah grasped my arm and slowly lifted it until it was fully extended. "It's hard going on these calls at night. Most of the studios do readings during the day, when I'm here. I just need to figure out a way to adjust my schedule to accommodate getting to the auditions."

I sat up a little straighter. "Well, Miss Priss, would you be willing to listen to a proposition?"

Karileah shook her head. "I'm not really in the mood to spar with you today."

"This is legit, I promise." I used my finger to crosss my heart. "I did a lot of thinking yesterday, and I made some phone calls. Marni even helped. I've got a solution to both our problems. Quit this place and come work for me."

"Stop fooling around."

"Seriously. I've already checked things out. The insurance will pay your wage, or at least a good portion of your current salary for up to a year. If you take the extra bedroom in the house, you can live there rent free, which should more than cover the difference in your pay."

Karileah stared at me. "Are you serious?"

"Hell, yes." I stopped her from working her arm. "I need you in order to get better and we both know it. I can't do this alone and I don't want to."

"You'll be fine. There are lots of—"

"I don't want them, Priss—I need *you*. You know me, you understand the injuries. You don't take any crap from me. Don't make me beg you. Please."

"This is crazy."

"Think about it. You can do my therapy at night. That frees your days up for the auditions you want to go on. My place is as close to the action as yours is. The extra room is sitting there empty . . . why let it go to waste?"

Karileah appeared to mull it over.

"Just to prove I'm serious. If you take the job, I promise no more sexual innuendos, ever."

"I need to think about this."

"Seriously? Come on. What's to think about? It's a win-win for you. No rent, you get paid slightly less than you're earning now, but you won't be paying any rent, or utilities. That's got to work out as more money in your pocket. I already pay for the food, so you wouldn't need to contribute to that either." Maddison recognized the moment that Priss started to fold. "Most important, your days are freed up to pursue your dream."

"You absolutely promise no funny business."

I crossed my heart again. "I give you my word, Miss Priss. You and I are good together. I need you nagging me. I need your expertise. You need more free time, I can give that to you. Please. I'll even try to curb my potty mouth."

Karileah chuckled. "Now that almost makes it worthwhile." She made the sign of the cross, then held out her hand. "Deal." We shook hands. "Thank you Maddison, this means a lot to me."

"Kiddo, it's me, that should be thanking you. I owe you, big time. We both know it."

Three days later, I was home in my own bed, Karileah was moved into the extra bedroom, and our new routine began.

Late that night, Karileah excused herself to compose a letter to her mother.

```
Hi Mom,
    The best thing's happened. I'm working
for crime novelist, L. M. Addison. Author
of 'Criminality'. The book might even be
turned into a movie-of-the-week. Anyway,
```

the insurance company hired me to provide extensive therapy.

We've struck a deal. I'm moving into the extra bedroom in the house and won't need to pay rent or utilities. I'll work with the patient at night, and have my days free to go on casting calls. My agent assures me I'm bound to get a recurring part on one of the sitcoms now that I'm available days to audition.

I'm so excited. I'll write more about it all next week. Take care, write back soon. Tell Nonie I said Hi.
Love
Karileah

Chapter Ten

October 23, 2008

ANOTHER EIGTH INCHES of snow had fallen. The skies appeared clear to the west, hopefully the inclement weather was behind us for now. Chance charged down the deck steps and jumped into the deep snow, leaping around, flattening down an area to make room for her morning needs. Her antics brought a smile to my face.

I opted to shovel the wrap-around walk all the way this time. I needed time to think and work helped me do that. I had worked myself down the stairs, and still no solution availed itself to me. Doc was going to be here at least a couple of more days and I needed to figure out how to deal with that without lashing out.

Under the landing, I reached for a pair of snowshoes that hung from one of the beams and strapped them on for our walk. Chance ran ahead, sniffing and exploring, at times needing my help to be rescued from the four-foot drifts, but finally we reached Priss's meadow, a plot of land, surrounded by century old ponderosa pines and alpine firs. The trees protect the area within from the inclement weather. I always felt humbled and insignificant when standing amid their splendor. I walked through the small gap in the branches into the lee, removed my snowshoes, and walked to the bench and memorial hidden just ten feet within. I swept the small monument of it's coating of white fluff, then sat on one of the handmade wooden benches.

"Morning, Miss. Priss." Chance came and sat beside me. Her head rested on my thigh. That's her custom while we sit here in the quiet. We visit Priss's ashes often. Anya loves to keep her Mama apprised of what's happening in our lives. Of course, Anya is always happy to talk with her Mama. She misses her badly. But there's a definite peacefulness that soothes us all whenever we're here. I think Chance feels something too. She never explores or does anything to desecrate the grounds in here.

Deep breaths. I take a couple and remember Priss teaching me this calming technique. For the moment, it works and the tension eases.

A memory of her forms in my mind. She had wanted me to learn yoga. I thought she was out of her mind. I could barely walk, never mind twist my body into a pretzel. Another recollection fills my conscious: Priss watching me, doleful eyes chiding me for some offense I'd committed. Likely, my potty mouth. She hated when I swore. We were so different, and yet, our lives melded together almost perfectly.

The enclosed space grew brighter. I gazed upward in time to see the skies turn from pale gray to blue. "Might be a nice day, after all, right girl?" Chance licked my hand in response.

I don't really believe in the hereafter, or in heaven and hell. I believe life on earth *is* our hell, and death is just the reward you've earned from surviving it. I don't believe in ghosts or spirits or whatever it is that so many people attribute to noises in old houses. Things that go bump in the night usually have a logical explanation, if you're willing to search them out. My problem is, Priss *did* believe. Emphatically so. She believed in God, sins, purgatory, heaven and hell, and the eternal afterlife.

"We had one hell of a storm," I said out loud, "and I'm not sure if you've noticed, but we've got a guest on the property." I sat there, my insides churning.

"Priss, I really miss you, and I suck at playing nice with strangers." I took another deep breath, but my errant heartbeat wouldn't settle.

"This woman, the one that got lost, there's something about her." I doubled over, putting my head between my knees. I felt like I was gonna pass out. "She scares me, Priss, I don't know why, and I'm always angry with her for some reason. Jesus, look at me talking to you like you can hear me! You'd probably like her just because I don't."

I sat there quietly, thinking about that. Priss liked everyone; she trusted everyone. Being a cop, I knew the seedier side of human nature and I wanted no part of people. Though Doc didn't fall into that category, I didn't like the way she made me feel, or the way my hormones automatically spiked when I was around her. I sat a bit longer, thinking.

"Hey, I think I made some headway on the edits. You always knew what was missing. What needed tweaking. I miss that. Anyway I got some of it done. I think Marni will be pleased. I know I said it, but I miss you. Anya does too. She's visiting with Sophia and Lorraine, but she'll be home later today. I'll try to get her up here then. I hope you're at peace, my friend."

As I walked toward the gap in the trees, a slight breeze buffeted me. I turned and smiled. Whenever this happened, I liked to believe it was Priss. Just in case, I responded. "I know. I'll see you soon."

We had been coming here to spend time and talk with Priss the last four months. Priss and I found this hidden gem on my great-grandfather's property four years ago when I inherited it from my grandmother. Priss had chosen this field for her remains mainly because wildflowers of all types and colors grew here in the summer and she said they reminded her of home . . . of the flowers in her mother's garden.

We knew her time was limited. I had hoped she'd get to spend a couple of years here with us before the illness took her. Her God had other plans. She died in my arms on a beautiful warm spring day, two weeks before we were scheduled to move from Los Angeles. Anya and I brought her remains with us five weeks later and we scattered her ashes as she had requested. I liked to think she's in a better place, that maybe she *can* hear me. That she's finally forgiven herself.

"Come on, mutt, we've got a guest at home that needs feeding." The walk back was easier since we had already forged the trail. Chance saw a deer in the distance and sped off. It's not like she'd attack it. I chuckled and went on my way. She'd come home soon enough; she hadn't eaten as yet.

Chapter Eleven

"BREAKFAST IS READY," Fiona called out as Maddison came through the door. "I hope you don't mind. I figured it's the least I can do, since you took such good care of me."

"You shouldn't be standing on that leg."

Fiona turned. "I am a doctor. I know what my limitations are." She smiled in an attempt to soften her tone.

"Guess you would. Sorry."

"Now hang your coat up. Everything's ready."

"Didn't expect this." Maddison hooked her coat on the rack and walked into the kitchen.

"About this morning . . . I'm not always eloquent—"

Maddison put up her hand. "My fault completely, I've been an ass. It's been a little stressful and I'm not used to having a stranger around. I should be the one to apologize and I do. Let's forget everything."

"As you wish." Fiona had set the counter with silverware, napkins and a pitcher of milk. "I thought we could serve up in here and carry our plates over to the table."

"I'll carry them, you go sit. Be careful." Maddison dished up the two plates. Fiona had made what appeared to be Spanish omelets, Canadian bacon, and a plate of multi-grain toast. "Smells great, thanks." She passed a plate to Fiona and put the other in front of her chair. "Would you like more coffee?"

"Please."

Maddison brought the carafe to fill both of their cups.

Just then, Chance pawed at the door, her odyssey apparently over, and her belly likely empty. "I'll just feed her so we can have some peace while we eat." Maddison went to the door and rubbed the dog down thoroughly with her special chamois towel, then led her into the kitchen to prepare her meal.

"You're limping, did you hurt yourself?" Fiona watched as she continued the prep of Chance's meal.

Leaving the question unanswered and Fiona silently waiting for one, Maddison put down fresh water before returning to the table.

"The carnage you saw yesterday is the issue. The leg gives me trouble from time to time."

"That's why you're off the force and have a set of crutches," Fiona said, her voice almost a whisper.

"Yup." Maddison reached for a piece of toast and dug into the meal.

"You should never have carried me that first day, that had to have put a strain on the leg."

Maddison shrugged. "I didn't exactly carry you. Just supported ya."

"I'm so sorry." Fiona felt awful. "After we eat, you should get in the Jacuzzi and let the jets massage your muscles. It'll do wonders."

Maddison raised her eyes to meet Fiona's. "After we eat, I have a slew of chores to complete to keep this place running smoothly. I'm behind three days' worth since I didn't want to leave your side during the fever episode. I told you, I was scared. I didn't know what was happening to you. Anyway, Anya should be home midday and I want to spend time with her. I've missed her. And at some point I need to start plowing out to the state highway . . . that is, unless you're okay with staying here indefinitely?"

Fiona shook her head, unsure how to respond. "Tell me about the house. Why an old church? Why so far from everything? What needs doing to maintain it?"

Maddison kept eating, her head down, her fork repeatedly filling her mouth every few seconds until her plate was empty. She sucked down the coffee then turned to Fiona who had silently watched her the entire time.

"I need to empty the coal dust from the coal furnace in the basement and load it up with more coal to keep it stoked. I managed to sneak down each day while you rested, because it's imperative I keep it going. It's the source of the hot water and supplemental heat. The stack pipe needs to be cleaned a couple of times a month to ensure no build ups that could allow carbon monoxide getting into the house. I'm behind on that and we don't need a problem. I usually run and test the generator weekly to be sure it's recycling properly. We're likely to lose power if the snow brings any trees down and that's a fairly common occurrence up here with the winter storms."

Fiona sipped her coffee as Maddison talked.

"We're gonna need more wood for the fire, I normally keep a minimum of two of the four rings out on the deck and the bin by the fireplace filled. The wood on the hearth is all that's here right now." Maddison took a deep breath.

"The church was my great grandfather's, it's been handed down to me by my grandmother. She raised me and felt I deserved it. I'm really not sure I do, since I'm not exactly religious. Now it's home." She shrugged. "*When* everything else is complete, I need to get some work done on the computer."

"I wish I could help."

"You already did, by making breakfast. That was a treat and very good, I would add. I'm used to handling the rest." Maddison stood and took the dishes to the kitchen to clean up. She repeated the steps until the table was wiped clean and ready for the next meal.

"I can do the dishes if you leave them in the sink," Fiona offered.

Maddison turned back to her. "Are you sure?"

"Yes." Fiona nodded her head firmly. "Doctor's orders."

"Okay, then. Thank you."

"Can I ask you something?"

Maddison waited.

"When do you think I might realistically get on my way and how exactly will I do that?"

Maddison moved to the window and looked down into the valley. Some light snow still fell. She could see the highway below and the town beyond if she squinted. "Early storms are always expected up here, but this one has dumped an inordinate amount of snow. That *is* unusual. The real problem for you is winter comes early to Montana. It can snow for a week steady without letup. As soon as I get the household chores set and you and Anya settled, I'll see about taking the tractor out and clearing the driveway and road out to the highway."

"So tomorrow?"

Maddison shook her head. "I already told you, It's gonna take me at least two days to clear the driveway and road. Add another day to tow your vehicle back here and see if I can get it running. Once I know that, I can give you a better idea. Remember the highway down there needs to be cleared before they'll bother with the National Forest roads that come up the mountain, and it's all dependent upon the weather."

"How can you stand being isolated like this?" Fiona shivered as she crossed her arms over her chest.

"That's exactly why we moved here, Doc, for the solitude. We wanted our daughter to grow up in a small town. I'm making sure that happens." Maddison moved to the door under the staircase. "I'll be downstairs for a while. Chance, stay."

I STOMPED MY feet on the deck before bringing in the last load of wood. As I approached the fireplace, Fiona was on the couch lovingly stroking Chance.

"You're limp is worse."

I filled the woodbin and placed the remaining four logs on the fire then turned to Fiona. "I know, don't worry about it. It's temperamental, much like me."

"The internal damage must have been significant to cause this much discomfort." Fiona's eyes followed me. "Or is it recent?"

"I told you, it was shattered in two places. There's rods and screws holding it together."

"You were shot, right?"

"Twice . . . in the leg."

"Twice. Yes, you said that yesterday." Fiona leaned forward, staring at my leg as if she could see beneath the material of my jeans.

"Three times actually."

"Three?"

"Once in the shoulder too."

"How long ago?"

"Seven years last month." I try not to recall that day or the loss it entailed.

"Have you seen another doctor, a specialist maybe, to see if something more can be done."

"Look, Doc, I'm lucky to be alive. The fact I still have my leg and am able to use it is a miracle. The doctor was good, but my therapist was heaven-sent." I thought about that statement. Priss truly was an angel. I hoped with all my heart she was *in* her heaven. I shook my head.

"Anyway, a little pain's a small price to pay for the luxury of my leg working normally."

"You're right, of course and it's none of my business." She leaned back in the chair and spread the afghan over her legs.

"I didn't mean that. I was simply explaining that my therapist is the reason I can walk. The doctors weren't sure it was possible. She made it happen and gave me my life back." I shrugged. "I'm gonna get out of these sweaty clothes, do you need anything before I do?"

"No, I'm fine."

I headed upstairs to gather clean clothes and passed the den on my way back to the bathroom. The tablet was plugged into the outlet, its light emitting a soft glow. That's a relief, Doc clearly was determined to keep busy, hopefully she'd stay out of my hair as well.

Chapter Twelve

Later That Afternoon

THE HUM OF the snowmobile drew me to the front door. Sophia pulled up the drive slowly and parked the unit in front of the steps. I turned to Fiona. "I'll be right back."

I stepped out on the landing and, smiling, held out my arms to Anastasia who couldn't move her short legs fast enough to get off the snowmobile. "Mam!" She took off her helmet and hung it on the railing before she clumsily ran up the steps and jumped into my arms.

"Hello, baby." I hugged her tight and kissed her cheek. "I missed you."

"Me too."

"Hey, Sophia. Don't just sit there. Come on in, I've got fresh coffee brewing."

"You sure?"

"Absolutely."

Sophia shut down the engine, unclipped Anya's backpack, and brought it with her.

"Mam, who's that?" I turned to see Anya pointing at Fiona. She stood upright on one crutch, looking back at us. "I'll introduce you both in a minute."

By this time, Sophia was on the landing with us. "I can't wait to meet this ninny."

"Don't start, I've been rude enough for both of us." I opened the door and Sophia walked in ahead of me. Anya tends to be shy around strangers and hid her face in my neck as I approached Fiona.

"Fiona, this is my daughter, Anastasia." Anya turned her head slightly. "Anya, I want you to say hello to Doc Fiona."

Anya's head shot back, tears formed quickly as she began to cry. "No doctor, no doctor." Her tiny fists flew up to her eyes as she swiped at her tears.

"Easy, easy. Doc Fiona is *not* here to see you, I promise."

"No doctor," she whimpered.

I gently gripped her hand. "Sweetie, look. Doc has the boo-boo. That's why she's here, not to see you."

Anya had buried her face in my neck, she peeked at Fiona.

"Anastasia, I'm not here to examine you, I promise. I fell down and got hurt. See my ankle." Fiona lifted her leg slightly.

"She has owie?"

"Yes, baby. Mam had to sew up a boo-boo on her leg and give her the brace for her foot. With the storm, she has nowhere else to go for a while." I leaned closer and whispered in her ear. "I promise, it's true."

Fiona smiled at Anya. "I hope we can be friends. It appears you know all about boo-boos."

Anya smiled tentatively. A small cough next to me, reminded me that Sophia was there. I half turned and beckoned her forward. "This is Nana Sophia, a phenomenal babysitter and all around good person and friend."

"Hi."

"Nice to meet you." Fiona put her hand out.

Sophia wiped her palm on the leg of her snow pants then took Fiona's hand. "Same here, Doctor."

"Call me Fiona, I'm not here in a professional capacity." She turned to Anya and smiled. "Right Anastasia?"

Anya looked suspiciously at Fiona.

"I'm not here to check on you. But you can examine me, if you like?" Fiona clarified.

Anya smiled, nodding enthusiastically.

"Then you're a medical doctor, and not one of them Phd's?" Sophia asked.

Fiona chuckled. "Medical, definitely. I work at a family practice back in Pennsylvania."

"Sophia, get some coffee and take your coat off. Stay awhile." I carried Anya to the side chair and sat with her in my lap. "So, tell me all about your weekend?" I unzipped her pink snow suit and removed it.

Chance arrived at the front door just then. "Sophia, could you let her in?"

"Got it."

Chance ran through the door, across the room and jumped into my lap. Anya laughed out loud as the dog licked her face and hands. She threw her arms around Chance's neck and kissed her nose. "I misseded, Chance."

"She *missed* you too." Chance got down and jumped on the couch next to Fiona, who immediately began petting her. "So you were telling me about your weekend."

"Nana Lorraine and I played checkers. And we bakeded a cake and shoveled snow and we—"

I glared at Sophia. "You shoveled snow?"

"Uh-huh," Anya stated proudly.

"Just the side walk," Sophia responded.

"Well, I have to say, there's no broken bones, no stitches and no black and blues, so how did you two manage that?" I pretended to examine Anya, lifting and probing her arms and legs as I spoke.

Anya giggled as she wiggled to be let down. "Nana Lorraine said you would kill Nana and me if I gots hurt. We had to be carefuls." She smiled mischievously.

"Nana Lorraine is right."

Anya went to the couch and started petting Chance on the opposite side that Fiona was petting her. The damned dog was in ecstasy.

"What brings you out this way?" Sophia asked.

Fiona looked up. "A wayward sister."

"Mam, know what else?"

I directed my attention to Anya. "What Munchkin?"

"Sunday, we wented to church." Anya climbed up on the couch to sit next to Chance.

"You did?"

"Uh-huh." She lay across the dog's back and hugged her tight forcing Fiona to remove her hand. "And I played with Jetson, Keaton, Gwen and Casey." She counted them off on her fingers before she jumped down off the couch and ran to the kitchen. "They have a new sister, but she's too little to go'd out."

I turned to Sophia.

"Poppy's just three months old," Sophia said in a low voice.

"Did you have fun with the kids?" I asked.

Anya called out, "Yes."

"They had a blast." Sophia took a sip of her coffee, her eyes watching me over the rim of the mug. "We go to church, you know that. Besides, they live next door, and everyone played at our place while we babysat them all."

"Anya, what are you doing?" She was on the other side of the island and out of sight. Suddenly she appeared with the Blankety-Blank jar and placed it in front of me on the floor.

"Did you put moneys in, Mam?"

I smirked at the little imp. "No. I didn't have too."

She stood with one hand on her hip and the other wagging a finger at me. She was the image of her mother in that pose.

Sophia laughed out loud. "She's got your number, that's for sure."

"I pulled three dollars from my pocket and handed them to Anya. She counted each one, then stuffed them into the slot at the top of the jar. "Is that really all?" She glared at me.

"Yes, you little monster." I reached out to tickle her.

"Should I even ask?" Fiona chortled.

"Mam says bad words and Mama makes her put money in the jar all'd the time." Anya carried the jar back to the cabinet and put it away.

"Yikes! I'm glad I'm not part of this. I'd owe a boat full of dollars after the week I had," Fiona whispered.

"Come here you little rascal." Anya ran over and climbed into my lap. "Did you take your medicine?"

"Uh-huh."

I raised my eyebrow. "Are you sure?"

"Yes." Anya crossed her heart.

I hugged her to me. "Good girl." I was thankful every day for her presence in my life.

Anya pushed against me. "Too tight, Mam."

I loosened my hold. "I really missed you."

She kissed my cheek. "Me, too."

"Are you hungry?"

"No, Nana and me eated."

"You ate. Not eated." I wouldn't ask what, better I don't know. I turned to Sophia. "How are things in town?"

She grimaced. "Like you'd expect. The small plow guys finally cleared the local roads, but now they've been assigned to help with the highways." Sophia shook her head. "The Department of Transportation can't keep up and it's only October."

"Typical," I said.

"They'll get 'er done, sooner or later."

"How are your supplies?"

She snickered. "We did like you suggested, bought a used freezer and fridge off the Andersons when they moved. So, I stocked up in September. I'm good, thanks."

"What about fuel?"

"Tank was filled last Wednesday before the storm. Wood pile is almost full."

"Excellent. Just remember you're both welcome up here if you get in trouble, or supplies get low."

"Thanks." She gulped her coffee down then stood up. "I'm going to head home. It was nice meeting you Doctor Fiona. If you ever need a change of scenery or a job, think about Yaak. We definitely need our own doctor. The job comes with a house and a small salary." She turned to Anya. "Come give Nana a kiss good-bye."

Anya ran to her. "Bye, Nana."

"What do you say, Anya?" I prodded.

"Thank you Nana. I had fun." She kissed Sophia on the cheek. "Will you come visit me soon?"

"Maybe. We'll see how the weather is." Sophia hugged Anya one more time.

"Thanks, Sophia, for everything. Drive careful. Say hi to Lorraine for me and thank her as well."

"Will do. Call if you need me. I'll let you know when I get home."

Sisters

Anya and I watched from the doorway as Sophia pulled the cord to start the engine. She climbed on the snowmobile and waved before pulling away down the drive.

Chapter Thirteen

March 2002

KARILEAH COUNTED MADDISON'S reps. When they reached fifty, she nodded her head. "Stop." She said a silent Hail Mary.

Maddison lowered the twenty-five pound weights to her sides and flopped back on the bed. "I told you I could do it."

"You did, but it's my job to be sure you don't *overdo* it." Kari took the weights and placed them on the floor.

"So pizza tonight to celebrate?" Maddison asked.

"Whatever you want."

"What time do you have to be on the set tomorrow?"

"Early, about four." She put the second pillow behind Maddison's head. "I'm not sure what time I'll get home. It could be late."

"You have the keys to the car. Just be sure to drive safe."

Kari removed the brace from Maddison's leg. "Thank you for understanding."

"It was part of our deal. I wanted to show you I really can do the upper body exercises without you."

"Please, just don't attempt to do the leg ones. You'll only undo the progress we've made." Kara put lotion on her hands and started the deep massage.

"I won't. I promise." Maddison remained quiet.

"What's wrong?"

"I'm trying to figure out how to ask you a question, and get the truth from you."

Karileah stopped her ministrations. "I've always been honest with you. Just ask."

Maddison took a deep breath. "Do you really believe I'll walk again?"

"I do." She nodded her head. Maddison had made great progress, but the damage to the muscles had been extensive. Normally she'd be happy for a patient to have gotten this far, but Maddison was different. Unless she regained full mobility, Kari knew the therapy would be judged a failure in both their eyes. "It won't be next week or even next month, but you will walk on your own two legs in the future. I promise you."

"You wouldn't kid a kidder, would you?"

"Gosh, Maddy, you're dating yourself. My Mom says that." Kari resumed the massage. "You'll walk, and when you do, you'll owe me a steak dinner."

"Miss Priss, if I walk, I'll owe you my life."

Sisters

Kari nodded shyly. She knew Maddison's ability to walk and care for herself was mandatory, and she was determined to make it happen for her friend.

Karileah,
   I am not happy with this living arrangement of yours. I did not raise you like that. Father Francis is praying for your salvation. He's very concerned about your soul.
   That place is corrupting your morals and I'm not pleased. I want you to come home. You'll never find a respectable man to marry if they discover this. The bible says to honor thy mother and thy father.
   Your sister has been named to the Board of Trustees at the facility she volunteers at, I worry she's working too hard, but that's always been her way.
   Think about what I said and about coming home. I love you, but I worry about your future. You're happiness means everything to me.
Love Mom

Mom,
   I have the best news. I'm playing a barista on Frasier next week. It might even turn into a repeat performance. I did it, I'm going to be an actress!
   My therapist job continues to go well. The hours are long, but I have my days free to pursue my dream. I'm not living in sin, or doing anything I'm ashamed of. Tell Father Francis to pray for someone who needs his prayers. I'm working hard to make my dream a reality, why can't you be happy for me?
   I'm glad about the new position for Fiona, that's wonderful news and I know you must be so proud of her.
   Take care of yourself and write soon.
Love
Karileah

Chapter Fourteen

October 23, 2008

LATE THAT EVENING after the dinner dishes had been cleared, Fiona and Chance sat on the couch while Anya knelt on the floor next to them. Fiona chuckled at the look of concentration on the little girl's face. They were playing checkers. Anya waited none too patiently for Fiona to make her move. So far it was a close match.

"How did you get so good at this, young lady?" Fiona asked. She was enjoying herself despite the circumstances, and the child was utterly charming. It made the ache in her heart hurt even more.

"Mama teached me." Anya never took her eyes off the board.

"She taught you." Maddison corrected as she stretched my arms over her head. "It's getting late, Munchkin. You can finish the game in the morning."

"But Mam, pleeeease."

"Uh-uh, you know the rules." Maddison stood up and advanced to where they played.

Anya climbed onto the couch, wrapped her arms around Fiona's neck and gave her a kiss on the cheek. "Goodnight, Fiona."

"Goodnight, Anastasia." Fiona smiled brightly. "Sleep tight and don't—"

"Let the bedbugs bite." Anya started giggling. "Mam, she knowed it too."

"Knows it too." Maddison held out her arms, and Anya stepped off the couch into them. "Most people do know it."

"But Mama knowed it best, right?"

"Yes, Mama did." Maddison turned to Fiona. "I'll be back in a bit."

Ten minutes later, Maddison stepped out of Anya's room, leaving the door slightly ajar behind her. "Would you like another cup of hot chocolate or some tea?"

"Chocolate, please." Fiona watched as Maddison moved around the kitchen preparing the drinks. The more she studied the woman, the more she was sure there was a deep sadness about her.

After fixing two mugs and adding mini marshmallows to one, Maddison walked into the nave and placed the mug into Fiona's waiting hands. "Here you go."

"Thank you." She took a sip. "This is so good, but I have to admit, I'm surprised you let Anastasia have it earlier."

Maddison chortled. "She doesn't. I heat up the milk for all of us, but she gets mostly milk, with a quarter-teaspoon of sugar and the marshmallows. She doesn't even realize there's a difference."

"It'll be our secret, promise."

Maddison got up and cleaned the residue from the fire pit, then loaded more logs onto the grate. Soon the flames leaped up and heat flowed into the room.

"I owe you an apology."

Maddison turned to Fiona. "Why?"

"I judged you by appearance. And I got it all totally wrong, I'm so sorry."

"Not an issue."

"Can I . . . I'd like to ask you something?"

Maddison sat down. "As long as you understand I might not answer."

Fiona nodded. "Fair enough."

Maddison waited.

"Sophia mentioned Yaak earlier. I thought I was in Libby?"

"Ah, that explains a lot. You took the first right instead of the second. Lots of people make that mistake at the fork. You're an hour off course and definitely near Yaak proper. This property is just outside the perimeter. Libby is south of here by almost twenty miles."

"Why was the church built so far from town?" Fiona waited, at first she didn't think Maddison would respond.

"Almost two hundred years ago the town was here on the mountain. Then a plague of some sort, I'm not sure which one, swept through. The townspeople burned the structures to get rid of the sickness, but the church didn't burn. My great grandfather felt it was an omen. He purchased the land and building from the town."

"Wow, that's . . . kind of eerie."

"Yup. If you believe in that sort of thing, it is."

"That doesn't excuse my stupid mistake." Fiona rubbed her forehead.

"It happens all the time, but mostly in the summer. The fork splits twice, the first right turn cuts up here, the second right turn is a U-turn, which would have taken you right into Libby."

"Thank you, but I still feel foolish." She shook her head.

"If that's the worst of what happens, you'll be fine." Maddison shrugged. "My turn. Why were you headed to Libby?"

"I think my sister might be there, or more accurately the person who can give me some answers regarding her, is there."

"Answers?"

"My sister is a dreamer, always has been. But she was consistently good about writing home. We haven't heard from her, not for a while and my mother is worried. I have reason to believe she may be dead. So I find myself traipsing across country trying to find answers."

"There's a lot of communes around here. Is that where you think this person is?"

"To be honest, no. I don't know what to think at this point. I'm sick of always chasing after her, trying to fix her mistakes, but my mother is older and wants answers."

"Ahh."

"Never mind. I'm just a typical older sister who's tired of being responsible." She shrugged her shoulders. "Anastasia is a beautiful little girl. She's so smart!"

Maddison's smile lit up her face. "Takes after her mama, that's for sure."

"Did you always want children?"

Maddison laughed acerbically. She turned, apparently to look toward Anya's room, then lowered her voice and whispered. "No. In fact, I never wanted to inflict these genes on the world. Once was more than enough, dontch ya' think?"

"Did your partner pressure you?"

"No, why?"

Fiona folded her hands in her lap, a cuticle absorbing all her attention. "My biological clock has been sounding for a while now. When I suggested children to my last partner, she packed up and left before the words were out of my mouth."

"Ouch."

Fiona grimaced. "It didn't help when my mother very sagely pointed out that I wasn't heartbroken, just angry that my plans had been usurped." She shrugged her shoulders. "Sadly, she was right."

"How old are you?"

"Thirty-eight."

"Hell, that's still young. Don't women have kids into their fifties now?"

"Yes, and then those fifty-year-old women are chasing after them into their seventies. I can't see myself doing that."

Quiet enveloped them, long moments of silence. Not awkward, but something definitely in the air.

"Can I ask you another question." Fiona held her breath, nervous to broach this subject.

"Same rules," Maddison said.

"Did you and your partner use insemination?"

Maddison sat quietly. She appeared to think long and hard before she responded. "No."

"A surrogate then?"

"No."

Fiona's brow furrowed. "I don't understand."

"My wife got pregnant the old-fashioned way."

That left Fiona with more questions than answers. The set of Maddison's shoulders warned her to tread lightly. "You were . . . okay with that?"

"I'm more than okay with the outcome. I have a remarkable daughter."

"Yes"—Fiona's eyes softened in the firelight—"you most certainly do."

Maddison took their empty mugs to the kitchen.

"I have another question, if you don't mind?" Fiona thumped to the counter while Maddison rinsed the cups and placed them in the dishwasher. "It's about Anastasia."

Maddison turned, her arms crossed over her chest.

"Why is she so afraid of doctors?" Fiona watched as Maddison clearly struggled to answer.

"Her immune system is susceptible to infection, so she's seen more than her share in her short life."

"Weak tonsils?"

"A couple different issues."

"That's why you had her stay with Sophia, in case I was contagious?"

Maddison nodded. "It's my job to protect her."

"Of course. I don't blame you. She's precious, and really bright." Fiona stared off into space. "I'm quite jealous. She's absolutely perfect."

"Are you thinking about having one by yourself?"

Fiona nodded. "I am. I had a procedure a while back. It didn't take." Tears filled her eyes.

"I'm sorry."

"I tried again recently, but I'm not feeling very confident about it."

"That's why you don't drink. Cause it's not good for a baby, right?"

Fiona nodded. "Also not good when you're trying to get pregnant."

"I'm really sorry."

"That's life, right?" Fiona shrugged and tried to blink her tears away. "I'm going to go to bed. Thank you for talking with me, and I'm sorry about misjudging you."

"Hey, Doc, I need a favor. I'm going to work here for a while." Maddison pointed to her laptop. "Then I'll catch a nap. I'd like to get out early to start clearing the roads. I need you to listen for Anya, maybe make breakfast for her if I'm not back."

"I am just screwing up your entire routine, aren't I?" Fiona tucked the crutches under her arms. "Wake me when you go out, I'll come down to the couch, that way I can listen for her. I'm glad to help with Anastasia and anything else if I can." She walked to the steps and opened the gate. "Goodnight, Maddison."

"Night, Doc."

Fiona lay in bed awake, listening to the clacking of the laptop. She fell asleep thinking of the little blue-eyed, raven-haired cherub asleep one floor below her. The little girl was endearing, and Fiona found herself wanting one just like her.

Chapter Fifteen

October 24, 2008

THREE HOURS LATER I closed down the Word program and shut off my laptop. My eyes were heavy and I needed a nap before venturing out. I slept until two-fifteen, then made sure the fire was fed and burning evenly before I climbed the stairs to wake Fiona.

I turned left and tapped lightly on the side wall. "Doc?"

"Hmmm?"

"Doc, you awake?"

"Yes. Yes, I'm awake."

I took one tentative step into the open space. "I'm going to head out to clear the roads. You said you'd listen for Anastasia."

Fiona sat up and I quickly averted my eyes. She wore a simple white T-shirt. Even in the dim firelight her plump breasts were clearly outlined, her dark nipples visible through the thin material.

"What time is it?"

"It's a little after two. I should be able to make headway and get back here by mid-morning if all goes well."

She pushed her hair back, and threw the covers aside. "Just let me throw some sweats on."

"I'll wait downstairs." I rushed away, the vision of her in my boxers and the wispy shirt would be burned into my memory for life. In the kitchen, I busied myself, trying to forget the image of Fiona half naked. That delectable portrait would be part of my erotic dreams for years to come I was sure. Full-figured women are how the female form was meant to be. Fiona represented the ideal lady in every aspect for this dyke.

"I'm here." She made her way down the stairs, then closed the gate securely. "Where's Chance?"

I tilted my head. "In with Anastasia, I told the dog to stay with her."

"Please be careful out there."

"Take care of my daughter, she's precious to me." I reached for my coat. I had dressed in layers to help offset the cold. Hours on the tractor meant wind and weather buffeting me while I worked to clear a path. Normally I wouldn't bother. Chance, Anya and I were snug and safe here on the mountain.

At the door, I paused. "Hey Doc?"

Fiona looked up from the book she had picked up. "Mmmm."

"I'm likely to be gone till midmorning, do you think you can handle Anya and Chance *and* stay out of trouble?"

She chuckled. "I promise not to let her play with sharp objects."

"There's left-over soup in the fridge if I'm not back by lunch. You handle breakfast. Make sure Anya eats. A fresh pot of coffee is all set. You need only turn it on."

"You're still limping, do you really think you should stress that leg?"

I had been rubbing my thigh reflexively. "Do you want to chance another snowstorm coming in before you can get out of here?"

She rubbed her forehead slowly. "No, but I also don't want to be responsible for you damaging your leg more than it already is."

"Don't fret, I'll be sitting for the most part. The tractor does the real work." I opened the door. "Be sure to feed Chance around five? It's in the bowl on the counter."

"Of course."

"Thanks. See you later."

MINUTES TURNED TO hours, the night noises reverberating and feeding Fiona's fears and imagination. She was edgy and unsettled ever since Maddison left the house. What if something went wrong? What if she had an accident? What if—the list was never ending.

Anastasia woke shortly after Maddison started up the tractor. The thundering noise disturbed the quiet of the night. Fiona was not surprised when Anya walked into the nave dragging her floppy-eared rabbit.

"Where's Mam?"

"She's out trying to clear the roads."

"Why?" The little girl moved next to the couch.

"So I can get out of your way and go home."

"Don't you like it here?"

Fiona grinned. "Come, sit with me." Anya climbed up on the couch and snuggled next to Fiona. She gladly embraced the child. Soon, Chance was up beside them.

"Why do you have to leaves?"

"Because, I have a job, and my Mom is back east." Fiona tugged the blanket and settled it over the dog and child. "Go back to sleep. Mam will be back when you wake up."

"We could be your family."

Before Fiona needed to respond, Anya's eyes closed, and she fell asleep, for which Fiona was very grateful.

The little girl and Chance blissfully snoozed while Fiona listened for every noise. At one point she swore she heard howling in the distance, and worried what it might be and if Maddison was safe out there alone . . . in the dark. She couldn't concentrate no matter how hard she tried and found herself re-reading the same words over and over again. She put the book aside having lost interest almost immediately.

She split her time, petting Chance and then gently touching Anya's downy hair. Playing with the long curly mop, pulling the silky strands between her fingers, she watched the child sleep with her thumb securely tucked between her lips and wished for the thousandth time she had a child of her own.

Fiona recalled Maddison's comment that Anya was conceived the old-fashioned way. What exactly did that mean? An open relationship? Fiona couldn't imagine Maddison tolerating such a thing. She was much too protective of the child, the dog, and the property. No, Fiona was sure, Maddison could never share a person she loved that way.

I STEPPED OUT onto the stoop, zipped my coat, pulled on my stocking cap and pulled the hood of the jacket up over that. As I slipped my hands into my gloves, I glanced back to see Fiona sitting on the couch, a book in her hand. Instantly an odd feeling of domesticity came over me and I found myself smiling.

Chance had taken an immediate liking to Fiona; that was unusual in itself. The dog was a rescue. Priss and I were told she had been mistreated and was horrifically skinny when first brought to the pound. The woman at the kennel assured us there wasn't a mean bone in her body, but she may be hesitant around unfamiliar people and places. Priss named her Chance as in second chance. The dog bonded with the three of us immediately and, with regular meals, soon became healthy and strong. Chance returned the favor by being very protective . . . almost aggressive with strangers. Mysteriously she never once reacted that way with Fiona. They were best friends from the start. Odd.

Another surprise was Anastasia. After her initial reaction to Fiona's being a doctor, she seemed to connect with the woman. Fiona talked to her for hours, patiently answering Anya's incessant questions. After dinner they'd played board games. The kiss good night surprised me as much as it appeared to surprise Fiona. It had only been five months since we lost her mother. Before that Anastasia had been an outgoing, chatty, happy child; after her mother died, she became quiet, distant and needy. I just hoped she wasn't bonding with Fiona to the point of having her heart broken when Doc went back East.

The two of them were connecting with this outsider as though they knew her. Puzzling behavior for sure. I prayed no one got hurt. I shook off the feeling and moved down the steps to walk around the side of the building toward the back of the lot.

The old, three-bay barn had been converted into a garage long before I took possession of the property. I used it to house my tractor, truck, and snow-mobiles. I entered through the side door, quickly closing it against the cold northwest winds. After undoing the heat plug on the diesel tractor, I climbed up into the cab and turned the key. The engine cranked hard against the icy temps, but turned over on the second try. I pushed the button to open the garage door, then pulled the tractor through the opening so the engine and fluids could warm up without carbon monoxide filling the bays.

Once outside, I looked westward. Stars glittered in the night sky. If I pushed hard, I might get the drive and roadway cleared by midmorning. Maybe even have a chance to take a look at Fiona's rental car. Ten minutes later, with the engine warmed and running smoothly, I popped the tractor into gear and lowered the front blade, ready to plow the drive.

It took an hour to finish the driveway and make all the bays of the barn accessible. I would need my truck if Doc's car was too far gone. Plowing the roads was going to delay my edits. That was something I didn't need. But it had to be done if Fiona was gonna get home before the spring thaw.

At the bottom of the drive, I turned right and started the grueling task of plowing twenty miles of snow. Accumulations were three-feet deep in places with nary a place to push it. I made pass after pass, plowing the white stuff until it wouldn't move any further, the drifts often higher than the blade of the tractor. As a last resort I used the bucket on the back to lift and dump the piles of snow into the ditch alongside the road. And so it went, using the plow for the most part, and relying on the scoop where the snow either drifted too high or was too compact.

The mindless task of clearing the roadway allowed me to think about my work-in-progress and the issues Marni had with the plotline. I spent the entire time reworking parts of the book in my head and imagining changes and what ifs to fill the holes and create the story arcs necessary for a mystery. I needed to add more miniscule details about each character to hint of possible connections to the murder, only to clear it all up in the final pages of the book. Now that the plot was going in a new direction, I'd have to look back and make sure all the changes blended. With the new details clear in my head, I'd start the rewrites tonight if I had time.

Many long hours later, I was finally headed home. Daylight brought a new beauty to the surrounding landscape. The white of the snow glistened in the sun, wildlife scurried about foraging for food. I could more than understand that need. I was cold, hungry, and tired with thoughts of curling up in front of the fire after a long, hot shower. With luck, Anya will have been fed, and completed her lessons in my absence. Basically, she's just reviewing for her upcoming on-line tests. Most of that work she can do on her own or with minimal help. Maybe she would even be ready for an afternoon nap. Then again, maybe Fiona would be in need of one herself.

THE WEE HOURS of morning finally turned to dawn. Chance awoke and wanted to be let out. Fiona gently nudged Anya aside so she could get up. She opened the door to let the dog out. "Hurry back, I'll have breakfast ready." Chance leaped through the door and down the steps.

Fiona kept watch until the dog was out of sight. The howling continued and she worried what it was and how close it might be. Would Chance be safe, was Maddison? She walked into the kitchen and flipped the switch on the coffeepot. Soon the sizzle and belch of the unit filled the room as coffee dripped into the carafe. Fiona moved to the fridge. She had never made breakfast for a child. She needed to know what her options were.

An hour after dawn, Fiona happily learned that Anastasia was an easy and willing guinea pig. The little girl ate the oatmeal that she had prepared without complaint, even though it was watery and tasteless. The child even peeled the skin off the apple that Fiona had cut up and neglected to mix in with the hot gooey mess. In the end, she asked for juice to finish the meal off. Fiona had even forgotten to provide a beverage.

"I'm sorry, Anya. I promise next time I'll do better." She took the empty bowl and rinsed it off.

"It's okay." Anya reached to the middle of the counter for a napkin, then wiped her mouth. "Thank you."

"You're very welcome." Fiona dried her hands on the towel after cleaning up. "What now, young lady?"

"I have to do lessons."

"Your lessons?"

"School, silly."

Fiona felt foolish. "You go . . . to school?" Maddison didn't mention getting her ready. "How do you get there?"

"I goes here. Mam teaches me."

"Is that because you're not old enough to go yet?"

"No, cause I learned here. Mam and I do lessons. I take tests on the 'puter."

She's homeschooled. Fiona released the breath she had been holding. "Do you have a lesson plan?" *Where the hell is Maddison?*

Anya ran into her room and returned shortly with a couple of different books. "I do reading first."

Fiona picked up the book, the title read *Book Fiesta*. She opened it to the first page and noted it was bi-lingual. "Do you speak Spanish?"

Anya nodded. "*Si, Fiona. Es lo que mamá quería.*"

Fiona put the book aside. "Mam will have to help you with that. I never learned Spanish. What else do you have here." She reached for the second book. The title was *What's Out There?* She turned to the foreword of the book. It dealt with space, the sun, moon and planets. Another subject Fiona was not knowledgeable in. She reached for the last book,. *Math Made Easy.* She opened it to the section marked with a post-it. The chapter dealt with fractions. Now this was a subject she felt confident about. "Let's do math first."

"Okay." Anya picked up her pencil and opened her notebook.

An hour later Fiona felt totally humiliated. Over the years she had become reliant on the dose-calculator app to provide the quick and easy answers when converting medicines. She was one of the first residents to get that program for her PDA, and soon all the doctors used it, tweaking it to suit their individual needs. The damned plug-in turned her brain to mush. She found herself unable to calculate the simplest conversion. Anastasia ended up teaching her the lesson. In disgust, Fiona let out a breath that scattered her bangs.

"Can we play now, Fiona?" Anya asked.

Fiona had been lost in thought. "Of course sweetheart, what do you want to do?"

"We could go outside and make snowmens?"

Fiona looked down at the girl's sweet smile. "Does Mam let you outside to make snowmen when it's this cold?"

Anya looked down at her feet.

"I didn't think so. How about I brush your hair for you?"

Anya peeked up. "Why?"

"Because that's what little girls do. They play dress-up."

"What's that?"

Fiona grinned. "Go get your brush and hair clips." Soon happy chatter filled the kitchen. They brushed and combed each other's hair. Anya ended up with a braid going down her back and Fiona received pigtails, slightly askew.

Anya giggled hysterically as she applied cream to Fiona's cheeks. "Can I put lips stuffs on too?"

Fiona seized a tube of lip balm and handed it to the child. "Here you go." As she anticipated, Anya covered a swath of skin from her nose almost to her chin. "I think that's enough for now."

"When's Mam coming back?"

"I'm not sure, sweetie, but soon." Fiona had been glancing out the window for hours, wondering the same thing. "*Where are you Maddison? Are you okay?*"

Chapter Sixteen

AS THE DRIVEWAY came into view, I made the decision to by-pass home and quick check on the rental car's condition. With luck I could save myself another trip later on. I plowed a single lane for the next mile and a half before noticing the vehicle resting on its side down in the ditch. I'd never have found it, if not for the tire sticking up out of the snow-covered mound.

I sat and stared at the wreckage for minutes, amazed Fiona had not been more seriously injured when she crashed and landed in the gully. It's obvious I'd never be able to get it out of the ditch and, even if I could, I wouldn't have the parts necessary to get it running again. The radiator was creased where the tree crushed the front of the vehicle.

That left only personal effects. They had to be in the car since she arrived with just the clothes she wore. I tied one of the ropes I carry in the cab to the plow end of the tractor, then used the other end to form a loop around my waist and under my thigh. Slowly I rappelled down the slope to the car. If her purse and clothing were in there, I'd retrieve them. The vehicle itself was going nowhere soon.

I used my gloved hand to clear the windshield and peek inside. A briefcase lay on the floor at an angle. I walked to the downed tree, gripped the branches to climb up and onto the damaged fender, then worked my way to the driver's door and started yanking. After a few tries I managed to wedge it open. The dented fender prevented full access, but I was able to reach inside and get the briefcase and started to climb back to the road. *Idiot. Where the hell are her clothes?* After checking the rear seat and finding nothing, I searched out the lever for the trunk and gave it a pull. The catch release was audible, but nothing happened. I'd have to dig the heavy snow from around the rear section of the car to get into the trunk. The more I maneuvered around the vehicle, the more compacted the snow became. As I drew closer to the rear and actually looked at the tire sticking up in the air, I became furious. The fucking thing was practically bald. That had me inspecting the rest of the car more closely. Compacts are fine if they come with front-wheel drive at a minimum, or better with all-wheel-drive. This piece of crap had neither. *What the hell was Fiona thinking?*

Forty-five minutes later, I had Doc's overnight bag slung across my back and her briefcase strapped to my side while I slowly and deftly made my way back up the incline to the tractor. I had left the engine running and the door of the cab closed, blocking some of the cold. The difference in temperature helped to warm my frozen extremities.

On the return trek, the sun was to my back, but so bright it nearly blinded me as it reflected off the snow-covered landscape. I kept the unit in four-wheel drive, even though the path was already cleared. It made forward progress slow going but provided better traction in the numerous slick spots. The final challenge would be the journey up the driveway, but the tractor climbed the hill effortlessly.

I GLIMPSED THE clock on the wall of the barn; it read after one. Fueled up and with engine and hydraulics fluids checked, the tractor was parked where it belonged with the engine heater plugged in. Satisfied that it was prepped and ready for the next time, I stepped out the side entrance in time to hear the generator kick on. At least I'd be here to ensure all was well inside.

My leg ached from the constant use of the clutch and that climb down and up from the rental car. Both contributed to making my gait unsteady. Overcome by exhaustion, I used the handrails to help pull my way up the front steps. Fiona's briefcase and backpack were still strapped to me. Hopefully, having her personal belongings would be a nice surprise. I pushed through the front door and dropped the luggage at my feet.

"You're back?" Fiona stood by the fire using one crutch while pushing a new log onto the grate with the poker.

"I am."

"Mam!" Anastasia ran and jumped into my arms. "I missed you."

I laughed out loud. "What the heck happened to you?"

"We played dress ups."

"You did, huh?"

Anya nodded. "Why we don't play dress ups?"

I kissed her powdered cheek and put her down. "Because if you dressed like me, you'd be in jeans and flannel all the time, and you wouldn't need that gunk."

Anya stood in her polka dot dress and hot pink leggings. "You can dressed up if you wanna."

"We'll see, Little One." I watched as Fiona finished feeding the fire. "I'll get more wood."

"No need, we did that already."

I turned to see the rings outside newly filled and the one inside packed part way. "We?"

Anya tugged on my hand. "I helpted," she said proudly.

"Yes, she did." Fiona said. "She kept herself busy at the counter, while I loaded the wood outside using the carpetbag, then when I brought up enough for here, we dragged it together to the hearth."

"You shouldn't be doing that with your leg."

"We both did what needed doing." She flinched when the refrigerator kicked back on. "I heard the electric go out. I wanted to make sure I kept the fire going. I guess I didn't need to worry. I didn't even hear the generator kick on."

"Yeah, I heard it when I was walking back from the barn. It has to cycle itself before the appliances will start up though." I looked down at my daughter. Anya was tugging on my pant leg. "What, Little One?"

"Can I have a cookie?" She stuck out her lower lip. She had that little girl pout down perfectly.

"I don't think we have any, baby."

"We could maked some?" she pleaded.

"How about you let me get a hot shower," I said as I removed my coat, gloves and boots. "And maybe if you've been good, we'll bake. How's that?"

"I did good all morning"—Anya turned to look at Fiona—"right?"

Fiona laughed out loud. "She's been a little angel." Then she gazed at me. "Is there anything I can do to help?"

There was much I wanted to say to her, but not in front of Anya. Chance ran to my side, then stopped to smell the unfamiliar gear I had dropped at my feet moments earlier. I reached for the door and let her out, then picked up the two pieces and placed them at Fiona's feet. "Here. I thought you'd want these. Sadly that car's not going anywhere."

Fiona leaned over to examine the items. "Thank you."

"Uh-huh." As I walked into the kitchen I began removing the outer layer of clothes and threw them into the washer, tomorrow would be soon enough to get the loads done. "Anya, wanna join me, maybe wash that gunk off your face?"

"No, uh-uh." She ran to Fiona's side. "I helps Fiona with her stuffs." Fiona had opened her briefcase and pulled an AC charger out. She attached it to her long dead phone.

"You still may not get service up here."

She looked up, "I know, but I should be able to use your Wi-Fi signal once it's charged. Then I can contact my office and explain things to my boss."

"Okay, then. Little One are you sure about the shower?"

She pushed into the chair next to Fiona. "I sure."

I grinned at her beautified face and worried how I would ever replicate it once Fiona was gone. "Okay, I'm heading in, behave yourselves."

"Yes, Mam."

Chapter Seventeen

June 2002

"HOW ARE YOU doing?" Karileah asked as she entered the room. Maddison had been working her legs for twenty minutes.

She sat on the exercise bike, her hands on the knees as she pedaled slowly. "It hurts like a mother."

"Ten more minutes, then I'll put the heat on your thigh." Kari watched as Maddison pushed herself even harder. She knew that Maddison wanted faster progress, but she worried at what cost. Patience was not Maddison's strong suit and her temper often flared when she couldn't physically do what her mind set out to accomplish. The sweat was pouring off Maddison's head and face. Her T-shirt was soaked and she was beginning to look a little gray. "Why don't we stop early?"

"No."

"If you hurt—"

"I won't." Maddison visible pushed down on her knees to keep her trembling legs going. "How's the new gig?"

Kari smiled. "It's wonderful. Everyone's been so nice to me and I love the character. It's a small part, and only for a couple of weeks, but I'm on TV and my mother gets to watch me for at least three episodes."

Maddison nodded. "I'm really proud of you and I'm sure she is too."

"I wish." Kari snorted. "Okay, time's up."

"Whadda ya mean by that?"

"My mother doesn't believe I'll ever be as accomplished as my sister. She feels that my dream of being an actress is foolish and she strongly disapproves of us living together."

"Why, we're just friends."

Kari shook her head. "It doesn't matter to her. And I'll never measure up in her eyes."

"You're not close then . . . with your sister?"

"We used to be." Kari helped Maddison off the bike. "Then when we hit high school it felt like I was suddenly in competition with Nonie. She got good grades, she was in all the clubs, and she had a job. I hung out with my friends and got in trouble a couple of times. My mother is super religious and believes that people— read that 'me'— are sinful every chance we get. She's convinced I'll end up pregnant and unmarried." Kari shrugged. "She never worried about my sister, because Miss Perfect never let on she had a life outside of school."

"Didn't you say your sister is gay?"

Sisters

"I don't want to talk about it anymore. It's too depressing." Kari settled Maddison in the chair. "You know you're pushing yourself too hard. You don't need to. Your leg is getting stronger all the time."

"It's been nine months and I still can't walk."

"I never promised you when, only that you *would* walk again. I stand by that." She took the heating pad and set it to high, then tucked it around Maddison's left thigh.

"I'm holding you to it." Maddison wagged her finger at her.

"If I'm wrong you get to keep the money in the BB jar."

"You must be sure. You'd never give that up willingly."

Kari laughed heartily and Maddison joined her.

TEARS RAN DOWN her cheeks as Karileah read her mother's letter a second time. When would she be good enough in her mother's eyes.

> Karileah,
> I watched you the other night on TV, you look like you've lost weight. Are you eating. You need a haircut, long hair was never becoming on you. I hope this part is over with. I don't appreciate you being on a comedy about gay people, it's not right. I just pray my friends don't recognize you. Father Francis was quite shocked that you would appear on such a show.
> Fiona and that woman broke up. I can't say I'm sorry, she was all wrong for your sister. Maybe now she'll meet a nice young man and get married.
> My flowers are blooming and the back yard is vivid in color, just as you always liked it. When are you coming home for a visit? I miss you, I miss us working together in the garden. Your sister never had your green thumb and never will. I love you, your room is always here for you.
> Write soon,
> Mom

Karileah had so many things she wanted to say in response to her mother's latest letter. Instead she tried to remain upbeat and confident. She took a sip of her water then picked up her pen and began her response.

Dear Momma

I'm glad you watched Will & Grace last week. It's so exciting and everyone on the show is so nice. I was thrilled that I said my lines right and they didn't need to do extra takes because of me. I'm eating three times a day and I honestly like my hair longer.

I'm sorry for Fiona, but I never liked Tasha, she was too snooty. Fiona will be better off without her. It will just take time. But, Mom, she's never going to find a man, she likes women, please try to accept that. Fiona will only find real happiness with a woman. Accept that I want to be an actress. It makes me happy. Please accept that.

My patient continues to improve, it's a process. I'm glad you bought the book, I hope you like it. Well I gotta go. Write soon.
Love Karileah

Chapter Eighteen

October 24, 2008

AN HOUR LATER Maddison placed the cookie sheet into the oven and set the timer. Anastasia knelt on a stool, licking the mixing bowl, while Fiona sat next to her observing the process. A warm feeling filled her. "I'm still trying to wrap my brain around the fact that you know how to bake."

Maddison looked up with a smirk. "Another of your incorrect assumptions?"

Fiona nodded. "Absolutely."

Maddison gathered the butter and eggs and placed them in the fridge. She put the canisters of flour, brown and white sugars in the cupboard and the vanilla extract on the second shelf along with the other spices. "I'll admit, baking is new to me. I promised Priss I'd learn so Anya would know how someday."

Fiona shook her head, truly impressed. "My mother is a baker. She tried for years to teach my sister and me. It's all Greek to me. I'm pretty useless in the kitchen, right Anya? But my sister, Kari, she got that gene. She can cook and bake."

"Carrie?"

"My sister."

"Ahh. I like cooking for the most part. Baking is trickier though. I'm still learning how."

"It's good." Anya had the bowl licked clean. Chocolate covered her cheeks and chin.

Maddison beamed at her daughter. "You're really going to need to clean up young lady."

Anya turned to Fiona. "We can play makeups again, right?"

Fiona's smiled. "We definitely will and this time, I actually have makeup for you to play with."

"Okay." Anya ran into the bathroom. Soon you could hear water running in the sink.

"She is a remarkable little girl. You're so lucky." Fiona's heart ached at the thought of never having a child.

Maddison nodded. "I am that."

"You're not mad about the makeup are you?"

"No, but I better go supervise the removal, or she'll need a bath as well. If the timer goes off, can you pull the cookies out of the oven?"

"As long as that's all I need to do. I'm telling you I have zip aptitude for the kitchen." Fiona chuckled.

"It can't be that bad."

"Trust me. I'm surprised Anya could eat the oatmeal I prepared. It was tasteless. My one and only specialty is an omelet and that's the full extent of my culinary skills."

Maddison shook her head as she made her way to check on her daughter.

I PUT THE last of the dinner plates in the dishwasher. "Anyone want dessert?"

"Me, me, meeeeee." Anya came running into the kitchen. She had been on the couch with Fiona, who was reading *The Cat in the Hat* to her from the tablet.

"Want milk with that?"

"Yes, please."

"What about you, Doc?"

"I'd love some milk and cookies."

"Powdered or frozen?"

"Which are you having?"

"Powdered, I keep the frozen for the Munchkin."

Fiona smiled at Anya. "Powdered for me, then."

I took the Mason jar out of the fridge and poured a glass, then poured two more from the jug and set the tray onto the coffee table. "Here you are, ladies."

Fiona reached for her glass. "Why the Mason jar?"

"I buy the whole milk in bulk, then freeze it in these so it lasts longer." Anya took a bite out of her cookie and had chocolate all over her face, again. "Use a napkin, young lady."

"I didn't know you could freeze milk?"

"As you've already concluded, you have to plan ahead when living up here. The shelf life for milk doesn't cut it, so I freeze it to make it last longer"

"Is the store in town able to replenish supplies during this weather?"

"Oh hell, no. That's why I stock non-fat powdered milk as well. I use the powdered to ensure a supply for other than her. Anya takes vitamins, so the powered should be safe for her, but I prefer her drinking the whole milk when possible."

Anya climbed down off the stool and ran to the bottom cabinet. She opened the door and pulled out the BB jar and carried it over to me. The little munchkin was grinning from chocolate-covered ear to chocolate-covered ear. I pulled a dollar out of my pocket and handed it to her. "Isn't it time for you to clean up and get ready for bed?"

"But Fiona is reading me." She wiped her mouth on her sleeve.

"You know the rules."

"Can Fiona read me in bed?"

"No. Now go get cleaned up. I'll read to you when you're ready." Anya hesitated only a moment before doing as she was told.

"I wouldn't mind reading to her." Fiona said.

"I mind."

Fiona's brow furrowed. "I don't understand."

I gazed toward the bathroom, the door was closed. "Anya is becoming attached to you . . . maybe too attached. I don't want her disillusioned or hurt. Her bedroom is her sanctuary. It's where she dreams and pretends. I can't have you sharing that with her when you intend to leave as soon as possible."

"I'd never hurt her. You can't believe I would."

"I cleaned the driveway and the road today, as soon as the plows clear the highway you're going to be out of here without a second thought. How do you think Anya's going to feel? Going to handle that?"

Fiona looked toward the bathroom, then leaned closer. "I've already told her I need to go home, she understands—"

"All she understands is that people she cares about leave." I went to the fireplace to add wood, then turned back to face Fiona. "She's very vulnerable right now. She's still grieving the loss of her mother . . . now you're here. She likes you and trusts you. I can't let you become BFFs and then have you abandon her. I won't."

"Do you honestly think I want to hurt her?"

"Not on purpose, but your decision-making is suspect at best. I have to protect my child from foolish choices."

"What the hell does that mean?"

I faced off with Fiona. "It means what the hell were you thinking, driving that piece of shit up here into the mountains?"

"What?"

"The fucking tires are bald. Did you know that? That piece of crap car doesn't even have front-wheel drive. What's the matter with you? Are you stupid?"

"Who the hell do you think you're talking to?" Fiona glared at me.

"I'm talking to you. You're a god-damned doctor. You're supposed to save lives, not throw them away. You're lucky to be alive. If that storm had hit earlier, I doubt you would be." I shook my head and made my way to the kitchen.

Fiona sat back down with a thump.

Chance came scurrying, her ears back, timid in her approach. "Hey girl." She jumped up and placed her front paws on my shoulders as she tried to lick my face.

"Easy does it, girl." I lifted her front legs down onto the floor. "Wanna go out?"

"Can I ask you something." Fiona sat staring at me.

"What?"

"Why are you so angry?" She held her hands outward. "What do you care what kind of car I drive? What does it matter to you?"

I ran my hand through my hair, frustrated and yes, angry. "It's like I said, you're a freakin' doctor. You're supposed to save lives, not compromise them. If you're really concerned about your mother back home, how in hell did you ever climb into that death machine?"

"Death machine?" Fiona shook her head slowly. "Isn't that a bit dramatic?"

"No. It's not." I walked closer.

"It's all the agency had. What was I supposed to do?"

"Next time find a fucking reputable rental company." My hands were fisted at my sides. "Jesus, don't you get storms where you come from? What the hell kind of car do you drive?"

"An Outback."

"Then how in hell did you end up with that piece of crap?"

"Desperation!" Fiona whispered. She looked directly into my eyes.

The way she said it, quiet-like, and sad, I almost felt guilty. "You should know better. Now I'm going to check on my daughter." I left her sitting there glaring after me.

Chapter Nineteen

October 2002

"I'M REALLY SCARED, Miss Priss."

Karileah took my hand. "I've never asked you to do anything you weren't ready for. You can do this, I promise."

I looked into her eyes, searching for anything that might warn me she was lying or overly confident. She calmly returned my gaze. "If I fall, it's on you."

"You won't."

I knew my progress to date was due to Priss's dedication and hard work. She didn't take any crap and she pushed me well beyond my comfort zone, but always safely. As the doctor noted, my progress was remarkable.

Once I was able to stand for short periods of time using a set of forearm crutches, she became relentless. Therapy took place all day long, even if she had to call it in from the studio. I knew the smiling therapist with her optimistic attitude and drill sergeant tactics was the reason for my recovery. Walking, though, still seemed impossible.

We had driven to the local Procare Physical Therapy center. Two trainee assistants stood at the ready. My wheelchair was locked at the edge of the parallel bars. I glared at the novices. "You better not let me fall, or I swear you'll fail this course."

Dani, the young blond, grinned. "You can't scare us, Kari's already threatened our lives if anything goes wrong."

"Okay, then"—I nodded to Priss—"let's do it." I gripped the armrests of the chair and pushed with all my might. Glenn and Dani each had a hold on my belt from behind. Once I was erect, I just stood there, terrified. Sweat began to form on my forehead and upper lip. My left leg trembled for the most part even with my right bearing my weight.

Karileah approached from the other end until she stood right in front of me. "Lift your left leg and step forward."

"You say that like it's nothing," I said through gritted teeth.

"It will become automatic. For now you need to think it through. Imagine it, send the impulses to your leg, then *let* it happen."

"You better be right."

She smiled that angelic smile, the one that always had me performing like a trained seal.

"Okay, here goes." I looked down the length of my injured leg, willing it to move. Thought waves focused on my foot. Minutes felt like hours but finally the toe of my sneaker lifted. My deadened limb lurched forward, banging into the edge of the one inch wooden platform.

"Lift higher."

I shook my head. "I'm trying." Sure, of course, just lift your leg, like it hasn't been useless for over a year. Like it hasn't been numb for almost as long. Like it isn't completely mutilated. I refused to look up. I knew Priss was watching. Again the toe of my shoe began to move. I dragged it up mentally as well as physically, willing it to lift the half inch needed to get me onto the platform.

"Now pull yourself along the bars," Kari said.

With my leg visibly unsteady, I gripped the bars tighter and pulled my good leg closer.

"See! I *knew* you could do it." Karileah beamed and backed up two feet. "Now, walk toward me."

I turned to be sure Glenn and Dani were still behind me. Dani smiled encouragement.

I peeked up at Priss. "No BB fines today."

Karileah pushed a loose strand of hair behind her ear, then nodded. "Deal. *Now walk.*"

And I did. I managed to negotiate the length of the platform, curses flying out of my mouth with each agonizing step. It wasn't pretty, and I was sweating like a pig by the time I reached the other end, but I had done it.

"You did it, Miss Priss. Thank you." Maddison had tears in her eyes, and her heart was beating rapidly.

"I didn't do anything, you're the one that worked hard." She glanced at me quickly before returning her concentration to the road. "I told you from the beginning, if you did as I said, you'd walk again." She beamed.

I shook my head incredulously. "How come you were so sure, when even the doctors doubted it was possible."

"I had a secret weapon."

"What was that?"

"You."

"Me?"

"Marni and I talked . . . a lot, before you woke up. She told me about you, about your stubbornness and about your reticence. She warned me you'd be a problem patient, but she also hoped you'd never settle for being confined to a chair. Especially if there was the slightest chance of you walking again."

We pulled into the driveway and she turned off the ignition. "I never doubted you would walk, because you're too darned ornery not too." She climbed out of the car, and retrieved my wheelchair from the trunk. As she held it for me, she smiled and said. "You know, pretty soon, I'm going to need to find a new place to live."

"Why?"

"Because you won't need me anymore."

"You can't believe that? You've save my life, Saved my soul. God, I don't know what I'd do without you. Priss, we're friends. I'd like to think after nine months, that you feel the same way."

"I do."

"Then why do you need to move?"

"Because you're not going to need a full-time therapist any longer."

"No, but I do need you in my life." I shook my head. "I don't mean romantically, but believe it or not, you've taught me a lot this last year and I don't want to lose you.

"I care about you too, you do know that, right."

"So. We become roommates, until you get that sitcom you're looking for."

"Are you serious? You'd let me stay?"

I grinned. "I never anticipated a different outcome."

"I'll start paying rent."

"It's not necessary. Just make sure I keep up with my exercises, and that I don't do anything wrong."

Karileah hugged me tight. "Thank you."

"Don't thank me . . . you're the one that made it all happen. I owe you my life and I'll never forget that, I promise." I shifted into the wheelchair, and rolled up to the back door.

KARI LAY IN bed reading her mother's latest letter. Nothing was ever going to change.

```
Karileah,
    Did I tell you Fiona bought a new car?
It's an Outback and it's just wonderful,
nice and roomy. I hope you're not still
driving that old clunker of mine. You know
I worry about you. I want you to be safe.
    The sweater you sent was beautiful, but
you shouldn't be wasting your money on me.
I know you don't make much. Fiona bought me
a flat screen TV, it's 30 inches and we
hung it on the wall over the fireplace.
    Father Francis has been after me, asking
questions about you and your acting career.
I tried to explain it's important to you.
He said to remind you family is important
too. That the commandments say to honor thy
Mother.
```

My arthritis continues to plague me, but that's to be expected with age. Have you thought about visiting? That's all I'd really like, to see you once more before I die. I love you, please take care of yourself.

Write soon,
Love Mom

Dear Mom,

I'm glad you liked your birthday present. I really wanted to fly home to see you, but with work and auditions, I just didn't have time, I'm sorry. I'll try later in the year.

I just got back from a casting call for a steady part in a new detective show called 'Monk'. I even read with two of the stars, Tony Shalhoub and Ted Levine. This could be the break I've been waiting for. I'm so excited.

Things are good here. I have a job I enjoy. I have good friends, time to go on casting calls and I've joined the choir at St Andrews, down the street. Maybe now Father Francis will stop nagging you and making you worry so.

I'm sorry to hear about your arthritis, and I know you don't want to hear it, but if you lost a little weight it might help.

Tell Nonie I said hi, and it wouldn't kill her to write once in a while. Talk to you soon.
Love
Karileah

Chapter Twenty

October 25, 2008

BY THE TIME I limped out of the Anya's bedroom, Fiona was squirreled away upstairs, my traitorous dog apparently with her. The lights were on and I could hear her murmuring softly while Chance play-growled in reply. *Dammit. Is everyone attracted to this woman?*

The hot pulsating shower I had taken earlier had done little to ease the queasy knot of anxiety that built in my stomach during the luggage retrieval. Yelling at Fiona wasn't the answer, but her lackadaisical attitude and foolish choices more than justified my pointing out the stupidity of her mistake. Jesus, I had trusted her to watch over my daughter. *What was I thinking?*

I poured some reheated soup into a thermal bowl, grabbed a spoon and walked into the nave to set them on the coffee table. After placing two more logs on the grate, I sat to eat. Three spoonfuls later and my appetite lost, I got up and dumped the remainder down the garbage disposal. *Desperation?* Why? What was so frigging important that Fiona would risk her life over it.

I sat with an oomph into the side chair and put my legs up on the coffee table. It's not like she was a friend. I'll never see her once the roads are clear and whatever the problem is, it's none of my business. *Why the hell do I care?* Exhaustion overtook me, I moved to the couch and stretched out, but sleep was intermittent at best. The word *desperation* and the look on Fiona's face when she said it haunted my lucid thoughts and my jumbled dreams. *Desperation.* I totally understood that feeling.

WHILE DEEP SLEEP never really came, I remained on the couch, eyes closed, too tired to move or to think about writing. My deadline was looming closer and closer, yet my focus failed me. A noise outside drew my attention, I looked up in time to see snow sliding off the corner of the roof. *Fuck!* It's snowing again . . . heavy. Any other time I loved to watch the snow fall, to see the landscape become blanketed in white, giving the surrounding area a Rockwell-type imagery. There's nothing more beautiful than freshly fallen snow that's undisturbed by man or beast, or tree branches laden down by the weight of the snow, or ice crystals sparkling in the next day's sunlight. Today I wouldn't get to enjoy any of that. At the rate the snow was falling, my labors of yesterday were already lost. Worse, it meant Fiona would remain our guest for the unforeseeable future.

I picked up the satellite phone from the coffee table and set it in its cradle to charge. With luck Doc would be able to call home before this latest front got much worse. *Crap.* Time for coffee. Lots and lots of coffee.

I STOOD IN the kitchen waiting on the brewer, trying to recall all Fiona and I had said to each other. *Fuck.* I could have been a little more tactful, but no, I just had to dive right in and tell her what I thought.

Obviously an apology was in order, even if my intentions had been good and justified. *The damn woman gets under my skin. She makes me want to run away as fast and as far as I possibly can!*

Hours later, dawn came and went without my awareness. I was too busy typing and, except to pour more coffee, I didn't stop. Though yesterday's efforts on the roadway were for naught, the time I spent re-thinking the plot for *Vigilante* had proved fruitful. With a new outline, more in-depth characterization, and additional clues, the story felt like it was coming together. After Priss got too sick to read my work, I found myself floundering without her input. Marni had read the first draft I submitted back in January and thought it flat. She wanted more complexity, more description, more hints of things to come. Most importantly, Marni wanted me to let the reader *see* the neighborhood where the slaying took place. She wanted me to show the events as they happened and the assassination.

"MADDISON, YOU NEED to stop looking at this story indifferently."

"What do you mean?"

"It's Karileah's story, and a big part of your life together, yet there's no emotion. No arcs, no pain."

"My other books didn't rely on cheap sentimentality."

"No, they didn't." I heard her sigh over the phone line. "This book is different from the others and we both know it. The reader needs to realize that upfront. They need to feel the gut reactions you went through. The jolt to everything you believed. The remorse, the despondency and most importantly the anger and how you dealt with it."

I thought about it for a moment. "I'm not sure I can do that."

"Of course you can. Stop thinking like a cop and try being Karileah's friend."

Silence filled the airwaves.

"Maddison?"

"I'm here."

"When you asked to tell this story, you knew you'd have to relive it. We discussed that at length. I tried to warn you."

"I know."

"Do it for Karileah. Tell the world what happened to that beautiful, innocent young woman. Show how her faith brought her to her knees.

Show how all too often women, young and old, are vulnerable without realizing it. Date rape is serious. It's happening across the nation on every college campus and no one's talking about it."

"I don't want to let her down."

"You won't. I have faith."

"Priss had faith too, look where that got her."

VIGILANTE WOULD IMMORTALIZE Priss's life and death. It would serve as a warning to all women, that Rohypnol is a dangerous weapon used against women. The drug is a tasteless, odorless and colorless paralytic that leaves the victim absolutely at the mercy of their assailant. Women need to know that just a few drops can leave the quarry totally defenseless for hours. I needed to do it right, both for her and for Anastasia. Marni was right.

The story neared the moment when the facts would meld together with all the pieces of the mystery seamlessly clicking to reveal the crime, the murderer, and his executioner. The end of this quest for Carey Troye, quirky private detective extraordinaire, would be very unlike my other books. Most importantly, Carey was a friend of the victim. That would be new. Previously, I had never allowed emotions to invade the plot. The private eye had always been portrayed as a jokester, a good-time partier, never as someone who cared about anything but solving the case.

Fortunately for me, the public appeared to embrace the detective's erratic but always accurate methods of getting to the truth. I think the wry humor helped in that. Blood and gore didn't appear in the pages of my stories. I had seen too much in real life. Details were what made a good mystery, and I strove to always make even the most innocuous fact become an important piece of the final unearthing of the truth.

With the January deadline lurking, I was comfortable that I'd be able to complete the changes and still go to print on time. In eight years, I'd only missed one production date, that was the month Priss died.

PRISS HATED HOSPICE. She especially hated the needles used to monitor her T-cells which kept dropping with every assessment. Most of all she hated herself. Her warped Catholic beliefs of heaven and hell, purgatory and divine intervention had her believing AIDs was a *just* punishment for her tribulations.

"Did . . . you call . . . Father Dominick?"

I leaned over the railing of the hospital bed. "I'm sorry, Priss, he wouldn't listen to reason. He's not coming." I took her hand in mine. "The priest here, Father Michael, is willing to hear your confession. He'll say all that mumbo jumbo about redemption. He knows none of this is your fault, and he wants to give you peace. Please . . . let him."

Kari moved her head from side to side. "No."

The area around her eyes was sunken in and blackened, her lips were cracked, her breathing shallow. "Tell me how to reach your family. Your mother—"

"Please . . . no." She squeezed my hand as tears trickled out the corners of her eyes.

"Don't you want them here with you? You're family—"

"No."

I nodded, not wanting to put more stress on her already labored breathing.

"Ana . . . stasia?"

"She's fine, she's with Dottie next door."

"Home."

"Home?" I leaned over to hear her better. "I don't understand."

"Home, you, dog, Anastasia."

"I'm not leaving you, Priss."

She slowly shook her head again. "Take . . . me . . . home." She licked her lips. "Ready."

"Ready?" My heart sped up.

"Die . . . home."

Her breathing was getting worse. The blasted disease had eaten her up. "Priss, you have to fight this. Anya needs you."

Her eyes closed. I watched her struggle for air, holding my own breath in fear.

She gripped my hand, opened her eyes. "Time."

Tears ran down my cheeks as I nodded. "I'll go get the doctor. I'll make the arrangements, hold on."

That evening Priss was back in her old room at the house. Anya was sitting on the bed next to her, reading from *Dog and Bear*, one of their favorite books. I sat in the chair close by, watching and silently talking with *her* god, trying to make a deal, anything to give Priss more time or a miracle.

"Picture."

I rose and moved closer. "What?"

"Picture."

"Now?"

She closed her eyes then opened them quickly. "Yes."

I smoothed back her thin wisps of hair and lifted her higher onto the pillow, pushing a second one behind her. "Okay, you two." I tapped my cell phone and opened the camera feature. "Smile pretty." I pushed the button three times, as Anya grinned happily sitting beside her beloved mother.

Later, after I put Anya to bed, I came back to sit with Priss. I held her hand and listened to her tortured breathing. During the night I supported her back when the coughing jags wracked her body. She held on even as blood and mucus filled the tissues I used to wipe her mouth.

I dozed in the chair when she jarred me awake.

"Water."

I picked up the glass on her bedside table and held it to her lips.

"No."

"I don't understand, what do you want?"

"Sun . . . rise." Her eyes closed.

I sat back and waited.

"Bea . . . ch."

"You want to see the sunrise at the beach?"

"Yes."

"Okay, give me a couple minutes."

I ran to Anya's room and woke her up, then made her a bowl of cereal and told her to eat quick, that we were all going to the beach. Chance ran through the door as soon as I opened it to the back yard. She would do her morning thing while I got everything else ready.

Back in the bedroom I stood beside the bed. "Take this first." I held the morphine pill in one hand and the glass of water in the other. "You'll need it."

"No."

"Then I won't take you."

"No."

"Priss, please. It will help with the pain."

She tried to lift her hand, but she was too weak.

"I'll get it." I put the pill on the back of her tongue, then lifted her shoulders and put the glass to her lips. "Drink." She took just enough to swallow the medicine, then pulled her head back.

"Beach."

"I'll get the car."

I let Chance into the back seat and strapped Anya into her childseat. "Stay here, I'm gonna get Mama."

"Yay." Anya clapped her hands together, ignorant of what was happening.

In the bedroom, Priss lay with her eyes closed. Her breaths nearly undetectable. "Priss?"

She lifted her lids and gave a weak smile. I pulled her into my arms, blanket and all and carried her to the car. The drive to the beach took less than twenty minutes, thankfully it was mostly deserted at this time of the morning. Dawn was just breaking, the grey light of morning stretching a thin line across the horizon. There was a rare jogger, but no crowds to intrude on our time. I opened the back door and Chance jumped out, then I unclipped Anya and put her on the ground. "You stay with Chance and don't go far. Stay away from the water, understand?"

"Yes, Mam."

"Okay."

I watched them go about twenty yards down the beach. Anya sat down and dug into the sand with her shovel and pail. I opened the front door. "Priss?"

"Yes."

"We're here."

"Good."

I scooped her into my arms and carried her down near the water's edge, then sat in the moist sand holding her in my lap. We waited quietly and watched as the sunrise and it's breathtaking display of radiant colors filled the sky. Bright streaks of red, pink, and orange reflected off the morning's blue backdrop. The sun rose up, its brilliant rays soon warming the air around us.

Priss turned her face to the sun's energies and a smile graced her face. I held her close as the sun continued its trip in the sky, the gentle warmth turning to intense heat. "Priss?"

She sighed deeply, her eyes closed, the sun shining on her pale mottled skin. Anya and Chance ran and joined us as the color display gave way to bright beautiful skies with white puffy clouds.

The four of us remained like that, quietly listening as the sea gulls flew overhead, watching as the waves lapped against the sand at our feet.

"Priss?"

I looked down at her tranquil face, the smile remained, but her last breath had been taken, just as she had been taken from us.

She had accepted her fate with humility and grace.

MARNI FLEW OUT from the East Coast for the funeral. She held my hand during the memorial and stayed with me while the cremation took place. We sat, waiting in the darkened room with the hum of the air conditioner the only outside noise.

"Have you contacted her family?"

I shook my head.

"Oh, Maddison." Marni squeezed my hand tight. "You need to let them know."

"Why? Nothing's changed. They didn't give a damn these last couple years. What's different now?"

"Look, I liked Karileah. She was a sweet girl. But you don't know her family and you don't know what transpired there. You owe them the courtesy."

"You don't understand. She didn't want them to know." I looked Marni in the eyes. "Evidently her mother would have disowned her."

"Why on earth—"

"Because of"—I dropped my head into my hands—"why did I insist she go out that night?"

"Don't go blaming yourself."

I shot up out of the chair. "And who should I blame? Certainly not Kari."

"Absolutely not!" Marni shook her head emphatically. "Blame that bastard, Ortiz, that raped her. He knew exactly what he was doing."

I slipped back onto my seat next to her. "That's going to cost you a dollar."

Marni laughed out loud. "You're right." She patted my hand. "Karileah would have marched right over with that infernal jar of hers."

We both chuckled, some of the tension and sadness eased momentarily.

"How's Anastasia doing?"

I shrugged. "I'm not sure how much she actually understands, but I've tried to explain that her mama went to heaven."

"I can't imagine how hard that must have been." Marni reached for my hand.

"If Kari was right, and there is a super being, I want Anya to believe she's with him. I don't want my daughter ever worrying about purgatory."

"You're absolutely right." She patted my hand.

"Thank you, Marni. You're a good friend. I'm not sure I could have gotten through this week without you."

"Karileah was my friend too."

I nodded. "Everyone that knew her, loved her."

Chapter Twenty-One

December 2002

"**WHAT DO YOU** think you're doing?" Karileah asked.

"Relax." I grinned as I pulled the door open. Standing on the other side was a longtime friend. "This is Juan Delgado, Anna's brother, and he was nice enough to pick up a tree for us."

Karileah shook hands with the man. "It's nice to meet you, I've heard a lot about you." She began to turn then pivoted back. "Mr. Delgado, I'm so sorry about your sister. Maddison speaks of her often. She misses her very much."

"Thank you. Call me, Juan, please." His eyes never left her face. "

Kari nodded. "And you can call me Kari—"

"Careful, Priss, he's a cop and a ladies man."

"I don't think that will be a problem." Kari laughed nervously. "Would either of you like coffee?"

"Yes, please," Juan said.

"Want me to make it," I asked.

"Yeah, right," Kari said.

We sat around the table sipping coffee and talking about the upcoming holiday and plans for the long weekends.

"If you need time to visit family, Kari, I could always stay here to help out," Juan offered. "I have time coming to me."

"That's very nice of you, but I can't trust Maddison to behave herself. She pushes too hard, and she's likely to do permanent damage."

I watched my friend blush under Juan's admiring gaze. "We should get the decorations out of the attic . . . make a party of it."

Kari smiled shyly. "I'm sure Juan has other things to do."

"No, I don't! Order a pizza, and tell me where the ornaments are. I'll get them.

"You're on," I said.

Juan and Kari had the lights on the tree and lit by the time the pizza arrived. Kari served it up and offered us each a beer. I requested a soda instead. Juan was laughing, and flirting with my cautious therapist. Clearly she wasn't immune to his attention. That fact made me chuckle to myself.

"Well you two, I'm going to call it a night," I said.

"Wait and I'll help you," Kari said.

I frowned. "Why? I've been putting myself to bed for months now."

She appeared nervous.

"I should be going," Juan said.

"Stay, finish the decorations. I'll be okay. And Juan, thanks for everything. I owe you."

Juan made a fist with his right hand and pounded his heart twice. I returned the gesture. "Good night my friend."

I wheeled myself into my bedroom, but left the door ajar.

MORNING MISS PRISS. The tree looks great. Did you have fun decorating it?"

Kari blushed profusely. "It does look pretty and Juan is very nice."

"He's a hell of a guy, and if you're ever looking for someone special, you couldn't do better."

She slapped Maddison's arm. "Now you're a matchmaker? Thank you but I'll find my own dates."

"Yes, ma'am."

She looked at Maddison strangely. "That's it?"

"You're a big girl. You can make your own decisions." Maddison rolled her chair into the living room. "It really does look nice."

"Are you okay?"

"I am. I just . . . I thought . . . I wanted to be walking by now."

"You are."

"I mean all the time. I'm sick of the chair."

"Then stop using it," Kari said.

"What?"

"You're ready. Use the full crutches, your arm is plenty strong enough. They'll give you better support when you're tired."

"You mean it?"

Kari grinned. "I do."

Maddison wheeled into the bedroom and returned with the crutches. "I can do this."

"You can." Kari chuckled.

The phone rang. Maddison reached for it. "Hello?" She listened for a second. "Hold on." She extended her arm to Kari. "It's for you."

"Hello?"

Maddison watched as Kari's face lit up.

"Yes, I'm interested." She listened, her head bobbing. "Yes, I'll take it." The silence on their end continued. "Thank you so much, I will. I'll be there."

Kari fell into the chair. "I got the part?" She looked at Maddison, then jumped up and ran to her arms. "I got the part!"

Maddison held her close. "Which one and when do you start?"

"Cold Case, and production starts in January. It premiers in September."

"We should celebrate."

"It's okay. We don't have to."

Maddison gripped her hand. "Yes, we do. This is huge. I'm walking with crutches, and you're on your way to stardom."

"I'm not the star, but it's a thirteen-week contract." She beamed. "I can't wait to tell my family."

A knock at the door interrupted the joyous moment. Kari answered it. A delivery man stood holding a vase filled with colorful flowers. "Ms. Kari Gallagher?"

"Yes, I'm Kari."

"These are for you."

Maddison walked closer, handed the guy a tip, and closed the door. Kari had taken the flowers to the kitchen. "So who are they from?"

She had the card in her hand "They're from Juan."

That night Karileah sat down to read her mother's latest missive and then tell her about her own good news.

> Karileah,
>
> I've not received a letter from you and worry that all is not going well there. Has something happened? You know your room will always be waiting. I do so worry about you out there among those people. Drugs and sex swapped like most people change their underwear. I don't know what you're thinking some times.
>
> Fiona and her friends are going skiing the weekend before Christmas. Remember how you used to love to ski? Did I tell you she got a raise. She's doing so well, but it took hard work and dedication.
>
> Your sister is thinking of having a child. I swear I don't know where I went wrong with you girls. She likes women, you, god knows what you're doing? I pray for your souls every day, but I don't seem to be getting answers. Father Francis prays with me.
>
> Write soon so I don't worry myself to death.
> Love Mom

"Something wrong?" I asked.

"It's not important." Kari folded the letter in her hand, then slipped it into her pocket.

"If something upsets you, I'm here. You can talk to me."

"My mother is on one of her guilt trips again." Kari shook her head. "I know she loves me, but she imagines I'm doing all these horrible things, like I'm doing drugs and . . . never mind." She let out a deep sigh.

"Doesn't she know you? You're the proverbial *Miss Clean*."

"I told you, she's religious and god-fearing."

"So are you."

"She doesn't see it that way." Kari rubbed her brow. "She sees evil at every turn, our priest back home preaches condemnation for the slightest offence."

"But you haven't done anything wrong."

Kari shook her head. "The minute I left home to try for a career out here, I committed a sin in their eyes."

"What the heck was that? Wanting to better yourself? Wanting a career? Wanting something of your own?" I walked closer and took her hand. "You're one of the sweetest, kindest women I've ever met. There's not a corrupt bone in your body."

She snorted. "Tell my mother that."

"I'd think she had bigger issues than you wanting to be a star. After all your sister is gay . . . that's gotta rank higher than you wanting to be an actress."

"Nonie gets enough grief from my mother believe me. Now that she's thinking about having a child, my mother is practically living at the church, wondering where she went wrong with us."

"Then stop writing her. Screw her. Screw your sister. You don't need them in your life."

Kari stepped closer and wrapped her arms around me. "I know you hate your mother, but I love mine, even if you can't understand that. I just . . . I want her to be proud of me."

I nodded. "You're right. I'm sorry."

"Don't be. Knowing your situation, reminds me how lucky I am."

"There you go again, being a nice person."

```
Dear Momma,
    It's finally happened. I've signed a
contract and we go into production in
January. It's a new crime series that will
air in September 2003. I told you I would
do it and I have. I am walking on air, I
can't stop grinning.
    Momma, I'm glad you're feeling better,
but Nonie is right, you need to take the
medicine. Listen to her, she's the doctor.
```

I know you worry about her, but she'll find the right woman someday. It doesn't matter if it's a man or woman as long as Nonie loves her and she loves Nonie. As for the baby, it's what you've always wanted, grandchildren. Can't you be happy for us? Must everything always be black and white with you?

I love you, I just wish you could love me too.

Write soon.

Love
Karileah

Chapter Twenty-Two

October 25, 2008

FIONA SLEPT FITFULLY through the night. Every time she awoke, Maddison was still rooted at the computer, the sound of her fingers rhythmic tapping on the keyboard echoing in the open space. When the smell of fresh-brewed coffee pervaded the upstairs, she threw off the covers with the intent of getting a cup for herself. She hesitated, not sure of what to expect when face-to-face with her host. At the top of the stairs, she paused. "May I come down to the inner sanctum?"

Without moving Maddison replied, "You might not want to when you get a gander outside." She turned on the stool and looked up. Fiona stood at the top of the stairs, her hair mussed from sleep, her eyes wary.

"No!" Fiona moaned. Chance scurried past as Fiona thumped down the steps closely behind the dog. "Tell me it's *not* frigging snowing again."

Maddison looked out the front door, then back at her. "Yup, it sure is."

"What am I going to do?"

Maddison reached for the coffee pot. She poured the hot liquid then set the mug and spoon on the counter. "I've charged the phone for you. You should call home, as soon as you're completely awake. I also jotted down the Wi-Fi service provider's name, and the password for the router so you can contact your boss." Maddison tilted her head down and captured Fiona's gaze. "First thing, you should probably call your mom and let her know it's snowing again."

"For God's sake, I have a job, you know. I was due back at work three days ago." She plopped on the couch and propped her foot up on the coffee table. "What about the roads? You cleared them yesterday, is there a chance we could reach a city before it's—"

"Sorry, but my truck will barely clear the fresh stuff that fell overnight, and this section of Route 93 hasn't been touched. We'd get stuck along the way and I won't chance it."

Fiona started to cry. "I can't believe it's friggin snowing again."

Maddison walked closer carrying tissues and the phone. "Call home, talk to your mom."

Fiona blew her nose, took a deep breath, then placed the call. "Mom, it's me." After a pause. "No I'm fine, just frustrated. It's snowing here, the roads aren't clear, and I don't know when I'm gonna get out." Tears ran down Fiona's face as she spoke.

"Mom?"

Fiona stared at the display screen. "Great! I've lost the connection."

Maddison looked outside. Patches of blue still showed on the horizon. "Call back. It might just be a blip."

THIRTY MINUTES LATER, I watched as Fiona walked to the counter and dropped the phone in the cradle.

"Thank you. My mother wanted to know if there's such a thing as search and rescue up here? A way that I might be able to get out before this gets any worse."

"You're welcome to call highway patrol, but they'd most likely tell you, you're not a priority. They have limited funds. They need to use their resources on people that are actually stranded in life-threatening situations. People without access to necessities due to the weather. You have a roof over your head, food in your belly, and no medical issues. I'm sorry, but they'll probably tell you to stay put." I poured coffee into my mug.

"Is food going to be an issue? You didn't exactly plan on a long-term houseguest."

"Nah, we're good. If things get too bad, you can share Chance's food."

Fiona maneuvered over to the doors and looked out. Another two inches of snow had accumulated just since she had come down stairs.

"How much snow is normal for this area."

"You sure you wanna know?" I took a sip of my coffee and waited.

She turned back and moved to the counter. "Back home, winter's snowfall amounts can average about seventy inches. Am I close?"

I gave a quick shake of my head. "Only if you quadruple that number. That's a conservative figure. It often goes higher here in the elevations."

Fiona added creamer and sugar to her coffee, then stirred the mixture. "Don't get mad, but how can you stand it?"

"I keep busy."

"Yeah, right." She took her cup and hobbled with one crutch over to the couch. "There's only so much reading I can do."

"There's movies upstairs or I can bring the TV down here, whichever you prefer."

She nodded without comment.

I walked over and sat on the coffee table in front of her. "Okay, Doc, let's face facts. I can't get you out safely, so you're stuck until the weather breaks. Give me a for instance. What would you be doing home, if you were there?"

"Working at the job I'm about to be fired from."

"Understood." I crossed my arms over my chest. "What else?"

She glared at me. "I have friends . . . I'd call them. Maybe set up a lunch date or make plans to see a movie together. I might ask a beautiful woman out and then screw her brains out under the right circumstances." She picked at the cuticle on her thumb.

"Well, since there's no beautiful women here, that's not an option. What else?"

"I have a membership to a gym. I try to work out five times a week whenever my schedule permits."

I peered closely at her. "Okay, I can help there. When your ankle is better you can use the equipment downstairs."

That appeared to pique her interest. "What's down there?"

"A treadmill, weights, a Bowflex, and some Pilates equipment."

She sat up straighter. "I could probably use parts of the Bowflex now and definitely the Pilates gear." She took a sip of her coffee. "Do you have the DVDs that go with them?"

"Yup. And there's a small TV down there that you can view them on."

She put her cup down. "Why are you being so nice to me all of a sudden?"

"Because I was out of line last night. I owe you an apology. I can be an ass sometimes. I'm not really a people person. It comes from being a cop and living alone most of my life."

I searched for the right words. "That car you crashed *is* a piece of crap. I'm absolutely right about that. The idiot at the rental agency should be hung for having sent you out in it. Montana, well most of the states here in the northwest, have laws about minimum safety standards for all means of transportation using the highway system in the winter. That vehicle doesn't meet any of them.

"I got upset . . . when I realized what could have happened to you. You keep telling me you're worried about your mother back home and her health. It doesn't make sense you would deliberately put yourself in danger driving that piece of shit." I put my hands up. "I know, you're on a mission of some sort. I get it. That implies you're anticipating a favorable outcome. It wouldn't be if you were dead."

Just the thought of it brought back my queasy stomach. "You evidently didn't think about the consequences of getting lost up here. Possibly getting hurt or trapped in the car during a snow-storm." I looked directly into her eyes. "If you hadn't remembered seeing the church, and if I wasn't here, how do you think you would have survived this past week?"

That brought tears to Fiona's eyes.

"I'm sorry for what I said . . . I had no right, but you need to take responsibility for compromising yourself like that. I wouldn't want to be the cop bringing the grim news of your demise to your mother."

I went back to the counter and sat at the computer. *Vigilante* awaited.

Chapter Twenty-Three

October 28, 2008

FIONA OPENED HER eyes and turned her head to look out the window. For the third day the skies were cloudy and dark. *More snow.* She peeked at the clock on the night stand and noted it read eight-fifteen. She shook her head in disgust. Though she felt stronger each day, she was still sleeping almost ten hours a night. *Incredible.* Her appetite was back to normal and there had been no indication of fever in days. Thankfully the scar on her leg was clear and only slightly pink.

It was time to remove the stitches. That meant asking Maddison for her help. Fiona was hesitant to add another chore to her workload. The woman never stopped. She cooked, handled the running of the house, walked Chance a couple of times a day and, most importantly, she doted on Anastasia.

Fiona stretched on the bed, then tested her ankle. The swelling had gone down, the bruising faded, but it was not healed yet. When she tried to stretch the injured ligaments, they hurt like hell. She needed the brace for continued support, but she could ditch the crutches now. She hated using them.

The days of rest since the high fever that wiped her out had helped to rejuvenate her. Today she was feeling like her old self—stronger and ready to work. Unfortunately, having nothing to do was driving her crazy. She needed something to occupy herself.

Fiona leaned up in bed and peeked over the stair railing—Maddison sat at her work station typing. Except for tending Anastasia or the chores, she was there day and night, working into the wee hours, on who-knew what. The accumulating snow didn't even faze her. Worse, it was clear adult conversation was problematic for her. While Anya was a delightful child, Fiona craved grown-up interaction, even if meant forcing her reticent host to participate.

She shook her head in disgust. *"How the hell did I let this happen?"* Maddison was right, she hadn't thought this trip through properly. She had acted foolishly and in haste. That could have ended with very different results, dire ones.

She thought back to the day she embarked on this trek. She remembered reading Addison's dedication and how fear had clutched at her. "In loving memory of my wife." Had Addison been writing about Kari? If not, who then? He didn't name names, but still, Kari

110

never mentioned a wife. The past books thanked Kari and Kari alone. Fiona turned to the acknowledgements, Kari's name was glaringly absent. How could that be? What happened to Kari and why didn't we know?

Fiona had hired a private investigator in Los Angeles. The advertisement claimed they were the best in the city. That combined with their state-of-the-art technology and extensive investigative experience, they would resolve all questions and issues quickly and cost effectively.

What a line of bullshit that was. She herself had uncovered the same information simply by Googling Addison. Worse she never got to retrieve the message the Publisher had left. That call might have proved fruitful.

What had she been thinking? She knew enough about cars that checking the tires should have been instinctive. At home, she drove a four-wheel drive for the traction, yet never thought twice about the rental car. The fact she'd never been to Montana before didn't excuse her with regards to the weather conditions . . . they were a given here in the Northwest.

If she were honest with herself, she'd have to admit she hadn't been acting judiciously. Between worrying about Kari, her baby clock clanging, the failed insemination, her mother's health . . . she just hadn't seemed able to think sensibly.

THE FIASCO WITH Tasha set everything off and only underscored Fiona's desire for a child. Fiona had wanted them to get an apartment together, maybe rent a house and start a family. She had thought they were on the same page. Tasha quickly dispelled that notion and spurned all talk of cohabitation and children. She claimed her career demanded all her time, this had been fun, blah, blah, blah. Tasha felt it better to end it as friends, rather than push what wasn't there.

Within days of the breakup, Fiona had started researching sperm banks and artificial insemination. However, her career and personal matters had forced her to put off the procedure indefinitely. Now, six years later and as many years older, she decided if a relationship wasn't in her future, then having a baby definitely would be. Raising a child alone wasn't a major concern in her decision-making process. Her mother was the perfect role model. Fiona felt sure she was equally equipped to do the job.

Her mother, Mary, hadn't been as receptive about the insemination process, and didn't want to debate sperm banks or "baster babies," as she called the procedure. But then she wasn't much for discussing what she didn't fully understand. She did comment that becoming a grandmother would be a dream come true.

FIONA SMILED AS she thought back to the day she finally came out to her mother. At twenty-five she had just completed her residency and was to begin working at a medical practice associated with Wilkes-Barre Hospital.

Her mother never minced words. For her, life was black or white according to the Catholic Church's doctrines and the man wearing the white cassock.

"Mom, I need to talk to you."

Mary stood at the stove, her back to Fiona, preparing their evening meal. "So talk?"

"I love you, and I never want to hurt you."

Mary turned from her task, spoon in her hand, sauce dripping onto the floor. She studied Fiona over the top rim of her glasses. "But?"

Fiona took a deep breath. "There's no easy way to tell you this, so I'll just say it. I'm a lesbian."

Mary nodded and turned back to the pot. "You'll be needing to confess to Father Francis. I'm sure he'll have a lot to say about it."

"I already have. I'm no longer allowed to receive communion." Fiona waited. Silence, except for the meat sizzling in the pan, and the water boiling for the noodles in another. She waited till she couldn't stand it any longer. "Mom?"

Mary put the spoon down and walked to the table. She sat and grasped Fiona's hand. "I've suspected since you were in eighth grade and found out Sue Ellen was dating little Tommy Richards from down the street. "

Fiona nodded and grinned. "I was so in love with her. She broke my heart."

"Hog wash. You didn't know what love was back then." Mary patted Fiona's hand. "I suspect you *think* you do now though, am I right?"

"I believe so, yes."

"When you know for sure, I'll be wanting to meet her."

And that was the end of the conversation. No drama, no hysterics, just Mom being Mom. Of course Fiona knew her mother went to church that night and prayed for her soul. Prayed that God would forgive her, but that didn't bother Fiona. What mattered is she knew her mother still loved her no matter what.

FIONA SHOOK HER head. Enough of the memories, it was time to accept what is and make changes, starting now. She rolled over in bed and peeked between the balusters. Maddison was still at the counter working on her computer. She headed downstairs.

"Do you have a minute?"

Maddison sat hunched over the computer, her fingers flying over the keys, as she chewed on the pen she used for making notes. "Huh?"

"I need your help?"

Maddison's hands stopped abruptly, and she turned to Fiona. "What's wrong?"

"It's time for the stitches to come out, so whenever you're up to it"— she took a deep breath—"I am too."

Maddison started laughing. "I didn't kill you when I put them in. Coming out should be a breeze."

Fiona bobbed her head. "I always tell my patients this is the easy part"—she grimaced—"but I'm finding that's not the case when it's yourself having the procedure done."

"It'll be fine. Let me get my supplies."

Anya was playing at the coffee table, drawing. "Hey, Little One, I need to sit there, can you move to the counter?"

"I'm not 'posed to when you working."

"I know. I'm sorry, but we have to take Doc's stitches out."

"Oh!" Anya's hand flew to her mouth. "It's gonna hurts."

Fiona smiled at the little girl. "No, it doesn't. It actually tickles." Maddison raised her brow, but continued toward the closet for the provisions.

"Can I help?" Anya asked.

Fiona watched as Maddison set the various objects on the table—a small scissor, a magnifying glass, tweezers, rubber gloves, a paper surgical mask and some disinfectant.

"You can. I need you to hold my hand while Mam removes my stitches." Anya grinned and climbed up on the couch next to Fiona.

"Okay, you two clean your hands with this." Maddison squirted a small amount of sanitizer in each of their hands. "Now put your gloves on." Anya slipped her hands into each glove like a pro, Fiona not so much.

"Need help there, Doc?"

"I've got it." She tugged the tip of the index finger and finally set the glove correctly on her hand.

Maddison put the surgical mask over Anastasia's nose and mouth, securing it snuggly with the ties.

"Look at you, you're like a little doctor." Fiona grinned at the child.

"Okay, here we go." Maddison cleaned the area of Fiona's leg, then snipped the end of the clear fishing line where the first knot was tied. She used the tweezers to pull the thread gently through the skin. Slowly and methodically, she worked her way to the other end of the wound till all the stitches were removed. Using the magnifying glass, she inspected the pale red line closely to ensure she hadn't missed any. She looked up and grinned. "There, see? It didn't even hurt."

Anya threw her arms around Maddison's neck. "I was so scareded!"

Behind Anastasia's back, Fiona wiped her brow and mouthed. "Thank you."

"No problem." Maddison set Anya back on the couch. "You stay with Doc, and make sure she doesn't pass out while I clean up." She pulled the gloves off Anya's hands, the mask from her face, and waited for Fiona to remove her gloves. "You ladies sit tight."

When she returned, she held the crutches in her hand. "You forget these?"

"No, I don't need them any longer. The brace is enough."

"Good, you're making progress then."

FIONA TESTED HER ankle by doing the dishes without the support of the crutches. Twenty minutes later, she walked into the nave and collected Anya's drink glass and snack plate.

"You don't have to clean up after her." Maddison reached for the items.

"I need something to do. I'm going crazy just sitting and reading."

Maddison looked down, then up into Fiona's eyes. "How's the leg holding up?"

"Okay so far, why?"

"I'm going to put you to work since you have so much energy."

Chapter Twenty-Four

MARCH 2003

"I DON'T REMEMBER telling you to leave the crutches behind." Kari stood with her arms crossed over her chest glaring at Maddison.

"Easy Miss Priss, I only do it in the house," she said. "And look, the leg is taking my weight."

Kari walked closer, concern evident on her face. "May I?"

Maddison nodded.

She placed her palm on the damaged thigh. Then ran her hand down the length of the scar and back up. She worked the muscle gently; it responded as well as could be expected. "Can you feel this?"

"I still get sick to my stomach when you do that, but yes, I can feel it."

Kari nodded, pleased. "It is getting stronger. You're right."

"So, can I ditch the crutches?"

"Not yet, but soon, I promise."

Maddison nodded. "You've been right so far, so I'm holding you to that."

"What are your plans for today?" Kari walked into the kitchen.

"I'm going to finish the edits on the new book. I made good headway with your notes last night, and I might even have it finished by next week."

Kari beamed. "I just told you what I liked. It's not rocket science."

"You have no idea how important your insights are. And you caught three different timeline errors and I'm not finished with your comments yet."

"They were glaring issues, I'm sure you would have caught them."

"But I didn't, you did." Maddison went to the fridge. "I'm gonna make a sandwich, want one?"

"No, uh-uh." She turned and looked at the clock.

"Got a hot date?"

"Don't tease me. I'm nervous enough."

"I'm not teasing. I want you to be happy. And I told you Juan is a great guy."

She nodded. "I think so too. I am happy."

"You don't look it."

"I just get scared that things are going too well, that something's going to go wrong and take it all away."

Maddison put her arm around Kari's shoulder. "That's just your Catholic guilt kicking in. Or did you get another letter from your mother?"

"No. I didn't."

"Enjoy your happiness then. Juan's in love with you, and I think it's mutual. If something does go wrong, these memories will boost your resolve to find happiness again."

Kari rested her head on Maddison's shoulder. "Thank you."

"Your date just pulled up." Maddison watched as Kari picked up her purse and ran to the door. "Have fun."

She turned in the doorway and wagged her finger at Maddison. "You behave."

LATE THAT NIGHT, Kari took the letter she had hidden from Maddison and ripped open the envelope. She knew Maddison would never understand Kari's desperate need for her mother's approval and she didn't want to fight with her about it. She pulled the single sheet of paper out and read it.

```
Karileah,
    What do you mean, you've met someone?
And what kind of name is Juan Delgado? You
tell me for years you don't have time to
date, that I shouldn't worry, your career
comes first and now I find out you've been
running around with this man. What do you
know about him? About his family? What does
he do for a living?
    Your sister is insistent that she's
going to have a child on her own, I swear
you girls will give me a heart attack. I
don't understand where I went wrong.
    I expect some answers and I don't want
any shotgun weddings in your future, do I
make myself clear? I'm going to church,
I'll pray for you and for Nonie.
Love Mom

Hi Mom,
    Production's been delayed. The female
star backed out at the last minute and they
had to find a replacement. We start
shooting April 13th. Based on the pilot,
the studio has ordered thirteen more
episodes. My contract's been extended.
That's a plus on my resume.
```

Sisters

Everything is going so perfect, I have to pinch myself to make sure I'm not dreaming.

Filming will take a break in May, I'm trying to make reservations to fly home for a visit, I have so much to tell you. Juan is trying to join me so you can meet him. Mom, you'll like him, I know you will.

Hope all is well, take care.
Love Karileah

Chapter Twenty-Five

October 31, 2008

"**ARE YOU EXTRA** hungry today or are we having a party you forgot to tell me about?"

I gazed at Fiona. "I cook because it's a necessary evil. It's also consumes a lot of my time, time I'd rather spend with Anya. My solution is to plan out good tasting, nutritious meals and to cook them all at once. Then I portion out the food and freeze the individual servings. That way I'm not slaving over the stove every day, and Anya is still getting balanced meals."

Fiona sat at the counter, watching Maddison slice and dice, dumping items into the four different pots currently on the stove. "I hate cooking."

"What are you going to do when you have a baby?"

"My mother will cook, or we'll eat out."

I shook my head, chuckling. "I doubt that's gonna work, but good luck with it."

She took a sip of her water. "So tell me, what are the chores you have for me?"

I quick looked at the clock, then turned back. "Ten minutes till the dryer will be done. You *can* fold wash, can't you?"

"I'm warning you, I don't do ironing."

"Let me guess, mom does that for you too?"

Fiona's face turned crimson. "She likes taking care of me."

"More likely, it's you that likes *her* taking care of you."

"Well, I knew it was one of those." She giggled.

Maddison dumped two cups of rice into the boiling water and stirred it. "I suppose you don't do diapers either?"

"I've never had to."

"No children in your life?"

"No."

"Ahh." Maddison poured the olive oil into the hot wok, then dropped the slices of beef in as well. She kept turning them until the sides were browned, then added a teaspoon of ground ginger, one diced onion, with garlic powder. Then placed the lid on top to let the meat simmer.

"What does that mean?"

"What does what mean?"

The buzzer went off on the dryer, I went and gathered the clothing and brought it to the counter. "Anya, come help Fiona fold the clothes."

"I don' want to," she whined.

"Anastasia!"

The girl came running and climbed on the stool next to Fiona. "I help." She pulled a T-shirt from the pile and flattened it out on the granite slab, then folded the two sides over themselves. "See, I helping." Anya gripped the bottom of the shirt and folded it upwards in thirds, creating a tidy little rectangle.

"Where did you learn to fold clothes like that?" Fiona asked.

"Mama taught me. I helped her all the time."

I beamed at my daughter. "Yes, you did baby."

Chance scratched at the door. I let her in. "It's snowing again."

Fiona looked out the window. "I refuse to get upset about something I have no control over." The shirt she was attempting to fold took a beating instead.

"That's not right," Anya said.

I burst out laughing.

Fiona looked down at the top, comparing it to the one Anya had done. "What am I doing wrong?"

"Letting your mother do everything for you, obviously," I said.

"Hush you."

Anya took the shirt and smoothed it all out. "See, this is how." She slowly showed Fiona the art of folding the sides and sleeves onto themselves. "You have to smoot it again, or you get winkles." Then she gripped the bottom and completed those folds, creating an exact duplicate of the first one she did. "See."

Fiona hugged her tight. "You are so smart, thank you."

"Welcome." Anya smiled broadly at the praise.

I stirred and spooned the rice out into a bowl to cool. "Anya, keep an eye on her, don't let her mess up our clothes."

Fiona threw a sock at me, luckily I caught it. "Careful you." With the sock back on the pile of clothes, I mixed a half cup of water with a quarter cup low-sodium soy sauce, and two tablespoons of oyster sauce then mixed it all into the wok. After stirring the ingredients together, I replaced the lid.

"I'll confess, I don't know how you do it all." Fiona was struggling with another shirt. She wasn't getting any better at it.

"Necessity. You do what you have to." The meatballs I had cooking in the fry pan were completely browned. I added the tomato sauce and chicken broth mixture to the pot. I lowered the heat and placed a lid on the pan.

"Dammit." Fiona pulled the shirt apart to start over.

Anya slid off the stool and ran to the cabinet. She brought the BB jar back around and placed it on the counter next to Fiona. "You hafta pay. You said a bad word."

I tried hard not to snicker, but the frustration on Fiona's face was impossible to ignore.

"Can I pay you later?" Fiona asked. "My wallet is upstairs."

Anya stood there with hands on her hips, not giving an inch. I pulled a one out of my pocket and handed it to her. "I'll pay for the Doc. She's good for it."

"Okay."

"Evidently your mother never made you or your sister do chores. Am I right?"

"Not true." Fiona batted her eyelashes at me. "I just always conned my sister into doing them for me."

"You haft a sister?"

"Yes, I do," Fiona said.

"I want a sister. Mam says I hafta wait." Anya started matching socks and pushing them into themselves.

"Why do you have to wait?" Fiona smirked at me.

"I asked too. She don't say."

"Cute, very cute." I murmured. "And that's not the way to fold the sweats." I laughed when she stuck her tongue out at me.

"Mam, why do I hafta wait? I want a sister. I'll be good wit her." Anya continued to gather the socks.

"I'll look online tonight . . . see if I can find one."

"Okay."

"Did you do your lessons?" I asked.

"Uh huh."

"Spanish, too?"

"Fiona don't talk Spanish. You were busy," Anya said.

"Fair enough. I'll help you later."

"Okay."

Fiona was smiling broadly as she continued folding the clothes. "How much more is there?"

"Two more loads. I got behind."

Fiona looked at the pile of items. "I'm sorry, it's because of me."

"Not everything is your fault, Doc." I covered the pot. "Though those wrinkles will definitely be blamed on you."

"Smart as—"

"Ah ah, careful, I'm almost out of singles."

"I was going to say, smart aleck."

"Sure you were, and the sun's gonna melt all the snow away . . . tomorrow." I pulled the dough out of the bread machine and shaped it. It needed to rise a second time before I could put it into the oven.

"I love that bread, it's wonderful." Fiona stacked the folded clothes on the side chair. "Okay, we're ready for the next load."

I brought the jeans, and work shirts out, along with Anya's dresses. "Here you go, ladies."

"You wash her dresses with your jeans?"

"Yeah, why not?"

Anya watched the exchange, her head bobbing back and forth.

"Because they'll get ruined by the dyes in the denim," Fiona said.

"Well looky at you knowing something about doing wash." I winked. "These jeans are probably older than you are . . . there's no dye left in 'em."

"How old are you?" Anastasia asked.

"Anya, that's not nice. You don't ask a woman that."

"Why not?"

"It's rude."

"How am I gonna knowd if I don't ask?" Her innocent eyes looked directly at me.

"It's just not polite."

"But why?"

"Because some women don't like talking about their age."

"Why?"

"Anastasia."

She sighed, but stopped asking. "I'm this many." She held up four fingers.

"In three months you'll be five."

"Will you come to my party?" Anya was looking at Fiona.

"At the rate this snow is falling, I probably will."

"How old is your sister?"

"Anastasia Aine."

"I didn't ask Fiona's age," she said.

I shook my head in exasperation.

"Aine?"

"It's her middle name. Priss picked it, it's Irish I think." I quick checked the meatballs.

"Nice."

"And my sister is thirty-six."

"Is she older than you?"

I walked around the counter and lifted Anya into my arms. "You are incorrigible." She giggled when I kissed her cheek.

Fiona was laughing too. "No, she's younger, for the record."

"Mam is old, right, Mam?"

"Do you want to go to bed without supper?" I threatened. I put her back on the stool next to Fiona.

Anya reached for one of my flannel shirts and started folding it. She put her fingers to her lips and made like she was locking them. Too late, but at least she tried.

"Can I ask you a question?"

"Sure." I drained the macaroni and deposited it in with the sauce and meatballs. That would be our dinner tonight and leftovers later in the week.

"How do you time all these different meals to finish at the same time."

"Practice, trust me." I took the stir fry off the burner and set it to cool on the cutting board. Later I would dole in frozen broccoli cuts with each portion, and a scoop of rice, then freeze the individual servings. The timer went off, I pulled the bread out of the oven, and replaced it with the whole chicken I had prepared earlier.

"How many meals will you cook at once?"

I thought about it. "I don't think I have a set number. I just try to ensure there's enough for the week, sometimes longer."

"And they stay fresh in the refrigerator?"

"You really have no clue, do you?" I laughed. "There's a freezer downstairs. Once everything is packaged up, I'll put them down there to store."

"I wonder if my mother does this?"

"Have you never watched her?"

She seemed to ponder the question. "No. Not in a long time at least. Between school and work, it's been years since I paid attention."

"Hmmm."

"I'm learning to hate those sounds you make."

I waggled my eyes. "I'm not lending you more cash."

LATER THAT NIGHT after dinner was done, the dishes rinsed and put in the dishwasher, we gathered in the living area.

"Mam, can I watch a movie?"

I looked at the read-out on the microwave. "It's too late tonight, maybe tomorrow."

"Okay." She climbed into my lap.

"You did good today, teaching Doc how to fold the clothes."

"Mama would be proud, right?"

"Right." I kissed her forehead. "It's time for your medicine."

"Okay. Can I have a cookie too?"

"I suppose you can." I stood up with her in my arms. "What about Doc, do you think she earned one today?"

Anya giggled and nodded her head. Fiona was on the couch reading a book.

"I don't think she heard us." I whispered. "Maybe we don't have to share?"

"I heard you, and I dare you to try having a cookie without me."

I plopped Anya on the counter and pulled her three pill bottles down from the top shelf of the cabinet. After removing one pill from each bottle, I poured a glass of water and handed it to her. "Okay, number one." She placed the pill on the back of her tongue and gulped the water. I put the medicine back on the top shelf and closed the cabinet door. "Okay?"

Anya nodded. "Yes."

"Okay, number two." She repeated the process, this time finishing the glass of water. I refilled it and waited.

"I'm gonna be very strong someday," she said solemnly.

"Yes, you are sweetheart."

She held her hand out, and I placed the last pill in her palm. "Number three." She started to gag almost immediately, then quickly swallowed more water.

"All gone." She stuck her tongue out to show me.

"Good job." I placed her Minnie Mouse glass in the sink. "Ready for that cookie?"

"Yes, Mam."

Fiona had approached during the last pill consumption. "You are a terrific patient, Anya. Good girl."

Anya reached into the cookie jar I was holding for her. "You can haft one too."

"Thank you very much." Fiona reached into the jar.

"When you finish that, go wash up for bed."

Anya finished her cookie and climbed down, then ran to the bathroom.

"She is absolutely amazing. What a sweet, clever, little girl." Fiona stared after her.

"She is."

"She *must* take after your wife, Priss, right?" she said with a smirk.

I laughed out loud. "She does. One hundred per-cent."

Fiona turned to me. "You mean that don't you?"

"Absolutely." I put the lid on the cookie jar and put it back on the counter. "Anastasia looks and acts just like her mother."

"How long has it been?"

Tears gathered in my eyes, I wasn't sure why. "Earlier this year."

Fiona placed her hand on my arm. "I'm so sorry, I had no idea."

I gazed down where her fingers grazed my skin, heat radiated off them.

"What medicine does she take?" Fiona asked.

"Vitamins."

"Three kinds?"

"Look, Doc, they're prescribed by her pediatrician, so don't worry about it."

"I was just curious—"

"Mam, I'm ready." Anya had her pajamas on and walked toward her room.

"Don't be," I said. Fiona's hand remained on my arm. It suddenly occurred to me, we were going to be alone later, and tomorrow, and maybe next week, possibly even next month. For some reason I found the thought quite unsettling.

"I'm coming, Munchkin."

Chapter Twenty-Six

November 1, 2008

THE FOLLOWING DAY Chance, Anya and I were returning from our visit to Kari's meadow when I heard a scream. I picked up Anya and ran the remainder of the way to the house. "You stay here, do you understand?" I lowered Anastasia onto the bottom step of the landing.

"Yes, Mam."

"I mean it." I pointed my finger in Anya's face. "Do not move until I say so."

She nodded her head and crossed her heart. "Chance, stay." The dog moved to Anya's side and sat.

I raced up the stairs and pushed open the door, then stood rooted to the spot at the spectacle before me.

Fiona was kneeling on one of the kitchen stools, swinging a broom as a field mouse ran across the floor. Every time she slammed the broom down, the mouse retreated in the opposite direction, only to have Fiona swing her weapon back again. Back and forth they continued, back and forth, Fiona shrieking with each pass of the broom.

I bit my lip. "Hey Doc, where's a camera when you need one?"

Fiona swung the broom one more time and managed to drop it precisely on the back of the mouse, stunning both of them. "Well don't just stand there, do something!" she yelled.

I could see Fiona apply pressure to the broom, resolute to hold her quarry down. I lost control and burst out laughing. Fiona shot daggers at me and I quickly swallowed the rest of the belly laugh.

"You want me to get my rifle?" The smirk on my face froze and I quick bit my lip to keep from chuckling more.

"I want you to get this damned rat out of the house." Fiona used two hands to maintain her hold on the mouse. "Then I want you to set traps in case there are any more of these damned things. I hate rodents, do you understand?" Fiona's chest was heaving, she was sweating, and her eyes blazed in anger. She never looked more beautiful.

I took a deep breath and walked to the fireplace, picked up the ash shovel, and slid it under the broom, trapping the quarry between the two. I eased the broom handle from Fiona's lethal grip and walked out onto the deck to release the prisoner into the snow. "It's okay, you two can come in now."

Anya ran up the steps, Chance at her side.

Sisters

As the three of us walked back into the house, Fiona slid off the stool, tears running down her face. "Don't you dare laugh, damn you! I hate rats! I mean it. Don't laugh at me."

I tried to maintain a solemn expression.

"What happened?" Anya asked.

"Doc, caught a mouse."

Anya jumped in place, her arms flapping. "Can I see it? Can I? Please?"

"No you cannot," Fiona screeched.

Anya peeked up at me.

"It's okay." I put my hand on Anya's shoulder. "I put the mouse outside, maybe next time."

"Next time. Are you mad?" Fiona said. "You have to set traps. There can be *no* next time."

"Doc, it was just a mouse . . . we get them all the time. You're in the mountains. They won't hurt you. They're just hungry and cold, honest."

Fiona stood, visibly shaking. She wrapped her arms around her middle. "I hate mice. Hate rodents of any kind and I'm sure that was a rat."

I walked closer and placed my hands on each of Fiona's arms, running them up and down, feeling the woman's distress. "Doc?"

Fiona moved into my embrace, burying her face. "I was so scared and I kept screaming for help. I forgot where you were. I needed you," she sobbed.

I held the trembling woman in my arms and walked her over to the sofa. "Sit, I'll get you something to drink." I turned to Anya. "Take your coat and snow pants off, then wash up before your milk and cookies."

"Is Fiona gonna be okay?" Anya's lip trembled.

"Yes, baby, I promise."

I removed my own coat and hung it on the hook at the door, then walked into the kitchen. "Whiskey or brandy?"

"Water."

Right. I filled a glass with water, then took it to Fiona. "Here you go."

Tears ran down Fiona's face as she reached for the glass. "Thank you."

I sat beside her and wrapped my arm around Fiona's shoulder. "Doc, I don't believe for one minute that this is about a little mouse. What's really wrong?"

Fiona buried her face in my neck. "I hate mice, I hate this incessant snow, I hate that I'm stuck in these mountains because my stupid sister forgot to write home, that she may be dead and I'll never find out one way or the other. I hate that I'm acting like a wimp, and I hate my life." We stayed like that wrapped in each other's embrace till Anya came running into the room. I gently withdrew.

Anya tentatively approached Fiona and patted her legs. "You okay, Fiona?"

The fear in the child's eyes touched me.

"I'm fine, Anya, I just got frightened."

Fiona wiped her face, then leaned over and kissed Anya's cheek. "I'm sorry I scared you."

"Wanna play makeups?"

"In a little while, okay?"

"Okay."

"Anya, after your snack, I want you to get your workbook and practice your letters."

"Okay, Mam."

I tilted my head till I caught Fiona's attention. "Want to join us for some milk and cookies?"

"Could you make me some tea instead?"

"Of course."

Fiona nodded her head. I stood and pulled her up on her feet. "Come on, come sit and talk to me." I walked her over to the counter. Fiona sat, her head bowed, while I went about brewing tea and giving Anya a glass of milk and her cookie.

FIONA'S MIND BATTLED with her heart. Fear, happiness, panic at the unknown. And now she discovered this new emotion— it was too much for her. She fought to understand these feelings, ones she was not yet ready for or able to put a name to.

She lifted her head and looked directly into Maddison's eyes. She expected to see amusement, instead she found concern.

Maddison returned Fiona's steady gaze. "You okay, Doc?"

"I got fired today."

"I'm sorry. How?"

"I emailed my boss yesterday and explained the situation. I offered to trade my vacation time for my continued absence."

"What did he say?"

"She." Fiona grimaced. "She basically said that after an administrative review, it's been determined that my future services will not be required. Then she offered to write me a letter of recommendation."

"Damn." Maddison wiped the counter in front of her. "I'm really sorry."

"It's not your fault. I should never have taken this blasted trip."

"There's got to be other jobs . . . I mean, medicine is a thriving business, right?"

"You mean, if I ever get out of here?"

"Well, spring is only five months away." Maddison smiled, the skin around her eyes crinkling.

Fiona had never noticed that before. Nor had she paid attention to the warmth and kindness in Maddison's eyes. The woman was stuck with her for who knew how long and she was trying to make her feel better. Fiona tore a napkin into tiny pieces, tears gathering in her eyes threatening to leak out.

"You know you're welcome to call home and talk with your mother, right?"

She nodded, but said nothing.

Maddison patted Fiona's hand. "I'm sorry I laughed about the mouse."

"You don't understand." Fiona spread her hands, the pieces of napkin flying in different directions.

"I'm trying to. Talk to me."

She shook her head, the tears escaping down her cheeks.

Maddison walked around the counter and gathered the weeping woman into her arms. "It can't be that bad."

"It's not, it's wonderful," Fiona wailed.

Maddison ran her hands up and down Fiona's back. "You're crying because something wonderful happened?"

She nodded her head against Maddison's neck. Maddison pulled back and tipped Fiona's chin up with her finger. "Wonderful is supposed to evoke joy and happiness, you know that, right?"

Fiona looked into Maddison's blue eyes. Apprehension and something else was reflected there. A moment later, she realized Maddison was staring at her lips. She looked back at Maddison's eyes, as a wave of lust ran through her body. She saw her own need reflected in Maddison's eyes. Fiona felt herself responding. She leaned closer, just a breath away, she closed her eyes in anticipation.

Maddison stepped back. "You okay . . . I'm . . . I . . . what can I do for you, Doc? To help I mean." She released Fiona and moved around the counter.

Fiona blew out a breath. "I think I'm pregnant."

"That's awesome!" Maddison beamed. "It's what you've wanted."

"I know." Fiona pushed her bangs out of her eyes. "Suddenly I'm terrified."

"Perfectly natural. Anya's mom was positive she'd suck at motherhood. I knew she was wrong, but she wouldn't listen. After thirty seconds even she realized she was meant to be a mother."

Fiona started to cry again, a look of alarm on her face.

"You're gonna be a great mom, look how good you are with Anya." Maddison picked up the satellite phone and laid it next to Fiona. "When you calm down, and by the way, that's hormones making you cry, call your mom. Let her know the good news."

AN HOUR LATER Fiona was back to normal and smiling. "My mother's going to start knitting right away," she reported.

"So, she's happy?"

"Yes. She's wanted to be a grandmother for as long as I can remember."

127

"Your sister doesn't have any kids?"

"No, not that I'm aware of."

"Ahh."

"There's that sound again." Fiona grimaced.

"What *is* the deal with your sister? It doesn't sound like you're close and yet you're here in the middle of nowhere looking for her. Why?"

Fiona rolled her eyes. "Because she's in—"

"Are you feeling bedder now, Fiona?" Anya asked.

Fiona reached down and picked her up. "I am, and I'm sorry I upset you. Wanna play makeups?"

"Yay!" Anya squirmed to get down and ran to her room. She returned with a compact, lipstick and a plastic palette that displayed an assortment of eye shadow in blues, greens and grays.

"You probably shouldn't lift her up anymore."

Fiona looked puzzled. "Why?"

Maddison indicated her stomach, but said nothing.

"It's okay for now, tell me again in two months, if I'm still here."

"Where did you get that stuff?" Maddison asked.

"Fiona gave them to me."

"Did you ever think Fiona might need them?"

"No, uh-uh. She said there's no one she has to 'press, so I can have them."

Fiona felt herself flush. She realized how unkind it sounded and immediately regretted her words. "I—"

"It's okay, I understand." Maddison made her way to the door. "I'm going to head out and shovel the deck and the roof. Have fun ladies."

Chapter Twenty-Seven

November 1, 2008

I RUSHED OUTSIDE and clutched the shovel. Physical labor would keep me busy, and my salacious mind in check. Because the snow was fluffy, the stairs and landing were quick and easy. The pathway around the church was a different story because the falling snow had piled up over the last couple of storms. Some mounds were over six feet tall. If only it would all slide off at the same time. After the initial turn around the building, I secured the ladder to the north corner and climbed up. As soon as the broom touched the edge, the bank of snow began its decent. The rumble was loud and shook the ground as it landed with a thud below. I was grateful that the ladder was securely latched to the side of the building.

I cleared the newly dumped snow and moved the ladder to the other side of the building. The snow on this side was already almost all off the roof, the partial southern exposure assisting with the thaw. Clean up on the ground was more difficult because the white fluff had melted and re-hardened multiple times, making it denser to handle.

A look toward the west revealed gray clouds swirling over the mountaintops below; more snow would fall by tomorrow.

Priss and I made the decision to move here knowing the winters would be hard and long. We never made provisions for a sexy stranger to share the abode with, and certainly never anticipated a pregnant woman being trapped here.

Up until a few hours ago, Fiona was just a guest sharing the house and dinner table, now unfortunately she was so much more. The image of her screaming and wrestling with the mouse undid me. I have never seen anyone more beautiful and sexy at the same time than she was at that moment. It didn't help when my body reacted to her trembling frame. *"What the fuck am I doing?"*

My intent was to offer comfort, next thing I knew I wanted to kiss her. It's that damned smile of hers . . . it's captivating. The longer these snows lasted—days, weeks or months—the harder it would be when Fiona finally went home. She had made a big enough impact on our lives as it was, and she would be sorely missed. I refused to kid myself, she *would* go home at some point no matter how much Anya or I wished differently. Regrettably now it wasn't just Anya who needed to be protected, but my own heart as well.

Snowflakes began to fall as I approached the front steps. Sophia's snowmobile was parked at the bottom of the landing. I hadn't expected her.

129

Maybe she could help the situation. I took a deep breath; more snow meant more time with Fiona, which meant I needed to harness my infatuation and maintain any and all interactions with her on a friends-only basis.

"You're back," Fiona said.

"I am."

"We have company."

Anya was sitting on Nana Lorraine's lap, applying green shadow to her eyelids.

"Hey Guys, I never even heard you ride up! What a nice surprise." I walked over and kissed Sophia, then to Lorraine and hugged and kissed her as well. "It's good to see you, how ya been?"

Lorraine grinned broadly. "My legs hurt, my hands don't work, and I can't remember sh— anything."

"And we both know the alternative is not an option. I'm glad you're here."

"You're looking good," Lorraine said.

"It's all this fresh air and clean living."

"Uh-huh." She snickered.

I looked at Anya's face, the skewed colorations made her eyes look bruised. "That *is* makeup on her, right?"

Fiona giggled. "We got a little carried away."

"Ya think?"

"Mam, I'm giving Nana Lorraine a makeups."

"I see that, but it's makeover, Little One." I kissed her cheek and went back to the front door.

Fiona watched as I removed my jacket and gloves. "We prepared dinner."

"You did?"

"Mam, I do you now?"

"You keep doing Nana Lorraine, I want to talk with Nana Sophia and Doc for a bit."

"Okay." Anya picked up the brush she had been using. "Closes your eyes Nana."

I walked into the kitchen area. "I didn't know to expect you," I said.

Sophia nodded her head. "I called and spoke with Fiona. The market got a delivery. I wanted to know if you needed milk or anything else." She tilted her head toward Fiona. "She mentioned a few things she needed, and then read me your list. We shopped and came up. I added the milk on my own."

I peeked at the list I usually post on the fridge. All the items had been checked off. "You got everything?"

Fiona nodded. "When Sophia mentioned she was coming up on other business. I asked if she'd pick up a few things for me and get those items for you as well. I gave her the money to cover the expense. It's the least I can do."

"I don't need you paying for my groceries, Doc."

"Fight nice you two, you have company." Sophia grinned.

"What's new in town? How are the roads?"

She put her coffee cup down. "I was just telling Fiona, US 2 is clear to Libby and beyond. MT 37 has one lane open in each direction, but Pipe Creek Road is a mess, and NF 5879 hasn't been touched as yet."

I nodded my head. "That's pretty typical."

"That's what I said." Sophia laughed, the action causing her belly to roll.

"With it snowing again, I wouldn't hold out much hope for those roads until they get the main ones cleared first."

"Snowing!" Fiona walked to the door. "I cannot believe this." She laid her head against the window pane and groaned.

Sophia chuckled some more. "That's what you get for getting lost in Gopher Crotch, Montana. Just be glad you're not in a hole."

Fiona walked back slowly. "I thought this was Yaak?"

I burst out laughing as Sophia tried to keep a straight face.

"It is Yaak. Gopher Crotch is a euphemism for 'the middle of nowhere,'" Sophia explained.

"Well Yaak, certainly qualifies for that. Do I want to know about the hole?"

"Hole, usually refers to a valley lodged between towering mountain ranges," I explained.

"And this isn't a hole?"

"Oh lordy, no, honey. If this were a hole, you'd be looking up at snow covered mountains on all four sides, praying for sunshine," Lorraine said.

"Are y'all having fun at my expense?" Fiona asked, her hand on her hip.

"A little bit, yeah," I admitted. I walked around the counter and poured myself some coffee. "So what other business?"

"Huh?" Sophia asked.

I looked her right in the eye. "What's wrong? You didn't come up here to bring me groceries."

She glanced at Lorraine, then looked back at me. "Alice White is dead."

"Good." I took a cleansing breath. "How?"

"Not sure. The sheriff down in Hot Springs called." Sophia took a sip of her coffee. "Alice had my number in her wallet."

"Ahh," I said.

"It's over"—Sophia tilted her head toward Anya—"you're both free."

Fiona's eyes bounced between Sophia and myself. "Who is Alice?

Sophia stood up, patted my arm, and walked into the living area. "What say you give Nana Sophia a makeover, Little One?"

Anya jumped off Lorraine's lap and moved to Sophia's. "What color you want, Nana?"

I watched the exchange and chuckled. Anya was perfectly happy with her Nana Lorraine and Nana Sophia as our family. We didn't need anyone else.

The hand on my back was warm to the touch. Heat radiated through my three shirts. "Who is Alice?" Fiona repeated.

I looked her in the eye. "My egg donor."

"Egg donor?"

"Biological carrier."

Fiona stared at me long seconds. "I'm so sorry for your loss."

"Don't be. I'm certainly not. In fact, I feel wonderful."

Fiona sat with an oomph. "Why . . . exactly?"

"It's a long story, and you don't need to know my dirty little secrets."

Fiona lay her hand on my arm. "Are you all right?"

I stared down at her hand, then back to her eyes. "I'm fine, thank you. Just don't ask me to mourn. I won't do it."

"Mam, what's morn?" Anya asked from across the way.

I put my finger up to my lips for Fiona's sake. "It means be sad."

Anya turned her head. "You sad, Mam?"

"No baby, I'm happy."

"Good."

"I don't understand." Fiona whispered.

I turned my back and lowered my voice. "I can't explain while Anya's awake, it will have to keep till later."

She nodded her head slowly. "Why don't you take a shower, while I finish dinner."

"You really don't want any help?"

"Even I can reheat a meal." She patted my arm.

"You're the one that said you were clueless in the kitchen."

"I'm a blue ribbon microwaver and that's all I'm required to do."

"Just checking, after all we do have guests. I can't have you poisoning them." I moved quickly before she could swing at me. "You ladies *are* staying for dinner?"

Sophia mumbled something, I couldn't distinguish due to Anya's artistic endeavors.

"We're here for the night, brought our bag with us," Lorraine said. "Hope that's okay?"

"It's always okay. You know that." I squeezed her shoulder. "I'm gonna take a shower. I'll be back in a bit."

"I'M MAKING PANCAKES, if anyone's interested," I yelled. While I mixed the batter, the cast iron griddle was on the stove heating up. Lorraine and Sophia were moving around upstairs, Fiona had run into the bathroom to brush her teeth and comb her hair. Anya came shuffling out of her bedroom, yawning and dragging her floppy-eared rabbit across the floor.

"Morning, Little One."

She came over and kissed my cheek. "Are the Nanas here?"

"We are, Munchkin." Sophia walked down the steps with Lorraine following right behind her.

"Yayyy." Anya ran and kissed both women.

"Go wash up Anya, and brush your teeth," I said. "Morning ladies."

"Where's your guest?"

"Right here." Fiona came out of the bathroom, dressed in my sweats, her hair pulled back in a ponytail.

"Didn't I recoup your clothes from the wreck for you?"

Fiona nodded. "Yours are more comfortable and so much warmer."

I poured coffee into four mugs and milk into Anya's glass. "I hope you slept well."

"Like a dream. Tells me we need a new mattress." She elbowed Sophia in the ribs.

"What? Sophia doesn't have any extra hay in the barn she can stuff the old one with?"

"Funny, you're always so hilarious," Sophia said. She turned to Fiona, "Did you sleep okay, Doc?"

"I did actually. That couch and I are good friends, and I love sleeping by the fire."

Anya came running out of the bathroom, toothpaste smeared on her face. "Come here, you." I wiped her mouth and picked her up to kiss her. "What do you have planned for your Nanas today?"

"We gonna make a snow'dman."

Fiona looked outside, and shook her head. "Is this turning into a blizzard?"

"Hard to tell right now," Lorraine said.

"All I know is, I'm out of places to shovel it to," I said. "It will just have to pile up from here on out."

"Can I use the phone?" Fiona asked.

"Of course. You don't have to ask."

Fiona took the phone and went up the stairs to the office.

"So, Doc's got a bun in the oven," Sophia said.

I shook my head, and put Anya down. "Not now." I indicated Anya.

"Well, if you had to get stuck with an unwanted guest, at least she's amicable, " Lorraine said. "Not hard on the eyes either." She snickered naughtily.

"She's okay. Particularly after she accepted the inevitable. Anya, why don't you get your Leapster and practice your words till the pancakes are done."

"Okay." Anya ran to her room and returned just as fast, then sat on the couch with her handheld children's tablet.

"She calling her husband?" Sophia asked.

I shook my head. "No."

"Who then?"

"Her mother. She's elderly and has a couple medical issues. Doc's worried about her." I poured the batter onto the hot griddle and began cooking the pancakes.

"Mom is doing fine and she says 'Hi' to all of you." Fiona came down the stairs slowly. I noticed she was putting more and more weight on the ankle.

"She doing okay?" I asked.

Fiona looked pleased. "She's a tough old bird. She's doing great." As she moved around the counter, her hand stroked my back, then she began gathering plates and silverware. "Thanks for asking."

"Uh-huh."

A look passed between Lorraine and Sophia, and I waved my spatula at them in warning.

"So Fiona, no husband waiting at home?" Lorraine asked.

She looked up from the drawer. "You didn't tell them. That's sweet." Fiona shifted her gaze between Lorraine and Sophia. "I'm gay, so there's definitely no husband waiting back there. And, unfortunately, no significant other, and now, there's no job either."

"Why not?" Sophia asked.

Fiona pointed out the window. "I was on personal leave. It was supposed to last for ten days. I'm here three plus weeks, plus my traveling time, with no idea when I can get back." She brought the silverware to the table. "They had no choice really."

"Bull. This weather has always been unpredictable. They could be a little understanding," Lorraine said.

"They have a business to run," Fiona replied. "Everything comes down to money in the end."

"Well, you can always apply for the position in town. I've got an in with the mayor," Sophia said with a big smirk.

"Really, who's that?"

I chuckled as I flipped the second helping of pancakes off the griddle and then poured more batter onto it.

Sophia put her hand on Lorraine's shoulder. "Mayor McCollum, meet Doc Fiona."

Fiona laughed along with the rest of us. "Honestly, I couldn't stand this weather every winter. It's absurd that you can't get out, get into town, visit friends, see a movie, something."

Lorraine leaned forward. "We get around, it's just not in a manner you're accustomed too."

"But I can't picture myself driving one of those machines for transportation or being cooped up for weeks on end voluntarily."

A sadness squeezed my chest. I knew it wasn't a life someone like Fiona would choose, and yet it hurt to hear her say it.

"Breakfast is ready, ladies."

Chapter Twenty-Eight

November 3, 2008

LATE THAT NIGHT Fiona lay in the bed, tossing and turning, frustrated and staring out the window. The night was clear for a change, the moon lighting the blackened sky. Stars twinkled, all was calm . . . weather-wise. She, however, could not erase the look on Maddison's face when she learned her mother was dead. Her entire body stiffened, and yet she never let on how she felt. If she felt. A shiver ran through Fiona. "What kind of person is so in control?" she mumbled.

She had been awake for hours, the night noises that usually soothed her instead trumpeted in her mind. She climbed out of bed, and walked to the balcony. Down below Maddison appeared to sleep peacefully. For once the old wooden steps didn't creak as she made her way down them, nor did the newly refinished plank flooring as she scooted through the living area into the kitchen.

"What's wrong with you tonight?"

Fiona fell against the counter. "Jesus, you scared the crap out of me." She stood upright, and glared at Maddison. "I thought you were asleep?"

"I was, except for the continuous bed creaking. If I didn't know better I'd have thought you were entertaining a lady up there. Especially with the mumbling and the sneaking down the stairs."

"Ha. Ha. I was not sneaking, I was trying to be quiet."

"Ever hear about the bull in the china shop?"

"You're just so very amusing, I could vomit." Fiona turned and opened the fridge.

"Warm some milk up, it'll help you sleep."

"I'm the damned doctor here, you don't have an answer for everything."

Maddison tossed the blanket aside and walked to the counter. "What has you so upset?"

Fiona filled the kettle with water and set it on the stove. "I realize I'm lucky you've taken me in and provided for me, but I have to be honest here, I can't forget your reaction when you heard your mother was dead. It was so cold. So uncaring, and it just doesn't fit. I don't understand." She drilled Maddison with her eyes.

Maddison sat at the counter and rested her head in her hand. "That woman is not my mother. Trust me."

"But she is! Or was." Fiona grasped a mug and slammed the cabinet door.

"Hey, the Munchkin is sleeping." Chance came running out of Anya's room, and Maddison petted the dog to soothe her.

Fiona felt like throwing something. She wanted to scream. "There's such an incongruity between the way you treat Anya, talk about your partner, and then this. I can't wrap my head around it," she hissed. "How can you have such diverse emotions?"

"Simple. I feel nothing where Alice is concerned."

"Please don't sit there like nothing happened." Fiona added honey to the mug. "Talk to me."

Maddison sighed. "I hated her okay. I hate everything she stood for and believed in. The fact she's dead is cause for celebration as far as I'm concerned."

"Can you please explain why?"

"Why do I have too?"

"She's your mother, grandmother to that child in there."

"She's nothing to Anya or me and never will be."

"Why is Anya afraid of her?"

"She's dropped by the house once. Called Priss despicable names, and yelled at Anya. Made her cry. She would have slapped her, but I got back in time to stop her."

"That's it, she called you names?"

"Do we need to go into all of this?"

"Yes, please."

"She made my life a living hell once she found out I was gay."

Fiona scowled at Maddison. "How?"

"Does it really matter. Am I not allowed to hold a grudge?"

"Have you never gotten along with her?" Fiona picked up the kettle as soon as it began to whistle and poured the boiling water into her mug.

"She wanted a son. I didn't have the right bits."

Fiona glared at Maddison. "I want a way home. A healthy child. A job, I'm stuck out in the middle of nowhere looking for an ungrateful sister, but I don't hate anyone." She stirred the tea.

"Well, see, that's 'cause you're nicer than I am."

"Why are you so fucking calm?" Fiona shook her head. "I'd be devastated if my mother died."

"I keep telling you, she's *not* my mother." Maddison slid off the stool and walked around the counter. She took Fiona's hand and pulled her toward the couch. "The day Alice found out I was gay, she set out paper plates for me at dinner."

"And?" Fiona was incredulous.

"We were having soup. She didn't want me contaminating her dishes. She put rubber gloves on to pick up the debris and threw everything I touched into the garbage."

"That's awful." Fiona sipped her tea. "I don't even know how to respond to that."

"I wanted to kill her when she upset Priss. She was already sick, barely had strength, and that bitch persecuted her."

"I'm sorry. Sophia said she was evil, but I didn't realize how bad it was."

"Why would you? If you've never known someone like that, you can't conceive it."

"I feel like I don't know you when you're like this."

"You *don't* know me. We're living together because you took a wrong turn. This is temporary. You wouldn't even be here if given an option. Simply put, we would never have met if you could read a map."

Fiona laid her hand on Maddison's arm. She felt the muscles under her fingers twitch. "Some would call that fate."

"Fate." Maddison snorted. "That's something people say to explain the decisions they've made. In your case, a trip you should never have embarked on."

Fiona said nothing. She held the cup with two hands and sipped the hot brew slowly.

"You know I'm right."

Long minutes passed in silence. "I believed, obviously I'm wrong, that we were getting to know each other. Becoming friends," Fiona said.

Maddison turned sideways on the couch, face to face with Fiona. "Let's be frank here, Doc. If you were back home in your comfort zone, would you even look at me twice?"

Fiona's face turned beet red before she was able to utter a response.

Maddison got up and moved to the fireplace, she poked the wood in the grate, then swept the ashes into the galvanized can before she turned back to Fiona. "I get it, honest." She walked back and sat on the edge of coffee table. "You're beautiful, part of the upper class or in-crowd, and naturally you gravitate toward your own kind."

Fiona put the mug of tea on the side table and leaned forward. She peered into Maddison's eyes, then wrapped her hand around the back of Maddison's neck and pulled her down, pressing their lips together. The kiss was sweet, tender and felt like so much more to her.

Maddison pulled away. "Now you're just slumming, Doc."

"Do you truly believe that?" Fiona moved back, sitting deeper into the cushion pulling her knees up and wrapping her arms around them. "Or is it because I'm pregnant."

"I found you attractive the minute you first appeared all disheveled and uppity about wanting to get home." Maddison chuckled as she spoke.

Fiona nodded her head. "I'll grant you, you're not the *type*"—she used her fingers to make quotation marks—"that I'm normally attracted too." Fiona reached her hand out and caught Maddison's. "And yes, let's be honest. The women I've dated in the past were shallow and had no staying power. They didn't want commitment, or families, and didn't have the wherewithal to stick with me when things got serious."

"It's their loss, Doc."

"See that's what I mean. You're so gentle and caring most of the time, but two days ago, your reaction to your moth— to Alice's death, I just don't understand."

"Wow"—Maddison shook her head—"that was a topic changer!"

"I need to know," Fiona said.

"Why, you'll be gone from here first chance you get, and you'll never even look back. So what does it matter?" Maddison got up and went to the fridge. She opened the door, looked at the six pack, then closed it, opting for water instead.

"Please come back here and talk to me."

Maddison returned, but sat in the side chair instead the couch. "Whadda ya want to talk about?"

"Did she always mistreat you?"

"Doc, I don't want to be rude about this, but Alice is not the issue. You're dealing with hormones, loneliness, and whatever is going on with your sister. Why don't we discuss that? What is going on with her?"

"I am dealing with all those things, you're right. But you missed one other important truth—I'm attracted to you." She spread her hands. "I can't explain it, I certainly don't understand why it happened, but I know the pull is there and that I feel it deeply."

"It's just the hormones, don't fret." Maddison reached over and pulled the blanket off the back of the couch to cover herself. "It's not catchy, I promise you."

"Are you always this difficult to talk to?"

"It's late and I'm tired. And pregnant ladies need their rest." Maddison ducked her head as the throw pillow flew across the space between them.

"You are the most aggravating, pig headed, obstinate pain-in-the-ass I've ever met." Fiona took her cup to the sink, stomped across the floor and started up the stairs.

"Doc." Fiona turned on the second step. "You're here short term. Maybe a quick romp in the sheets is enough for you. I need to think about Anya."

"Until we understand what's happening, she wouldn't need to know . . . about any of this."

Maddison stared at Fiona. They remained that way until Maddison looked away. "Then I guess it's me I need to protect. My heart could get broken by you, and I'm not up to that either."

"So you'd rather *not* explore what we're both clearly feeling." Fiona waved her hand between them. "Even if it meant possibly finding true happiness?"

"Okay, say we do examine this, and we like the outcome. Are you ready to move here? Leave your family and life behind to live in Montana?"

"You could come East. We have mountains there, too."

"Sorry Doc, that will never be an option for me."

Fiona felt the air leave her chest. "Then, you're right, we have nothing else to discuss." She turned and continued up the stairs.

Chapter Twenty-Nine

April 2003

BANG, BANG, BANG. Someone was pounding on the front door. I turned to the clock on the nightstand. What the fuck?

After pulling on a pair of jeans, I limped toward the door, and yanked it open. "Juan? What the hell is going on?"

"Kari's in the hospital."

"What? Why?"

"She was attacked out back of Tanner's, downtown."

"Let me get my phone and wallet"

The time it took to get to the hospital felt like an eternity. My mind raced. I wanted to vomit. "How did it happen?"

"We're working on it."

"Who's handling the investigation?"

"Lieutenant Sanderson."

"Good, she'll stay with this. Tell her I want to be kept in the loop."

"Will do." Juan turned left, then a sharp right and drove the patrol car into the lot and let me off at the emergency room door. "I'll be in as soon as I park."

I shuffled my way to the counter, flipped my badge to the nurse on duty. "I'm here to see Karileah Gallagher."

"The doctors are with her now."

"Where?" I started around the counter.

"You can't go back there."

"I'm a *rape* counselor." The lie was necessary in order to get to Priss.

She nodded. "Curtain three."

I pushed through the double doors, then scoped out the area. Number three was on the left. "Priss? . . . Honey, I'm coming in."

"Noooo," she cried from behind the curtain.

"I'm here to help." I tugged the curtain aside and stepped within the cramped space. Kari turned away and buried her face in the pillow. I stepped closer, leaned down and wrapped the sobbing woman in my arms. Her eyes were blackened, her jaw appeared broken and there were cuts and scrapes on her hands and face.

"Who are you?" A man in scrubs demanded. His plastic ID identified him as Doctor Thomas Alvarez.

"I'm her sister. How is she?"

The doctor seemed unsure. "Is that true, Miss?"

Kari nodded.

"We're doing tests, I'll let you know when we do." He walked out without another word.

Five hours later, Dr. Alvarez reappeared with a nurse at his side. "How are you feeling Ms. Gallagher?"

"It hurts," she mumbled.

"We'll give you something shortly. Do you remember anything that happened?"

Kari shook her head, I looked on stunned. "You don't remember?"

The doctor put his hand up. "That's not unusual under the circumstances. She was under the influence—"

"Bull shit." I released her hand and stood up straight. "She doesn't do drugs. God damn it, I know for a fact—"

"Have you heard of the drug Rohypnol?"

I gazed at Priss, then back to him. "You mean—"

He nodded. "We're going to keep her overnight. We've set the leg and sutured the laceration on her arm. The ankle will require an air cast, which I've ordered. Her ribs will eventually heal on their own, but it will take a while. We've wired her jaw, and cleaned her cuts." He made a note in a binder. "Can I speak to you . . .outside?"

"Of course." I patted Priss's hand. "I'll be right back."

Out in the corridor, the doctor waited. "She's been worked over pretty severely as you can see. The rape was brutal. She has extensive vaginal tearing on top of the other injuries. I recommend she see a counselor as soon as possible."

"I'll make sure of it."

"Normally, I would prescribe anti-retroviral medication without making an issue of it. In this case, I strongly recommend she also be tested for HIV every six months for a year. She suffered a lot of blood loss and possible transfer from the beating she took. If her rapist carries the virus, she's in danger of contracting it."

I nodded, as my stomach constricted. "I'll make sure."

"I'll get those pain meds for her."

"Thank you, Doctor."

THE NEXT DAY I brought Priss home in a cab. She walked into her room and closed the door behind her. I let her grieve for two days before I barged in and demanded she talk to me.

"You can't just give up and die."

"I don't care," She mumbled through her wired teeth.

"Priss, please, let me get take you to a doctor, someone you'll feel comfortable talking to about this."

"No. I've talked to God and that's all that's important."

"God!"

"It brings me comfort."

"You need to talk with a therapist, someone who deals with rape victims."

"I've confessed to God. It's in his hands now."

"Are you freakin' kidding me?"

"I'm gonna sleep now." She rolled away from me and closed her eyes. "Leave me alone, please."

Over the next three weeks, I begged, yelled and begged her again till she finally began to drink her liquid meals.

Two days after that I walked into her room. "Juan is on the phone. He's been calling every day."

She shook her head and closed her eyes.

I went to the phone. "Try back tomorrow. She's sleeping now."

I went back into her room and sat on the edge of the bed. "Priss, you can't survive like this. You need to eat, your agent's called three times. Juan calls every day and stops by. Let me get someone to help you?"

"No."

"What about your mother or sister?"

"No."

I walked out of her room more frightened than I had been the day I was shot.

Chapter Thirty

November 5, 2008

TWO DAYS LATER I walked through the front door with an armload of wood just as Fiona threw a book across the room.

"God . . .dam . . . ng it."

I searched for Anya. She was at the table doing her letters.

"Problem?" I asked.

Fiona shook her head. "I started another book." She blew a breath out her mouth that scattered her ebony locks.

After dumping the wood by the fireplace, I hung my coat on the rack by the door. "And?"

"The author is a misogynist pig." She clomped over and picked up the offending book.

"Who is it?"

"L. M. Addison. It's his latest mystery. And can I just say, I'm shocked you read this crap." She sat with a thud. "He's a"—she took a deep breath—"butt hole if there ever was one."

"I'm out of singles . . . be careful." I studied her closely, searching her eyes; she apparently had no clue. *She's thinks I'm a guy?* "And why exactly is Addison so bad?"

"There isn't enough time in the world to explain it to you how despicable I think he is."

"Okay, then." I turned to check on Anya's progress. "How you doing baby?" I was looking down at her numbers when Fiona chose to answer me.

"His men are wholly developed characters, with brains, depth, quirks and varying degrees of good looks. Maybe the occasional scar. A tick. A limp once. But they're real and you relate in them, maybe care about them. His PI is a zany buffoon, and still, he's beloved by the public."

"And that's bad?.." I sat across from her a little unnerved to be discussing my own works. I hadn't had the opportunity since Kari became too sick to help me.

"He's turned into a pig." She slammed the book down on the end table. "His first books were good, the people ordinary. This last one, his women are caricatures and totally unbelievable."

I took a moment before responding. "Why do you say that?"

"The women in this book . . . well they're superficial." She gazed at Anya, then lowered her voice. "They're just fuck-bunnies. Not one of them has any brains. Or if they do, you won't read about it. The female suspects are all described as having big tits, or bazzooms, or mammories. Well, you

144

get the idea. Oh, and they have a shapely rounded ass. The women are only there to feed his macho detective's sexual appetite. None of them appear capable of thinking for themselves. If they get into trouble, they're saved by the big bad-ass hero and they scream like ninnies, or faint."

"Isn't that a little harsh?"

"You think so?" She picked up the book. "Listen to this crap. 'Carey motioned for the woman to go first, then waited to see the direction she would take. The statuesque woman turned toward the stairs. After just a few steps, the facts of the case as Carey knew them were obscured by the sensuous energy of Ms. Jones' shapely hips and ass. The silk of her nightgown clung to her with each progressive footstep. She reached for the door knob, her hand slender, the movement graceful. A seductive smile and gentle push found Carey alone with Ms. Jones in the master suite. Carey's hormones took over.'" Fiona stopped reading.

I stared numbly.

"Can you believe that drivel?" She tossed the book a second time.

"Isn't sexual tension part of every genre? I mean even when it's not explicit, there's still a hint, right?"

"Yes and that's the problem." She took a sip of her tea. "In his first books the detective was kind—a little crazy, definitely unorthodox—but he respected women and they found him cute in a nerdy sort of way. The sex scenes were just an afterthought and could just as easily been deleted without hurting the plot. The last book, the bonehead has done a complete one-eighty. Maybe his girlfriend left him, maybe he's always been a jerk, or maybe he had a better editor the first couple of times, but it feels as if a different writer is creating this work." She shook her head. "You would think an author would improve with time, not get worse. That they'd have the decency to write for women as well as men."

"I've . . .ahh read the books. I can't remember one actual sex scene."

"Then you were skimming, because they're there in graphic detail."

I studied her eyes closely, she *was* serious. And I didn't know how to tell her. "How about we make a bet, whoever wins does the household chores for a week."

She looked at me inquisitively. "What's the bet?"

"That there's no real physical sex in Addison's books."

Fiona retrieved the abandoned volume off the floor. "Are you crazy? I just read a scene to you."

"There was no kissing. No touching. Just a natural reaction to the woman's sex appeal."

She sat on the couch and flipped till she found the page again. I watched as she reread the scene. "Maybe not here, but trust me, these books are filled with hot monkey sex and you're on. I expect breakfast in bed every morning."

"And I expect the wash to be done *before* we run out of clothes."

"Since I have no intention of losing, that won't be a problem. Addison is a pig, and I'll prove it to you." Fiona put the book aside. "Seriously, it's no wonder I prefer lesbian fiction. Some of those women really know how to write for other women and they stay consistent."

I took exception to her comments. "Like who?" I turned to work the fire and clear the debris.

She rubbed her forehead unconsciously. "Well, how about *Handmaid's Tale* by Margaret Atwood, or *Onion*, by Kate Braestrup, *The Sealed Letter* by Emma Donoghue, *Water Mark* by J.M. Redmann, *My Sweet Untraceable You* by Sandra Scoppettone, *anything* by Lee Lynch or—"

"I get it." I put my hand up to stop her. I had heard enough and not for the first time.

"Wait, there's more. There's *Solitaire* by Kelley Eskridge, or *The Blue Place* by Nicola Griffith. These women know how to develop characters and build tension. They tell a story that draws you in from the first page." Fiona sat back and stared at me. "I'm sure there's more but that's off the top of my head."

"You obviously prefer lesbian fiction written by lesbians, and Addison doesn't do that."

"What I prefer is a good story, romance or not. I want believable people that are fleshed out, not distortions of this pinhead's opinion." Fiona stared daggers back at me.

"Lesbian authors earn crap. At least Addison seems to be doing well, right?"

"You think making money makes it okay to write like crap?" Fiona crossed her arms and glared at me. "That housewife was on the *Time's* best seller list, I hope you don't think that means she deserved it?"

"*Who*?"

"Never mind." She shook her head in frustration. "Without cable TV you wouldn't understand. Even with cable, I doubt it would be your style."

I needed to distance myself from this conversation . . . to think about all she had said. Did other readers feel as she did? I got up and went to the kitchen. "Want more tea?"

"Yes, please." She brought her cup and placed it on the counter. "Please tell me you do not approve of his portrayal of the females in this latest book?"

I put the kettle on to boil then turned to face Fiona. "I believe . . . that an author writes what . . . the public is craving at that moment in time. What they expect, whether you agree with the assessment or not. Male readers have an image of private eyes as these macho-type, whiskey-drinking, brawling brethren. And those type of men expect women to be fragile, sexual, and not overly bright." I put my hand up to stop her before she could reply. "This Addison . . . has a lot of women followers, so

146

apparently the stories are meeting both sides of the public's gender requirements."

"Tell me you don't actually enjoy his writing?"

This was such a surreal conversation and so difficult to participate in without revealing what I didn't want known and what my publisher had worked tirelessly to keep hidden.

"I think Addison does a decent job with the mystery-murder aspects of the plots. It's been written they're comparable to that of Agatha Christie and Arthur Conan Doyle's style. You see all the clues, but initially they're banal. It's only at the end when the villain is revealed that the evidence comes together to prove his or her guilt, and that, my dear lady, takes a certain modicum of talent."

"Fine." Fiona stomped away, apparently annoyed. At least that's the impression she gave.

I stretched my arms over my head and twisted my back from side to side. "Well, you can't argue with success, but what do I know?"

"I can't believe you're defending him."

"Look, Doc, most people who write hope to reap the benefits of their musings. You can't tell me that they shouldn't write what sells. Besides, right now, you're sounding a little like a man-hater yourself."

"Bull. If you ask me, the whole book is drivel." She sat with a whoosh.

"Tell that to Addison, not me." I fixed her tea and made myself another pot of coffee. I still needed to work on the rewrites of the next installment of said drivel.

Chapter Thirty-One

November 8, 2008

"WERE YOU TOGETHER long?" Fiona asked.

Fiona and Maddison sat opposite each other in the living area, drinking tea and coffee respectively.

"Almost seven years."

Fiona took a sip of her drink. "Was it love at first sight?"

Thinking back to her initial reaction to Miss Priss, Maddison burst out laughing. "Not hardly."

"I'm so jealous." Fiona looked up quickly. "I'm sorry, I didn't mean that the way it came out. It's awful that your wife is gone, but at least you had that time together, and you and Anastasia have your memories of her. I don't think I'll ever have that and I worry if I'm cheating this one." She looked down and rubbed her stomach.

"Are you even sure you're pregnant?"

Fiona nodded. "I am. Yes."

"How can you be positive?"

"One of the things I asked Sophia to pick up was a pregnancy test, three in fact. And prenatal vitamins."

Maddison got up and walked over to Fiona. She leaned down and kissed her cheek. "Congrats. You're gonna be a terrific mother."

"Yeah, right."

"You will. It will take you all of thirty seconds and you'll be in love with the baby in your arms. After that, it's just providing what the child needs."

"I certainly hope you're right." Fiona rested one hand on her stomach.

"How far along do you think?"

"Almost five months, without an ultrasound I'm only guessing."

"You know when you had the procedure right?"

"Yes, based on that, I'd say just over four months."

"You didn't suspect before this?"

"I've never had a regular menstrual cycle, so it was difficult to be sure. Honestly, I was afraid to hope."

Maddison counted on her fingers. "So you're due in March sometime?"

Fiona nodded. "I sure hope so."

"Crap, that's before Spring thaw up here." Maddison chuckled as she returned to her chair. "You better know how to do this, cause I sure don't."

Quiet filled the space, the crackling fire the only distraction to the stillness.

"How long did you know each other till you fell in love?" Fiona asked.

Maddison sat in the chair, her fingers steepled. She stared into the fire as she spoke. "There are lots of forms of love and many reasons for people to get married or create a partnership. It's not always like they write in the romance novels."

Fiona regarded Maddison with a surprised look on her face. "That was deep. Now what the hell did it mean?"

"I'm just saying people don't always get together for the same reasons. Sometimes they do it for pragmatic purposes, or because they're friends, or because it's the only option left open to them."

"Wow, next you're gonna tell me you hooked up with a straight woman."

Maddison didn't respond.

"Oh. My. God. Is there anything more pathetic than a butch falling for the straight girl next door." Fiona laughed. "How stereotypical can you get?"

"It wasn't like that."

"Yeah, right. You obviously loved her, and you claim to miss her. If that doesn't define romance, what does?"

"She was my friend, and a damned good one. We were never lovers." Maddison glared at Fiona. "I loved her. I was not *in love* with her. There's a big difference between the two." Maddison hissed.

"Maddison, you lived with a woman for six years and you're telling me nothing sexual transpired?" She sniggered to herself. "That's just sad."

Maddison leaned forward, hands on her knees and stared at Fiona. "There is nothing sad about it. She was my best friend, someone I trusted implicitly."

Fiona took in the set of Maddison's shoulders, the angle of her jaw. "She must have been super special then."

"She was." Maddison walked to the door, grasped her coat, and called to Chance. She left without another word.

Fiona sat in the side chair till just after midnight. Maddison hadn't returned and she was just as glad, since she had no idea what to say to her. Fiona fed the fire, turned the lights out, and lay on the couch so she could listen for Anastasia. She'd apologize in the morning if it wasn't already too late.

I WOKE TO the sound of Fiona's brace moving across the hardwood floor upstairs. After stretching in place to loosen the kinks, I swung my feet over the side of the couch and moved to the hearth to tend the glowing embers.

A little after one, I had ventured in from the barn, expecting Fiona to have gone to bed. Instead I discovered her dozing on the couch, seemingly listening for Anya. I should have known she would. No words were exchanged between us, she stood and walked away, climbing the stairs posthaste. I couldn't put words to how I was feeling or why I felt so damned guilty.

I never meant to reveal the complicated status of my relationship with Priss. It felt like a betrayal and that was the last thing I wanted for Anya's memory of her mother. Things were getting dicey to say the least, between Fiona and myself. The mutual attraction was awkward. I just had to accept what couldn't be. Between Fiona's pregnancy and her family being back East, anything more between us seemed futile. She would go home as soon as the weather broke and as she kept reminding anyone who would listen, she hated Montana and all its weather-related restrictions. All valid motives to douse my titillation. Now I just needed to convince my heart it would never work.

Chance nudged my hand, checking to be sure I was okay, clearly sensing my disquiet. The dog rested her head on my thigh, offering canine comfort as she often did. I rubbed her head and ears, sure that the dog truly understood my feelings and my dilemma.

"It's okay girl." I stroked the dog's head lovingly. "Come on, let's get breakfast, okay?" Her ears perked up as she raced to the kitchen. I fixed her bowl and set it down, then went about getting her fresh water. Once she finished her meal, I let her out for her morning ritual. The sky was dark gray and the cold felt damp on my skin. The winds had howled all night and today the clouds promised another storm was imminent. In years past, I hadn't paid attention to the constant snows, the inability to get around, or the cabin fever so many complained about. Fiona's presence changed all that.

"I WANT TO apologize for what I said last night," Fiona said.

I was preparing breakfast, when she came down the stairs and approached me.

"I shouldn't have been so touchy. It was me who betrayed Priss's memory.

"You don't really believe that, do you?" she asked.

I poured her a cup of coffee and topped my own mug off. I waited while she fixed hers.

"A lot of people will tell you they're your friend. The word is bandied about just like the word love. It doesn't mean anything. It's just an expression that has no depth or real significance to it. Friendship, for me, is and must always be a two way street. One that includes loyalty." I took a sip of my coffee.

Fiona nodded her head. "I'm pretty sure my ex was one of those other people."

"Well Priss, wasn't. When I say she was a saint, I mean it, literally. Our friendship was the result of years of helping and depending on each other.

Being there when we were needed. Laughing, enjoying life, delighting in the same experiences, but most importantly, sharing adversity together."

"You were very lucky to have that."

"I was. I've had people that called themselves friends who deceived me. When I give someone my word, I keep it. Integrity is everything." I poured more coffee in each of our mugs.

Tears formed in Fiona's eyes. "I believe that. I've witnessed it myself."

"Don't get me wrong . . . I'm no saint, and I have a lot of bad traits, but I can be counted on and am faithful."

"Still, I shouldn't have teased you about your relationship. At least you stayed with Priss, my ex ran as fast as she could without stopping at GO."

"She's a damned fool."

"Thank you for saying that."

"So, now that you're officially eating for two, what would you like for breakfast?"

"Surprise me."

"I'll just get my daughter up and dressed and I'll be back."

Chapter Thirty-Two

November 10, 2008

FIONA SIPPED HER coffee as she watched Maddison return to the kitchen.

"Anya, be sure to brush your teeth, then come meet us in the kitchen." Maddison made her way to the counter area. "Well, I've decided on cheese omelets, bacon, toast, orange juice and, of course, more coffee. You better be hungry! And, just to be nice, I'll let you choose the jelly." Maddison ducked down to grab something from the bottom cabinet.

Fiona was relieved that the uncomfortable feelings between them had passed.

"Do you need anything right now?"

Fiona shook her head and held up the mug of hot coffee. "No, this will hold me, thanks."

The meal was pleasant by anyone's standards. Talk around the table consisted of updates on Anya's daily lessons, the need for her to complete her latest skill tests on line, and Fiona's desire to call her mother later in the day.

"If she's only four what kind of testing is required?"

"Anya's mother had her identifying whole words at three. She could do simple math using her fingers. We took her to be tested. The results suggested that we start her on a cross between kindergarten and first grade as soon as possible. Priss and I discussed it at length. We agreed that we wanted her homeschooled. I took some computer courses and here we are." Maddison kissed Anya's cheek.

"I gonna be a doctor when I growed big," Anya said.

"When did you decide this?" Maddison asked.

"When Fiona tolded me about makeups and stuffs," she said.

Fiona giggled into her hand. "We may have discussed the benefits of being a financially independent liberated woman."

"Wow, very cool, Munchkin. Then you can take care of me in my old age," Maddison said.

She kissed my cheek. "I will, Mam."

With the meal consumed, Maddison began the process of cleaning the table. Fiona remained seated, sipping her coffee and wondering what she could do with herself. The inactivity was something new and was driving her nuts. She watched Maddison move around the kitchen. Arousal was instantaneous. She shook her head hard.

"I hate to ask, but is it a big deal to move the flat screen down here?"

"No, I can do it soon as I finish here," Maddison said.

Fiona nodded. "Thanks, I just need something to occupy myself."

"It's not a big deal, only takes a couple minutes."

Fiona approached as the last dish was put in the rack. "And do you think I could go downstairs to exercise?"

"Sure"

"Fiona waved her hand at the computer. "You're apparently busy, but I need to start moving."

"No problem." Maddison hung the towel from her waistband on the hook. "This door"—Maddison pointed to the left one under the stairs— "takes you right down."

Fiona wrinkled her brow. "Can I take a towel down with me."

"Sure thing, I'll get you one."

UNHOOKING THE TV would prove easy, easier than dealing with my attraction to Fiona. It was getting out of hand and becoming downright embarrassing. The more time I spent with her, the more I wanted to. Having a four-year-old was not exactly conducive to romance or seduction, and Fiona's pregnancy added another layer of concern, yet the more I knew about her, the more we talked—it was like a magnet was pulling me toward her.

"Mam, you gonna move the TV?" Anya stood there holding my small tool-kit.

"Sorry, Munchkin, I was daydreaming." I pulled the screwdriver out of the kit and undid the bolts holding the flat screen to the wall bracket. I undid the plug and handed the tool back to my able assistant. "I think that does it."

"Can I pick out some movies?"

I had to chuckle, poor Fiona was liable to be watching cartoons the rest of the day. "Go ahead. I'll take this downstairs and hook it up." I started out of the room, but stopped. "You wait for me before you come down those stairs, you hear me?"

"Yes, Mam."

Downstairs I made quick work of mounting the TV on the second bracket high up on the fireplace. Once I had made sure that the stonework would not get hot enough to melt the television, I'd ordered the extra support to make moving the TV easier.

"You *are* done," Fiona said as she walked out of the steamy bathroom.

"Not quite, but I'm getting there. Anya's picking out movies, I sure hope you like cartoons." I pulled the socket end of the wire and plugged the unit into the power.

"That's fine, as long as she sits with me."

I turned from my chore. Her face was flushed from the hot water, her hair slicked back. She had on a pair of my older sweats that did little to hide the feminine outline beneath.

"There's popcorn in the jar in the cabinet. Brown bags are in the drawer. Put one quarter cup in the bag, fold over the edge and put it in the microwave to pop. Should take about four minutes."

"Mam, I'm here." Anya stood at the top of the stairs, her arms filled with DVDs.

"Wait there, I'm coming." I climbed the stairs two at a time, afraid my independent daughter would attempt to meet me half way. "Let me carry them and you hold on as you come down." Anya handed the cases to me and grasped the banister. At the bottom, I high-fived her. "Well done."

She grinned proudly.

"Okay, ladies, I'm going to go take a shower. You have fun and stay out of trouble."

LATER THAT EVENING, after Anya had gone to bed, Fiona said. "I have a question."

Maddison turned on her stool at the counter where she was working on the computer. "What's that?"

"You pay for a satellite phone but not TV reception? I don't understand."

"People pay good money for up to five-hundred channels and then continually surf because there's nothing on that interests them. I abhor what I'll refer to as the news channels. When someone getting a new hair style or growing a beard makes *news* headlines, I get angry. That's not news, it's gossip. It doesn't take a rocket scientist to know that today's reporters rely on the internet for things to discuss instead of getting out there and doing their own research. The majority of the studios are simply remaking the old movies, and they do them badly. I can't be bothered."

"Why have a TV then?"

Maddison hesitated before explaining. "Various reasons. When Priss was sick, it brought her comfort to hear the noise in the background. She told me she knew she was still alive as long as she heard the din." Maddison shrugged. "Chance hates when the winds come up the mountain during storms. It catches the end of the metal roof and whistles throughout the house. You commented yourself that the night noises are eerie. Maybe it hurts her ears, because she whines when it happens. I'll run the TV to block out the noise, it seems to calm her." Maddison leaned over and petted the dog's head. "And Anya's mother introduced her to some wonderful old movies. She likes watching them from time to time. She tells me it reminds her of her mama. And, as long as everyone is occupied, I can get some work done here."

"You really are so sweet," Fiona said.

"The only problem you're facing as I see it is that Anya and Chance like to watch *101 Dalmatians*, but they might be willing to expand their viewing tastes to accommodate their new best friend."

"I couldn't believe when Anya brought down all those old Bette Davis tearjerkers. I haven't seen some of those since my mother used to make us watch them with her." Fiona nuzzled the dog that was resting in her lap. She couldn't stifle the yawn that escaped her.

"Why don't you go to bed. You need your rest. I'll take Chance out, then I'm going to work for a while longer. Good night, Doc."

As much as Fiona wanted to continue talking, she was exhausted. Dinner had been wonderful and she ate too much. It made her lethargic. She nodded her assent and headed up the stairs. "If I haven't said it already, thank you for today."

"No problem, I managed to get a lot done." Maddison indicated her computer.

"I had so much fun with Anya and Chance watching the movies. The popcorn was much better once you showed me how to get the melted butter on it. It was a perfect afternoon." Shocked that her body was twitching in ways she didn't normally react to other women, Fiona stared at Maddison from her place on the upper landing. She felt sure that all the intricate parts of Maddison's persona would haunt her for a long time to come. She hoped it hadn't ruined her for other women. "Good night then."

"Night, Doc."

Chapter Thirty-Three

November 11, 2008

OVER THE NEXT two days the four of us established a doable routine. I tended the daily chores, while Fiona fixed breakfast. Anya loved Fiona's many omelet recipes, often asking for more, but she specified that I was to be in charge on the oatmeal days.

When the weather permitted, Anya, Chance and I went for our walks to visit her mother's meadow.

Afternoons, Fiona and Anya spent time playing board games, watching movies, or my personal favorite, Anya teaching Doc to speak Spanish. I sometimes stopped my work just to watch and listen.

Despite the service interruptions due to weather, I managed to finally open my e-mail. It had been more than a week since I had checked it and I promised Marni I would never let it go longer than that. After clearing the spam, I found a message from Marni, that was marked 'Urgent'. It wasn't like her to nag, so I opened that first.

> To: Maddison Delanie
> From: Marni Roberts
> Subject: Urgent
> Something's wrong with your damned e-mail again, I've sent this message numerous times and it keeps coming back to me.
> Thought you should know, Karileah's family might be looking for her. A woman, claiming to be a relative, left a message for me asking for information about you and Karileah.
> I'm not sure how you want to handle this, please advise as soon as possible, so I'm prepared.
> Hope all is well in God's country. Give Anastasia a kiss from her auntie and tell her I love her.
> Talk to you soon if you ever open your damned emails.
> Marni

I responded immediately since the initial message was already close to two weeks old.

> To: Marni Roberts
> From: Maddison Delanie

Sisters

Subject: RE: Urgent
    Tell them to go to hell. Karileah survived without them for seven years, and died surrounded by the people who loved her.
    Fuck them.
    Call if you need to,
Maddison

I WENT BACK to my work in progress, making the revisions quickly. All in all, since Fiona's arrival, I had gone from remote ramblings to actual chronicled notes, from not writing to creating a living testament for Kari and all the women like her who become victims of our male-privileged society. Instead of persecuting the men who perpetrate the sexual attacks on innocent prey, society—and often the law—treat the female victims with disdain and subject their lives and experiences to harsh review and judgments.

I took to heart Fiona's comments about the women in my stories. I needed to improve my characterization of them. If I was to do justice to *Vigilante*, I especially needed to be able to show the strength of character that epitomized Priss. As long as my brain kept working and didn't flip into vapor-lock mode, I hoped to get the book and the dedications finished this week and off to Marni.

I worked into the wee hours, finalizing the last chapter. This book would end differently than the others. Though the reader would learn the name of the man who killed Priss, they would never discover the person responsible for his execution. That would be the first loose end I had ever left, the only question to remain unanswered. I knew it might create a stir, but the truth would solve nothing, and most certainly would cause pain to innocent people.

I typed the two little words that any author has the most anxiety writing—*The End*. Then I saved the document and closed down my computer.

I would wait a day or two and think about what to write in the foreword. I had already informed Marni that a portion of the royalties was to go to AIDS research. She promised that the publishing house would match my contributions in Kari's memory.

AFTER STOKING THE fire, fixing a glass of milk, and stealing a cookie, I sat in my chair watching the flames and thinking. The fireplace was my personal signature on this structure for generations to come. Besides providing the primary heat, I had a metal chimney crane installed during construction. The simple steel L-bracketed arm and hook allows me to cook in the hearth when needed. It also fit the time period of the church perfectly, which was an architectural bonus for me.

I stared at the inferno, mesmerized by it. My mind was restless. I had felt this way before when finishing the other books. This book, however had been more difficult for all the reasons it might also end up being my best work to date. Time would tell.

I got up and walked to the doors to look out into the night. The sky was clear after today's storm. Another couple of inches of snow had fallen. No longer angry about her predicament, Fiona was taking it all in stride.

A falling star swept across the inky sky. If I believed in wishes I'd have made one. I shook my head and moved back toward the hearth. Fiona was standing at the railing above watching me.

"You okay?" she asked.

"Fine, thanks. Why aren't you sleeping?"

She shrugged her shoulders as she moved down the stairs.

"Hey, where's the air cast?"

She glanced down. "I forgot all about it." She stopped midway and moved her ankle in a tight circle. "Guess I'm healed."

"Want some warm milk?"

She went to the kitchen counter and set the kettle on the stove. "Not everyone likes warm milk." Fiona grimaced as she spoke.

"I hate it, myself." I returned to the chair and watched the flames flicker, anything to help divert my attention from Fiona.

"What are you thinking about?" she asked.

"Lots of stuff."

"You're done working earlier than usual."

I turned to watch her sit on the couch. "Yes, I'm finished for now."

"Are you consulting on an old case?"

"Old case?" I looked at her. "What do you mean?"

"When I was cleaning the counter, I had to move your notes and computer. I couldn't help reading some of the gibberish."

I steepled my fingers and stared at her. "Gibberish?"

"Well, you write one word references, rape, manslaughter, execution, death sentence"—she hesitated, ostensibly trying to recall more—"bar, Rohypnol, paralysis." Fiona leaned forward. "Is it a campus rape you're dealing with?"

"Something like that." I turned my attention back to the fire.

Silence filled the room, noisy in its own way. Words unspoken, emotions bubbling just below the surface, fear of the unknown hung in the air, unsettled and charged.

"How is Anastasia related to Sophia and Lorraine?"

I tried to rub out the stiffness in my neck from hours hunched over the computer. I sighed. Fiona was determined to make me talk. "Sophia is Alice White's sister, my aunt. Since there was no one else, we—Priss and I—decided that we wanted Sophia and Lorraine to be part of Anya's family."

"What about Priss's relations?"

I shook my head. "She didn't get along with them. I never met them; they never called or visited . . . not when Anya was born, not even after her mother got sick."

"How awful."

"There's a lot of extenuating circumstances, but yeah, when someone's dying you would think the petty shit shouldn't matter."

"I'm sorry they did that to her."

I nodded my head. "Me too, Doc." I watched her from the corner of my eye. There was something on her mind, some issue that she was having a hard time bringing up. I waited.

"I watch you with Anastasia, the life you're providing her. Homeschooling her. I know you spend hours helping her with the course work, patiently teaching her Spanish. Reading to her even though she recognizes most words herself. Praising her when she does well. You're providing her with family values, yet letting her be a child by playing silly games that make me laugh so hard my sides hurt when I watch you. Then I listen as you work all hours into the night, and even then you're never short or ill-tempered with her."

"It's not Anya's fault I have deadlines— What's really bothering you, Doc?"

She grimaced. "I don't think I can do this. Be a mother, I mean."

I got up and sat on the edge of the coffee table. "It is a little daunting, and you're always going to second guess yourself. It's the nature of the beast. But you're gonna be terrific at motherhood."

I took her hand in mine and held it. "You've wanted this for a long time. You went out and made it happen. This wasn't a mistake or a foolish whim or an act beyond your control."

Fiona started to cry, and I slipped onto the couch next to her and lent her my shoulder.

Time passed, Fiona wept softly. She leaned away from me. "Thank you, I needed to know you didn't think I was making a colossal mistake."

"Nope, you're just moving on to the next chapter in your life. A very exciting one." I stood and went toward the fire. I needed distance. I enjoyed holding her way too much. I knocked the tinder down with the poker, shifted the burning logs, then added more.

When I turned back, Fiona had removed her sweatshirt. The T-shirt she wore underneath did nothing to hide her ripening breasts.

"What are you doing?"

She stood and slipped out of her sweat pants, standing before me in just her underwear. "I'm trying to seduce you. Am I doing it right?"

"Doc, please." I couldn't control the stir of desire, the fire that was heating my core. Want surged so strong it took my breath away. "Don't do this."

Fiona pulled the flimsy cotton shirt from her torso. "I know you want this as much as I do."

"I want . . . I so fucking want you. But I need it to be more . . . I need it to mean something. I . . . Don't you understand? You'll break my heart." I spread my hands outward. "You already own it."

Fiona approached. "And you, mine."

I gazed at Fiona, her words resonating in my head. "Are you sure?"

"Yes." She kicked out of her panties.

My eyes were glued to her body, the flawlessness of every lush curve. She pressed against me, wrapping her arms around my shoulders, her breasts mashed against my front. My vision blurred, my heart raced. Words were no longer possible—I wasn't sure anything was! I gulped loudly.

"You are so many things. First and foremost, adorable comes to mind." Fiona's searing gaze caused my knees to buckle.

"I need to sit down." We moved to the couch.

Fiona unbuttoned my flannel shirt and tugged it out of my jeans.

"You're way too overdressed."

Next she pulled on the hem of my thermal top and removed that as well.

"I knew you'd be like this."

She ran her hands up my stomach, between my nonexistent breasts and then down, flat over my nipples. They immediately hardened with her caress. She bent her head and took the right one between her moist lips. A moan resonated from deep inside her.

I blew out a breath. My insides quaked. I had envisioned this moment for days, possibly weeks and still the reality was more than I ever dreamed. The time had come—I wrapped my arms around her, pulled her closer, tilted my head and captured her mouth in a fiery kiss. My hands stroked Fiona's back, my fingers itching to be buried deep inside her, a need to possess her stronger than I had ever felt. Arousal singed my depths, desire so robust, that release was already looming.

Fiona used her fingers to draw dizzying designs over my shoulders, back, and arms. Everywhere she moved her hands, heat flared up. She insinuated her leg between my thighs, and used a rocking motion as she gripped my biceps.

"Sweet Jesus."

"I need you," she said.

"You *own* me."

"In that case, I insist you be naked." She nipped my lips as she tugged the flap of my belt and unhooked it. Next she undid the button on my jeans, and slowly pulled the zipper downward. Her next move had my skivvies and jeans on the floor, and she ordered that I step out of them.

160

I pulled her down onto the couch beside me. I began to explore her curved hips, the gentle swell of a baby bump just above the dark triangle of her sex, the lush plump orb of her breast . . . something I'd fantasized about for weeks. The soft globe fit within my mouth perfectly, the taste divine as I lavished attention to her nipple. It tightened with each sweep of my tongue. Fiona let out a moan that nearly caused me to come on the spot.

"Fuck me. Please."

I gulped for air, sanity vying for dominance in my sex-deprived brain. "Is this safe?"

Fiona stared at me. "Safe?"

I spread my hand and fingers across the rounded area between her hips where her unborn child was cocooned. "For the baby."

Fiona bobbed her head. "If you know what's good for you, you'll listen to the doctor now." She leaned in and kissed me. Hard.

I plundered her mouth in return. All my tension, desire, and anxiety merged together in that kiss. Fiona met each thrust of my tongue, giving and taking with equal fervor. She whimpered as I cupped the apex between her thighs. I slid my fingers through the mass of curls, savoring the wetness waiting there. Fiona's arousal heightened my own. I stroked the swollen flesh, dipping a finger between the soft folds, then pushing deep inside with one stroke.

"Yes. Deeper. More." Fiona murmured as she bit my shoulder.

I pushed another digit into her heat.

She spread her legs further apart and arched her back. "More, please."

I pumped my fingers in and out, matching the rise and fall of her hips. And still she asked for more. I slid down until I rested between her thighs, the scent of her arousal drawing me in. I lowered my mouth, extended my tongue and greedily lapped the nectar she offered.

FIONA PANTED AS Maddison used her warm wet lips and vigorous tongue to tease the bundle of nerves centered between her legs. Maddison was merciless with her attention to the throbbing pulse between her folds. Fiona gasped in pleasure, shuddering as the tension built deep within. Maddison inserted a finger, then another. She probed deep within Fiona's heat. Precise steady thrusts and her voracious tongue had Fiona unabashedly thrashing about. All too soon the anticipated shudder exploded through Fiona's overheated body, incredible pleasure curling her toes as all control abandoned her.

Maddison held on tight, firmly laving Fiona's need with her tongue, till the last moan vibrated through Fiona's body and the contractions stilled around her buried fingers. Maddison looked up lovingly into Fiona's eyes. She had a fist jammed against her mouth in an attempt to stifle her cry of ecstasy.

They stayed like that, both overcome and spent. Fiona had never responded like that before. Her legs quivered for long moments, rocked by the intensity of her orgasm.

Maddison placed a gentle kiss on the tangled curls, laid her cheek against the overheated space, and sighed. She watched as Fiona floated back to herself.

Fiona opened her eyes. "Thank you," she whispered. "That was amazing."

Maddison climbed up and lay beside her. "You're amazing. You're beautiful and sexy and luscious, and—"

Fiona leaned up and captured her lover's lips, wrapping her arms around Maddison, pulling her closer, needing and relishing her strength. When the kiss ended they were both gasping for air. Ready for more.

"CAN PEOPLE DIE from too much sex?" I asked.

Fiona nuzzled my neck as her head rested on my shoulder. "Define too much."

"How did I get so lucky?" I leaned over her and grinned.

"It's easy, hot shot. I couldn't resist your carnal charms." Fiona batted her eyes at me.

Our lips met instantly. The kiss was deep; our tongues dueled. My mind was willing, but my body failed to keep the promise. I fell back exhausted. "I'm sorry, I need to rest."

"Did I break you already?"

I wrapped my arms around her, pulling her tight against me. "Give me thirty minutes, and I'll show you broke."

Oomph! I doubled over as Anya used my groin as a step up and jumped onto the couch between Fiona and me.

"Munchkin, what are you doing up so early?"

"Not early. Sun's out." She snuggled down between us pulling the tiny corner of the blanket Fiona had allotted me.

I swiveled my head, the digital read-out on the microwave read six-forty-five. *Crap.*

"Okay, baby. I'll get dressed and then start breakfast. While I'm in the bathroom, you go into your room and get dressed too."

"Why's Fiona sleepin here?" Anya asked.

I looked over at Doc's startled eyes. "She had a nightmare. She got scared."

Anya turned to her and patted Fiona's head. "I get mares too. Mam always makes them better, right?"

"Yes, she does," Fiona murmured.

I lifted Anya out from between us and lowered her to the floor. "Scoot. Go get dressed, then I'll fix something to eat."

"Okay."

Anya ran from the room. I looked at Fiona. "Sorry about that."

"I'm just glad you thought to pull the blanket over us this morning."

I stood up. "You take it with you, but I strongly suggest you do it quickly or my daughter will be getting a lesson about the birds and the bees way too early."

The nap had revitalized me, and right now, Fiona's naked silhouette had me thinking about making love, not cooking and caring for Anya.

"Later?" she said as she stood.

"You can bet on it."

Chapter Thirty-Four

July 2003

THE RETCHING SOUND woke me for the second time that week. I climbed out of bed and walked into the bathroom. I wet a facecloth and handed it to Priss. "I think you need to see a doctor."

"I know what's wrong." She flushed the toilet, wiped her mouth and set the rag in the sink. I watched as she stumbled back to bed.

After pulling up the blanket, I sat beside her. "Care to share?"

"I'm pregnant." Priss looked miserable. She'd lost weight, her hair was greasy, and she was in need of a bath. It's like she'd stopped caring about everything after the night of the rape.

"We can get that taken care of. You don't need to be concerned."

"Taken care of it?" Priss stared at me. "I'm going to have this baby— I have to."

"No, you don't. You can get rid of it, move on with your life."

"You don't understand, I can't. My religion says—"

"Fuck your religion! Do you really want a rapist's child?"

Priss touched my cheek. "It's not the baby's fault. You can't believe it is."

"I understand that. You're barely living now, what will you do with a child? You quit a job that you struggled and waited years for. You've lost so much weight that you're nearly a skeleton. You look ghastly and you won't let me take care of you. You've ditched Juan. You can't possibly think you can raise a baby inside these four walls."

"I have savings . . . I can pay you."

"Priss, I don't want your money. I want the happy sweet girl back, the one who always had a smile on her face."

She turned her head from me. "She's gone. Dead." When she turned back there were tears in her eyes. "Will you help me?"

"Yes."

MORNING SICKNESS LASTED through the end of August, by then I feared Priss would never deliver a healthy child. Her appetite was lacking; she hadn't gained the weight she lost after the attack and none related to the child she carried.

"What did the doctor say?"

She grimaced as she climbed into the car. "Eat more, get lots of rest, take the vitamins and hope for the best."

"Only two more months, then you can be tested."

"I already know what the test will show. I have the virus." She gripped my hand. "I just pray my child doesn't get it."

"Me too."

I drove us home. When we pulled up, Juan was sitting on the porch. "Will you be okay?"

She nodded. He opened her door and tried to hug her when she exited the vehicle, but she stepped sideways and quickly put distance between them.

"Kari, please talk to me. I miss you," Juan said.

Since he was still in uniform, he clearly had just come from work. Even this dyed-in-the-wool dyke could appreciate the impressive sight he made.

"Maddison, I need to talk with Juan. Could you wait inside?"

"Of course." I patted Juan's back as I walked past.

I watched from the kitchen as Priss and Juan made their way up onto the porch. She never looked at him, just shook her head repeatedly. Juan was clearly pleading his case, his arms moving, his face animated. It hurt to watch two friends brokenhearted over something so horrid.

Priss walked in the front door moments later. She went directly to her room and shut the door. I watched as Juan kicked a garbage can, then climbed in his cruiser and sped away.

"PRISS? I MADE you dinner."

I stood at the door, but received no response. I pushed it open. She lay on the bed, her eyes staring at the ceiling.

"Priss, if you intend to have this child, then you've got to take care of it. No more bullshit."

"I'm having my baby. I told you that."

"Then get your ass up and eat." I pulled the afghan off of her. "You're gonna start taking care of yourself, and you're gonna do what the doctor said. This baby deserves a mother who loves it. Start acting like it."

She sat up, furious. "I do love it."

"Then come eat, start exercising, come back to the land of the living."

She glared at me, but nodded. "It doesn't mean I want Juan back in my life. He deserves better."

"You do too. You didn't do anything wrong . . . that bastard Ortiz did." I pulled her gently into the kitchen.

"I don't want to talk about it."

"Priss, why are you cutting Juan off." I squeezed her hand. "I thought you really cared about him."

"I do, don't you understand?"

"No, honey, I don't."

"He wants to get married."

"I thought you did too?"

"Maddy, we both know I'm sick, that I'm going to die. I can't marry him . . . have relations with him. And nothing is a hundred percent safe, you know that."

"Don't say that." I pulled her into my arms. "Don't ever say that again."

"I can't talk about this anymore."

"If you promise to eat, to shower, to do what the doctor says, I won't bring it up again."

She nodded in resignation. "I promise."

Sadly she kept her word and I had to keep mine.

TWO DAYS LATER, Kari received a letter from her mother. She took it into her room to read.

> Karileah,
>   What's going on with you? Either I don't hear from you or the letter doesn't make sense. Is it this young man you were seeing? Has something happened? You had promised to come home in June, then I don't hear from you. I'm praying for you. I'm worried, about you. You've not spoken of your series, or any other parts you've tried for. What happened.
>   Fiona just returned from the Bahamas. That girl travels more a year than I have my entire life. It was one of those lesbian cruises, I pray my friends never hear about it. But when you have money, transgressions are forgiven. I always tell you that.
>   Write soon, I love you.
> Love Mom

Kari read the letter over and over, but couldn't bring herself to respond. Her mother would blame her for everything. Rape was something her mother believed was an excuse for bad behavior and not an act of violence. When Kari went to her priest to confess, he basically concurred with that judgment. She put the letter in her nightstand and turned out the light.

Chapter Thirty-Five

November 13, 2008

"MAM, WHAT'S THAT word?" Anya asked for the third time.

I rubbed my face briskly to dispel the cobwebs. "Sorry, sweetie. Can we do your Spanish later?"

"Okay." She began packing up her lesson books.

"Uh-uh, do your letters and numbers, and I want to see your name and address too."

"Awe, Mam. I don't wanna," she whined.

I picked her up and kissed her cheek. "Trust me, Little One, I don't wanna do lots of things . . . doesn't mean we don't have too." I hugged her close. "Now back to your schoolwork."

She giggled when I tickled her belly. "Yes, Mam."

Fiona watched our exchange with hooded eyes and a smug look on her face. "Didn't you sleep well last night?"

I drilled her with red, tired eyes. "I slept fine, just not long enough."

"That's too bad. You should probably get to bed early. Get some rest, you're clearly out of shape," she said.

Her devilish smile reminded me of a cat on the prowl. "That's exactly what I intend to do, thanks."

Fiona's chuckle had an evil cadence to it.

I poured coffee into my mug. The phone rang as I put the carafe back on the hot plate.

"Hello." I waited for the echo of my voice to bounce between the satellites.

"Hey, thought I'd call and tell you the roads should be cleared any day now," Sophia said. "They started your way early this morning."

"Thanks for letting me know." I waited for her to continue.

"You and the munchkin gonna join us for the Thanksgiving feast?"

"Not sure right now, depends on the weather and stuff. Can I get back to you?"

She continued talking, advised that the plows had finished the major routes, supplies were being delivered, and life was once again back to normal in Yaak.

"Thanks for that, I'll tell Doc."

Fiona walked to the counter. "Tell me what?"

I put my finger up. "Yeah, Sophia, and thanks for calling." I hung up the phone.

"What's going on?"

167

Though it hurt more than I wanted to admit, I had to relate the news. I took a sip of my coffee before saying the words that would break my heart. "That was Sophia. She wanted me to tell you the plows have started the back roads and, as long as the weather holds, should be here in a day or two."

"A day or two?" she asked.

"Most likely tomorrow . . . the latest the day after."

She sat on the stool. "How soon . . . when will . . . how long after that?"

"Of course, it all depends on the weather."

"Of course." Fiona stood and went to the door. "Skies look clear to the west."

I walked up behind her. "Yup."

She turned and buried her face in my shoulder. Her hands gripping my arms, holding me tight.

I kissed the top of her head, my mind trying to memorize the feel of her in my embrace, the vision of her when she cried out from orgasmic release, the smile she bestowed on me just that morning when she promised me tonight. *Tonight.* I wanted forever.

"What are we going to do?"

Anya ran over to us. "Mam, what's wrong?" Her little voice shook.

I picked her up and held her between us. "Fiona's gonna go home soon. We need to celebrate." My voice cracked.

"I don't want her to go." Anya put her arm about Fiona's neck and pulled her closer.

"Her mom is back East and she really misses her."

"But she's s'posed to be our family now." Tears trickled from Anya's eyes.

Fiona pulled away and ran up the stairs.

"Mam, make her stay. I don't want her to go," Anya cried.

"I can't do that, baby. Doc, has her own family . . . friends. She needs to go home." The words tore at my heart.

It took quite a while to settle Anya down, to explain that we couldn't just keep Fiona here against her will. In the end she stopped crying, but I knew she had been hurt. This was just one more loss in her short life, and I let it happen.

DINNER WAS A quiet, dismal affair. Fiona came down the stairs only after I called to her for the third time. Anya was angry or hurt and acting out for the duration of the meal. Both of them had red eyes from crying, and I had no solution or advice for either of them.

After the dishes were cleared and rinsed, I sat in the side chair with Anya in my lap. Fiona had retreated upstairs as soon as clean-up was complete.

"Mam, can't we marrieded Fiona?" Anya asked.

168

"It doesn't work like that, baby."

"You marrieded mama."

"Sorry, Munchkin, I know you're going to miss her, but Doc doesn't like living in the cold with all this snow. She wants a job back East and her mother and friends are there."

"We could put more woods on the fire. Couldn't her mama come live with us? Then we be family."

"I wish it was that simple, Little One." I held her close and gazed into the fire. Anastasia fluctuated between pouting, crying, and begging. The offer of cookies or games held no interest. She finally fell asleep in my arms around six-thirty. I held her close, taking comfort from her since I was hurting as much or more than she was.

I never wanted to think of last night as a mistake, but right now my heart told me I had been a fool. I rocked Anya for another thirty minutes, making plans, working out the details in my mind, and creating a list of things to be done.

"Wake-up, Munchkin."

"Mmm."

"Anya, you need to take your medicine and then I'll put you to bed."

"Don't wanna."

"Munchkin wake up." I stood up with her still in my arms and walked into the kitchen. I pulled her pills out, ran water to get it cold, then filled the glass. "Here, Sweetie. This is number one."

She took the pill and swallowed the water. We quickly got through the following two and I carried her into her bedroom and laid her on the bed. "Help me get your dress off."

"No."

I untied and removed her shoes. Anya lay there, eyes closed, sucking on her thumb. I tugged her tights down her legs, then pulled her dress off as well. It wasn't worth waking her to do more, so I let her sleep in her undies. For now she needed rest and time to heal. I covered her with the blankets and tucked her Betty Bunny under her arm.

I sat watching my child sleep, grateful to Priss for entrusting her to me. For a nanosecond in time I'd actually thought I'd have another child in my life. A wife to share the ups and downs with. What a fool I had been.

Leaving the door ajar, I walked out of Anya's room and went to the entranceway. The night sky appeared to be clear, the moon shown brilliantly against the inky landscape, and there was not a cloud to be found. *Fuck!* Chance came and stood at my side, her head nuzzling my thigh. "It's okay girl, we'll get through this." I hoped I was right.

FIONA CRIED HERSELF to sleep. Fatigue and anxiety zapped her of what energy she could muster after a night of making love and little rest. Maddison had sworn Fiona owned her heart, owned her. They hadn't pledged themselves or mentioned the L word, and yet Fiona knew that's what she would be walking away from. Love. The lasting kind. The reason people vowed eternity to each other.

The dreams came. Scattered, out of order, and frustrating.

Weeks passed since Kari's last letter. No emails, no phone calls, nothing. The private investigator took her money. There was nothing to go on. Kari had not left a paper trail. Fiona called Kari's emergency number. It was disconnected. Laughter sounded in the background.

She heard a child crying. It was Anastasia, but Fiona couldn't reach her. Couldn't see her. She kept calling. Addison's latest release hit the shelves. Fiona bought a copy. She opened the dedication page. It started, 'In loving memory.' Her vision blurred as she repeated the words. A small sob escaped her.

Maddison was walking up the mountain. She was sad and hurt. Fiona called to her, but she didn't hear . . . wouldn't turn around.

Her mother's face, as she read the words, 'In Loving Memory.'

Fiona surged upward, gasping. *A dream.* She leaned against the headboard for long minutes trying to quell her beating heart. The house was quiet except for her own breathing. She glanced at the clock on the nightstand; it was ten after one. She rubbed her fist over her chest trying to massage the ache, to erase the look on Maddison's face when she told Fiona the roads would soon be clear. *How did I let this happen?*

She got up and walked into the den. She didn't want to think, to remember how she got to this place or why. She didn't want to imagine never finding out the truth about Kari. The baby, however, made it unsafe to continue her nomadic search. Though money wasn't an immediate concern, she needed to find a job to provide for her child and their future. Who was going to hire a pregnant doctor?

Fiona resigned herself to going home, even if it meant without answers. She had done everything in her power, including taking the damned leave to go traipsing across the country.

After landing at LAX, she had rented a car and driven to the house on Las Cruces Avenue. It was deserted, a sold sign posted on the weed-filled lawn. She had written down the name of the realty company and their phone number. After a couple of hours of playing phone tag with the sales agent, she had been informed the house sold back in March. He had let slip that the belongings had been shipped to Libby, Montana. The realtor had refused Fiona further information based on privacy laws, though he had said that L. M. Addison was merely a pen name. By the time Fiona got off the phone, the tax office at City Hall had already closed for the day. She had not wanted to waste another day of her leave slogging through public records when the answers were in Montana.

She had called home and had her mother re-read all of Kari's letters. They all referred to Addison. Suddenly her resolve wavered. Was she on the wrong track? The only person that could answer her questions appeared to be the author, Addison. And that's how she ended up here.

Fiona was desolate. She hated the thought of leaving Anya and Maddison and all they signified. Maddison had warned her that Anya was getting too attached. The child's crying and heartbreaking pleas that Fiona stay and become their family tore at her soul. Maddison tried to explain to her daughter it was impossible. Fiona could hear the pain in Maddison's voice. She stoically explained to Anya about Fiona's responsibilities and family. Just talking calmly, trying to sooth the little girl till she fell asleep. *Why did I let this happen?*

She had to go back, find a job, help her mother cope with the not knowing, and prepare to start the next part of her life. Motherhood . . . alone.

She sat in the rocker, a book in her hands. She opened it to the first page, stared at the words, but her mind kept going back to Kari. Kari screwing up, or Kari acting out, or Kari not towing the line her mother expected both of them to follow. Truth was, Fiona was tired of it all. Tired of hearing her mother complain how Kari would ruin her life out in Los Angeles, that being an actress was not suitable. Mostly she was tired of watching her mother decline with each passing year and not being able to do anything to stop it.

Fiona growled in anger. She loved her sister, but not knowing what happened to her was driving her mad. She feared the truth would kill her mother. She blew out a breath in frustration.

THE SCRATCHING AT the door pulled me back from my ponderings. "I'm coming, girl." Chance came through the door soaked. I rubbed her down with the towel and gave the dog a biscuit for standing so patiently. A chill raced through me, the temperature in the room had dropped, I must have zoned out because I never even noticed. I went to the hearth, the grate needed to be cleaned and restocked. After shaking down the ash, I loaded it with wood. Within seconds, the flames shot up and warmth started to fill the space.

"Come on girl, come sit by me." Chance didn't need to be invited twice, the dog jumped up on the chair and settled in my lap. "You know what the worse part of this is?" I murmured. Chance sat up as if to listen. I ruffled her head. "I miss her and she hasn't even left yet." The dog licked my face, then settled down, her attention elsewhere. I stared into the flames, contemplating without Fiona in it.

Chapter Thirty-Six

November 2003

PRISS AND I sat in the doctor's office, holding hands. Hers were cold, mine sweaty. "What's taking so long?"

She squeezed my fingers. "Relax, we know what she's going to say, so it doesn't really matter."

"You could be wrong, ya know."

"I'm not."

"Fine." I swallowed my retort; she wouldn't listen anyway.

"Afternoon ladies." Doctor Taylor, Priss's OBGYN, came through the door. "How you doing today?"

I leaned forward. "You tell us." Priss gripped my arm and pulled me back.

"The doctor sat behind her desk, opened the file, lifted a sheet of paper then let it fall. She folded her hands in front of her. A pained expression passed across her face. "I'm afraid the tests were positive for HIV." She shook her head. "I'm so sorry."

"Can you do it again?" I asked. "Test her again. Do it now."

"Stop," Priss said. "I'm sorry, Doctor, she's just upset."

"That's understandable, Kari." Doctor Taylor turned to me. "We tested her blood twice, then we sent it for the Western blot test. There's no mistake, Kari tested positive."

I took a deep breath. This was not what I wanted to hear. "So, what do we do now?"

"We monitor her. We'll test her again in six months and we start her on a regimen of medicines immediately."

"What about the baby?" Kari asked.

Doctor Taylor looked at her. "Most of the cocktails are perfectly safe for you and the child. Each individual case is different, but I strongly believe you'll do well as long as you follow instructions. Starting with getting your weight up."

"She won't eat, I try—"

"Kari, we've discussed this. You need to take care of yourself, if you want to have a healthy baby. That includes eating three healthy meals a day."

"I'm not hungry."

"Do you want a healthy child?"

Priss stared at her feet. "Yes."

"I presume it's not too late, but you two should be practicing safe sex now that we know Kari is a carrier. I can make arrangements to test you."

Kari's face turned crimson.

"It's not an issue, but thank you." We left shortly afterward with three scripts. I drove directly to the pharmacy. "Wait here."

"No, I need a couple of things, I'll come with you."

We walked to the back, handed the scripts to the pharmacist, and went to do some other shopping while they were being filled.

Kari picked up shampoo, more vitamins, and toothpaste. I threw a bag of chocolates and a new electric toothbrush into the cart. We strolled around till her name was called.

I placed the items from our basket on the counter, then waited for it all to be rung up.

"That will be two thousand, three hundred sixty-five dollars and seventy-two cents."

I looked at him slack-jawed. "Are you kidding me?"

He tilted his head, leaned closer. "The medicine is expensive. You might try getting some assistance."

I felt the blood drain from my body. "You take charge cards?"

He nodded. "Yes."

I signed the slip, stuck it in my pocket, and turned to find Kari looking at a display of diapers. "All ready?"

"What's wrong?"

"Nothing. Let's get home and get dinner. We need to fatten you up and get you healthy for this baby. "

Chapter Thirty-Seven

November 13, 2008

FIONA CAST THE book aside. She paced the small office, concentrating on the particulars as she knew them. First of all, Kari hadn't been heard from in months. That much was fact. Even when they did receive letters, they weren't her usual cheery anecdotes. Second, Kari or Addison, or both were hiding something. Their silence proved that. Third was Addison's dedication to his wife. Kari never mentioned a wife. Any further speculation would be just that. Fiona threw herself into the chair and tried to recall everything that Kari might have said that had been corroborated through other means. Her letters were limited to parts she auditioned for, parts she got, and Addison. That left Addison's books, and his repeated acknowledgements of her sister in them. Which meant Addison held the key to Kari—where she was and what happened. *How could she and her mother have known so little about Kari's life and not realized it?*

I LAY ON the couch listening as Fiona paced upstairs. Anger echoed as she cursed and mumbled to herself. Though the words were not distinct, the emotional outbursts were. Like me, she was dealing with many issues, not the least of which, were her unborn child and an ailing mother eagerly awaiting her return.

My heart screamed at me. *Go to her! Tell her you love her. Beg her to stay.* Logic and fairness had me tethered where I lay, unwilling to influence a woman already under extreme stress. An older mother-to-be at that. And in the early months of pregnancy, a time when things can so easily go wrong.

The grumbling went on for what seemed like hours. I'd hear her drop into the recliner, then minutes later be up and walking again. I couldn't imagine the angst she felt. I only knew I was paralyzed to help her.

The shadows of the flickering flames on the ceiling helped to focus my attention. I needed to ignore my pain, the sense of loss, and concentrate on what I had to get done. I prepared a mental list, then reviewed each item. Maybe if I concentrated on mundane chores, I'd forget the fact my heart was breaking. I'd need adequate time to complete the most essential tasks. Preparing the house to be empty for a couple of days was not a biggie. A strategy to get Fiona safely aboard a plane headed east and home to her mother and life was. Most important was ensuring Anya was cared for during my absence and not made to feel abandoned. The final and simplest issue would be to e-mail the revised manuscript to Marni for review. The plans were set in my mind, implementation was the next step, and it needed to begin soon.

First chore, remove the snow from the driveway and roadway out to NF5879. As soon as the National Forest road was plowed by the county workers, we could drive to Kalispell or even Missoula. I wanted to start plowing as soon as Fiona settled down. Then I'd ask if she could listen for Anya while I was outside.

The last thing I remembered was Fiona stomping into the bathroom.

"ARE YOU SLEEPING?"
I lifted my head and squinted at the clock on the microwave. An hour had passed. "No, just waiting."

"You *could* have come to me."

"You don't need that kind of pressure." I tilted my head to meet her eyes.

Fiona sat on the edge of the couch. "Could you hold me?"

I opened my arms wide. She moved into them and stretched out beside me. "I wish it would snow," she murmured.

I kissed the top of her head but said nothing.

Fiona turned to me. "Don't you?"

I pulled her closer, wrapping my arms tight around her. "I'm a realist."

"What does that mean?"

"It means that whether it's tomorrow or next week or next month, you're still going to leave. You're still going to hurt Anastasia whether that was your intention or not. She's sensitive and she's come to care for you a great deal"—I took a deep breath—"and you're going to break my heart."

She ducked her head tight between my jaw and neck. I felt her tears on my skin.

"I don't know what else to do." she muttered.

"If that's the case, can I suggest an option?"

"Yes," she whispered.

"Go back East, talk to your mom. Be sure she's okay. Then pack up your belongings and come *home* to Anya and me." I tightened my hold on her. "You don't have to give me an answer right now, or at all, but you have to know I love you." I kissed the crown of her head. "I need you and I think you need me. We could have a good life to—"

"I can't."

I didn't bother continuing. There was nothing more to be said.

WE STAYED LIKE that for over an hour—neither talking, just holding on tight. I'm not sure what Fiona was thinking or feeling, but I was making memories for the long empty life moving forward without her. I lifted my head and checked the clock. "I should get up and start plowing."

176

"Stay with me." Fiona punctuated her words with a deep, searing kiss. Delicate hands roamed over my body, touching my back, arms and chest. She pulled at my clothes, her fingers deft, her intent clear. I wasn't sure I wanted this, but my body answered for me. Fiona pressed me back against the cushions, settling herself between my legs.

"I need you," she said. Her tongue teased my stiffening nipples. She didn't play favorites, just kept moving from one to the other till I thought I'd scream. Her hand played havoc within my curls. Her skillful touch drove me mad. My hips thrust against her palm. Her long fingers were buried deep inside me. I moaned as she pumped life into my center. We exchanged passionate kisses. Our tongues dueled as she fought for my release. Closer and closer, I worked my way toward deliverance. Fiona curled her fingers, plunging deep as I arched to meet her. The explosion raced through my body, the vibrations extending to every limb. I lay gasping, my need spent.

Time stood still as we lay in each other's embrace. I wanted to make love to her, to show her how I felt. She stilled my hand.

"I love you."

She turned away.

I waited and hoped she would say something, anything. Instead she stood up, and tugged my arm. "You should probably get going."

My gut reaction was to fight. I felt used and abused. I wanted her to hurt like I did. I wanted her to *want* to stay . . . to make a family with Anya, the baby, and me. My eyes burned with unshed tears. Anger and disillusion welled up inside me. I wouldn't give her the satisfaction. Anya and I had lost enough this year. My child didn't deserve more grief. I had no intention of letting this stranger cause any more disruption to our lives. I nodded and gathered my clothes.

Chapter Thirty-Eight

November 14, 2008

THE BRIGHT SUN against the fallen, brilliantly white snow was blinding. I tugged my sunglasses off the hook in the cab and put them on. I had a headache beating at the back of my skull that rivaled the ache in my chest. I shook my head in disgust and dropped the gear box into drive. *What the fuck had I been thinking?*

The tractor lurched forward, the plow unearthing the snow and depositing it onto the side of the roadway. The driveway took thirty-five minutes to clear. I hoped the road surface would be as easy. Tall timbers and little sunshine till today left piles of drifting, frozen snow. It took three passes the entire nineteen-point-seven miles to clear a path wide enough for my truck. It would take another three to create the two-way traffic it was meant to handle.

The first return pass seemed to take forever. I was tired, angry and most importantly worried about Anastasia. I stopped after the first trip. I could get my truck out to the road, and no one else belonged coming in—that would have to be good enough.

As I climbed the driveway, I spied Fiona looking out the front door. I drove by without acknowledging her, just as she had dismissed me earlier that morning. I spent the usual time prepping the tractor for its next use. All too soon it was road worthy, and I had no excuse to avoid what was ahead of me.

AT THE LANDING, I made a vapid attempt at kicking the snow off my boots. My arms laden with firewood were grateful when the unlatched door swung in with a gentle push.

"Mam!" Anastasia ran to me.

"One minute, Munchkin, I need to put this on the hearth first." She followed me. As soon as I deposited my load, I picked her up and kissed her cheek. "Good morning."

"Guess what, Mam? Guess."

I would have guessed a million times if it meant my little girl kept smiling, as she was now. "What?"

"Fiona can play games on her phone. Did you know that?"

"No, I didn't. That's way cool."

Anya nodded. "How come our phone don't do that?"

"Doc must have a very special phone."

"Can we get one, too?" she pleaded.

"Maybe it's only for doctors?"

"Fiona, that true?" Anya asked.

She winked at my daughter. "Maybe you should look online?"

"Mam?"

"You play games on your learning tablet, don't you?"

She shook her head soberly. "Not nakes."

"Nakes?"

"She means Snakes."

Anya nodded her head, her eyes sad, her bottom lip pouting.

"Well, we'll see, okay?"

"Okay." She squirmed out of my arms and ran back to the couch where Fiona sat reading.

After hanging my coat and gloves at the door, I dropped my boots by the hearth to dry. "Anya you be careful with that."

"I am."

She never even looked up. "Anastasia, I mean it. Don't break Doc's phone."

"I won't!"

"Did you have breakfast?"

"Uh-huh." The game had her full attention.

"Did you honestly think I'd forget to feed her?" Fiona asked.

The comment was snippy. I opted to ignore it. "I'm going to take a shower." I walked away rather than fight.

THE STEAMING SHOWER rained down on my tired, aching muscles, and I reveled in the warmth of the hot water rinsing over my body. While soaping up, I had a long chat with myself. My egocentric reaction to the events of the last two days was not the example I wanted to set for Anya. People don't always get what they want, and acting out solves nothing and only causes more hurt feelings. What I want versus what will be does not warrant a meltdown on my part. My daughter's sting of loss could be a lesson learned, but not if she were to emulate me. Thirty minutes later, I began feeling like a new person.

Time with Fiona was limited, something to savor and there is no logic in spending these last precious hours or days fighting. I walked out of the bath with a smile plastered on my face. My heart may ache, but my attitude didn't have to show it.

Anya was still on the couch, playing with Fiona's phone. I quick looked around. Fiona had disappeared. "You want some lunch, Munchkin?"

"I'm already fixing it," Fiona said.

I turned in the direction of her voice. She was in the kitchen, but out of sight.

"I hope soup and grilled cheese is to your liking?"

"Sounds great."

179

Fiona popped up from behind the counter with a pot in her hand. "Anya suggested it."

"Probably because it's her favorite," I said as I approached. "Want help?"

Fiona's eyes stopped me. "Are you suggesting I'm not capable of a putting together a simple meal?"

I put my hands up. "I just thought you may want help. You've been dealing with Anya, Chance, and the fire since early morning."

"And you've been dealing with the plowing for endless hours."

"Yes, I have and if you're curious, it's done."

She turned away and pulled bread from the drawer.

"Once the main thoroughfares are clear, you'll be able to get out of here and back home." I walked around the counter and reached up in the cabinet for a can of tomato soup. I poured equal parts of skim milk in the pot with it and put it on the stove to heat.

"How exactly am I going to do that?" Fiona asked. "The rental is still down in the gulley, last I knew."

"I'm going to drive you." I put the lid on the pot.

"You must know I don't want to leave," Fiona whispered.

Having tried this conversation during the wee hours of the morning, and being shot down, I wasn't willing to put myself out there again. The cabinet next to Fiona held the soup bowls, I reached over her and pulled them down.

"I'm so sorry," she murmured.

"It's all good." I took the bowls to the other counter and set them down next to the stove. "We'll serve up in here, okay?"

Fiona nodded her head.

"Anya, put the game down and go clean up. Lunch will be ready shortly." Anya continued to play. "Anastasia!"

"Just a minute, I'm winning."

I walked toward the couch and stood over her. "Give me the phone, now." She glared at me, handed the cell over, and crossed her arms over her chest.

"I was winning."

"And now you're not. Go clean up."

She stomped into the bathroom and slammed the door.

THE WORDS BLURRED on the page before me. I had gone over the manuscript one last time, written the acknowledgements, finished the dedication page, and provided the information for donations to the Elizabeth Glaser Pediatric AIDS Foundation where portions of the royalties would go. It had taken three and a half hours, but I was finally done. All that was left was the e-mail to Marni going over the details and changes she could expect to see. Thirty minutes later, I hit the send button for *Vigilante*. It felt oddly redeeming.

I closed the laptop and turned to see what the other residents were up to. Anya was still playing with Fiona's phone, and Chance lay next to Doc, lapping up the attention she was showering her with. Allowing me to continue my work, Fiona had fixed omelets for herself and Anya for dinner. With that behind me, it was family time. "Anyone want dessert?"

Fiona looked up with a smile. "I thought you'd never ask."

"Anya?"

"What, Mam?"

"Do you want dessert."

"Yes, please."

"Then put the game down and come help me."

She put the phone down immediately and jumped up to assist. "Come here, you." I picked her up and sat her on the counter, then pulled down the three bottles of medicine. "Let's get these out of the way."

Fiona walked closer, she reached for one of the bottles.

"What are you doing?" I snatched the bottle back.

"I was just curious?"

"Don't be. It's none of your concern."

"I didn't mean—"

"Ready, Munchkin?"

She nodded. I dispensed the pills, and a glass of water. She swallowed them one, two, three without incident. "Good girl." I lifted her down. "You get the cookie jar." I poured the three glasses of milk, and put a plate out for the cookies. Anya carefully picked out three from the jar, one for each of us. "Good job, Little One."

She gazed up at me.

I carried the tray into the living area, and placed it on the coffee table. "Enjoy, ladies."

"I'm sorry,." Fiona said.

"Uh-huh"

Fiona reached over and snagged a cookie. I swear she hummed as she bit into it. Anya had picked up Fiona's phone again. "Anastasia, I'm sure Doc, doesn't want chocolate smeared all over her phone."

"I'm clean." She held up her hand to prove it.

"The game can wait, have your dessert. It's gonna be time for bed soon."

"Mam, I'm not playing. I watching movies of Mama," Anya said.

Fiona peeked at the phone, then me. "She's just looking at pictures of my mother and sister."

"You can look at them later or tomorrow, now put it down," I said.

Anya placed the phone on the couch between Fiona and herself. "Mama looks real pretty, Mam."

"I'm sure she does, but eat your cookie and drink your milk, before Fiona does."

Anya gasped and quickly nibbled her cookie. Fiona chuckled and even I had to laugh.

When everyone was done, I rinsed off the plates and glasses and placed them in the dishwasher.

"Anastasia, time for bed."

"I wanna see more of Mama first."

I was tired and getting annoyed with Anya's new stubborn streak. "I said it's bedtime. If Doc says it's okay, you can look some more tomorrow, but for now, put it down."

"But Mam, I want—"

"That's it. I'm tired of telling you things twice. Give the phone to Fiona. You're not to play with it again."

"No." She gripped the phone in two hands and swung it away from me.

"Go to your room, now."

Anya started to cry. Tears tracked down her cheeks. "I want to see more Mama."

"Now, Anya, or else." I raised my voice, my temper quickly matching it.

She tossed the phone onto the cushion next to Fiona and ran to her room crying.

"I don't want her playing with that thing again," I said.

"She wasn't doing anything wrong," Fiona said.

"I've seen too many kids with those things glued to their ear or their hands. They'll text to people in the same room rather than putting the freakin things down and talking face to face. They forget there's a real world out there, that people can interact with . . . without those damned gadgets. She's not going to be one of them."

Fiona nodded. "I'll put it away when I go upstairs tonight."

"Thank you."

Chapter Thirty-Nine

November 14, 2008

ANYA LAY FACE down on the bed crying when I entered her room. "What has gotten into you today, young lady?"

"I miss Mama, and I just wanted to watch her pictures," she mumbled.

I pulled her up and into my arms. "I know you miss your mama, but that's no excuse to misbehave."

"I want Mama," she cried. I held her close and waited for her sobs to subside. Her little body was racked with grief.

"We've talked about this. You know she's in heaven, sweetie." I held Anya close as she continued to weep.

"Why Fiona got Mama in her phone?"

"It's not your Mama, honey, it's her mother."

"It is too, Mama."

"Anya, you're mistaken."

"Nuh-uh, it's Mama. I knowed it."

"That's not possible."

"Mam, it's Mama in there. I sawed her. There's lots of pictures of her."

This was not a simple case of defiance. My daughter believed what she was saying. I'd have to correct that assumption, but not tonight. "I'll look into it, okay."

"You promise." Her eyes, brimmed with tears, held mine.

"Yes, I promise, baby." I kissed her downy cheek. "You need to sleep. I love you."

"Love you too."

We exchanged her clothes for pajamas and she lay down. I pulled the covers up tight and kissed her once more.

"Sweet dreams." I tucked Betty Bunny under her arm.

At the doorway, I peered back. Anya was holding her rabbit tight. Guilt washed over me. Over the years, I had taken thousands of pictures to chronicle our lives, but had never hung them. Priss wanted these memories for Anya and I completely failed her. I had feared they would upset Anya, that the constant reminder would extend Anya's grief and sense of loss. Instead, I was cheating her of the celebration of happier times. Tomorrow, I would remedy that mistake.

There was a large box of pictures of Priss and Anya hidden away in Anya's closet. So many memories of happier times. Some were images of them building sand castles on the beach at sunrise. Two were of Chance splashing in the water with Anya and Priss. Dozens of Priss teaching Anya about planting bulbs in the flowerbeds at the front of the house. Most showed them covered in mud and laughing like fools. My favorites were of Priss and Anya sitting on the front porch at sunset, reading books, in the swing seat I installed for just that reason.

I walked out of the bedroom with a queasy feeling in my stomach.

"Did she finally settle down?"

"Yes." I walked into the kitchen and pulled the bottle of scotch off the shelf and poured two fingers in a glass. Back in the nave, I sat next to Fiona on the couch.

"I've never seen you drink before. Don't get me wrong, I know you've offered it to me on occasion, but you've never imbibed yourself."

"That's because I rarely do."

"Something bothering you?"

I turned my head and glared at her. "What do you think?"

Fiona laid her hand over mine. "I'm sorry, that was a stupid question."

"Yeah, it was." I took a sip of my drink. "Could I see the pictures Anya was looking at?"

"Of course."

Fiona turned her phone on, then tapped the icon for the photo gallery. An array of images came into view. She flipped through them, and finally tapped on one in the middle, then handed the phone to me. First picture up was an elderly woman with stark white hair, steely blue eyes behind clear rims. A little portly, but definitely Fiona's mother. The same smile, and eyes for sure. I'd have recognized her anywhere. Another picture of Fiona and her mother, but from years earlier. The fifth picture of the album was Fiona, her mother and another younger girl. It was taken sometime in the eighties based on the hair styles and clothing. The quality was poor, the image blurry. I tapped the arrow for next. This image was grainy, but I knew who it was, without a doubt. My heart sank. I tapped again, the same young girl appeared, but from years earlier.

My stomach clenched tight, I tapped the screen, this time a more current photo popped up. This one revealed a small craftsman's style home as the backdrop with the woman standing out front. A surround porch was encased by flowers of all colors and varieties. The house was the one Priss and I had shared for six years, the one I sold this past spring. The woman standing out front *was* Priss. My stomach soured, my heart rate sped up.

I kept flipping through the photos, trying to understand how they got on Fiona's phone. She had said Anya was looking at pictures of her mother and sister? *Priss was her sister? The missing sister. The screw-up.*

A sharp pain, tore through my chest. *Priss was Fiona's sister.* That could only mean one thing. Fiona had lied about getting lost, about pretending not to know who I was, *about us.* I handed the phone back to Fiona, then finished my drink in one gulp. "I need to go check on Anya." I walked away, the bile choking me. I knew deep down inside that nothing could ever fix this.

FIONA WAITED FOR Maddison to emerge from Anya's room. They needed to talk. *She* needed to apologize for this morning. She hadn't meant to make love to Maddison. She just wanted to be held. To feel the strength Maddison emitted, to feel cherished for just a little longer. To revel in her warm embrace.

"I love you," Maddison had said. Fiona felt in her heart it was true. Knew that Maddison was already committed and looking at long term. That Maddison meant it when she said they could make a life together. Why hadn't she responded? Why did she treat Maddison like a, a . . . a what?

Fiona got up and began pacing. What was taking her so long? Any other night Maddison might have spent upwards of thirty minutes with Anya, but never longer. It had already been an hour since she entered the little girl's room. Surely nothing was wrong?

Fiona walked the floor, worrying, thinking, and praying. At the front entrance she stared out the windows. The skies were clear, stars twinkled everywhere she looked. Where was the blasted snow when she needed it?

Another hour passed, Fiona took her phone and slowly climbed the stairs. Tomorrow she would talk with Maddison. Explain that Kari was missing and presumably dead. That she needed to find Addison to clarify the details. Then she needed to help her mother grieve.

THE PRINCESS NIGHT light in Anastasia's room emitted enough illumination for me to sit and study the pictures from the box that I removed from the shelf. There were images of Anya and Kari that had been blown up to eighteen by twenty-four and pasted to foamboard for hanging. Photos of the three of us together laughing and making memories. Five-by-seven pictures mounted as well. Sixty photos in all filled the box. Anya had been cheated of these by my foolishness.

I sat there a long time trying to defend Fiona's betrayal. The story about searching for her sister was one thing, making me fall in love with her, fucking me to get closer, was another. The woman I thought she was, clearly didn't exist. This one would stop at nothing to get what she wanted. Whatever that was. I listened to the creak of the stair as she climbed up them, then waited to be sure she'd stay there.

Anya rested peacefully, the much-loved and mangled bunny in her arms, her thumb in her mouth. Priss had given her the stuffed animal as a baby, and she slept with it every night. I leaned over and kissed her cheek. "I'm sorry I didn't believe you, sweetie,." I whispered.

After waiting another thirty minutes, I tiptoed into the kitchen, picked up the phone and walked outside to place my call. It rang three times before it was answered. "Hi, I'm sorry to be calling so late."

"What's going on, it's after midnight," Sophia said. "Is Anya sick?"

"Yes, something's wrong, and no, she's fine. How are the roads?"

"They should be clear by morning. What's going on?"

That was exactly what I wanted to hear. "I need a favor." I briefly explained the situation and my request. We made the arrangements and set the time schedule. "Thank you, see you in a little while." Chance kept looking at me quizzically. She didn't understand what was going on any more than I did.

I walked back into the house and looked up the number for the airlines, then went outside again to place that call. A very pleasant and knowledgeable reservation clerk helped me book the most direct flight from Montana to the northeast quadrant of Pennsylvania. She advised anything out of Kalispell would require longer waiting times at the two or three scheduled stop-offs and could add an entire day to the trip. I booked a First Class seat out of Missoula, charged it to my credit card, and printed up the boarding pass the woman e-mailed me.

Back in Anastasia's room, I pulled her backpack from the closet, and packed enough clothes for two days and added three photos of her mom. When I returned, I would hang every picture we had so my daughter wouldn't need a stranger's phone to see her mama. I took the backpack with me into the kitchen and stuffed her meds in the front pocket. A quick look around confirmed everything was set for the time being. Now all I had to do was wait.

Chapter Forty

FIONA CAME DOWN the stairs just as the coffee finished brewing. I poured two cups and slid one across the counter.

"Gawd, what time is it?" she asked.

"Ten-to-five, drink fast, we're leaving here in an hour. That should give us plenty of time to reach Missoula before your flight this afternoon."

"What?"

"I said—"

"I heard what you said. When did you make reservations? Where's Anastasia and Chance."

"They're safe."

"Safe?" Fiona shook her head. "From what?"

"The joke is over *Doctor*. I know who you are and what you're up to."

Fiona stared at me. "What the hell are you talking about?"

I walked around the counter, gripped her wrist and began pulling.

"Don't you handle me." She slapped at my hand, and I released my grip. "What is wrong with you?"

"Like you don't know."

She reached out and moved to touch my arm, but I jerked backwards. "What the hell is going on?"

"Come on, follow me."

We walked to Anya's door. I pushed it open, flipped the light switch on and held out my arm. Fiona walked into the space. She moved toward the bed where I had spread the pictures out—all images of Anya, Priss, and myself.

"Where did you get these?"

"Fuck you. You know damned well how I got them."

Fiona turned pained eyes to me. "You're . . . you're L. M. Addison."

"Damned right I am. That was one hell of a performance you put on, lady."

She sat on the edge of the bed, staring at the pictures. "Anya's my niece. My sister's child."

"Like you care," I roared. I stormed out of the room, afraid my anger would have me doing something I'd regret.

Fiona followed on my heels. "Where is she?"

I stood at the door, staring out, anger coursing through me.

"Where is my sister?"

I turned to her. "She's dead. I already told you that."

Fiona slumped onto the couch and began to sob.

FIONA CONTINUED CRYING. She had known in her heart Kari was gone, but hearing the words spoken so coldly added a finality to the fact. She pulled herself together. "How?"

Maddison had been watching her. "She was sick a long time. She ultimately surrendered to her fate."

"Why didn't you tell us?"

"Why should I? It's not like her family ever gave a damn about her. You never visited, or called. Hell, you never even congratulated her on the birth of our child. She wasn't worth so much as an afterthought from you people."

Fiona jumped up and slapped her across the face before Maddison saw what was happening. Maddison caught Fiona's arm as she attempted to swing a second time.

"We had a right to know, you son-of-a-bitch. To bury her. To grieve," she screamed.

"Instead, Priss was surrounded by people that knew and loved her . . . by people she shared her life with."

They stood at odds, rage radiating from both. Fiona walked back into Anya's room and sat on the bed, eyeing the pictures. So many images of Kari and her daughter! Maddison was right—Anastasia *was* a miniature Kari. How had she not seen that before?

Fiona sat stunned. All this time, the answers were in here. The proof less than ten feet from where they made love. Kari looked so happy. Motherhood and Maddison agreed with her. She picked up the small five-by-seven frame from the nightstand, her finger lightly touching Kari's image. She'd smiled for the camera, but there were circles under her eyes, her cheeks were drawn, her skin gray. Kari was dying when this was taken; Fiona felt it.

Maddison walked into the room behind Fiona, she yanked the frame out of her hands. "You better pack. We're leaving in twenty minutes." She put the picture on the nightstand and walked into the kitchen.

The snapshot back in her hand, Fiona followed. "When was this taken?"

Maddison gazed at the picture. "Middle of May. Why?"

Fiona touched the photo. It clearly wasn't taken here. "You lied to me."

Maddison threw the towel onto the counter. "How exactly did I fucking lie?"

"You knew I was looking for Addison."

"Really? Think about it. Try to get the facts straight for a change. You complained about *his* writing. You never once said you were trying to find him. You said I was a misogynist jerk."

"You conveniently neglected to mention your last name."

"Once more, you're perverting the truths, Doc. You introduced yourself as Fiona and mentioned you were a doctor. I told you my name was Maddison. You figured out I was a cop. How is that a lie?"

"You knew I was looking for my sister."

Maddison nodded. "I did and I asked you about her, a number of times. You didn't want to discuss it. Remember?" Maddison loomed large over her.

"What about the debate about your books? Why didn't you admit you were Addison then?"

"You were under the misconception L. M. Addison was a man. I knew you never read any of them, since you missed the fact that Carey Troye is, in fact, a woman and a lesbian and that there's absolutely no sex on any of the god damned pages."

"You're twisting my words."

"How? How am I twisting my fucking words? You never once talked about your sister in the same sentence as Addison or the damned books. Why? What were you hiding? Worse you kept calling her a screw-up. Fuck you, she was an angel. If Anya hadn't found the pictures on your phone, none of this would have come out, because you didn't want to chat about your pain-in-the-ass sister." Maddison was furious and spitting the words out heatedly.

"Well, I want to talk about her now."

"There's nothing more to say." Maddison walked to the entrance.

"Why didn't you just tell me you're an author?"

"What difference would it have made? Would you have finally admitted your ruse?"

"Me! Deceptive?" Fiona screamed. "Your entire life is a sham."

I turned around at that. "How do you figure?"

"The great author L. M. Addison doesn't lower herself to do interviews. Refuses to sign autographs, or do appearances. What are you hiding?"

"I'm not hiding anything. My publisher felt it would behoove us if the public didn't know a woman wrote the mysteries." Maddison shook her head. "Some stupid idea that a female wouldn't be taken seriously. They absolutely balked at letting it be known that Carey is a dyke."

"Bullshit."

"Think what you will."

"Believe me, I'm going to discover your secret. You'll regret this."

"Yeah, fine." I glared at her. "My turn. Why the fuck did you sleep with me? Was it all a sick joke to you? Or do you get off fucking you're sister's partner? What possible reason could you have to prostitute yourself like that? What did you get out of it?"

"You bastard."

She threw the bulky picture frame at Maddison's head. There was no time to duck. It caught Maddison on the cheekbone, ripping a deep gash on her cheek and shattering the glass on impact.

Chapter Forty-One

I REMAINED STILL, too shocked to move. "What the fuck?"

Blood seeped down my cheek, tiny glass shards littered my shirt, the counter, and floor.

"Did you have a good laugh using me, lying to me?" Fiona screamed. "God what an idiot I've been! I believed you when you said you loved me. I even considered coming back here."

Fiona was out of control, her anger palpable. She kept circling the room, screaming at me. "I hate you! How could you do this to me, to Kari?"

I cleaned up the glass from the counter and floor, and dumped it into the metal garbage can. "Go get dressed and pack your shit, or so help me, I'll throw you in the friggin' truck as is," I hissed.

Fiona stepped in front of me. "Answer me something first. Tell me why you lied about Kari. How did she die? Make me understand why you didn't have the decency to tell us she was dead. Did she mean so little to you?" She waved her arms. "What the hell, c'est la vie? Is that it?" Fiona yelled. "She was a human being. How could you discard her like that, ignore her family? Do you even have a heart, you miserable bitch?"

Fiona turned and ran up the stairs.

I picked up the broken picture frame and photo. Papers slipped out from behind the matting. I shoved it all together, brought it all back to Anya's room, and laid it out on the nightstand. Priss had never liked the heavy dark wood frame and had begged me to replace it months ago, but it slipped my mind with all that happened. I'd get a new frame in town and repair it when I got back.

Priss, Fiona's sister? Why didn't I see it? I took a deep breath, my heart was pounding in my chest. Blood oozed down my cheek. I used my shirt sleeve to wipe it dry.

Fiona moved around upstairs.

"I'm going to get the truck." I yelled up to her. "Hurry the hell up."

FIONA PACKED HER suitcase, then checked the drawers, bathroom and den three more times to make sure she had everything. Outside she heard the rumble of an engine. It had to be Maddison or Addison or whatever the hell her name was. The motor was loud even in here. She quick e-mailed her mother advising she would be on a flight later this morning. She told her not to worry about meeting the plane, that she would get a cab once she landed in Wilkes-Barre, sometime late tonight or early tomorrow.

She sat on the bed trying to understand. Fiona never suspected anything was amiss. Anya had stated it was her mama; Fiona couldn't fathom, not for a minute. She believed Maddison's story about her wife, her child and even living on this god forsaken mountaintop. *How could I have been so gullible? Maddison lied to me. Used me.*

The truck horn honked three times. Fiona picked up her briefcase and bag and started down the steps. Maddison came in the front door, met her half way and grabbed the larger of the pieces. "Let's get a move on."

Maddison had banked the fire earlier, now she closed the damper on the hearth, set the thermostat in the kitchen to fifty-eight, turned the lights out and waited at the door. Fiona slipped through. After setting the alarm, Maddison locked the doors behind them.

As soon as they were settled in the vehicle, Maddison dropped the gear shift into drive, released the brake and turned the wheel.

"Wait!"

Maddison slammed on the brakes and turned to Fiona, "What now?"

"Where is Kari buried? I need to be able to tell my mother."

Maddison stared out the window. They had plenty of time, and her anger was not going to resolve the issues between them. Maybe simply showing Fiona would provide some closure. Maddison pulled the emergency brake and turned the engine off. She climbed out of the truck, walked around the building and disappeared into the barn. A few minutes later, Fiona heard the roar of a snowmobile. Maddison pulled up next to the truck, climbed off and opened the passenger door. "Come on."

"Where are we going?"

"Just get the fuck on, okay."

Fiona swung her leg over the back, then Maddison climbed on the front and revved the engine. She turned around. "You need to hold on."

Fiona understood that to mean onto Maddison. She gripped the back of her vest tightly and off they went. The machine negotiated the snow easily. Between the moonlit sky and the headlights, the path was easily visible. They climbed up the foothill behind the church, almost to the peak of the mountain. Maddison stopped along the well-worn path and shut the engine off. She held her hand out, but Fiona swatted it away.

Maddison reached for a large flashlight and led the way to an opening between two evergreens. Had she not walked through it, Fiona would have sworn it didn't exist. Ten feet on the other side was like visiting a different realm. Patches of brown grass dusted with snow greeted them. Moon beams slanted through the tree branches, shimmering in the breeze. Winter seemed to have missed this piece of ground except for the perimeter where the snow was deeper. A small stone marker took center stage in the open meadow, two wooden benches faced it. Fiona took the light from Maddison and stepped closer. The inscription on the stone read 'Kari's Meadow.' She kneeled, bowed her head and clasped her hands together.

Maddison listened as Fiona prayed. Maddison bowed her head and said "amen" at the appropriate time.

Fiona stood and moved to the bench where she sat quietly.

"I'll give you a minute, but we've gotta leave soon." Maddison walked to the exit and waited there.

Fiona gazed around the meadow. She felt peaceful and calm as though she were able to commune with her surroundings. She nodded her head, satisfied that Kari was at rest here.

She stood and followed Maddison out of the meadow and back to their ride.

They finally left the property shortly before six. An hour later, their headlights illuminated the sign as they were passing the town of Libby. Fiona sighed. What if she hadn't gotten lost? What if she had never found Maddison and most importantly Anya. She had a niece. Her mother was a grandmother. She rubbed her stomach as a frown formed on her brow. My son or daughter will have a cousin. Fiona stared out the side window, recalling the events of the past weeks. She couldn't let go of the notion that something was wrong, but what?

Maddison kept her eyes straight ahead.

ANYA HAD BALKED earlier that morning when Sophia came to pick her up. She didn't want to go.

"Why do I hafto?"

"Because, baby, Mam needs to get Fiona to the airport and you can't go with us."

"But I don' want to, please."

"I promise when I get back, we'll do whatever you want."

"Can I say goodbyes to Fiona?"

"She's still sleeping. You can call her later, okay?"

"Okay."

The fact that Chance was going with her only made her more mistrustful. I vowed to call her later and talk to her. I told her I loved her and needed her to be a big girl.

If things went according to plan, Fiona would be on a plane headed home before noon. Then I would wash my hands of her and all that had transpired between us. I vowed to forget the woman who stole my heart, forget the memories we made, and overlook my foolish declaration of love.

FIONA REACHED FOR her briefcase. She had placed it on the floor when she climbed into the truck. She leaned down and rifled around till she came up with her phone. She stared at the device, and recalled the sadness on Anya's face as the child flipped through her family photos. The little girl was adamant it was mama. Why didn't she question that?

She fleetingly looked sideways. Maddison's appearance took her breath away. Overnight, circles had appeared. Her normally ruddy complexion was pale and splotchy. Fiona flinched at the sight of the ragged skin near her right eye. Dried blood still coated her cheek. "You need stitches."

Maddison didn't respond, didn't even acknowledge her.

"Tell me how Kari died?"

I WAS LOST in thought. Priss rarely spoke about her family. Only that she came from the East Coast. That her mother was a religious diehard who never questioned a priest or a papal edict. Because of her illness, and the truth surrounding Anya's conception, Priss believed her mother would reject her and the child. The fact that the priest blamed Priss for the rape and declared Anya unclean only added to her anxiety.

Dammit, we lived together for six years. In all that time, Priss had been adamant that her mother would judge her . . . her and Anya. That she'd proclaim the illness God's punishment. Priss swore she feared her mother's incriminations and she refused to subject Anya to one of her mother's denouncements. Then why keep in touch? Why subject yourself to that shit. *"Because I love my mother."* That's what Priss had said, she loved her mother. It didn't make sense. Was it our unorthodox relationship? Priss insisted she was at peace with her fate. That her family, if they knew, would only interfere with her final wishes.

"I'M TALKING TO you!" Fiona said.

Maddison glared at the stranger beside her. "What?"

"I asked how Kari died."

"Peacefully."

"Don't do that. Stop deflecting the damned truth. I want answers." Fiona took a breath. "I want to know what killed her?"

Maddison kept her eyes straight ahead. "What the hell do you care? Where were you when Kari needed someone, when our daughter was born? I'll tell you where, no place to be found."

Fiona blew a breath out. "How long was she sick?"

Maddison thought long and hard before she responded. "Almost five years."

"How did she die?"

"I already told you she was sick."

"Damn you, tell me what she died from?"

"No."

"No?" Don't you think her family deserves answers?"

"No."

"You better have more to say than no," Fiona spewed.

"If Priss had wanted you to know, she would have told you. It's not my place."

Fiona knew that was the truth. Why hadn't Kari told them. How could they not know?

"Did she see a specialist? Did she—"

"We explored every option open to her."

"When?"

Maddison shook her head. "Whenever the fucking doctors came up with another opinion." Her voice shook with anger.

"I meant . . . when did she die?"

"Oh." Maddison slipped her sunglasses on, the swelling around her eye set them askew. "She died Wednesday, May twenty-eighth."

Maddison's eyes welled up. She furiously blinked the tears away.

"My mother is not going to be happy to hear that you buried her in unconsecrated grounds."

"I frankly don't give a fuck what you or your mother think. Besides, she's not buried there. I spread her ashes there and the cremation was your sister's choice, I merely complied." Maddison took the bottle of water from the cup holder and took a swig. "For the record, Kari also chose where her ashes would be spread."

"She was only thirty-six. How did she die?"

"If you've been in communication all this time like you claim, why aren't you curious that she didn't tell you herself?" Maddison slammed the bottle back in the cup holder. "Besides, we lived together for six years. I don't recall you visiting her or calling. Maybe that's why you were never informed."

The next two hours passed in silence.

FIONA FELT SICK to her stomach. She had made the mistake of falling in love with Maddison. Someone with secrets. Someone who knew more than she was letting on about Kari. Now Friona was walking away. Away from her niece and the last connection to her sister. Away from her chance at happiness.

She hadn't started this journey with thoughts of finding love. She certainly hadn't realized that the last treatment had been successful and she was already pregnant. She also hadn't expected Maddison to want to embrace this unborn baby. Instead of rejecting the child, Maddison wanted to create a family.

If her inner circle knew she had even considered the notion of life with a flannel wearing dyke, they would shriek with laughter.

But things with Maddison had been different. They talked and shared chores that didn't feel like work. They laughed together. Maddison made love to her. She had seemed so open and loving with Fiona, so willing to give of herself. Why did she lie about who she was? How could she have kept Kari's death a secret?

194

Maddison was adamant that she was Anastasia's legal guardian and mother. Fiona intended to get a lawyer and challenge that fact. Make sure it was her sister's wishes, and maybe get some answers along the way.

"Did Kari have life insurance? Are you living up on that mountain off the proceeds of my sister's death?" Fiona was angry all over again.

Maddison stared straight ahead, her eyes never leaving the road. "No."

"And I'm supposed to believe you? You can't even look at me."

"I have a pension from the police department. There's royalties from the sale of my books. Between the two there's enough for us to get by on. It's all public record. Look it up."

"I don't believe you. You're hiding something, and I'm going to figure out what it is. I'm not the naïve fool that came to the mountains five weeks ago." Fiona felt her temper mount.

After a while Maddison finally responded. "What difference does any of that make ? The bottom line is you got your damned answers. You're finally going home, and you will put this all behind you. In the end you'll believe what you want, and that's your right. But getting upset or angry is not good for the baby. You need to worry about that little one." Maddison sighed.

Chapter Forty-Two

AT THE TOWN of Kalispell, I stopped for gas, and handed money to Fiona. "Would you go get something for us to drink and snack on? We still have a long way to go."

When Fiona climbed back into the truck, she had two large coffees and a bag with cookies.

"Thank you," I said. I drove to the bank a half mile down the road and visited the ATM. I wanted to be sure Fiona had money for a cab and meals at the lay-overs.

I was gone all of ten minutes. When I climbed into the driver's seat, I handed Fiona an envelope with five hundred dollars in it.

"What's this for?

"I couldn't get you a direct flight so there's gonna be layovers in both Denver and Detroit, and that means time stuck in the airports. You'll need money if you want something to eat or even just coffee or a paper and when you finally arrive in Pennsylvania, you'll need cash for the taxi to get home.

"I have money of my own, you know."

"Look, it's going to take the better part of the day to get back home. I don't know, maybe you'll want a book to read, or a meal, since you didn't eat. Or just maybe you don't have enough cash with you. Just take the fucking money, okay?"

"I'll send you a check." Fiona tucked the envelope into her pocket.

There was no use in arguing. "You have your boarding pass?"

"Yes, for the umpteenth time, I have it."

I nodded and put the truck into gear.

"I didn't need to fly First Class. I'm perfectly fine in coach."

"It's going to be a long and tiring trip. You're pregnant. There's two layovers and you won't be home until midnight. You'll get better service in First Class, and more comfortable seats. Let's not get pissy. You wanna pay me back, fine. Go for it. In the meantime enjoy the amenities.

"There you go again. So sure you know what's best for me and my baby. *I'm*, the doctor. I'll worry about taking care of *my* child." Fiona's anger was choking her. "Did you do that to Kari too—make all her decisions for her?"

I turned to her. "Like you've done such a good job, thus far. Traveling across country, getting lost, driving that piece of crap, relying on a stranger for help?" I chuckled. "You have no idea how lucky you were it was me that you found." I turned my attention back to the road, but wasn't seeing it. All I saw was the hate in Fiona's eyes.

There were no further attempts at conversation. Four hours later we pulled into the Missoula airport, parked, and went directly to the ticket

196

counter. I insisted on carrying her luggage so Fiona's hands were free to show ID at check-in.

"I'll take that." Fiona pointed to her briefcase. She checked the other piece of luggage. We walked toward the security gate together.

"Fiona, we haven't eaten all day, at least you didn't. Be reasonable. Let's get something before you board. You still have an hour before the flight is scheduled to leave.

"Can you understand I don't want to be around you?" Fiona hissed. "That the sight of you makes me physically ill."

The venom in her voice made me cringe. I put my hands up, turned, and walked away.

FIONA STOOD WAITING for her turn through security. Maddison walked up to her and offered one of the two cups of coffee she carried. "I didn't like how we parted."

No further words were spoken. Everything that needed saying had been expressed. Fiona sipped the coffee, marveling that Maddison remembered how she drank it. Even after three years together, Tasha had to ask each time. Fiona stood abruptly, the sense of loss overwhelming her. "There's no point in both of us waiting. I'd rather be alone. Go home— That's what I'm going to do."

She picked up a newspaper at the kiosk, then went and sat, waiting for her flight to be called.

The flight was called fifteen minutes later. Fiona stood and reached for her briefcase. Maddison was seated across the aisle back two rows. She remained there, watching Fiona. She didn't move. She didn't make an attempt at talk. She wasn't even embarrassed at having been discovered.

Fiona almost went to her. Almost. Instead she turned to the gate, gave the TSA agent her ticket, then stepped to the doors. She turned back fleetingly to find Maddison on her feet, apparently straining to see. Fiona looked away and walked down the gang way.

THE SIGHT OF Fiona walking away was gut-wrenching. The pain of loss swamped me. I waited for the remaining passengers to finish boarding, then for the plane to taxi out. I ran to the sky café and watched as it coasted to the end of the runway, and finally as it began the takeoff. I stayed at the window watching until the plane rose up and out of view. My hand rested on the glass, my heart thundered in my chest. I whispered. "I love you."

Outside the airport, I placed a call to Anya and talked with her, promising that I'd be home by dinner time. I quick bought a cup of coffee at the local McDonalds and headed home.

I still had a four-hour trip to Yaak, then another hour up the mountain once I picked up Anya and Chance. I refueled in Missoula and again in

Kalispell. The final leg of the trip was in sight. My daughter and dog were waiting.

MADDISON WAS CORRECT about one thing, First Class afforded Fiona the privacy she needed to sort things out. She wasn't up to idle chit-chat or dealing with seatmates who were noisy or tiresome. She was more than glad to be alone with her thoughts.

Okay, let's look at the facts. Something is wrong; she could feel it. That Maddison lied by omission doesn't negate the falsehood. What else isn't she telling me? Kari wrote home faithfully over the years. How could she purposely omit her illness or the fact she had a child? A baby. Why would she hide that beautiful little girl? What did Maddison say? Kari got pregnant the old fashioned way. It didn't make any more sense now than it had when she first said it. How was Fiona going to explain it all to her mother?

Fiona wanted to blame Maddison for everything—Kari's illness, that she and her mother hadn't known about Anastasia, that they weren't there when Kari needed them most. It would be so easy to make Maddison the bad guy.

Each time she tried, Fiona would recall an act of kindness that seemed ingrained in Maddison. Like when she was afraid to make love for fear of hurting the unborn baby. Or the time she spent patiently teaching Anastasia her studies. Hours expended calmly cooking and cleaning and still patiently taking time to play with her daughter when other chores needed her attention. Another piece of the puzzle.

What is missing? Think, Fiona, think.

She recalled their meeting. She was the first to introduce herself, and Maddison was correct, she hadn't offered a surname. She only mentioned being a doctor because she needed treatment and didn't believe Maddison qualified. That had proven to be a wrong deduction. Another misconception.

Just as judging Maddison by her mannish clothing had been an injustice. She dressed for comfort and warmth. Fiona had gladly followed her example during the arctic blasts that came up the mountain.

The fact Maddison was Addison, the writer, was trickier. They had talked about the writing and the way women were depicted. Fiona wanted to believe it was subterfuge on Maddison's part when she failed to declare herself the author. In fairness, Fiona had assumed Addison to be a man. Kari had implied as much. She would have bet her life that sex was a vital part of every book, and yet Fiona would have been wrong. To have Maddison declare Carey Troye a dyke cleared up so many of the questions Fiona had while reading the books, but it still didn't clear up the omissions.

Ten hours and fifteen minutes later, Fiona sighed as the plane taxied to the arrival gate back in Wilkes-Barre. Nothing was ever going to be right again. She had to break the news to her mother that Kari was dead, that she had a granddaughter named Anastasia, and that Kari's ashes, of all things, were scattered on Maddison's mountain.

Fiona had no intention of revealing more than necessary. Definitely not that she had fallen in love, or that Maddison was Kari's partner. Certainly not that Fiona felt there was more to the story.

FIONA WAS ONE of the last to depart the plane. As she moved along the gangway, she noted other passengers meeting up with loved ones, families hugging, kisses exchanged. Business people approaching limo drivers with names on placards. She yelped when her arm was pulled and her body turned in one swift movement. She raised her hand in defense. "Mom?"

"Who else would it be?"

"What are you doing here?" Fiona wasn't prepared for her mother, and she sure hadn't yet decided what all to reveal to her.

"You called with your flight information. I wanted to surprise you." She held Fiona at arm's length, studying her. Fiona's eyes filled with tears. Mary pulled Fiona into her embrace and held her tight as she burst into tears.

"So, we have our answers then, is that it?"

Fiona wiped her eyes with a tissue and dabbed her nose. "I'm sorry, Mom, Karileah's— She's dead."

"Dead?"

"I'm so sorry, Momma."

Mary started to cry. It soon turned to sobs. Fiona walked them to a stand of empty chairs. "When?"

"Back in May."

Mary sat quietly weeping as Fiona held her close. "It shouldn't be a such a shock. We knew something was wrong. We knew she had gone quiet, but I hoped and prayed for a simple explanation. Then the dedication, but that was to his wife?" She pulled a tissue from her purse and blew her nose. "Tell me everything."

"Mom, let's get my luggage and head home. There's time to explain later and this really isn't the place.

They didn't attempt to talk till they were seated in the back of the taxi and driving north on Interstate 81.

"I certainly know how to ruin a homecoming, don't I?" Fiona wiped at her eyes. "I'm sorry, it's just a culmination of everything. Discovering the truth about Kari, the baby, the long trip home. There's so much I have to tell you." Fiona gripped her mother's hand. "You're a grandmother. She's a beautiful little four-year-old girl. Her name's Anastasia. She's the image of

Kari and the brightest little girl you'll ever meet." Fiona pulled her phone from her purse and pulled up the pictures she had taken. "See here."

Mary squinted at the photo, smiling. "She's the image of your sister, God rest her soul." Mary scrolled through the pictures. "Isn't that the name of the woman's little girl you were staying with?" Mary asked.

"Yes, Maddison." Fiona looked out the window. "It's a long story, but she's the author, the woman Kari lived with."

"Woman? But I thought the author was a man." Mary stared at Fiona. "Why wouldn't your sister have clarified that? Why didn't we know about her daughter."

"Apparently, Kari withheld a lot of truths from us."

"Such as?"

Fiona didn't respond. The back of the cab was not the place to have this conversation and she wanted to choose the details carefully.

"What is it?" Mary gripped Fiona's hand. "You're not telling me something. Tell me?"

"No, not really. I'm hungry and tired. Can it wait till we get home? Anastasia is amazing." Fiona's eyes shone with love.

"You're always were a softy when it came to kids?" Mary patted Fiona's arm. "I've prepared one of your favorite meals. Then you can soak in a hot tub. After a good night's sleep in your own bed, you'll feel like yourself again."

"Mom, there's so much I need to tell you. I don't know where to start." Fiona was staring at her mother, wishing she could share the truth of Maddison and their passion.

"Honey, nothing is more important than that you're safe, reasonably well cared for, and home. I'll grieve your sister's death but celebrate the fact that I have a granddaughter. When can I meet her?" Mary reached in her purse and wrestled to get her wallet.

"It's okay, Mom, I've got money for the cab. Maddison made sure before she dropped me off."

Mary looked at Fiona over the top of her glasses. "She did, did she?"

Chapter Forty-Three

November 15, 2008

I PULLED UP in front of Sophia and Lorraine's house. Anya was on the front porch waiting. "Mam," she called.

"Hello, Little One." I swung her up in my arms and hugged her close. "I missed you."

"Mam has owie?" Anya patted my cheek.

"It's okay, I just fell."

Lorraine and Sophia stood in the doorway. "We made soup and fresh bread," Lorraine said.

I knew better than to refuse. "Sounds good." We walked into the kitchen, and I sat at their table with Anya on my lap.

Sophia had disappeared. She returned with a medical emergency kit. "Let me take a look at Mam's eye, Munchkin."

"It's fine, don't worry about it."

"I think I'll be the judge of that." Sophia gripped my jaw tightly and turned my head. "She's got one hell of a temper, I'll give her that. What'd she hit ya with?"

I just glared at her.

"Ain't love grand?" Lorraine chuckled.

Sophia cleaned the wound around my eye, claimed she was looking for broken glass. The probing hurt more than the initial injury.

"You're such a baby." It stung like hell when she poured antiseptic directly into the wound. She placed two steri-strips over the cut. "That is one hell of a black eye. She's a feisty little one."

"Don't start."

Lorraine served the soup and bread. I was hungry, and the bread would hopefully soak up the acid in my nervous stomach.

"So did you have fun with the Nanas?"

Anya nodded. "We sure did."

Sophia sat beside her, and helped Anya butter her bread. Lorraine sat beside me. "Out with it."

I kept my head down, trying to ignore her.

"You woke us at two in the morning, requested we pick up the baby and Chance as soon as possible. I think you owe us an explanation," Lorraine said.

I nodded my head. "Anya, why don't you go pack your knapsack while I talk to Nana?"

"Okay," Anya said. She jumped down and ran to her room.

Sophia stood up.

"Sit, you'll want to hear this too," Lorraine said.

I shook my head in defeat. "Anya had been using Fiona's phone. I thought she was playing games. She told me she was looking at pictures. Fiona said they were of her mother and sister . . . just family photos."

They both nodded.

"Anastasia insisted there were images of Mama in Fiona's phone. I lost my temper with her. I sent her to her room"—I took a deep breath—"but when I went in to check on her, she was crying, claimed she just wanted to look at the pictures of her Mama. She was so insistent. I went out and asked to see the photos. Fiona opened the album, I flipped through it for five minutes. Kari was in almost every picture."

Lorraine gasped.

"What the fuck?" Sophia asked.

"She told us she was looking for her sister. I just never imagined the wayward sister was Priss. And she certainly never wanted to talk about her sister with me."

Lorraine touched my hand. "I'm sorry, I know you really cared for her."

"That's life, right." I shook my head. "I'll get over it."

"So everything she told us was a lie?" Sophia asked.

"I honestly don't know. But remember what she said about her sister, that she was a fuck-up and irresponsible. Does that sound like Priss to you?"

"No, not at all," Lorraine said.

"I agree," Sophia said, "Priss was an amazing young woman."

"Exactly. I can't worry about it, but I owe the baby an apology. Most importantly I'm going to hang all the pictures of Priss for her."

Sophia nodded. "I think that's a great idea."

"Yeah, I totally handled that wrong." I sighed.

THE THREE OF us returned home later that day, and I went through the motions of normalcy for my daughter's sake. Over the next two months, Anya and I worked on her studies every morning. We practiced her Spanish and she became proficient with her numbers and letters.

Most importantly, we hung Priss's pictures throughout the house.

"Mam, why we not have these before?"

I had just hung my favorite photo of Priss and Anya digging in the garden. They were both laughing for the camera and, in the background, Chance was undoing all their hard work. I picked up Anya.

"Because, Munchkin, I made a mistake and I'm sorry."

She slapped her hand over her mouth. "What?" she said wide-eyed.

"I thought it would hurt you to see Mama's pictures, so I hid them away. I was wrong."

Anya hugged my neck. "I loves Mama. I like these."

"Let's go hang some in your bedroom too. That way Mama will be looking over you at night."

I let her down, and she ran in ahead of me. We finished hanging the remaining pictures in her room. Earlier, we had made sure to hang pictures of Priss in every other room as well. The final photo was the one from the broken frame. I had forgotten about it. I took all the pieces and placed them in the kitchen drawer to work on later that night.

FIONA BARELY TOUCHED the meal her mother had prepared. Shortly after arriving home, she claimed exhaustion and, begging to be excused, went to her room. She remained hidden away and didn't emerge for the next two days. Her mother brought her tea and toast, hovering as much as Fiona would allow.

On the third day her mother came into the room. "Well, you ready to join the living?"

Fiona knew her mother had heard her crying and was worried. Last night she'd woken Fiona from a dream and asked why she was calling out for Maddison.

"I'm sorry, Mom, I guess the ordeal took more out of me than I realized. Fiona shrugged, but suspected Mary wasn't fooled. "I'll fix something later."

"*I'll* fix breakfast. I still value my home and wouldn't be pleased if it burned down. Why don't you come keep me company. We can talk while you eat." Mary put her arm around Fiona and guided her to the kitchen. "Coffee?"

"Yes, please."

Mary poured a cup, and handed it to Fiona. "You'll need to be cutting back on the caffeine soon." Then she turned back to the refrigerator to get the provisions.

"Why does everyone think they know what's best for my child?"

"I wasn't aware *everyone* was giving counsel to you."

"Sorry," Fiona mumbled. It seemed surreal to be back sitting in her mother's kitchen and having Mom stand at the stove as she had for as long as Fiona could remember. She could almost imagine the last few weeks were a dream, except her heart wouldn't cooperate.

After Mary prepared the sausages and pancakes with butter and syrup, she put the plate in front of Fiona and poured them both more coffee.

Fiona smiled. "God, I'm hungry, and this looks great. Thanks, Mom."

Mary sipped her coffee, never taking her eyes off her daughter.

Lost in thought, Fiona played with her food pushing it around the plate. "Okay, out with it!"

Fiona looked up from her plate. "What do you mean?"

Mary leaned closer. "I'm grieving for your sister just like you. It hurts that she didn't feel she could tell us about Anastasia. I'll never understand that since all I ever wanted was for both of you to settle down and give me grandbabies. I can't fathom that she didn't tell us she was sick. And why did she allow me to believe that the author was a man?" Mary patted Fiona's hand. "There's something you're not telling me. I feel it. Was she murdered?"

"No, absolutely not." Fiona stared at her mother. If she told everything she knew, her mother would come to the same conclusions she had, that something was off. She didn't want her mother's golden years spent questioning the facts surrounding Kari's death. "You know I got lost. I hurt my ankle getting out of the car after I went off the road. I remember it was so cold searching for help. I was lucky I found the church, lucky I made it that far on my ankle. Maddison sewed the gash and gave me an air cast for support. She even had crutches from her own injury." Fiona remembered when she got the crutches. What was it Maddison had said? "I had an Angel who worked her magic. The therapy was intense but as you can see, she got it right." The words were spoken with such emotion. That wasn't a lie. Fiona was sure of it.

"And..."

Fiona looked up. "I developed a fever. Must have been pretty bad because I don't remember anything from the first three days." She took a bite of pancake, chewed it slowly, and swallowed.

"You were lucky she took care of you. That she wasn't some kook."

"She said that too!" Fiona nodded as she remembered the words.

"And?" Mary repeated.

"The fever broke, it kept snowing, and we worked out a plan to share the house until I could get home again."

"Must have been hard, no way to get around? Being cooped up with a stranger."

"I thought that too, initially. But they do get around. They use snowmobiles to shop and visit."

"They?"

"Anastasia's . . . well actually Maddison's aunt and her partner."

"How's the little girl get along with them?"

"She absolutely adores them and they her."

Mary poured more coffee into her cup and put the carafe back . "So how did you find out about your sister?"

"Anastasia actually discovered the truth." Fiona thought about it, that was fact. "I had taken a number of pictures of her. I wanted to show you how beautiful she was. She asked to see them. When I brought up the images, she flipped through them. Our family pictures were there too. She asked who you were. There's older pictures of Kari in the album, and Anya asked about them. She looked at all the pictures. I didn't realize it at the time, but she insisted to Maddison that her Mama was in the phone. Later, after putting Anastasia to bed, Maddison asked to see the phone. I opened the photo gallery and that was that."

"Not quite. I have a sense that you didn't handle it well?"

Fiona shook her head. "It's true, I didn't. Even though I already knew that Anya's mother was dead, I blasted Maddison about hiding her identity."

"Did she?"

"Before I answer that, let me ask you something. Did you think Addison was a man or a woman?"

Mary appeared to think about it. "All along I thought he was a man. I even nagged your sister about living in sin. Now that you ask though, I'd say definitely a woman. Makes more sense she'd hide that fact."

"Because you already know Maddison is a woman."

"No, because Kari kept it ambiguous, just like the private eye in those stories. There were never pronouns used, and that bothered me."

Fiona was surprised at her mother's astuteness. "You're right, the private eye is a woman. A lesbian."

"Makes sense to lie about it. Opens the readership up to a larger audience."

Fiona hated to admit it, but her mother was right again.

"Mom, why would Kari need to hide that she's living with a woman?"

Mary looked down at her folded hands. It seemed as if she wouldn't answer. "Because it would have broken my heart to think both my girls were lesbians."

"I see."

"No, you don't see. Father Francis says—"

"I don't give a fuck what Father Francis says or thinks. My sister is dead, I have a niece, and Kari was afraid to tell me about her illness and her beautiful daughter because that man spews fire and brimstone at will. It's all bullshit and I can't believe you even listen to him."

"Fiona!"

"Don't Fiona me, mother. Kari might not have been perfect, but who the hell is. She died afraid to tell us she was sick or that she had a daughter. We were her family and she couldn't tell us because she didn't want to disappoint you."

"Is that what the author told you?"

Fiona shook her head. "No, but she was pretty pissed that we weren't around during the most important events in Kari's life. You know what's worse, she's right."

"I always told her I loved her."

"And I'm sure you also lectured her about living in sin and what God Almighty Father Francis believes." Fiona threw down her fork. "Maddison was right about that much."

Mary gasped. "So how bad did it end, between you and this Maddison person?"

"Bad."

It was Mary's turn to shake her head. "I would have liked to meet my granddaughter. You've probably made that more difficult."

Fiona took her plate to the sink, then turned to her mother. "I'm going to sue for custody of Anastasia."

"Why?"

"Because she's Kari's daughter, because I'm a blood relative, and because I love her."

"You don't believe Maddison loves the child?"

Fiona turned away. "It doesn't matter."

Mary approached. "You told me Anya is loved and well cared for—what's changed?"

"She's our blood. Kari would have wanted us to raise her daughter."

"If that were true, why didn't we know of her existence?"

"It doesn't matter. She belongs with us."

"Is this about the little girl, or her mother?"

Fiona stormed away leaving the question unanswered and her mother sitting at the table.

Chapter Forty-Four

November 20, 2008

I KEPT MY laptop open and set up on the counter. E-mail notifications were set to chime if one came in. I hoped against hope that Fiona would make contact, if not with me, then to chat with Anastasia as she had promised.

The only e-mails I received were from Marni. She loved the revisions and wanted me to come to New York as soon as possible. She felt we needed to address the issue of interviews and book signings. That it might be time for full disclosure. She had a new contract for me to sign for my next novel, and wanted my approval on the book jacket for *Vigilante*. I needed time to think on it and the repercussions of hiding my gender from the public all these years.

Since arriving home, I had taken to keeping the phone charged and carrying it with me throughout the day in case a call came in. On Tuesday, in late-November, the phone rang, unfortunately I picked it up immediately.

"Hello," the male voice boomed through the handset, "may I speak with Ms. Delanie?"

"Yes, this is her."

"My name is Leyden Scibilia. I'm an attorney representing Ms. Fiona Gallagher."

"What!"

"Ms. Gallagher wants to explore your claims as legal guardian to one Anastasia A. Delanie."

I slammed my hand down on the counter, anger pulsing through me. "Tell Ms. Gallagher to fuck herself. I have the law on my side. So fuck you, too." I slammed the phone into the cradle.

"Mam?"

Anya was standing in the doorway to her room. I had thought she was still taking her nap. "It's okay, Munchkin, I just lost my temper."

"You said bad words." She approached slowly. When she reached me, I swung her up in my arms.

"I'm sorry, baby, here." I handed her a ten from my pocket. I hugged her tight to me, relishing the smell of her hair. I needed a moment to gather myself.

"Mam, too tight." She pushed against me.

"Sorry." I let her down and watched as she ran to put the money in the BB jar. "Why don't you take Chance out on the stoop and play ball with her."

"Can I?"

"Yes, but don't leave that area, understand?"

"Yes, Mam."

"I have to make a phone call, then I'll join you and we can go see Mama, okay?"

She nodded. I helped her with her jacket and gloves, then let her and Chance out the door.

AFTER TAKING A moment to calm down, I phoned the lawyer who advised Kari and me through each step of our legal arrangements. Samuel Banyon came highly recommended as a member of Lambda Legal and an advocate of GLBT rights. He was confident he could help us protect ourselves and our child once Anya was born. He ensured we took proper precautions, that we guarded each other and Anastasia against just such an event.

His soft, gentle voice came through the phone. "How's life up in the hills?"

"Sam we've got a problem?" My voice sounded tight, even to me. My heart beat rapidly.

"Tell me what's going on."

"Some hot-shot lawyer from Pennsylvania called. He's representing Priss's sister. She's looking into my legal standing as Anastasia's guardian and mother."

"Calm down and breathe. Kari covered all the bases and so did you. I made sure of it. They can huff and puff all they want—that little girl is yours."

I took a deep breath. "There's more."

"Start from the beginning."

I explained how Fiona showed up and claimed to have gotten lost. That she was stranded in the house for weeks, that not once did she divulge her last name or true purpose for being there. I took another deep breath. "I slept with her."

"Well hell, you just like making things interesting, don't you?"

"We just had this connection, or at least I did. I thought I loved her."

"I'm sorry, Maddison. Nothing on earth would have made Kari happier than you finding someone to share your life with."

"I bet she never imagined it would be her sister."

Sam laughed on the other end. "Maybe not! You're right."

Before we hung up, he assured me there was nothing to be concerned about. My daughter would never be the subject of a custody battle. He took the number of the lawyer who had phoned and promised to get back to me.

After the call ended I reached for my jacket and went out the door. Anastasia and Chance were waiting for me on the steps. It was time to visit Priss.

OVER THE NEXT two weeks, Fiona answered most of her mother's questions in an effort to let her learn more about Maddison and her grandbaby, Anastasia. She provided the minimal amount of information to soothe her mother's need to know, but she did it succinctly.

The biggest blow for her mother, besides Kari's death, was that she had been cremated and the ashes scattered. Regardless of it being against her mother's preference, Mary mourned not having a place to visit, to plant flowers. Her mother depended on the ritualistic rites to grieve a loved one.

"It's not right, I tell you," Mary said.

"Her ashes were spread in this beautiful meadow, high up on the mountain. It's surrounded by magnificent alpine and fir trees. A stone memorial, with an inscription sits in the middle of the field. There's two wooden benches to sit on and visit."

"But it's not our way."

"Maddison claims Kari picked the spot out herself. She wanted a place that Maddison could bring Anastasia to visit." As she thought about that statement, a shudder ran down her spine. She fought back tears thinking how excited Anya would get when told she could visit her Mama. "She takes Anya almost every day."

Even after the explanation, she understood her mother's dismay. Cemetery visits had been a part of their life for as long as Fiona could remember. Her mother was too old to learn new ways.

FIONA SPENT HER days filling out job applications, going on interviews, and preparing for the birth of her child.

Her friends pretended to rally round her. Lunch dates were made, and cancelled and made again. Most of the girls commiserated on the dreadful experience of being trapped with a stranger for weeks. They felt sure the isolation would leave scars for life. Fiona didn't dare mention that Maddison was a dyke or that she had gotten romantically involved with her. Few if any mentioned the loss of Kari, or asked about the health of her unborn child. They brought her up to date on the latest gossip and news within their ranks. None offered sympathy or support to her. Fiona came away from her latest luncheon with the group of them disgusted by their elitist attitude and narcissistic comments. She couldn't believe that these were the very people she had considered friends before her trip west.

"Mom I need to buy a few things for the baby . . . want to come along?"

"Can we stop for ice cream on the way home?"

"Sure, why not?"

They left the house and headed to Dickson City Mall. "Why do you think Kari never told Maddison about us, but we knew about her?"

The question stunned Fiona. "I got the impression Kari talked about us, but it apparently wasn't always flattering. And we didn't know about Maddison, we thought she was a he. Kari was sick for a while . . . maybe she wasn't thinking?"

"Hmph. You don't believe that any more than I do."

They rode the remainder of the way in silence. After Fiona turned the engine off, Mary asked. "Are you sleeping any better?"

Fiona nodded. "Yes, thanks."

"Why do you call out for this Maddison then?"

"I don't know."

"Does the lawyer you hired have anything to do with it? Or the custody suit you've initiated?"

"How did you know that?"

"You left the papers on the table."

"You didn't need to read them," Fiona huffed.

Mary glared at her. "I didn't read them, just the return address. What other reason would you have to contact a lawyer?"

Fiona rubbed her hand over her growing stomach. "Maybe I'm making arrangements for my child."

"Are you?" Mary drilled Fiona with a stare over the top of her glasses.

"No"—Fiona shook her head—"you're right. I'm suing Maddison for custody of Anastasia."

"It's wrong to do this."

"I love that little girl."

"And Maddison doesn't?"

"I don't want to lose her. She's the last connection we have to Kari."

"Seems to me for Maddison as well."

"I won't change my mind. That little girl needs me."

"Of course you'll not change your mind. Not as long as you stick with the notion you're in the right." Mary reached for her hand. "This is wrong, Fiona. You know it. *If* you've told me everything, the whole truth, it would appear your sister made very definitive decisions and plans. All of which didn't include *us*. I'll have to live with that the rest of my life, that your sister didn't want us to know her child or about her illness, but that little girl has lost enough it would appear."

Chapter Forty-Five

December 2, 2008

THE BEGINNING OF December, Fiona started working at a clinic in Scranton. For the time being, she was scheduled for four days a week. Once the baby was born, management was willing to discuss more hours.

Over the two weeks, Fiona had mostly cried herself to sleep nights. The memory of making love with Maddison and having her reciprocate kept her awake long after nightfall.

Upon her return to Pennsylvania, she had written a check and mailed it. To date it hadn't been cashed, leaving just one thread holding them together.

Working helped. She spent less time remembering, less time wondering about what ifs, and less time asking questions that only Maddison could answer and wouldn't. But work was exhausting. Her doctor assured her it was the pregnancy and she was healthy as an ox.

"Come and get it," Mary called.

Fiona walked into the kitchen. "Smells great."

"I fixed your favorite." Mary turned to the stove and began loading up a plate. "We've got to talk."

Shit. Fiona walked around the table and sat. "I'm not real hungry, Mom. I ate a big meal at the office today."

"Fiona, enough! I want you to tell me the truth about Maddison. What are you hiding." Mary sat beside Fiona, her hands clasped together.

"I can't do this. I'm sorry." Fiona stood and walked away. She never imagined anything could hurt so much. Talking about Maddison would only make it worse. She went to her bedroom and, for the first time in her life, it felt claustrophobic. After ten horrid minutes, she grabbed a coat and left the house.

FIRST THING THAT Saturday morning, Mary ambushed Fiona while she was still in bed.

"I know you want to protect me. That you think I'm too old to handle whatever it is you're not telling, but believe me, the not knowing is what will kill me. Not the truth."

Fiona thought about it, then nodded. "Let me get dressed."

Mary was in the kitchen, sipping coffee when Fiona came in. She started to get up.

"Sit, I can get my own coffee." She did just that, then sat across from her mother. "What do you want to know?"

211

"Tell me about my grandbaby."

Fiona smiled brilliantly. "She's so smart, Mom. She's learning Spanish at four can you believe it? And she learning about the universe, and she's terrific in math. Kari had her tested at three years old. She was found to already be reading at kindergarten level! That's when she and Maddison decided to home school her."

"Why? They could have just put her in an advanced class." Mary wiped her teary eyes.

Fiona nodded. "Seems she had some medical issues when she was younger. She doesn't like doctors."

"Is she a happy child?"

"She is. She's nothing like we were. She's bright, funny, and easygoing. Anya even tried teaching me Spanish, can you imagine? And I don't ever remember Kari and I being so obedient."

"Does she ask about us?"

"I don't know." Fiona sipped the coffee. It was decaf; she hated decaf. "I know there's lots of pictures of her and Kari. Some at the beach, Disneyland, hiking. And gardening. You should see the flowers they planted, almost as beautiful as yours."

"Are you in love with Maddison?"

"I don't want to talk about it."

"Because she was your sister's lover?"

"That's not true . . . they were never physical with each other."

Mary shook her head. "It's not? They lived together for years. The author dedicated his, well her book . . . to her wife."

Fiona thought about it . . . about Maddison. "Yes, but I'm telling you they were just friends," she said confidently. She believed it.

"Then why can't you discuss Maddison?"

"She lied to me, Mom. Kari died without our knowing. Maddison never admitted to being Addison until everything hit the fan."

"From what little you have told me, she didn't lie. She didn't admit to being the author, but you were looking for a man. You might have confused her."

"What excuse can she make for not notifying us Kari was dead?"

"I think you'd have to ask Kari that? Why didn't we know about her daughter? That she was married? Or that she was sick?" Mary leaned closer. "Why didn't *we* ask sooner?"

"What do you mean?"

"Well, think about it, back in 2003 she was going to be on that series, then all of a sudden it didn't happen. I don't think she ever tried for another part after that and she never explained why. And I didn't ask. Why? How could I do that to her. Karileah's letters started to wane almost two years ago, back in the fall of 2007. We both commented on the gibberish that filled the pages." Mary made the sign of the cross. "I thought she was mixed up in drugs. I didn't want to know."

"Oh, Mom"—Fiona got up and came around to hug her mother—"I'm sure it's not that." And if it was, Fiona didn't want her mother to ever find out.

"Did Maddison explain how she died?"

Fiona thought about her conversation with Maddison. She had withheld all specifics regarding Kari's death. "No"—she shook her head—"Maddison said she accepted her fate."

"Fate? What an odd way to describe someone's death."

OVER THE COURSE of the next week, via e-mail, I received copies of correspondence between the two legal eagles. My copies were always accompanied by notes of encouragement and faith. Samuel was confident that the laws were on our side, that Anya would never be taken from me. He reminded me of the letter Kari had written.

The end of the following week, I received a call from Sam's private secretary. He came on the line after a moment. "It's over," he said.

"Are you sure?"

"The sister wanted to be sure that Kari was, in fact, the one making the custody decisions. As soon as she saw all the documents with Kari's signatures and Kari's handwritten letter, it was over. She never had legal status to begin with, but I knew you wanted this resolved quickly so I turned copies of everything over to them."

"You're sure it's over."

"Have I ever led you astray?"

"No, but Fiona's a fighter. She's not the type to just give up."

"Kari was too, that's why you're on the birth certificate and have legal guardianship."

I nodded. "Thank you, Sam. I can't tell you what this means to me."

"Hey, I promised Kari I'd take care of this if it ever came up. I'm just keeping my word."

"Send me the bill. I'll make the transfer later today."

"Give Anya a kiss from her Uncle Sam."

I took my first deep breath since the initial call from Fiona's attorney. "I will, Sam, and don't forget you're expected to visit."

TWO WEEKS LATER, Anastasia was away visiting her two Nanas. They were going to drive down to Libby, see a movie, eat out, have a sleep over and bring her back tomorrow. The weather had turned mild and the three of them were eager to be out and about.

I looked around the house. It hadn't been cleaned in weeks. Marni wanted an outline for the new book. I hadn't even thought about it. Wallowing in self-pity had to stop and now.

First, the house needed attention, as did Chance. I took her for a long run up the mountain, then let her loose on the return trip. Back inside, I looked around. There were dishes in the sink. Dust coated everything in sight. I shook my head in disgust. All for the love of a woman who obviously didn't care about me or my daughter.

I tackled the dirty dishes in the sink first, putting them in the dishwasher and starting the load. Next, I dusted all the furniture and vacuumed the floors. Upstairs, I changed the bed sheets, scrubbed the shower and sink and tidied the den.

After I loaded the washing machine with dirty clothes, I worked on the remainder of the kitchen. The broken picture frame and photo still lay in the drawer exactly where I had placed them the day I hung the other photos. Every time I saw it there I meant to change the frame, and yet, I never did.

Memories of that morning flashed by—Fiona looking at the photos, her anger erupting, the frame striking me. I touched the raised scar dispassionately. Then I took the broken pieces out of the drawer and carefully dismantled the frame so the picture didn't get damaged.

Two envelopes with a note clipped on top were obscured between the picture and the mat backing. The script was Kari's. They were addressed to Fiona and her mother back in Pennsylvania. *Fuck!* The note requested that I deliver them in person, that I take Anya with me and introduce her to Kari's family. Her last words were to apologize for being a coward.

I looked at the envelopes and suddenly remembered Priss's insistence that I change that frame out after our move. The frame hadn't been the damned issue, the contents were. *Fuck!*

Sisters

Chapter Forty-Six

THE REST OF the house cleaning would have to wait. After finding the envelopes nothing else seemed important. I set them on the kitchen counter with the note, and fixed a drink. A stiff one. I read the note from Priss over and over.

```
Maddy, dear sweet Maddy,
    I need a favor from you and it's a big
one. I've pondered this for weeks, and now
I fear time has run out. Please don't mourn
me too long—I wish nothing but happiness
for you and our baby. Anastasia represents
the best of you, and I want her happy
always.
    I'm enclosing two envelopes addressed to
my family. One for Mom and one for Nonie. I
should have written these long ago, but my
illness and fear for Anya held me back.
    "You're stronger than I ever could be.
You won't tolerate any horse-pucky from my
mother or my sister. I so admire that about
you and hope our baby grows up to be just
as strong.
    Please deliver these in person. Take
Anastasia so my mother can see what a
beautiful child she is. Maybe even be proud
of my greatest accomplishment, our amazing
daughter. Fiona will fuss—she always does—
but she's a good woman, someone you could
be friends with once they're over the
initial anger.
    So my last request, because, yes, I am a
coward, please deliver these for me.
Love Always
Karileah, (Miss Priss)
```

Her usual high spirits were lacking. There was no flourish of bold letters or colorful inks, and the writing was tiny and cramped. I finished the drink and poured another as I stared at the two packets for more than an hour. The US Postal Service deems it a federal crime to open another's mail; I hoped curiosity about the contents didn't carry the same sentence.

What did she want her family to know that she wasn't willing to share herself? Why? Why make me do the deed?

So much had happened since Fiona and I shared our two nights of passion. I didn't exactly lie, but I certainly couldn't take my words back. I omitted important details that now felt like deceptions. Fiona wanted truths, but that could have wide-reaching ramifications that could hurt her, her mother, and certainly my daughter.

Most importantly Fiona tried to steal my child, I couldn't forgive that. None of this helped me choose what the right thing to do was.

AS WINTER MADE itself known in other areas of Montana, Anastasia, Chance, and I dealt with milder weather in our part of the state. Unusual for this area, especially after the start of the season, but much appreciated nonetheless. Snow still covered the mountain peaks, but down in the valley, grass began to show through.

On just such a sunny day, my e-mail notification chirped. I went to the computer to find a note from Marni.

To: Maddison Delaney
From: Marni Roberts
Date: January 9, 2009
Subject: Contract, Cover Art, and PR Appearances

Knowing how you love mornings, I've made reservations out of Kalispell at 5:45 a.m. for you and Anya. There's one stop-over in Seattle, then direct to the city. Your arrival in New York is anticipated at 5:11 p.m. our time. There'll be a car waiting for you that will take you directly to the hotel. I'll call for you at seven. We can have dinner and talk. The next day we'll sign the new contracts in my office, and you can meet with the graphic artist on the cover. I've set up one interview with GLADD network to make the 'BIG' reveal and start to promote *Vigilante*. A local radio station is looking for an interview with a promo spot. I'll leave that up to you. After that you're free for two days of fun, on me. Take my niece to a Broadway show, visit a museum, do something to broaden her education. There's more to life than that damned wilderness you love so much.

Please don't piss me off—be on the plane, Maddison. I can't come out there this time.

See you soon,
Marni

I knew the trip was inevitable. As soon as I told Marni that Fiona was aware of my identity, she wanted to get ahead of the facts surrounding the disclosure. Like it or not, from now on, L. M. Addison would forever be identified as a lesbian author. At this point, I insisted that Carey Troye also be exposed for the dyke she is. The public would either accept it or dump us both, but I didn't want to continue skirting the truth. It was time for full disclosure.

I knew Marni was concerned about what the revelation would mean for sales. At this point, it was more important to me to just be frank. Public appearances were not my forte, but as Kari used to threaten when I got away with it for a number of years, it was now time to pay the piper.

I needed to make arrangements. Chance would stay with Sophia and Lorraine. Instead of waking Anya at three in the morning to catch our flight, I booked a hotel room in Kalispell. We would arrive the day before, eat out, see a movie, spend the night and be at the airport on time, and hopefully not with a cranky child. My truck could stay in long-term parking. That left the house. Sophia promised to drive up and let Chance run while she made like a tenant for anyone paying close attention.

The only decision left to make was what to do with the envelopes? Do I take the chance? Do I fulfill Kari's request. Do I put my heart on the line?

FIONA WAS ON the sun porch reclining in a lounger resting. She knew she looked like hell. The ten-pound weight loss didn't help. Sleepless nights provided the raccoon eyes, as her mother referred to them. She had no appetite and was exhausted all the time.

"Welcome to motherhood," her OBGYN had said at their last visit.

Fiona's ankles were swollen, her back ached, and she couldn't get comfortable.

Mary walked out and sat down on the chair next to her. "I made more ice tea if you're interested."

"Thanks, Mom."

"I want to talk to you about Maddison." Mary put her hand up before Fiona could argue. "Just listen to what I have to say. That's all I ask."

Fiona folded her arms over her chest, but made no move to get up.

Mary pushed on. "When your sister ran off to Hollywood, I didn't know what to think. Was it me, was I a bad mother? Should I have done something different? I came to accept she just wanted a different life than the one she had here. She wrote home faithfully, said she was attending church. She so wanted to be on TV, to make us proud of her." Mary paused and took a sip of her tea. "I already was proud of her, and she didn't know it. That's my fault. I let that girl down in more ways than one. I have to live with that."

"Mom, it wasn't—"

"Hush, I've been thinking about this a long time. Remember the day you told me you were a lesbian?"

Fiona nodded. "I remember. I was so scared."

"I thought I had done something wrong raising you, that it was my fault you were like that. I read everything I could. The Church would have us believe it's wrong, medical science says it's genetic. *You* made me understand that love between two women or men could be just as satisfying as what your father and I had." Mary reached out and clasped Fiona's hand. "If that's true, then the heartbreak can be just as painful. I don't know what Maddison did, but short of physically hurting you, are you really sure she isn't hurting too. Are you absolutely positive that there's nothing that can be done to fix this?"

Fiona obstinately remained mute.

"Fiona Margaret . . . you are not a trusting person, and you're pigheaded. You get that from me. Don't be so inflexible that you throw away true love."

"You don't understand."

"Maybe I don't. Maybe I'm wrong. But at least I'm willing to give her the benefit of the doubt. If she made Karileah happy, if the child is happy, that's not a woman who would trample someone's feelings."

"She lied to me."

"Did she?" Mary asked. "Or did you hear what you wanted to hear?"

"We had a right to know Kari was dead."

"Did she know how to reach us?"

Fiona turned her head trying to hide the tears from her mother.

"Well I've had my say." Mary patted Fiona's hand. "I'm going to the market."

Fiona fell asleep that afternoon, and for the first time in months didn't dream of Maddison. She dreamt of Kari instead. Kari laughing, smiling, and happier than she had ever seen her. Kari, Anya and Maddison in the pictures of their life together . . . they appeared so content. So very happy.

She woke up famished, truly hungry. She wandered into the kitchen. Her mother was at the stove.

"I'm hungry."

"Praise the lord."

218

Chapter Forty-Seven

January 25, 2009

WITH ONLY TWO days till departure, Anya and I decided to plant the bulbs in her mama's field a little early. The brilliant rays of the morning sun warmed the earth and Anya was excited to make the pretty colors appear for her mama.

Years ago, I hired a man from Kalispell, a horticulturist who knew all about the flowers. I paid him to travel up the mountain to see the area. He visited the patch of land, studied the sunlight filtering down between the trees and made a diagram for the plantings. He took care to follow the pictures I provided, ensuring the inclusion of the same flowers Priss so lovingly cared for back in LA. He suggested some perennials and low-lying shrubs to help during the winter months. They would maintain an illusion of color long after the flowers died. The last two years, he showed up multiple times between spring and fall with different bulbs, labels attached, and instructions on how to plant them and where. The theory was we'd have brilliant color through late fall.

Today we used the ATV to drag the utility cart up with us. Anya was excited to be visiting her mama. I was simply happy to be performing physical labor. My nerves were on edge with the upcoming trip, and I still hadn't decided what do about the envelopes.

"Mam, can I plant pretty flowers?"

We were outside the meadow, I turned the engine off and stepped off our ride. "You absolutely can. We just have to follow Mr. Yee's instructions."

"Like we did other time, right?" Anya asked.

"Right." I removed her helmet and gloves, then helped her down.

"I visit Mama." She ran into the meadow ahead of me. I quickly followed behind, carrying the tools and bulbs.

Priss loved flowers. It was the only thing she ever asked to spend money on. When she felt strong enough, she would spend time in the yard weeding, planting bulbs, and talking with her creations. I came home more than once to find Anya and her laughing and up to their elbows in dirt with their faces smeared. I hoped Anya would inherit Priss's green thumb.

A small patch of color bloomed directly in front of the memorial. Bright yellow bulbs reached for the sun, leaning into its warmth.

"Mam, what kinds are these?"

"I don't know, Sweetie. We'll look them up when we get home."

"Okay."

After we buried the plants in the ground, we had a long visit with Priss. It was peaceful up here and Anya and I both seemed in harmony with our surroundings. Chance had followed us up the mountain, but took off after a rabbit. Most likely, she'd be waiting at home.

THE NEXT NIGHT I packed my oversized briefcase and Anya's backpack. Her pack held her clothes, her medicines and an extra pair of shoes. My piece contained my clothes, our toiletries and an outfit for Anastasia, in the event we went somewhere nice. At least I wouldn't be lugging the heavy laptop this time. If I felt inspired, or my muse returned, I'd use the notepad app on my tablet and either e-mail or print it up when we got back. That left the two letters sitting on the counter. They haunted me, reminding me daily of the mission Priss entrusted to me.

Anya and I arrived in Kalispell shortly after the noon hour. We had dropped Chance off at the Nana's house first thing, then headed out on our adventure. Anya was strapped into the booster seat in the quad cab of my truck.

"When do we flied?"

"Tomorrow, very early in the morning."

"Can we get McDonald's?"

"I think you need something a little healthier than McDonald's."

"Pizza!"

"We'll see." I pulled into the lot of the Holiday Inn. After parking, I lifted Anya out of the back and we went to check in. An elderly woman, with salt and pepper hair, was sitting behind the front desk.

"Hi, ma'am. My name's, Maddison Delanie, and I've got a reservation."

The woman tapped her keyboard. "Yes, Ms. Delanie, one room with two queen size beds, correct?"

"Yes, ma'am." I provided my photo ID and filled out the form she handed me.

"Mam, I gets a bed too?"

"I looked down at her. "Yes, baby, you're a big girl now."

"Aren't you a sweet little thing?" The woman behind the counter said.

Anya looked up innocently. "Yes, I am."

The woman handed her a cookie while I provided my charge card. Afterward we took our bags to the room, and Anya washed her hands and face of cookie crumbs.

"Ready to see a movie?"

"I sure am." She held my hand as we walked across the lot.

The selection of movies proved to be tricky, we settled on *Marley and Me*. Afterward we went to a nearby diner for dinner and by seven that night, Anya was fast asleep in one queen-size bed while I reclined in the other. The TV was on, but remained muted. I looked over the itinerary that I had printed out before leaving the house. Besides the one for *Curve* magazine, Marni had snuck in another interview. I jotted down notes and questions that I'd go over with Marni before the interviews. It was important we be on the same page with regards to this announcement. When I ran out of questions, I pushed the paper back into my briefcase.

The letters for Priss's family were in the same pouch. I hadn't intended to bring them. The postal service could have done the same task with less stress. Then the call came late yesterday afternoon.

"MAM, PHONE CALL." Anya ran into the bathroom with the phone. "Hello."

I heard the echo in the line and quick checked the number on the screen. My heart stopped as the voice came through loud and clear.

"Is this Maddison Delanie?"

I was too shocked to speak.

"Hello? Are you there?"

"Yes, Mrs. Gallagher, I'm here."

"So . . . You know who I am?"

"I do."

"I read where you'll be in New York City doing an interview. I want to meet my grandbaby. And I have some questions for you. I'd like you to come visit."

"Yes, I'll be in the city. However, I'm not sure a face-to-face meeting is a good idea." Again I listened. Be it out of respect, fear, or a need to know, I wasn't sure.

She spoke at length and finally. "So, that's my proposition. Do we have a deal?"

"I'll not put my daughter at risk if the situation turns ugly." Every argument I presented she countered.

"I give you my word. Anastasia will be safe."

In the end I promised to think about it.

THE AIRPORT WAS humming with activity the next morning. Anya had risen with little issue, and we were there thirty minutes ahead of schedule. I let her order an Egg McMuffin and juice for breakfast. Two large coffees was all I could handle after a night of no sleep and a stomach knotted with anxiety.

Having sped through security without a problem, we now stood at the departure gate. I held our boarding passes at the ready. My briefcase was slung over my back. Anya's pack was strapped to her and I held her in my arms. Though not a neurotic flier, I do believe in being aware of my surroundings. As I took in our fellow travelers and the area, I was reminded of the day Fiona left. I groaned inwardly, as memories of that morning painfully flashed in my mind.

"**MAM, I CAN** see the houses." Anya had slept the last hour of our trip. She woke when the captain came on the loudspeaker and told us to fasten our seatbelts.

"Those are office buildings and apartments. People live differently here in the city."

"Why?"

"Did you put your tablet in your backpack?"

"Uh-huh."

"Good, cause you're going to need it later."

We landed without incident. That part of a trip was always a nail biter for me. I love the surge of takeoff, but hate the thump of landings. Anya stood up, eager to deplane.

"Wait your turn, you can't go without me. Take my hand."

She did and I was glad she listened. Without a need to recover luggage, we headed to the arrival area. A tired looking, uniformed chauffeur held a placard for the "Addison Party."

I pulled Anya along. "Hi, I'm L. M. Addison."

He hesitated only a minute. "I'll take those, Ms."

I turned over my case, but held onto Anya's. Her medicines were too important to chance losing.

"This way, ma'am."

The limo was parked in the designated area, and Anya was super excited to climb in and have all that room. I let her take a soda pop, something she's not normally allowed back home. At the hotel, I tipped and thanked the driver for a smooth and quick journey. As soon as we checked in, we took the elevator up to the tenth floor. Anya was undergoing a number of firsts and enjoying every one in a different way. The electronic keycard was one of those new experiences. She tried three times before it clicked open.

"I did it, Mam."

"Yes, you did. I'm proud of you."

The room turned out to be a suite, and was more than adequate for our needs over the next few days. Anya ran from room to room, exploring. The view is what finally caught her imagination.

"Mam, look . . . it's so big."

"It is, sweetie."

I called home to Sophia. "We're here and safe."

She advised that Chance was worn out after walking the mountain, that all was calm in our absence, and she'd have dinner ready on our return.

"Take care and thank you. I'll bring you some bagels to make up for this." Sophia had a weakness for Manhattan Bagels, and I intended to bring home two dozen.

Sisters

A COUPLE OF hours later Anya was on the couch watching TV. I sat at the small desk and checked my messages. The knock on the door came earlier than expected. With the chain still engaged I pulled it ajar. Marni waited on the other side.

"Dayum . . . I hope the other guy looks worse. You look like—" She looked to see where Anastasia was "Shit," she whispered.

I just groaned. "Hey we're hungry. I hope you brought your wallet. Who votes for Chinese? You know it's my favorite."

Anya ran to kiss Marni hello. They chatted for a few minutes while I pulled our jackets out of the closet.

Marni waited until we were seated. "Okay, what's wrong? You're not sick, are you?" she asked.

Anya happily played on her Leapster. We had bought a cartridge with two games on it before we left home, she was busy saving the damsel in distress. It kept her occupied when I couldn't. "I'm fine. Just a little tired."

"Bull, I know better." Marni opened her napkin, but never took her eyes off of me.

I leaned closer. "I'm in love, doesn't it show." My eyes filled despite my best efforts at humor.

Marni shook her head. "Honey, if this is what love does to you, you're doing it *wrong*."

I started laughing, head back, deep guffaws. Leave it to Marni to tell me I'm doing love wrong.

"It's fine, really. I'm having a hard time with the new story and choosing a location. I'm not sleeping because of it. This break in routine should shake things up."

"This is about the *sister*, isn't it?"

"So . . . ahh. . . Marni, tell me what's new. How's the family?"

Marni nodded, her eyes never leaving mine. She loved to talk. After publishing, her family was her favorite subject. "First tell me about that, it's new."

She pointed to my eye.

"I zigged when I should have zagged."

Marni took my cue. She talked about Kate, her beleaguered wife and biggest fan, and about construction taking place at their home and the need to stay on top of the workers at all times lest mistakes happen. She talked about the four-legged fur babies she and Kate shared their home with. About the latest novel she'd contracted by an unknown. She continued to talk straight through to dessert.

"So, you wanna tell me about it? You know you can," Marni said. She shook her head when I remained mute. "Do you need me to beat her up or something? Just tell me so I can dress appropriately."

I started laughing again. "And what would that entail? Designer jeans and high heels?"

223

Marni stuck her tongue out. "You'll talk when you're ready. I can be patient."

"Since when?"

We walked back to the hotel. It was pleasantly warm, the night was clear, and the city alive with people. I enjoyed watching it all rush by. It also made me homesick for our mountain, where peace and quiet awaited.

"Let them use makeup on you, it'll take ten years off when the cameras are rolling."

"No way."

"Way." She leaned closer, kissed my cheek and Anya's forehead. "I'll see you in the morning. Night, Little One."

"Night, Aunt Marni."

"Eight sharp, I'll be there."

THE NEXT MORNING Anya and I were waiting for the offices to open. Marni had the contracts for my next book ready. Anya sat at Marni's desk with her Leapfrog while we reviewed the new contract together on the couch. I would receive larger percentages for e-Books, but the tradeoff would be smaller runs for initial print copies. I had no issue with that, most people preferred the electronic product versus a hard copy. I was glad I wasn't most people. Nothing matched the feel and smell of a printed book. Once I signed on the dotted line, Marni sent me off to the Creative department, specifically Nichol's office.

Nichol, the graphic artist, had the final version of the book jacket for *Vigilante*. Normally, they could and would override me if time or cost was a factor. However, I had stipulated that this book, Priss's tribute, would not go forward without my input and approval. I was there to do just that, approve the final copy. At last *Vigilante* was ready. The printer would have copies in our hands by tomorrow at noon. After that, POD—print on demand—would be available by the fifteenth. The e-books were already formatted, and the office assistant would have the covers in place within the hour.

I stopped back at Marni's office to verify the time for the GLAAD interview. Marni informed me that the GLAAD people were having some difficulties and needed to postpone for two days. Marni said there was nothing to worry about. With the airing two weeks away, they had plenty of time.

The albatross hanging around my neck was marring Anya's and my trip. Her enthusiasm normally engaged me, but the sealed envelopes made it impossible for me to think of anything but Fiona, her mother, and Priss's request.

"Marni, what's the chance of renting a vehicle here in town. I need to take a trip, and I hate those puddle jumpers the rental companies normally hand out."

Marni stared at me. "Something important?"

I didn't answer.

"How about a car service? I can have one here in an hour. It'll take you anywhere you want, wait, then bring you back."

"Ahh . . . no, thanks . . . I want to do the driving myself." I stared out the window of Marni's 12th floor office on Broadway, watching the hustle below. A spark of a story trickled into my head.

"So okay. You'll take mine. Try not to beat it up, I just got it. It's the white BMW-X6 across the street, first floor of the parking garage. It's got a GPS thingy, it's supposed to help you navigate. It might if I could figure out how to get it to work. I'll take the car service and enjoy the luxury of being taxied about." She tossed the keys at me. "Registration and insurance cards are in the glove box."

"Thanks, Marni, I promise to get it back to you good as new."

She waved me off as her phone rang. "Don't worry about it. You'll need gas and take care of my niece."

I could feel her eyes on me as Anya and I walked to the elevator.

Chapter Forty-Eight

January 26, 2009

FIONA GLANCED AT the clock. She still had three hours till the end of her shift. She was tired, a headache pounded in her temples, and she desperately wanted to go home and soak her aching feet.

"Buck up, Doc, you wanted to be busy. Now you are," Sharon the receptionist said.

"Busy yes, dead from exhaustion, no." Fiona leaned closer, lowered her voice. "Sharon, could you call me Doctor, please."

"I'm sorry, I didn't mean any disresp—"

"It's not you, it's me." Fiona shook her head. "A long story, but suffice it to say, I don't want to hear the nickname. Too many memories attached to it."

Life was getting back to normal, or as normal as a woman in her eighth month of pregnancy could expect. Gradually the haze of loss was easing. The journey had been a long and difficult one. She ached for Maddison. Her touch. Her tenderness. The companionship they shared. That was behind her now. After the debacle with the custody matter, Fiona was sure Maddison hated her.

She had gained her ten pounds back, and then another five. The circles under her eyes were almost gone. Unfortunately the pain was still as prevalent as that infamous morning back in November. Not a day went by that she didn't think of Maddison, picture her smiling, hear her tease Anya, or remember the look in her eyes when she came, or when she said "I love you."

Then there were the moments when Fiona would remember the lies and omissions that felt deceptive. That made it difficult to trust anything Maddison said. Not knowing how Kari died was a topic of much contemplation. Why hadn't Maddison explained it better? Why was she so circumspect about Kari in general, and her death, specifically? More deception? More secrets? What is she hiding? Fiona hated the enigmas.

The last patient of the day left the clinic at seven thirty, Fiona wrote in the chart then put it in the outbox for the clerical staff. She picked up her purse and jacket and headed home.

"HOW MUCH LONGER will you work?" Mary asked.

"I'd like to continue right up to the birth, that way I can take the three months to be with the baby, not waiting for it." Fiona had her feet up, and was reading the paper.

"And after that?"

"I'm hoping the clinic will offer me more hours."

"Why?"

Fiona turned the page on the paper she was reading. "Because I need to support myself and my child?"

"Have you given thought to contacting Maddison?"

Fiona set the paper down and glared at her mother. "Do you honestly believe she'd accept a call from me after the debacle with Anastasia's custody?"

"I told you it was a mistake."

"Yes, Mom, you did. And you were right and I was wrong, I get it."

"You're too stubborn for your own good. Where do you think you get that from? Not your father, that's for sure."

"It doesn't matter. There's too many questions Maddison left unanswered."

"How do you intend to get your answers if not from her?"

"I'm not sure. Someone else has to know the truth."

"What about the child's grandmother?"

"Sophia?" Fiona shook her head. "She'd never betray Maddison, and if she tried, she'd never see Anya again."

"What's your alternative then?"

"I'm not sure, but I'll think of something." She picked up the paper, but nothing she tried reading stuck. She thought back to the day the package arrived from her lawyer. He had advised her to expect it. He explained that Kari and Maddison had taken every precaution to ensure Anastasia's custody could never be rescinded, and that further legal strategies would only drain Fiona's bank account with no chance of getting a different outcome.

Fiona had gone through the paperwork diligently. Maddison hadn't lied—her name was on the birth certificate along with Kari's. Document after document clearly stated that Karileah Ann Gallagher wanted her child to be raised by Maddison Delanie. The signatures were plainly Kari's on all the paperwork provided. Two items among the numerous volumes surprised her. The first, a marriage certificate, dated February 24, 2004. It was made out to Kari and Maddison. They apparently had gone to San Francisco and taken advantage of Mayor Gavin Newsom's political maneuver. With a statement supporting equality for all, he had started allowing same-sex marriages on the 12th. Maddison had never mentioned they were legally married. Fiona wondered why.

After extensive research, Fiona discovered the marriage was legal for just a few months. The hate mongers went to court and eventually the marriages were declared null and void. She felt a stab of anger and pain, and could only imagine what her sister and Maddison had felt about having their union voided by strangers.

The final document had been a letter written by Kari. Fiona couldn't bear to read it for days, but the not knowing was worse. That evening, after she had gone to bed, she pulled the letter from her nightstand and opened the envelope.

```
Dear Fiona,
    And yes, I knew it would be you staking
a claim, wanting Anastasia for yourself. I
sincerely hope you do get to meet her
someday, mother, too. She's an amazing
child, and so very bright. She reminds me
of you.
    But, and I've done everything our lawyer
has suggested, she's not yours and I don't
want her taken away from Maddison, ever.
    Maddison loves Anya, as much as I do.
She's raised her from birth, and if you're
reading this, since my death as well.
    This is not about you or Mom, but about
what's best for my daughter, please don't
fight this. Maddison knows what Anya needs,
she will provide a good life for her. Trust
that I knew what was best for my child.
    I'm sorry you had to find out this way,
but I had my reasons.
Love Karileah
```

Fiona put the letter back in its envelope and placed it in her closet along with the other paperwork. She accepted her defeat, more upset by her sister's words than by any decision a court could have made.

Why did Kari not trust her own family? How could she marry, have a child, and never bother to tell them? In the end, Maddison had not lied about Anastasia or her sister's wishes. Why, then, wouldn't she explain how Kari died?

Chapter Forty-Nine

December 2003

WHEN I RETURNED from the pharmacy, I went to the kitchen where Priss was sitting. "I got your medicine."

Priss took the bag and pulled the bottles out. "Tell me how much, I'll write you a check."

I sat down. I had been avoiding this conversation for as long as I could. "We need to talk."

Priss's eyes widened.

"I've been thinking about this a while, so hear me out, please,"

"Should I make coffee?"

"I'll make it— You sit, rest."

We remained quiet while the coffee brewed, then I filled our cups and sat across from Priss.

Priss pulled her mug closer. "I understand if you want me to move out."

I reached across the table and took her hand. "I don't want that. This is about money, I'm sorry to say. I hate bringing this up, but your medicines are expensive."

"How expensive?"

"Twenty-four-hundred a month."

"Dear God. I can't afford that! What am I going to do? I need to worry about the baby. If I don't have that—"

"Relax, I've been doing research. I've had a month to come up with a plan— I just hope you'll listen to it." I took a deep breath.

"Is it legal?"

"Actually, the legal aspect is what will eventually pay the bills. Most importantly we have to worry about the baby. If she's born with the virus, she'll need medicine too."

"That's five thousand dollars a month! Where will I get that?" Priss got up and started to pace.

I jumped up and led her back to the chair. "I need to ask you something?"

"Go ahead." She looked terrified.

"We've never talked about Ortiz or his death."

Priss shook her head. "What does that have to do with my medicine?"

"I know how frightened you were when the police took us in for questioning."

"It just never occurred to me they would accuse you."

"Luckily we were able to prove I was out of town when it happened."

"I know that. Why are we talking about this?"

"Because I need to know you believe I didn't plan it either."

"I do." Priss stared at me. "At first I wasn't sure, but of course I am now."

"Okay then, here goes." I took a deep breath. "We're good friends, right?"

Priss looked at her quizzically. "Yes, of course."

"I love you as a friend, and I think you love me the same way."

"That's true," Priss said.

I flattened my hands on the table. "Then let's set up a domestic partnership, one that's recognized by the state and most importantly by my medical provider."

"What?"

"We already live together. No one has to know you have your own room. We've been together for years. It's documented. Hell, the police tried to use it as the motive for me to kill Ortiz. We could make it legal and after the initial penalty for the pre-existing conditions, you'd be covered under my coverage."

"That can't be legal?"

"I've done a lot of research. Medicare or Social Security disability might pay for part of your meds, but not as long as you're living with me. My income's too high for you to qualify. You lost your own coverage when you stopped paying dues to SAG and quit the show. I refuse to think about you moving out. The medicine can save your life, but the cost is exorbitant."

"I had no idea." Priss sipped her coffee.

"What other choice do we have?"

"I can't let you do this."

"Priss, think about it. What other avenue is open to us? Consider the baby. Once she's born that could double the cost. Nothing needs to change. It's not like we'd suddenly start sleeping together. We'd simply legalize our living arrangements and in the process get help paying for your medicine."

"Is this legal?"

I took a long sip of coffee. "It's skirting the issue real close, but I believe we can get away with it."

"And if we don't?"

"Then we're in the same place we were before we sat down to talk."

"I have to think about it. This is a big step. I'm not sure."

"Just think about the baby, please." I knew she'd be against it initially, but I hoped she'd consider all aspects..

Two days later, the phone rang. Priss picked it up. She identified herself and listened. She began to cry, I took the phone from her and guided her back to the chair.

"Who's this?" It was my turn to listen.

"Maddison, I was calling for you. This is Tomas, Juan and Anna's brother."

"What's wrong?" Obviously something since Priss was crying.

"Juan . . . well . . . he swallowed his gun last night."

"Oh fuck!" I said. "I'm sorry. So sorry for your loss." After another minute of conversation. "Let me know when the arrangements are made, I'd like to be there." I hung up the phone up and went to Priss.

"I'm sorry, Priss, really and truly sorry."

As tears ran down her cheeks, she shook her head. "It's all my fault."

"Not everything is your fault. People need to take responsibility for their own actions."

I helped her into her room to rest.

The next morning, Priss walked into the kitchen. "I've been thinking about your proposal."

I was sitting at the table, reading the paper and sipping my first cup of coffee. "And."

"I have a question for you?"

"Shoot."

"If we did this, and if I die, what happens to my baby?"

"She'd be mine, I'd raise her."

"Just like that?"

"What did you expect?"

"I guess I didn't expect unconditional acceptance." She reached her hand out, and I took it. "I want my child to be loved. If I'm not here to do it, I know you will. Thank you."

"Does this mean you're willing to make us legal?"

"Yes." She made the sign of the cross and nodded her head.

The following week, I filled out the necessary documents. Priss and I brought them downtown to a lawyer who came highly recommended. Samuel Banyon was a known crusader for equal rights. He helped us with the paperwork and would do the filing himself. Then he suggested other protections for our status as a couple, for our future child's guardianship, and for each of us as individuals. Afterward, as we left Sam's office and road the elevator down to the first floor, I said, "I feel better, don't you?"

Priss nodded. "Yes, I do."

"But?"

She shook her head from side to side. "I never imagined myself with another woman."

"And you don't have to. We're friends . . . nothing is going to change."

"You've given up so much for me, I'll never be able to pay—"

"Do you see me standing here?" I spread my arms and stamped my left foot. "If not for you, this wouldn't have been possible."

231

Priss took my arm and led us toward the car. "You know what I mean."

I opened the door and helped her in. "I'm the winner in all this—my best friend, a child soon—what more could I want?"

"Love."

I walked around the car and climbed in the driver's seat. "I *have* everything I want, or will want, once the baby is born." I patted her hand, then started the car.

Chapter Fifty

January 29, 2009

I DROVE WEST on I-84, my mind a jumble. I wasn't sure why I had agreed to do this and hoped it wouldn't be a colossal mistake.

Marni's BMW did come with a GPS system, and I took advantage of it. As soon as I punched in the address, the little machine started spewing instructions out of the speaker. "Go four hundred feet turn right. Blah, Blah, Blah. " If this thing was correct we should arrive at Mrs. Gallagher's house in less than twenty-five minutes.

"Where we going, Mam?"

I peeked in the rear view mirror at Anastasia and smiled. "We're going to see your grandmother."

"But Nana is home. We didn't flied yet."

"We're going to see Mama's mother."

Anya seemed to absorb this information easily, and shortly began to sing along with the radio.

The interchange for I-81 N was on the right, I pulled into the lane and proceeded cautiously. My stomach was in a knot, but a deal was a deal. Mrs. Gallagher had promised no funny business and assured me she just wanted to meet her granddaughter. Unfortunately, Priss wanted the same thing. I was obligated either way. As we approached Exit 18, for PA 247, I felt my chest constrict. Fear gripped me so tightly, I had trouble breathing. Seven miles up the highway, we turned onto Moosic Lake Road passing Holy Ghost Cemetery on the right. So far the directions had been correct. Two more turns and the female voice announced I was arriving at my destination on the left. I pulled up in front of a small, white, Cape Cod structure with green trim and shutters. The front lawn brought a smile to my face. Flowers in every color and type filled the landscape, reminding me of Kari's meadow. A woman knelt to the right of the walkway. She was pulling weeds. A shock of silver hair and a pleasantly plump figure was all I could make out from this distance.

"Is that my grandma?"

I turned the engine off and looked into the mirror. "I think so, baby. Let's go find out."

I exited the front seat and opened the rear door, unbuckling Anastasia and lifting her out of the car. Before we went toward the house, I smoothed down her hair and straightened her dress. First impressions and all. I quickly grabbed my briefcase before closing the door.

"Come on, Little One." I held my hand out and we walked around the car and down the front walk. The woman must have heard us approach. Using the porch railing for leverage, she struggled to her feet and turned to watch us .

"Mrs. Gallagher?" I'm not sure what I expected, but it certainly was not those crystal blue eyes peering at us over the top of her glasses.

The woman never took her eyes off Anastasia. Her smile reminding me so much of Priss's. This was definitely her mother.

"You must be Anastasia?" Mrs. Gallagher leaned over and grinned.

Anya looked at her quizzically. "Are you really my grandma?"

"Anya!" I chided. "I'm sorry about that. I'm Maddison Delanie."

Mrs. Gallagher briefly glanced at me, and held her hand out toward Anya. "Yes, I am your grandmother, and I'm very glad to finally meet you."

"How come I didn't knowed about you?"

"Anya, behave, please."

"I just asked—"

"Well, I'm happy to know about you. A friendly leprechaun told me you like chocolate chip cookies and milk. Is that right?"

Her shyness finally kicked in. Anya nodded.

"Well then, let's all go in the house and have some. I spent the entire morning baking."

She led us through the front door and down a narrow hallway into the large, eat-in kitchen. The walls were painted a pale yellow with a colorful flowered border just below the crown molding. The cabinets were bright white, and the appliances were older models. The linoleum floor had seen better days, but it was all clean. The table was a plank style with benches along each side with chairs at the ends.

I lifted Anya onto a bench and stood next to her while Mrs. Gallagher poured milk into a glass and placed a plate of cookies in the middle of the table.

"Sit. I don't bite."

She lowered herself on the bench across from us. Kari definitely had her mother's eyes. The difference was Kari's reflected compassion and naiveté. Mrs. Gallagher's were sharp, no nonsense. I felt my stomach tighten.

"Well, go on, help yourself," she said.

Anya reached over and gripped two cookies. I quickly took one from her hand and placed it on her plate and put the other back. "Just one."

Suddenly a loud bang caught our attention. A large yellow lab came springing through a doggie door. "That's just Abby. Ignore her . . . I do."

"Oh, doggie." Anya moved to get down.

I held her in place. "Remember the rule about strange animals." Meanwhile Abby was at our side, licking Anya's chocolate covered fingers and making my daughter giggle.

234

"She's pretty. Can I play with her? Please!"

I stared at Mrs. Gallagher. "They can go out in the back . . . plenty of room there for them to romp around."

I kept my hand on Anya's shoulder holding her still. "Is it fenced in?"

Mrs. Gallagher's eyes narrowed. "Course it is."

It felt like a power struggle, but I hoped I was imagining it. "Okay, but stay where I can see you."

"Yes, Mam." Anastasia took the rest of her cookie and ran to the door. Giggling, she followed Abby out through the doggie hatch.

Mrs. Gallagher chuckled heartily. "She's a beautiful little girl."

"I think so."

"She's the image of Karileah at that age."

I stood staring out the window watching Anya throw a Frisbee and Abby run to catch it. "I've always said she was Priss's twin." My voice hitched.

"I want to talk—"

The front door banged open.

"Mom, I'm home," Fiona's voice called out.

"In the kitchen." Mrs. Gallagher never took her eyes off me.

I walked back around the table and leaned against the counter just to the right of the doorway.

"I stopped and got your prescription. You'll need to see the doctor before it can be filled—" Fiona stopped dead in her tracks, and the bag slipped from her hand. "What the hell are you doing here?"

I leaned down, picked up the package, and handed it to Mary.

"I invited her. Sit down. We were just about to talk some."

"I want you to leave—"

Mary gripped Fiona's arm. "No one's leaving. I gave Maddison my word we'll be giving her no trouble, and I intend to keep it. Now sit!"

"Your word . . . you promised her . . . I don't understand?"

Mary pointed, and Fiona lowered her heavy, rounded figure into the chair at the end of the table. "I wanted to meet my grandbaby. I want to know about Karileah's life. Why she was taken from us. I called Maddison and made her an offer she couldn't refuse."

I watched the exchange between mother and daughter and wondered if it had been the same when Priss was here. Clearly, Mrs. Gallagher ruled the roost. Priss would not have stood a chance against this formidable woman.

"You." Mrs. Gallagher pointed at me. "Sit down, you're making me jumpy." I peeked out the window, then moved to the chair at the opposite end of the table from Fiona.

"Now, we're all going to behave like adults and talk."

"Where's Anastasia?" Fiona asked.

Before I could answer, Abby bolted through the doggie door, and Anya crawled in after her. "Fiona!" Anya ran over and climbed onto her lap. "I misseded you." She kissed Fiona on the cheek and hugged her tight.

With tears in her eyes, Fiona pulled her close. "I missed you too, sweetheart. Very much."

I rose and lifted Anya off Fiona's extended stomach and plopped her down on the bench next to her. "You have to be careful, Munchkin, Aunt Fiona is having a baby."

"She is?" Anya looked on in awe.

I gazed into Fiona's eyes and felt the final door slam shut. "Yes, she is."

"I gonna have a sister?"

"It might be a boy. Either way it would be your cousin, sweetheart," Fiona explained.

"But I want a sister," Anya said.

"Anya, please come here." I pulled her onto my lap at the other end of the table and handed her a cookie.

"Whether it's a boy or girl, Anastasia, I hope you'll be good friends. After all you're family," Mrs. Gallagher said.

"Please go," Fiona whispered.

I nodded. "Okay."

"Is Fiona mad at us, Mam?"

"No, she's tired and needs to rest."

"Hush, Fiona. This is still my home. I decide who stays or goes." Mary stared Fiona down. "I want to hear what she has to say. If you don't want answers, then leave the room." Mrs. Gallagher stood up and turned to the stove. "I'm making coffee, would you like some?" She was looking at me.

I remained transfixed, torn between wanting to settle this and needing to run. "Yes, ma'am."

After fixing the pot, Mrs. Gallagher turned to Fiona. "What do you want to drink?"

"This is why you wanted the damned cookie recipe, you knew they were coming?" Fiona said.

Anya's hand flew to her mouth. "You said a bad word, Fiona!"

Fiona slapped her hand over her own mouth. "I did! I'm sorry."

"You hafta pay." Anya smugly bit into her cookie.

"You're right." Fiona dug in her purse and pulled a dollar bill out. "Here, sweetie."

Anya jumped down and ran around the table to collect the money.

"If you ever cared for me, if you did love me, leave. Prove to me you have a shred of decency in you." Fiona had tears in her eyes.

"Mam?" Anya returned to my side and I picked her up.

"Love it is. I knew it." Mary shot Fiona a stern look. "*I* called her. *I* invited her here. She's not leaving until I talk with her. Now what are you drinking?"

236

"Tea."

"Mam, why is Fiona crying?" She buried her face in my shoulder.

"She just misses Mama." Anya nodded her head into my neck.

I pushed the plate of cookies closer to Fiona's end of the table. She just glared at me.

As soon as the coffee was poured, Mrs. Gallagher addressed Anya. "Little girl." She waited for Anya to lift her head and listen. "I need to talk to your mama in private. Is that okay with you."

Anya's eyes grew big and they quickly filled up with tears as she wrapped her arms around my neck burying her face.

"It's okay, baby, she means me. Don't cry. Grandma wants to talk to me."

Anya turned her wet eyes to Mrs. Gallagher. "My Mama's in heaven."

Tears glistened in Mrs. Gallagher's eyes. "I hope she is, darling girl, believe me."

"She. Is. In. Heaven." I said through gritted teeth. "You can be sure of it."

Fiona pushed herself up from the chair using the table. "That's right, Anya. Tell Grandma how you go to visit with her in the meadow."

Anya nodded solemnly. "We go'd every day. And we plant flowers and—"

"Later Sweetie, Grandma Mary wants to talk with Mam, so how about you play with some of your mama's old dolls?" Fiona held out her hand to Anya.

I stared hard at her, hoping this wasn't a ruse.

"Kari's room is right down the hall here. She and Abby can play there while we all talk."

I turned to Mrs. Gallagher, who was watching me in return, as if testing me. That's how it felt, like another test. "Okay, but don't wander around, Anya. You come back here if you leave that room, hear me."

"Yes, Mam." Anya took Fiona's hand, then she and Abby walked down the hall with Fiona.

"You're good with her," Mrs. Gallagher said.

I took a sip of my coffee. "She means everything to me."

"It shows." She drank her coffee, moments later Fiona was back and lowering herself into the chair again.

"What have I missed."

I shook my head.

"Nothing yet. I waited for you." Mrs. Gallagher turned to me. "Where's Anya's father? She must have one."

I held the coffee cup with two hands, a lie or the truth. It was time for truth, all of it. "He's dead."

"What happened?" Mrs. Gallagher asked.

"It's not relevant to your daughter or Anastasia."

"Anya's father is not relevant? You have an odd way of stating things. Did he not want her?"

"He never knew about her."

I watched Mary absorb that information. "Then tell me about my daughter."

My eyes met Fiona's. She drilled me with hers. "Mrs. Gallagher." I flicked my eyes toward her, then back at Fiona. "Do you care about the truth, or do you want the respectable version?"

Silence filled the kitchen; the second hand of the wall clock the only noise. I kept my eyes focused on Fiona, waiting.

"Don't do this, I'm begging you," Fiona said, her voice low and gravelly.

Mary watched the exchange between her daughter and me. She laid her hand over Fiona's. "It's clear you've suspected Karileah of sinning. To be honest so have I. You see where that's gotten us. We need to rely on a stranger to tell us how your sister died." She wrapped her two hands around Fiona's and turned to me. "I want the truth, young lady, now."

"Fiona?"

"Please, my mother should be allowed her memories. I don't want you—"

All the months of hurt since Fiona left, and the pain of Priss's death joined together and exploded within me. "I don't fucking understand you. What exactly is it you could possibly believe? Your sister was the sweetest, kindest, most caring woman, I ever met and she wouldn't hurt a soul. She went to church every damned week, even when she was too sick to walk. She'd make me carry her inside so she could pray to her god." I realized I was on my feet, my hands fisted at my sides. "And don't ever tell my daughter her mama's not in heaven. If there *is* a damned God and he's this supposed omnipresent being, he knows Priss deserves to be right there beside him." I walked to the windows and looked out on the back yard. I took a cleansing breath as I gazed at the colorful flowers along each side of the fence.

"Mam." Anya came running into the room calling for me, I swooped down and picked up her. "Mam, what's wrong, why are you yelling?"

"Nothing's wrong. I'm sorry, baby." I kissed her cheek and took a deep breath. "Everything's fine . . . I just lost my temper. You go back and play with the dolls, okay?"

"You hafta pay for bad words when we get home." Her little smile was sweet and innocent, so like her mother's.

"She doesn't miss much," Mary said, chuckling at Anya.

"She'll be a millionaire by the time she's ready for college." I put her down, and pulled two ones from my pocket. "Here, you hold these till we get home, okay?"

She rolled them up with Fiona's money and shoved them in her pocket, then nodded and ran down the hallway. I walked back to the table and sat down.

Fiona looked shocked. "I thought . . . I was afraid—" She shook her head. Her mother patted her hand.

"You were in love with Karileah."

"No, ma'am." I picked up my coffee. It was cold. "I owed her my life. We became friends during my therapy. She's the reason I can walk. I loved her for that, but I was never in love with her."

After a short lull, Mrs. Gallagher said, "Maybe you should start from the beginning . . . and please, why do you call her Priss?"

I had to smile. "Your daughter was my therapist. I used to have a real potty mouth, cursed when I was mad, in pain, whatever. She put her foot down, threatened not to work with me unless I changed my ways. It started out as Miss Priss." I shook my head. "Eventually she was just Priss."

Mary smiled. "I like that. Go on."

"Please, don't destroy my sister's memory," Fiona hissed.

"I won't, trust me."

"Trust you! That's rich."

"I'd never betray Priss, and you know that's a fact."

Fiona's only answer was to nod her head.

"Your mom deserves to know what a wonderful person she was. To understand about us, Anya, and what happened. To know how she—"

"My mother doesn't need to know ugly details. She doesn't need to know about addiction, and the ramifications of drug abuse."

"What the hell are you talking about?" I shook my head. "She wasn't an addict and there was nothing ugly about Priss. What happened to her was not her fault."

"Enough." Mary got up and poured more coffee into our cups. "Was Karileah a lesbian."

"What? She wasn't— No!"

Mary shook her head. "You dedicated the last book to your wife, wasn't that Karileah?"

I looked at Fiona. "It *was* dedicated to Karileah. Yes, under the eyes of the law in California, she was my wife for a short time." I took a sip of the hot coffee and tried to choose my words carefully. "Kari and I were never romantically involved. I didn't lie about that. We married for financial reasons."

"That makes no sense. She had a job. She was signed to be on a detective series," Mary said.

"I didn't mean money, I meant expenditures."

"I don't understand."

"I'm an ex-cop. The city provides excellent medical benefits, and as my RDP—"

"You're what?"

"My recognized domestic partner and later wife, she received those same benefits." I said the words softly, knowing the next part would be more difficult.

"Why did you need a therapist?"

That question caught me off guard. Clearly Fiona had told her mother nothing. "I was shot . . . in the line of duty, my leg . . . was damaged." I unconsciously rubbed my thigh. "The doctors doubted I'd walk again."

"But you can." Mrs. Gallagher stared over the top of her glasses at me.

"Yes, ma'am. Because your daughter was like a drill sergeant. She never gave me a moment's rest or allowed me to feel sorry for myself."

"Then you are the person she moved in with." Mrs. Gallagher said the words into her cup, her eyes downcast.

"Yes, ma'am."

"Mary."

I stared at her blankly.

"Call me Mary."

"Yes, ma'am."

"What happened to my daughter's dream of stardom?"

"A man by the name of Roberto Ortiz happened."

No one said a word. The second hand of the clock ticked off the seconds and still no one said anything.

I looked across the table at Fiona. She was gazing at the wall.

I took a deep breath. "It was my fault, ma'am. Everything that happened was my fault." I sipped from the cup trying to quell the quiver in my voice.

"You'll need to explain that to me."

Chapter Fifty-One

January 29, 2009

I NODDED YES, ma'am. You deserve to know." I set the cup down and pushed it away. "Priss was my therapist for just over a year, before I was finally able to take my first steps. Five months later, I was almost fully mobile. She lived in the extra bedroom. Always had, always did. I refused to take money for rent, the utilities or food. In return she did all the cooking and cleaning. On top of that she helped me with my exercises every night. It gave her the opportunity to go on auditions during the day, take parts as they came up, and follow her dream. The only time she left me alone was for church, shopping, or casting calls."

Mary clasped her hands on the table.

"Friends from her old job called one day. One of the girls was getting married. They were going out for drinks to celebrate. They invited Kari to join them"—a shudder ran through me as I remembered our conversation—"I pushed her to go. She had been stuck in the house with me almost eighteen months . . . she deserved a break. I promised her I wouldn't venture out of my room. You see, she cared about me, worried I'd do something stupid and hurt my leg again."

Mary blew her nose, then nodded for me to continue.

"The other women, Georgia and Sharon, picked her up at seven on Friday night. They went to a bar downtown to celebrate. I had given Kari money and told her to call a cab when she wanted to come home."

Fiona slammed her hand down. "She had money of her own."

"She did. And she was saving to get an apartment of her own, now that I was almost back to normal and she had the new series."

"Go on," Mary said.

"Once they were at the bar, Georgia's fiancé showed up. After a couple of rounds of drinks, she left with him. Sharon met someone on the dance floor. She asked Kari if she wanted a ride, because they were leaving. Kari told her she'd call a cab. Sharon left her there by herself." I drank my coffee down, dreading the next part of the story. Needing a moment to before I continued.

"Around midnight, my ex-partner's brother, an LA patrolman came to the house to tell me Kari was in the emergency room."

I got up and went to the doorway to listen for Anya. I could hear her talking to the dog and the dolls. I walked back to the chair and sat. I lowered my voice.

"When I got to the hospital, the responding officer told me Kari had been assaulted. They found her naked and unconscious in an alley behind the bar. The doctor let me in once I told him I was family. She was a mess. Physically she had taken a vicious beating, mentally she . . . well . . . she never really recovered from that night."

"My god, she was just raped!" Fiona slammed her hand on the table. "What the hell did you expect from her?"

"You don't understand." I stared at Mary, but she remained mute. "Priss, I mean Kari, blamed herself for what happened and for everything . . . well, for later, too."

"Herself? Why for the love of God?"

"What exactly did happen to her?" Mary asked.

"You have to keep in mind the assault took place, six years ago, medicine and science change daily. Women, who've been attacked are treated differently now than back then." I looked to see if Fiona would say anything, but she didn't.

"You promised me the truth. Don't gloss over it," Mary said.

"Yes, ma'am. I took Kari home the next morning and I . . . I became the caregiver. She withdrew into herself, backed out of the contract she had just signed. She even stopped going to church for a while. She lost weight, barely left her room. Then, two months after the attack, she told me she thought she was pregnant. I went and got the pregnancy tests from the pharmacy. She was . . . with Anya."

I stood to stretch my legs. "Under the circumstances, I thought she'd want an abortion. I couldn't believe when she didn't. She stressed it was against her religion. She refused to blame the baby. For the record it was the same damned religion that turned its back on her. The same God that preaches purgatory for sins beyond her control."

Fiona turned in the chair and stared at me. "What sins?"

"Exactly. That's always been my question." I sat back down.

"You're not Catholic," Mary said.

"No ma'am, I'm not."

"And Anya?"

"She goes to church with her Nanas. They're Episcopalians."

Mary nodded, then asked, "Did Karileah tell Anya's father?"

I clasped my hands together and locked eyes with Mary. "Don't you get it? Kari was raped."

"*He* was the father?"

"Yes, because it was his sperm that impregnated Kari." My head dropped to my chest. "No, because sperm doesn't make a man a father." I slammed my hand on the table. "That bastard drugged and raped Kari. He nearly got away with it."

Mary's hand flew to her mouth as tears trickled down her cheeks.

"Kari couldn't possibly believe that was her fault," Fiona said.

"That's exactly what she believed, because *your* mother told her there's no such thing as rape. That a woman uses her wiles to entice a man or to trick him." The words spewed from my lips; my anger flowed with them.

"I never said that," Mary said.

I took a deep breath. "I mean no disrespect, but Kari repeated those words to me too many times over the years. How you felt about women who claimed to be assaulted. How they set innocent men up then used sex to trap them."

Mary started to cry, sobs wracking her body. I almost felt sorry for her.

"What are you thinking, saying that to her?" Fiona pushed her chair closer and tried to comfort her mother. "That's enough . . . go!"

"No," Mary said. "If Kari believed that, it still doesn't explain how she died. Why is my daughter dead?" Mary wiped her eyes and stared at me.

I took a deep breath, my eyes darting from Fiona to her mother. "The bastard that raped her had AIDs."

Fiona gasped.

"AIDs? That's transmitted through—"

"Mom, you don't need to know this part."

"But I want, too." Mary looked at me. "He gave . . . the disease . . . to Karileah?"

"Yes, ma'am."

Tears tracked down Fiona's face. Mary fought to hold hers back. "I thought people could live with HIV? That medicine and research were making a difference."

"His virus was active and already mutated. He was in the final stages of the disease at the time of the rape."

"Oh. My. God." Fiona started to cry harder. "That's why, oh nooo—" She began rocking back and forth, tears flowing down her cheeks. "No, no, nooooo."

I nodded, because I knew she finally figured it out.

"What, I don't understand. What are you two not saying?" Mary demanded.

Fiona took her mother's hand. "If Karileah died of AIDs."— tears ran down her face, dripping onto her shirt—"that means Anastasia is likely HIV positive at the minimum."

Mary's head swiveled back and forth between Fiona and myself. "That sweet little girl is sick?"

"No"—I shook my head—"not yet. With luck, maybe never. Science is coming up with new medicines all the time. I have her on the prescribed regimen of drugs. We see a specialist every three months."

"That's why she hates doctors. Why she's homeschooled. Why you wouldn't let me near her till you knew I wasn't contagious," Fiona said.

"I couldn't take a chance."

"That's the vitamins you hid from me?"

"I didn't think it was your business."

Silence filled the room. I could hear Anya down the hall playing. I was grateful she didn't have to hear these details. Time passed. Mary and Fiona grieved silently. I waited.

Mary addressed me. "I have one last question for you."

"Yes, ma'am."

"Why are you so angry at God, why is my daughter dead if there's medicine that can help, and why did Karileah concern herself with purgatory?"

"That's three questions."

Mary nodded. "So it is."

"I'll start with Kari's death. The bastard that drugged and raped her knew he was HIV positive, that it had progressed to AIDs. He knew he was likely sentencing her and every other woman he had sex with to death. He didn't give a damn. I can't begin to explain all the medical terms and science. Fiona probably can do it better. The doctor told us that because the disease had progressed to the end stages, it was more virulent. With Kari's history of lung and throat infections from childhood, she was susceptible and her system less able to fight back. That's why we set up the domestic partnership and married when we could. The medicines are exorbitantly expensive. I was able to help with the cost through my coverage."

"Which is why she left Anastasia to you?" Fiona asked.

"No. She left Anya with me, because she knew I'd love her no matter what. And that I'd take care of her. I don't care that she carries the virus. She's my little girl and I adore her."

"Did she honestly think we wouldn't love that child?" Mary asked.

I turned to Mary. "She worried you would make her live in fear of other people finding out. Or worse, make her believe that she somehow deserved the illness because of the circumstances surrounding her conception."

Mary nodded her head slowly. "Karileah was very wise. More so than I gave her credit for."

"How can you say that?" Fiona asked. "You'd never blame that sweet little girl for what happened."

Mary shrugged. "I'd like to think you're right, but I might have."

"Kari, loved her daughter with all her heart. She never wanted Anya to suffer or have to hide."

"Mom, I swear I don't understand you sometimes."

"And the Church?" Mary said.

"Kari went to church faithfully and prayed for guidance. She believed there was a reason for everything. That it wasn't always easy to understand why bad things happened, but that you just had to believe that God would show you the way through the tough times in the end.

"The damned priest knew she had been raped, and he still called her a sinner. He wanted her to repent because she bore a child out of wedlock. He didn't give a damn that she was drugged. He claimed she had relations with a man not her husband. That she got AIDs because she put herself in a position to be drugged and raped. He forbid her the sacraments when he discovered she married a woman. Kari and I rarely disagreed about things, but on this we out and out fought."

"How did he, the attacker, convince her to trust him enough to drug and rape her?" Mary asked.

"Don't even go there. Kari, didn't do anything to *let* this happen. He was the bartender at the tavern they went to that night. When he realized Georgia and Sharon left Kari alone, he put the drug in the one and only drink she had nursed all evening. In case you didn't know, just a couple of sips with that drug in it, can incapacitate a person."

"And him? Where is he?"

"He's dead."

"The disease killed him?"

"No ma'am, he was found shot to death in an alley."

Fiona gasped, but said nothing.

"Purgatory. You said she believed in purgatory." Mary gazed at me quizzically. "She thought God wouldn't let her into heaven because she was raped? Because of Anya?"

I nodded. "Yes, ma'am. See, the priest refused to baptize Anastasia. It broke Kari's heart. She took it really hard. We went to another church, but that priest wouldn't go against the first one."

"Fucking bastard," Fiona said.

"Language, young lady."

"Mama, please, that's unconscionable."

"When Kari was at the hospice, her priest at the church refused her the last rites. I almost killed him with my bare hands. The priest from the hospice offered to perform the ritual, but Kari believed if her own priest wouldn't, then it didn't count. Anya finds comfort believing her mother *is* in heaven. I'll not have her worrying about her mother's soul."

"And her death?"

"The virus killed her. There was nothing more medicine could do. She begged to leave the hospice. I made the arrangements. That morning we were on the beach, the four of us, for sunrise. She loved the ocean and sitting there watching the sun come up or set. I carried her down to the water's edge and held her. I thought she had fallen asleep . . . she slipped away." Tears ran down my cheeks.

I waited as Fiona and her mother absorbed all I had told them.

"If there's nothing else, I'd like to get Anastasia back to the hotel. We have a long trip back and plans to see a show and museum tomorrow. She needs a good night's rest."

Mary took her glasses off and reached for my hand. "One more question. How is this your fault?"

I looked her right in the eye. "Because I insisted she go out that night. I told her she deserved to have fun, to enjoy herself. She had just signed the contract for that role on that detective show, and I told her to go and celebrate."

Mary shook her head. "I guess I should explain something. I hope you'll both understand. When I was a very young girl, there was a boy in town accused of rape. My mother refused to believe it. It split our small village—some believed his guilt, some didn't. My mother believed he had been tricked, that the woman was to blame. She said that a woman was always to blame." Mary took a cleansing breath. "His family tried to cover it up. The situation disgraced the family. People stared and pointed when they were out and about. That lie hurt many innocent people, destroyed relationships, caused a suicide, and now I find my own daughter has been hurt by it. When will it stop?"

"When people stop making excuses for the animals that rape women," I said.

She stared at me for a long time before saying anything. "Fiona told me about the meadow where Kari's ashes are spread. I'd like to see it sometime, if you'd allow me."

"Does our deal still apply?"

She tipped her head. "It does."

"Then you don't need an invitation. Come anytime you want. I'm normally there, but if not, Fiona knows where the key is."

"I'd also like to keep in touch with Anastasia . . . if you'll allow it?"

"You're welcome to call anytime, as long as you understand the rules about Kari and heaven. I never want Anya's memories destroyed. She loves her mama."

Mary held Fiona's hand. "I give you my word. Maybe I'll learn to Skype . . . that way I can watch her grow."

I watched Mary squeeze Fiona's hand.

I blew out a breath, blowing the hair off my forehead. "I'm not very good at handling . . . what I mean is . . . when Kari died, I . . . it . . . was a difficult time."

I lifted my briefcase off the floor and placed it on the table to retrieve the yellowed envelopes carrying Kari's scribbling on the front. I gently placed them in front of each woman.

"We were in the process of moving when she passed. We planned on her living long enough to reach the new house. When I packed up the old place, I just threw things in boxes. Once we got there, I stuck the box with her pictures in Anya's closet and never paid attention. I'm sorry this took so long. I didn't even know of their existence until I found them hidden behind a broken picture frame recently."

Fiona looked up, a moment of clarity visibly shot through her as her eyes got big in understanding.

"Kari left a note with them." I laid it on the table for viewing. "She asked that I deliver the letters in person to ensure you each receive 'em and that you meet Anastasia. I've complied with her final request."

Mary picked up the envelope addressed to her. She appeared to recognize Kari's script and immediately held it against her chest as tears gathered in her eyes.

"If there's nothing else, I really need to get Anya back to the hotel, give her some dinner, and let her have a good night's sleep. We have a busy day ahead of us."

Mary put her hand up. "Just one more question please."

"Yes, ma'am."

"Are you in love with my daughter?"

I glanced at Fiona then quickly back to Mary. "I swear to you, Kari was my friend, nothing more."

Mary nodded. "I didn't ask if you *loved* my daughter. I asked if you're *in* love with my daughter. Present tense. Daughter present here."

I had to admire this woman. She was truly daunting.

"I am. Yes." I looked her right in the eye, so there'd be no question in her mind. "I miss her, but circumstances have created an insurmountable abyss. For obvious reasons, I didn't disclose certain information about Kari. I don't talk about Anya's HIV status, because it's no one's business. As for lying about my identity, it wasn't my intention, but it's what happened."

Mary nodded her head.

"Is there anything else?"

"No, I think you've been very forthcoming, thank you." Mary stood, as did I.

"Okay, then. Anya! Come on, baby, we're leaving."

Abby and Anastasia ran down the hall side by side. "Say good-bye to your aunt and grandmother and thank her for the cookies."

Anya hugged and kissed each woman, and thanked Mary for the bag with two extra cookies for the ride home. Mary was talking to Anastasia as they walked to the front door. I held back. "I'll be there in a minute."

Fiona remained seated, staring at her hands.

"I know you don't want to hear it, but I *do* love you. I'm sorry about your sister. I'm more sorry you believe I purposely deceived you."

She kept her eyes averted, her hands crossed on her stomach.

"I'll go. I hope you have a healthy baby and that you find the happiness you deserve." I leaned over and kissed her forehead. "Take care." I straightened up and walked to the doorway. "Good-bye."

At the front door, Anya was telling Mary about Chance and the meadow. I picked her up and kissed her cheek. "Mary, take care of— What

247

I mean is— " I shook my head. "She's made her decision. I hope you know you had two amazing daughters. You're very lucky."

"Don't cry, Mam." Anya patted my face.

I shook my head. "I'm not . . . it's okay."

I turned back to Mary and handed her my card. "If you ever need anything, don't hesitate to call.

Chapter Fifty-Two

January 29, 2009

"WELL," MARY SAID. "Do you believe her?"

Fiona nodded her head. "Yes. It all fits. I think she's told us everything."

"She's an interesting character. Don't you think?"

"How do you mean?"

"She's so loving, protective when talking about Karilcah and Anastasia. But when discussing that priest, the church, and Karileah's attacker, she turns murderous."

"What did you expect? That bastard raped Kari. He knew he was sick and he didn't care. He might as well have shot her dead that night."

"But then we wouldn't have Anya." Mary laid her hand over Fiona's. "Maybe that's the same conclusion Kari came to. Maybe she accepted the gift as God's reasoning."

Fiona turned to look at her mother. "You're right, we have Anya. I hope Kari found comfort in that as well."

"She must have."

"Why do you say that?"

"You said there's pictures of their life together and that Kari is smiling in them. That she loved Anastasia. What more proof do you need?"

As Mary set about making dinner, Fiona came into the kitchen and sat at the table.

"Just eggs, Mom, I'm not up to anything heavy."

Mary put their place settings out. "What are you thinking about?"

"Everything."

"About Maddison?"

"Yes. She looks awful."

"How so?"

"She's lost weight, and she . . . she just . . . that scar is ghastly."

"You're the reason for it, aren't you?"

"Yes."

"Wanna talk about it?"

"It was the last morning I was there. She was furious. She thought I had tricked her. She accused me of lying about who I was. I was just as mad. I called *her* a liar. I lost my temper. I knew she wasn't telling me everything. I was so frustrated that I threw the picture at her."

"The frame she claimed was broken?"

"I believe so, yes. It was the only one not in the box. It was on the nightstand next to Anya's bed when I picked it up. I vaguely remember the frame cracking open and papers slipping out after I threw it. But I couldn't swear to it."

"So you both told the truth, and yet neither is willing to apologize? You just might have met your match for mulishness."

Fiona didn't answer; she knew it wasn't true. Maddison came, she explained everything, answered all questions, pledged her love. Maddison had nothing left to apologize for.

"Mom?"

"Hmmm."

"What was the offer she couldn't refuse?"

"You"—Mary smiled—"I promised her she'd get to see you."

Over the next ten days, Fiona found herself constantly recalling everything Maddison told them. It all fit once she separated her anger and looked at the facts. Maddison had omitted some truths, but she hadn't lied. On the other hand, Fiona was a stranger, why would Maddison share personal details surrounding Anya's birth. She had already admitted that she and her wife weren't in love. That they were just friends. How many times had she referred to her therapist as an angel? How did Fiona miss that? As for the pen name, it probably was because women authors aren't always taken as seriously as their counterparts. Hell, women in general are never taken as seriously as their counterparts, no matter the profession.

That's what the missing pieces were—the facts. That's why Fiona always thought something was off. It was. Maddison protected the specifics. The rape, the virus, Anya's test results. She did it for her daughter and for Kari's memory.

TWO WEEKS LATER Fiona emerged from her room waddling slowly, one hand on her back the other holding her stomach. "Mom?"

Mary was in the living room reading the Sunday paper. "Hmmm?"

"It's time. I need to get to the hospital."

"Are you sure, you're not due—

"My water broke and I'm having this baby, now!"

Mary jumped up and reached for the phone. She called her next door neighbor. Helena said she would be outside in two minutes with the engine running.

"Where's your bag?"

"On my bed."

"I'll get it."

Eleven hours later, a baby girl made her appearance. Mary watched the birth, sweating along with Fiona during each contraction. Fiona yelled and cursed throughout the birthing process. Mary kept a mental record, she intended to remind Fiona about it later.

"Arghhhh."

"Once more, Fiona, stay with me."

She gritted her teeth and pushed. A second baby slipped from her womb.

"Holy mother of God," Mary said.

"What's wrong?" Fiona leaned up to see.

Frances Baker, Fiona's friend and OB-GYN, looked over the sterile mask. "It's another girl."

Fiona fell backwards. "Twins! I had friggin' twins?"

Mary started chuckling. "I'm thinking Anya has the sister she always wanted, plus a spare."

Fiona glared at her. "Cousins, mother, cousins."

"Time will tell."

Mother and daughters were kept in the hospital for two days. The next morning, after stopping on the way to buy a second baby carrier, Mary arrived in a taxi to take them home.

She entered Fiona's room, eager to see her grandbabies.

"Arghhh."

"That's where I left you yesterday."

"Not funny, Mom." Fiona settled one of the girls against her breast. "Shouldn't this just happen?"

Mary used her finger to nudge the child, and soon she was suckling with ease. "Have you picked names yet?"

"Thank you. Yes." Fiona said. "This is Kaylah, and that one is Kadyn."

Mary picked up Kadyn and peeked under the blanket. "And now the fun begins."

"How am I going to handle two babies?"

"Same as you would have one."

"You know what I mean."

"It will work out." Mary cooed at the baby. "I have faith."

I have faith. That's what Maddison had said as well. Fiona had thought of her all through the delivery and last night before sleep took her.

The nurse entered the room. "Are our new mommy and babies ready to go home?"

Fiona groaned. She sure hoped so.

THE NEXT TWO weeks proved to be a learning experience for all. Fiona found she *could* handle motherhood and that caring for the girls was exactly what she'd dreamed of. Mary helped only when asked, and enjoyed watching her grandbabies come into their own.

"How'd the checkup go?" Mary asked.

Fiona had insisted on going to the doctor's alone. The girls needed to be able to depend on her and she needed to be up to the task. "Well

Kadyn's diaper needed changing and Kaylah threw up on me, but we're all alive and safe."

"It won't be the last time they get dirty, or that your upchucked on."

Fiona set them on the changing table. "Mom, could you help?"

"Gladly."

After each child was changed, fed, and burped, Fiona put them down for their nap.

"What did the doctor say?"

"They're healthy, growing, and perfect." Fiona laughed.

"I doubt she said perfect, but we'll let it slide. Want some tea?"

"Please."

They sat at the kitchen table with a baby monitor next to Fiona's cup. "I resigned my position at the clinic this morning."

Mary sipped from her cup.

"You're not going to say anything?"

"You'll tell me when you're ready."

"I've been doing a lot of thinking."

"So you've figured it all out, have you?" Mary watched Fiona's eyes.

"I've accepted another position."

"I wasn't aware you were looking?"

"I know someone who knows someone who does the hiring. The position is mine if I want it."

"And you do?"

Fiona placed her hand over her mother's. "I do."

"When do you leave?"

Fiona shook her head. "How did you know?"

"The worried look on your face. Can't be about the job or you wouldn't take it. That leaves me. I'll miss you and the girls, but I want you to be happy."

"We will be."

"Have you told Maddison?"

"This isn't about her—it's about me and the girls. What's best for us."

"I don't understand."

"I can't beg Maddison for forgiveness. It's too much to ask of her. But I *am* taking the position in Yaak. They'll provide a house and a stipend. I won't get rich, but I'll be able to take care of the girls full time. They won't grow up in the care of you or a baby sitter. "

"You do intend to tell Maddison, don't you?"

"Mom, I know she said she loves me, but so much has happened. I hurt her . . . terribly."

"The last thing Maddison said before she left here, was for me to take care of you. Does that sound like she's mad? You need to talk to her, to let her know how you feel. Let her know you love her—she deserves that much."

"I can't. I—I'll think about it."

Mary glared at Fiona. "What do you have to lose? Your pride? Maybe, but think of what you might gain."

Fiona stared at her mother a moment, then shook her head. "I'm going to take a shower and a nap while the girls are still down." She turned and walked out of the room.

Chapter Fifty-Three

AFTER LEAVING PENNSYLVANIA, Anya and I returned to the city early that evening. We parked Marni's car in her parking slot. Tomorrow we would return her keys.

"Mam, can we visit Fiona again?"

"Maybe someday. What do you want for dinner?"

"Pizza."

"Pizza it is then. Come on."

Two days later, I did the interview for the GLAAD network. As much as I hated doing a personal appearance, I understood the necessity now that I had been outed as a woman. At least the truth was out there and I was telling it. Marni and I discussed every possible scenario and believed we had them covered. In the end the public would make the final determination about my books. The sticky part was when the interviewer asked about the dedication in *Vigilante*.

I smiled. "My wife was a very special woman that no one could ever replace in my heart or in my life. But I've been lucky enough to find another true love. That's priceless for me." After that exchange, I refused to comment on any other personal matters.

"Why hide your sexuality?"

"I think you mean sex. The easy answer is, publishers treat women as lesser human beings. Unless the book is a romance, we have no credence in their estimation."

"Is Carey Troye a lesbian as well?"

"Yes."

"Do you expect a backlash because of your gender or your character's? Do you believe the public can't handle it?"

"I believe the patriarchal publishers would have you believe a person of my gender can't possibly write sound crime mysteries, that only men are capable of doing so. In fact, Agatha Christie proved she could write mysteries many years ago. Patricia Cornwell does crime mysteries better than most men. JK Rowling wasn't famous using Joanne, but as JK, she's known worldwide and has become a billionaire. As for what the public's perception will be, only time will tell."

"Will we see Carey Troye involved romantically?"

"Not romantically, no. But for the first time you will see an emotional response from the character. She's friends with the victim in *Vigilante*."

After the almost two-hour interview, I headed back to Marni's office to pick up Anya. Tomorrow we would travel back to Montana. I looked forward to the flight home. I needed time to think about all that had happened.

The flight *was* a time of reflection for me. I thought a lot about Fiona and her mother. About the way they handled the news regarding Priss. Fiona had believed she was addicted to drugs; she evidently didn't know her sister at all. I'm not sure exactly what her mother imagined, but I hoped I had put their minds at ease. Losing a child or sister is one thing, finding out that the person died through no fault of their own would eventually bring peace. And maybe that was Priss's intention all along. To give them peace.

"YOU'RE BACK."

"We are." Chance nearly knocked us down in excitement and had Anya giggling at the dog's antics.

"Come in. I've been cooking all day. You need to eat better, start taking care of yourself," Lorraine said.

"This is for you." I handed her the bag of bagels.

"I will be your slave forever." Sophia kissed my cheek.

At the dinner table, I heaped my plate with chili and rice. I bit into my second piece of bread as Anya regaled her Nanas with stories of our trip.

"Did you know'd I have 'nother grandma?"

Sophia nodded. "I did. Was she nice?"

"She made me cookies. I see'd Fiona too. She's having my sister."

"Your sister?" Lorraine asked.

"Uh-huh," Anya answered.

"Anya, I told you, the baby will be your cousin."

"But I want a sister," she whined.

I shook my head. "Help me out, will ya?"

"Anya, did you ask Mam for a sister?"

Anya nodded emphatically.

"Well, maybe try Santa Claus this time," Sophia said. "He's much more powerful."

"Well *that* was helpful."

"Relax, it was a joke."

"Does she look like she's laughing?"

Later, Anya helped Lorraine with the dishes while Sophia and I had coffee and talked. "How did everything go?"

I grimaced. "It's over with for another year, or until I write a new book. The interview should air in a couple weeks. The good news is, I no longer have to struggle to avoid pronouns." I shrugged.

"I meant with the lady doctor."

"Oh. Not as bad as it could have."

"Did you two talk?"

"We did. I answered all her mother's questions."

"The truth?"

"Yes. They know everything . . . all of it."

"Anya?"

"Yup."

"And?"

"I don't know what you want." I stood and walked to the window, dusk was coming on fast.

"Did it affect the way they look at her? Anya?"

I turned and sat back down. "No, I don't think it did."

"Even the mother?"

"She's not happy with the diagnosis, but she didn't hold it against Anya or appear put off by it."

"Good."

"She wants to keep in touch."

"Understandable. It's her grandchild."

"Yeah, but soon she'll have another. Doc looked like she was about to pop any moment now. Time will tell."

"Did you tell her you loved her?"

I stared at Sophia. "She's known since November."

"Did you say it?"

"Yes."

"And?"

"Nothing."

"Nothing? Could you elaborate a little?"

I sighed deeply. "I told her I loved her. That I was sorry for what happened. She didn't respond."

"Then I'm sorry. This will pass. You'll get over her in time."

"I know."

Chapter Fifty-Four

March 16, 2009

MARY AND FIONA had talked in depth about the move and about whether or not to notify Maddison, but Fiona remained adamant about not informing her. One evening, as Mary was searching for something to watch on TV, Maddison's face quickly flashed on, then off the screen. Mary hit the back button—it was the GLAAD interview with Maddison promoting *Vigilante.*

"Fiona! Come in here!"

"Mom, are you trying to wake the bab—" She spotted Maddison on the television and sat down. "Turn it up, please."

Mary raised the volume.

The interviewer was commenting about the gender of the author. She prodded Maddison to discuss the dedication in the book. Maddison said she loved a very special woman just before the program went to commercial. Fiona sat silent till the commercial ended.

The host was back smiling, she mentioned that the GLAAD interview had been previously recorded.

Based on the details Maddison provided, the new book was clearly an adaptation of Karileah's story. Maddison told the host that part of the proceeds from the book would go to AIDs research.

The last revelation Maddison provided about the new book was that her private investigator, Carey Troye, would be emotionally involved for the first time.

"So the new book is a romance then?"

"No, I don't write romances."

"But you just said—"

"I said Carey would be emotionally involved. In my previous books, she's never reacted to a murder. She follows the facts, deciphers truth from fiction, and determines the guilty party. This time she'll deal with the pain of losing a friend and investigating her death."

"Care to tell our viewers more about your special lady?"

Maddison steepled her fingers and looked directly into the camera. "She knows who she is. That's all I need to say."

The show ended on that note.

MARY STEPPED OUT onto the sun porch and handed an iced tea to Fiona. She had been resting there while the twins napped.

"Fiona Margaret, I love you. You've been a good daughter and I'm proud of you, but you can think a thing to death."

Fiona said nothing and sipped from her tea.

"Well?"

Fiona gazed up. "Once again mother, you're right."

"And?"

"And I guess I have shopping to do."

"Shopping?"

"I have to prepare for my new life. She had been mulling over everything ever since her mother revealed Maddison's parting words about taking care of Fiona and that she, Fiona had made her decision. Now with the interview and Maddison saying it herself, she felt hopeful. *I love her. She loves me.* Fiona repeated the mantra until she almost believed a future together was possible.

OVER THE NEXT month and a half, Fiona was too busy making arrangements and following through to worry whether the decision was right or not. She had made it and now she would live with it.

The first task was to sell her Outback in lieu of a truck worthy of the Montana winters.

"I assure you this vehicle will meet all your needs, and that you'll like the terms."

Fiona turned to the salesman. "Listen, *I know it will.* I've done my due diligence—I did my research." And she had. The truck would give her twenty-three miles per gallon while still providing the heft and power she needed. The cab would easily accommodate two adults, the twins, Abby, and their paraphernalia. The new ride had a heavy-duty heater, heated seats, and a GPS system. Nothing else was necessary.

"How much?"

The salesman ran his finger around the inside of his collar. "I'll run the numbers."

"Don't bother, I have a print-out off the internet. Beat it and we have a deal."

He took the proffered paperwork and stared at it. "I'll need to run this by my manager."

"Tell him it's a cash deal."

The manager came back with the contract ready for signature. Forty-five minutes later, Fiona drove home in her new truck. She would register it in Montana and avoid duplicate sales taxes.

"What do you think, Mom?"

Mary walked around the truck.

It was huge in comparison to the crossover she had traded in, but clearly would better fit Fiona's needs.

"I like it."

Fiona nodded. "Me too. I thought I'd have trouble driving it, but it was a breeze. Best of all, there's side airbags to protect the girls."

"I'm glad." Mary nodded. "What's next?"

"We start packing." Fiona led the way into the house. "I'll have most of the items shipped, but the girls' stuff will come with me."

"That's smart."

MARY WATCHED THE girls, while Fiona took charge of packing. "I'm going to miss you, and these little angels."

Fiona looked up from the box she was stuffing clothes into. "I have to try, Mom. I'll never rest if I don't."

"I agree." Mary looked up from changing Kadyn's diaper. "What would you say if I took the trip out with you? I'd get to see Karileah's meadow before another year goes by and see the place you and the girls will be calling home."

"I'd love the company."

"And don't worry, once you're settled, I'll fly back."

"You know there's always a chance Maddison may not welcome us."

Mary peeked over the rim of her glasses. "You don't really believe that."

"I can't get my hopes raised. I need to stay focused. I have a job waiting, if nothing else."

"Want some tea?"

"Yes, please."

Fiona continued packing. She wanted to be on the road by May 6th. She anticipated the trip taking between six and seven days. Less time would be too hard on her and not safe, and longer was just delaying the inevitable.

"Tea's ready."

"Coming."

"I'm glad you're coming with me. It will make the time go faster, and you'll be there to help me with the girls. Most importantly, though, you can keep me calm. My nerves are frazzled already."

"Selfishly, I want more time with my grandbabies."

"And I want more time with you."

"Have you called her to say you're coming?"

Fiona shook her head. "No. I want it to be a surprise. I need to see her face when I talk to her. I need to watch her eyes. I'm making all these plans for a life together, and she may say it's too late. That she hates me."

Fiona put aside the list she used to check off her chores and grasped her mother's hand, needing the comfort as well as the connection. "Oh God, what am I going to do if Maddison's changed her mind about us?"

"Fiona, you know damn well Maddison loves you. She will welcome you with open arms. So . . . when do we leave?"

Fiona nodded. "We'll leave end of next week. If I've calculated everything correctly, we should arrive at the cabin by May twelfth the latest." *Two more weeks before I find out if she's still wants me.*

Chapter Fifty-Five

May 8th, 2009

"MAM?" ANYA CALLED.

"Yes, baby." I was in the kitchen cooking.

"Did my sister get borned?"

I walked around the counter and picked up her. "Munchkin, you have to listen to me. Fiona's baby will not be your sister or brother. It will be a cousin."

"But—"

"It will never change. I can't make the baby be a sister for you."

Anya's bottom lip began to tremble.

"I'm sorry, Munchkin, but there's nothing I can do."

"You marries Fiona like with Mama."

"Where did you get your single-mindedness?"

"What's that?"

"It means you don't listen to reason." I kissed her cheek. "Did you do your lessons?"

"All but my letters."

"Then go do them, so I can finish up in the kitchen."

"Okay."

I went back to cooking. Today's plan was to prepare meals and use the time to work out the details for my upcoming book. A scrap of an idea kept replaying itself in my head. The morsel had been trifling with me for weeks but my mind refused to let it grow. It needed to blossom so I could expand the fundamentals into a full blown book.

Instead of following the plan, my mind kept wandering back to that little town in Pennsylvania. Fiona should have had the baby months ago. Hopefully it was healthy and everything she wanted.

I shook my head and concentrated on cooking. At least that was something I knew I could handle.

LIFE ON THE mountain got back to normal. Upon waking each day I handled the chores for the running of the house. After breakfast, Anya, Chance and I went to the meadow to visit Kari. The flowers we planted bloomed along with the wild ones Mother Nature provided. The entire field popped with bright colors and the flowers swayed in the gentle breeze.

"Mam?"

"Yes."

"Can we visit the Nanas soon?"

"What a good idea. We need to fill the pantry and it's a perfect time for a visit."

"I want to teach them my letters."

"Show them, Sweetie."

"I wanna see their new puppy too."

"I knew you had an ulterior motive." Anya had been talking about the puppy for three weeks. I was surprised she waited this long.

"When can we go?"

"How about Tuesday."

"Okay."

Anya sat beside the stone marker, chatting to Kari as if she were sitting there listening. It was heartwarming to see exactly what Priss had hoped for.

THE WEATHER WAS turning warmer quickly. Buds were blooming, the grass was green and thriving. Propane and coal deliveries were due any day now. A storm was predicted to hit by the middle of the following week. Late squalls normally left after a day, but they could still be a nuisance.

I called Sophia to check if Tuesday would be a good time to go to town for supplies and let Anya visit with them. I discovered Lorraine would be tied up with the new doctor who had been hired, but Sophia was more than happy to babysit while I went into Libby.

"Have you heard from the sister of late?" Sophia asked

"No, why?"

"No reason. Just curious."

After chatting a few minutes longer, I offered to pick up anything they might need while I was in Libby.

TUESDAY, AFTER DROPPING off Anya, I headed down the mountain. It was a quick trip, as I had already faxed in the order with my credit card information. The supplies were waiting when I arrived, and the round trip took less than four hours.

"Mam, Mam, come see." Anya ran to meet me, while Sophia held the door.

I walked into the kitchen. Chance and the puppy were playing tug of war with a knotted old towel.

"Wow, what a cutie."

"When my sister comes, we're gonna get a new puppy, too."

Sophia arched her eyebrow.

"Anya, we talked about this." She ignored my admonition and turned to play with the dogs.

"What's with that?" Sophia asked.

"I think she's just lonely."

"You knew that was a possibility here, but she's so insistent about a sister. Something I should know about?"

"She . . . she's convinced Fiona's child will be her sister. I've been telling her that's not going to happen, but . . . "

"You haven't heard from the Doc at all?"

"No, and I don't expect to."

"You never know, she could change her mind."

"Not gonna happen, and what's worse is Anya has the same stubborn streak in her."

Sophia gave my shoulder a reassuring squeeze.

"Come on, Anya, we need to head home."

After having gotten up early and then playing with the dogs all day, Anya fell asleep on the ride home. I was glad as it gave me time to ponder the issue of Fiona's child being Anya's sister. We'd discussed it, and I had explained that the baby would be a cousin and yet it fell on deaf ears. I needed a new strategy to get through to Anya. First I needed gas, I stopped at the station on the edge of town.

I turned into the drive and slowly made our way up the slope and around to the barn. A new four-wheel-drive, quad-cab truck was parked on the side of the church. I didn't recognize it, and the only identification was the new dealer sticker in the rear window.

After the automatic garage door slowly opened, I pulled into the slot and turned the engine off.

"Come on, baby, we're home." I lifted Anya out of the back and put her down. "Wanna help with the groceries?"

She rubbed her eyes, but nodded. "Okay."

I handed her the paper products. "Be careful and wait for me."

"Who's that?"

I focused on the truck again. Frankie, the park ranger, had mentioned a new vehicle last spring. "I'm not sure, maybe it's Uncle Frankie."

"Yay." Anya started to run, the bag dragged behind her.

"Wait for me!" I gripped two bags then hurried after her.

Chapter Fifty-Six

May 12, 2009

I JOGGED PAST the unfamiliar truck and rounded the building. Must be Frankie, probably wants to play some chess. "Anya, wait up."

While in town, I had picked up our mail. I carried that as well as the bags as I made my way to the door. The TV was on, obviously Frankie was making himself at home. As I climbed the stairs I realized I was glad for the adult company. I missed Fiona like hell and Frankie would provide an opportunity to vent freely. Sophia and Lorraine were insistent I reach out and they refused to believe that door had been slammed shut.

"Anya, I think Uncle Frankie is here."

"Yay." She ran up the stairs and pushed through the door. "Uncle Frankie, where are—"

I looked up, nearly falling against the door jam. A yellow lab burst through the opening with Chance happily racing after it.

Fiona croaked. "Hello."

"Fiona! Fiona! Is my sister here?" Anya ran to her.

I couldn't stop staring at Fiona. She nodded to Anya and bent to hug her hello, but her eyes never left mine. She picked up Anya and kissed her.

"That was Abby, right?" I asked.

"Yes, we brought her with us."

"Where's my sister? Can I see her? Is she here?"

I walked further into the room. "Anastasia! We've talked about this, I want you to stop this nonsense."

Fiona lowered her to the floor. "I do have a surprise for you, honey."

Dejectedly, Anya looked between us.

"Well, hello there." Mrs. Gallagher walked out of the bathroom.

"Grandma!" Anya ran to her.

"Hello, Anastasia, how are you." Mary Gallagher bent to kiss her hello.

"Hi." I walked to the counter and dropped the mail and my bags there. "What . . . umm . . . I mean . . . what." My heart was racing, I was sure she could hear it thumping in my chest.

"Mam, can I have my surprise?" Anya asked.

"Yeah, sure. Go ahead. I've got groceries in the truck and I need to get the rest of them."

"I can help." Fiona said.

"Nah, it's okay. Anastasia will burst if you don't let her see the baby."

Fiona nodded. "Okay."

Forty minutes later I returned with the last of the bags.

"You feeding an army?"

I rolled my eyes. "I hate shopping, so I stock up when I go."

"Good idea." She poured a cup of coffee and handed it to me.

"Where's Anya and your mother?"

"They're in Anya's room. She's showing Mom Kari's pictures. They look really nice hung up."

I shrugged. "I should have done it when we moved here. I wasn't sure it was good for Anya, but I was wrong. She needs to see her mother, to remember their good times."

"I agree. I'm glad you changed your mind for Anya's sake."

I placed the final box of cereal on the shelf and rolled up the shopping bag for the next time. "You look good. I mean . . . because . . . well the baby."

"I thought you forgot about the baby."

"Never." My voice cracked. She looked so damned good it hurt.

"Mam, Mam, did you see'd." Anya ran out of the bedroom.

"Anya, remember what I told you about shouting," Fiona said.

"Sorry, Fiona." Anya tiptoed closer and began pulling on my arm. "Come see. Wait till you see." She held her finger up to her lips.

I let Anya tug me into her room. A bassinet had been placed in the corner under the window, fading sunlight sifted through the glass. As we approached my breath caught and I turned back to Fiona who followed us. "Two? Twins?"

She nodded her head, grinning from ear to ear.

"Twins!" I leaned down and peeked at them closer. "They're beautiful," I whispered, "just like their mama."

"I gots two sisters," Anya said.

I picked her up. "You have to be quiet, or you'll wake them."

She covered her mouth with her hand.

Mary sat on Anya's bed staring at the pictures of our life with Kari.

"Karileah was very happy. The pictures don't lie." Tears rolled down her cheeks.

I stepped closer and squeezed her shoulder. "She was, I promise you. Stay, and visit awhile." Anya and I walked out into the nave, with Fiona right behind us.

"Twins. I never imagined." I put Anya down. "I don't know what to say, but it's . . . it's perfect. Congratulations. Did you know in advance?"

"No."

"No?"

"Last fall when I lost my job, I lost my medical coverage. The clinic I found work with offered to do an ultrasound for me at cost. After the initial one, there wasn't a medical need for more. Ironically the doctor never heard a second heart beat."

"Is that normal?"

"Maybe not normal, but it happens. Not often, but it definitely happens."

"Wow. It's terrific. I'm really glad for you."

"So, who's Frankie?" Fiona asked.

"He's . . . I told you about him. The park ranger. He comes and plays cards with us. He's teaching Anya how to play chess." My hands were sweaty and I could barely catch my breath.

Fiona nodded. "Hmm that's right. I remember now."

Mary walked out and sat on the couch. "Can I get a cup of coffee?"

I nodded unable to speak.

"I've got it." Fiona poured the coffee and brought it to her mother. "Here you go."

Mary looked from one of us to the other. "I asked Fiona to bring me here so I could visit Karileah's meadow. I'm not sure how many more years I have, and I didn't want to miss it. I hope you don't mind."

"What? You're not sick . . . I mean . . .You're okay aren't you? Is anything wrong?"

Fiona sighed.

Mary shook her head. "I'm not sick, but I *am* getting older. I wanted to be sure I visited her resting place before I die." She lowered her voice and leaned closer to me. "Breathe. You look like you're going to pass out."

"Oh."

Mary set her mug on the table. "I saw the interview you did. Heard you talk about the book, that drug, and the danger to young women. You were so vehement about it. Thank you for telling Kari's story."

"The interview"—my voice rose a few octaves—"you watched that?"

"I bought the book too. I'm half way through it."

"And I finished last night before falling asleep," Fiona said.

FIONA TOUCHED MY arm. "Mom's pretty tired from the trip. Would it be okay if we stayed the night. She can share Anya's room, you can go upstairs, and I'll take the couch. Tomorrow, we'll visit the meadow and then we'll get out of your hair . . . I promise."

I frowned. "It's fine. You know that." I looked down where Fiona was touching me and shivered. "You're welcome here as long as you want. Uh . . . the sheets need to be changed down here. Chance sleeps with Anya at times. The hair—" I rubbed my forehead. "I better go find the dogs."

Fiona went to the front door, opened it, and whistled loudly. Within minutes Chance and Abby bounded into the house, both of them panting. They flopped down by the hearth and quickly fell asleep.

"Okay." I started for the linen closet. "There is another choice of sleeping arrangements."

Fiona looked on. "What's that?"

Sisters

"After I change the sheets in Anya's room, your mom can take her nap. But we could move the crib upstairs to the den, and Anya can sleep with the twins in there on the roll away."

"You have a new bed?"

"I got one this spring."

"And who's taking the master?" Fiona asked.

"You are. You need to be near the babies"—a thought ran through my head—"unless . . . if you're worried about Anya being near the girls?"

Fiona looked confused, then shook her head. "The only issue I have, they tend to wake up at least twice a night to be fed. Can she sleep through that?"

"I don't know. There's only one way to find out."

She nodded. "I'll fix dinner while you get everything set up,"

"You're cooking?" I looked at Mrs. Gallagher. "I guess a lot of things have changed."

Fiona threw the sponge at me that she was using to wipe down the counter. "Don't get smart."

"You're the one who said you can't cook."

"But I do ready-made meals like a French chef."

I turned to go get the clean sheets.

"Maddison, is there makings for the chocolate chip cookies?"

"Depends on who's baking them? " I said.

"I help," Anya volunteered.

"Make sure she does it right, Munchkin."

Anya giggled as she climbed up on the counter. "Structions is on the bags."

"Big mouth," I said.

"Here I thought it was your recipe, you big phony," Fiona said.

I chuckled, grateful I had remembered to get the components. "I just bought six bags of the chips. They're in the cabinet with everything else."

"Excellent. Anya and I will whip them up."

I entered the bedroom as quietly as possible. Soon both babies were either fussing or crying. I ran out. "They're awake!"

Fiona peeked at the clock. "They're hungry and probably need to be changed." She washed her hands. "Could you get the beige duffle bag and a package of diapers out of the truck for me?"

I quickly went and got the requested items. Back in the bedroom, both babies were on Anya's bed, Fiona was undoing the diaper on one, and Anya was talking to the other.

"Here."

"Thanks."

"You bought a truck?"

"Hmm, yeah, I need it for my job."

"Mam, look how small," Anya whispered.

"Okay, we're gonna switch now." Fiona had swapped out a dry diaper on the baby before her.

"Want help?" I asked.

"Can you remember how to do it?" Fiona asked.

I nodded. Then walked around the bed and undid the tape on the other baby's diaper.

Anya wrinkled her nose. "Eww!."

"You did the same thing when you were little."

I used a wipe, cleaned the baby's bottom, then sprinkled powder and lifted her legs to slide a clean diaper under her butt.

"You're good at that." Fiona said. "I need to feed them before I fix dinner." She began unbuttoning her shirt.

I turned my back quickly. "I'll move the crib upstairs. Anya you help Fiona with the babies."

"What are you doing?" Anya asked.

"This is how I feed the babies."

"Can I watch?"

I collapsed the crib, and rolled it toward the door. "Anya, don't become a pest."

"I won't, Mam."

As I was leaving, Mrs. Gallagher came to the door. "I thought you all got lost in there."

"Fiona changed the babies, and now she's feeding them."

I continued up the stairs to the den where I put the crib under the window and set up the fold-away against the desk. Then I changed the sheets and put clean towels in the bath.

FIONA SAT ON the couch, one baby in her arm, the other lying on the cushion next to her.

"It's a little cool in here. Would you like me to start a fire?" I asked. Everything was set so I simply lit the match, and pulled the damper. The flame caught quickly.

"Thank you," Fiona set the baby on the couch, pushed the coffee table up against it and went to the kitchen. "I'll go start dinner."

"Will they be okay, there?"

She laughed. "They're not mobile as yet, and Anya is watching them for me.

"I helped," Anya said nodding. She sat on the edge of the couch, ogling the girls. "They don't do much."

"That's cause they're little yet. Give them a few months."

I followed Fiona into the kitchen. "I can do the cooking, you can be with them."

"Let's do it together. It will go quicker."

I nodded. "What are their names?"

"The one closest to Anya is Kaylah, the other Kadyn."

"Nice. They really are beautiful. And you're terrific with them. I told you, you would be."

"You did."

"Your mom sleeping?"

"Yes."

I walked to the wall and turned the ceiling fans on low. "That will send some of the heat into her room."

"Thank you."

DINNER SIMMERED ON the stove, a united effort for sure. "Want me to make the cookies?"

"Do you mind?"

"It's fine. Go check on the babies."

"Actually, I'm going to get my luggage and change. I've been in these clothes for two days," Fiona said.

"Why not take a nice hot shower?"

Fiona turned to the couch. "My number one babysitter appears to be sleeping on the job."

I looked up and chuckled. Anya slept next to the twins. "Go on, I can watch them all."

"Are you sure?"

"I remember how to deal with a crying baby. Go, relax."

"Thank you." Fiona leaned closer and kissed my cheek. "I'll hurry."

"No rush."

Fifteen minutes later she came down the stairs in sweats, looking fresh and relaxed.

"I love those shower heads. And the dial to set the hot water—it's to die for."

"Get a grip, it's just hot water."

She went to the babies, repositioned one of the twins on the cushion to provide more room for Anya.

"I'm guessing Kaylah will be walking soon."

Fiona looked at me strangely.

"What did I say?"

"You said Kaylah, how did you know?"

"You told me?"

"But how did you remember who was who?" Fiona asked.

"It's not that hard to tell the difference. Kaylah is a little bigger and she has more hair."

Fiona nodded. "You're right?"

"I pay attention."

"Yes, you do. Your turn—go take a shower and relax. You look tense."

I nodded and headed upstairs.

FIONA WAS ON the couch nursing Kadyn when Mary entered the living area.

"What'd you do with Maddison."

"She's in the shower."

"You're smiling, I assume you've talked?"

"Actually no, she's trying to avoid that. She assumes we're here so you can visit the meadow."

"Why is that good?"

"Because she still loves me." Fiona sighed.

"Hell, I could have told you that weeks ago." Mary sat in the chair across from her. "When are you going to put her out of her misery?"

"Tonight, Mother, tonight." Fiona was already scheming.

Chapter Fifty-Seven

May 12, 2009

DINNER WAS A quiet affair. Fiona had the table set to make room for the twins to be next to her in their carriers. The meal was linguini with Alfredo sauce, garlic bread and salad. I opened a bottle of Merlot for all of us.

"Fiona tells me there's an extensive collection of movies upstairs. That you have a library in your den."

"Yes"—I gazed at Fiona—"I've always loved to read, and I can never part with a book, so the collection just keeps getting bigger and bigger."

"Don't you get lonely here all alone?"

I hesitated before answering. "In the past, it never really bothered me." I shifted my eyes toward Mary. "I love this place. Kari and I had plans for it. Now, Anya, Chance, and I have a workable routine." I shrugged. "Anyway, with my writing, I'm not always very good company. I get driven."

"Did she distract you from your work last year?" Mary asked, tilting her head toward Fiona.

"Ahh . . . no. Once she was mobile, I worked almost every day. Some of her comments even had me rethinking the women in my stories."

After Fiona and I cleared the table, we brought out the coffee, cookies, and milk for Anya.

"These are good, very good," Mary said. "Mine didn't turn out this well."

"Mam says it's the love." Anya's face was smeared with chocolate.

During dessert I tried to tell entertaining stories about the church, the renovations that were done and about learning to run the guts of the house. Fiona yawned at one point and I took that as a cue.

"Anya, go clean up, it's time for bed."

"Okay."

The twins were already upstairs. I had remembered a baby monitor Kari had insisted we buy. I found it in the basement and set it up for Fiona.

I was upstairs settling Anya in for the night. "Remember . . . you have to be quiet," I whispered.

"I will."

"And if you hear a noise, it's Fiona coming to feed the babies or change them. Don't get up."

"Okay."

"I love you, Munchkin."

"Love you, Mam."

BACK DOWNSTAIRS, I peeked around and saw only Fiona. "Where's your mom?"

"She went to bed. Could we talk a minute?"

"Yeah, sure." I sat in the side chair.

"I'm sorry about your eye." She held her hands out in an almost pleading gesture. "I have a temper and . . . I was wrong. I feel awful."

"It's no big deal. I'm fine."

"But I could have blinded you!"

"But you didn't. It was a crazy time. We both said things in the heat of anger."

Fiona moved to the end of the couch closer to me. "I'm worried about you. You don't seem to be taking care of yourself."

"I'm fine."

"You've lost weight."

"I was overweight to begin with."

"I don't know how to talk to you anymore."

I avoided meeting her eyes. "I get it. You think I lied, or at the very least avoided the truth. I understand you can't forgive that." I stood up. "I'm gonna take the dogs out, then get some sleep. It's been a long day."

At the door, I called to the dogs. They both jumped up and ran through the door ahead of me.

HOURS LATER, I came through the front door with the dogs. We had walked to the meadow and back, because I needed to think . I needed a distraction.

"Mrs. Gallagher, I didn't see you there," I said, startled. The dogs bounded up the stairs, and I heard the thump when they jumped on Fiona's bed.

"Can I get you anything?"

"It's Mary, remember? And I'd love a drink . . . something with a kick."

"I'm a scotch drinker."

"What else you got?"

"Brandy or wine"

"I'll take the brandy, and bring the bottle." Mary plopped down on the couch and turned on the TV. A DVD of a Bette Davis black and white movie was cued up .

I sat in the side chair facing her. "Something bothering you? I thought you were tired."

"To be honest, I wasn't tired. I had hoped that you and my daughter would talk"

"We did. She's worried about my health. I've lost some weight, but I needed too. So, it's all good."

"Jeeze Louise, is that all she said to you?"

I felt the color drain from my face. "If this is about custody—"

She threw up her hand. "It's not, I promise you."

"What did I do wrong?"

"Why are you so sure it was you?"

I shrugged.

Mary sighed. "You know it's not any of my business, but a blind person can see you love my daughter."

"I do. I already said as much."

"Fiona loves you too. That's why she's here." Mary sipped her drink.

"I don't believe that."

Mary slapped her hand on her leg. "I swear you and Fiona are the two most pig-headed people I know."

"Mom, can you give Maddison and me some privacy?"

I jumped up, surprised to see Fiona at the top of the steps. "Were you listening?"

"That's my cue. Mind if I take the bottle?" Mary asked.

"Yeah, it's fine." I watched Fiona come down the stairs, baby monitor in hand. She kept coming until she was inches away.

"I love you," she said. "I should have started today with that."

"Whadda ya mean?"

"I mean, I love you. I'm in love with you. I'm here because you are. Because I'm hoping we can start over"—she tilted her head—"and because of the job in town."

"The job in town? They hired a doctor. Lorraine was showing her around . . . today." My eyes grew wide as the truth dawned on me. "That was you!"

"It's a terrific opportunity for me. They'll provide a house if I need it and a small salary so I can stay at home and raise my girls."

"You're moving here? But you hate the weather, hated being housebound, and missed having people around."

"I'm told a snowmobile is the transportation of choice."

"I thought you hated the cold?"

"I'll get used to it. I have two daughters that I can't stand to be away from. This job allows me to be a full-time mom and to earn a living."

I shook my head. "You're just full of surprises."

Fiona backed up.

I watched her eyes. "Wait. I love you too."

"Took you long enough to say it." She stopped retreating.

"I just . . . I can't believe . . . your friends . . . your mom—"

"Those people I missed so much last year, other than my mother?" She pulled me to the couch. "They're all hypocrites. I got to see them with different eyes when I returned. It made me think about a lot of things. Things I once felt were important just don't matter anymore."

"Like?"

"I was sure I'd want to go back to work once the baby was here. Back to my career. After the girls were born, I didn't want them out of my sight. You were right—it kicks in and I would kill anyone who tried to get between us."

I nodded knowingly.

"I discovered we don't need a lot of money to be happy. Enough to feed us and provide for their education. But *I* want to raise them. I want to be there every day watching them grow. Like you do Anya. I won't pay a nanny to be a substitute mother."

I reached over and gripped her hand. "And us?"

"There's a couple of things you need to know."

"Okay."

"Did you ever wonder why Kari asked you to deliver the letters to Mom and me?"

"To be honest, I was a little pissed off about it." I shrugged. "She should have done her own dirty work."

"She wanted us to meet."

"Then she should have introduced us."

"She knew you'd never allow yourself to become attracted to me or anyone else while she was still alive. She also said you deserved happiness, and someone who loved you. She told me I'd be a fool to let you get away."

"She was playing matchmaker?" It was hard to absorb what Fiona was saying. I shook my head. How could Kari have known? I got up and walked to the fire. I shoveled ash away from around the hot coals, then loaded three logs onto the grate. Then I remembered a conversation we'd had before Anastasia was born.

"You don't need to do this," Priss said.

"Are you kidding me? I get to marry my best friend, and I get a full-time therapist and a beautiful daughter—what more could I ask for?"

"Someone to love you?"

"Think about it. You *do* love me, and I love you . . . just not that way. It's still a gift."

She nodded. "I do love you. You realize you're gonna have a hard time explaining me to your dates."

"We've lived together for three years. How many women have you seen banging down my door?"

Priss reached out and cupped my face. "They're fools. I wish—"

"No regrets, just say, yes."

She closed her eyes, and when she opened them, there were tears. "Yes"—she took a deep breath—"but I want you to be happy, to find someone special to love you, and not as a friend."

"We'll have a good life for as long as it lasts. And Anya will want for nothing. I give you my word."

"Kari was incredible," I said.

"She thought the world of you. She loved you—"

"I told you it wasn't like that."

"I know." Fiona nodded. "I've *always* believed that part of your story. I never doubted your protectiveness toward Kari and Anya."

"But there is something that's bothering you. I can tell."

She pushed her hair behind her ears. "Yes, this has been troubling me since I finished the book last night. First, let me say, I love you. I accept whatever the truth is, but I need to know."

"Go on?"

"Did you kill him?"

"Who?"

"Roberto Ortiz."

"Is that what's bothering you? You think I killed the bastard?"

"Your book describes his last moments pretty graphically."

I took a deep breath. "It wasn't me."

Fiona nodded her head and averted her eyes. "Okay. We won't talk of this again."

I tipped her face up forcing her to meet my eyes. "It honestly wasn't me. But I never shed a tear about his passing."

I grasped Fiona's hand and walked toward the counter to turn on my computer. I pulled up a copy of the police blotter for the night Ortiz died. Then I pulled up the itinerary from our trip to Mexico. "Here, read this. Please."

Fiona leaned closer.

"This is the report surrounding Roberto's death, note the date." Fiona nodded. "This is a trip your sister and I took. She had read about a new procedure being tested down in Juarez. We flew to Mexico to meet with the doctors and staff. We were there for a week. Feel free to call and verify any of this."

Fiona threw her arms around my neck. "Thank you." She kissed me on the lips and pulled me closer.

After the kiss, I pulled back. "You believe me?"

"I do." She kissed me quickly. "I just needed to know. I love you no matter what. I don't want there to be secrets between us."

"Then you should know, I *was* a suspect. The police took me in for questioning. I told them I was innocent. At first, Kari questioned my guilt, too. She knew how much I hated that bastard. I had sworn to kill him a number of times, believe me. And I would have, given a chance. The police interrogated Kari across the hall from me. That's when she realized she was my alibi and I, hers. She gave them all the info for the trip to Mexico and the doctor's name. They checked it out, and I was cleared. Well, we both were."

"Did they find your vigilante?"

"They were close, but he died. The case was dropped after that."

"Do I want to know?"

"The gunshot was self-inflicted."

"Officer Delgado?"

I looked at her in shock. "How do you know about him?"

"You mentioned him in one of your books. I tried to get in touch with him when I was in LA. They told me he died back in 2003. Everything fits."

"He was in love with your sister and I'm pretty sure she loved him too."

"Then why . . . why commit suicide?"

"They met the December before her attack. They started dating almost immediately. It was getting serious." I took a deep breath. "Kari never came back from the rape. He came to visit often . . . she just couldn't let go of what happened. He told her he didn't care about the assault, that he loved her and her baby. He wanted to marry her. He didn't care about the illness. He tried everything to convince her. In the end, he did the one thing that gave her a modicum of peace."

"He killed her attacker."

I nodded. "Once the investigation turned away from me, and Kari still couldn't return his feelings, he . . . well . . . he ended it."

"That's when you and Kari became a couple?"

"The medicine really was prohibitive. We needed a way to get it legally."

"I hope they're together now."

"Do you believe all that crap? In the afterlife?"

She nodded. "I do."

"Damn, you're just like her."

Fiona giggled. "What can I say? We were raised together."

"Heaven help me."

Chapter Fifty-Eight

FIONA ROSE EARLY the next morning. By the time Maddison came up from working on the coal furnace, Fiona already had the bacon frying and the coffee made. She poured a cup when Maddison walked into the kitchen. "Here you go." Fiona handed it to her and leaned over and kissed her cheek.

Maddison almost dropped the cup. "I'm not complaining mind you but what was that for."

"For being willing to watch a movie with my mother. For taking time to talk to her when I know you probably wanted to work. So, thank you. After all, we did just drop in on you."

"Jeeze, you don't have to thank me. Your mother's a nice lady. I like a woman who can hold her liquor."

Mary walked into the kitchen. "Am I interrupting?"

Fiona looked up. "No mother we were just talking about all your bad habits, and how you need to clean up your act."

"Humph, first I need coffee. Then you can tell me about my faults. Just remember I know yours as well. And, I have a bone to pick with you."

Fiona was scrambling the eggs for omelets when the baby monitor squawked. "Damn."

"I'll go." Maddison said.

"Do you mind?"

"I'd mind more if I had to cook the omelets. You do them much better than I do." Maddison headed upstairs.

"You need to talk to that poor girl," Mary said.

"I did."

"And?"

"She loves me."

"Humph, tell me something I don't know."

"We talked—"

The dogs suddenly bounded down the stairs.

"The girls are hungry and I can't do that," Maddison said. She came down the stairs, a baby in each arm, and Anya holding onto her shirt. "They're dry and clean though."

Anya ran to Mary. "Grandma, we're going to see Mama today."

"I know, I can't wait." Mary clapped her hands in excitement for Anya.

Fiona reached out. "Give me Kaylah . . . she's the loudmouth."

Mary went around the counter and took the spatula. "I'll finish these."

Maddison turned Kaylah over to her mother, and cooed at Kadyn. "Kaylah must take after your Momma, huh Little One?"

"You'll pay for that one," Fiona said as she pulled her shirt aside and tugged at the cup on her bra. Maddison whirled around, putting her back to Fiona.

"You might as well get used to this."

Maddison nodded, but never turned back.

"Can I watch?" Anya asked.

"Of course you can, Sweetie."

"Mam, did Mama feed me this way?"

"No"—Maddison blinked away her tears—"she couldn't."

"Why?"

"Ahh—"

"Some mommies don't make milk," Fiona said.

"Oh, okay."

Maddison turned and mouthed a thank you to Fiona.

ONCE BREAKFAST WAS over, I went out to get the ATV. I hooked the jitney up and securely strapped the baby carriers in the back, then pulled the ride up to the front steps.

Fiona was standing on the landing watching. "What's this?" She asked.

"This is our ride up the mountain."

She laughed. "I see the girls are going with us?"

"They have to get used to how things are done up here."

"I'll go get Mom and the girls."

Anya passed Fiona on the landing and asked me. "We go now?"

"In a minute, Munchkin." I went inside and scooped up Kaylah from her place on the couch. Fiona already had Kadyn in her arms.

Mary looked from one to the other of us. "Looks like you two settled things."

"Are we ready?" I asked.

I helped Fiona strap the girls into their carriers. We placed Anya in the middle to protect her as well. Then I laid a blanket across the three of them to keep the wind off them. Fiona sat sideways across the back of the jitney, and I helped Mary into the passenger seat up front.

"Wait," Fiona said. "Can I cut some flowers from out front to take for Mom? I think she wants to put something at the memorial, you know, for Kari."

"You've never seen the meadow except in winter. Trust me, she'll be pleased with how it looks. I promise."

The trip was short, and I took it slowly so as not to bounce the girls around too much.

"That's one hell of a slope," Mary said. She held on with two hands, but seemed to be enjoying herself.

"It is, but it's great exercise." I pulled up next to the opening and turned the engine off. Both dogs ran up as I climbed down. "Wait for me to help you."

I walked around the back of the unit. "Everyone okay back here?"

"Next time, I need a cushion," Fiona said. Anya giggled.

We released the carriers and lifted the twins down. "They can stay in these. I'll carry them, you go with your Mom."

"I don't remember where the opening is." Fiona said.

Anya took her hand. "I'll show you, Fiona, this way."

Mary gasped at the array of color that greeted them as they walked through the narrow opening.

Flowers of many species and colors covered the grounds. Some were annuals, many were wild perennials, all were beautiful. Pathways cut between the plantings were for walking and inspecting. The sun, high in the sky, lit the area brilliantly.

"This is not what I expected. Fiona described the meadow to me, explained about the trees towering around the area, but this . . . this is amazing. This goes way beyond anything I imagined. Karileah would have been so happy with this."

Fiona's eyes filled with tears as she looked out over the landscape. "Look, Mom, there are paths throughout the plantings over the entire meadow." Fiona turned to me. "You did all this?"

"Not by myself. Kari found this spot. She loved it here. She'd sit here for hours. Said she found peace here. After she was too sick . . . well . . . later, I hired a professional. I gave him pictures of the flowers that Kari planted at our LA house. I asked him to replicate it . . . he did."

Fiona threw her arms around me. "Thank you, it's beautiful."

"Careful, I'm carrying precious cargo here."

Fiona leaned in and whispered. "You're just lucky Mom and Anya are here."

After walking along the paths, Mary and Fiona sat on the bench with Anya between them. Mary proceeded to name every plant and told of its origins. "It's so beautiful here," she said. "I can see why you come here to talk to her. I can feel her spirit." Mary turned her face to the sun and let the rays warm her skin. "I think she's truly at peace."

Tears ran down my face. I hoped Mary was right.

Fiona stood up and told her mother it was time to get back. The emotional impact of the meadow had taken its toll on both of them, but Mary did not want to leave. Fiona looked at me pleading.

"We'll come back tomorrow for another visit. This place belongs to both of you as much as to Anya and me. If Kari's soul is here, she would want both of you here with her."

Mary gripped my arm. "Maddison you did a fine job with this place. It's a real tribute, I thank you." She pulled me into her arms and held me tight. I stood there, arms at my sides, holding the twins in their carriers.

"I'm glad you approve and I'm happy you think Kari would have too."

WHEN WE ARRIVED back at the church, Sophia's truck was parked out front. "We apparently have company," I said.

Fiona nodded as I helped her with the babies. "They're here to give me the key to the house."

"Oh. I thought . . . I hoped—"

"It's about time you got back here." Lorraine was at the door, holding it open.

"Nana!" Anya ran up the stairs.

I looked up. "I wasn't expecting you."

"We're here to see the doc."

I helped Mary up the stairs, and Fiona to the door with the twins. "I've got chores to do, I'll be in, in a while."

"Maddison?"

"It's all good. I understand."

Fiona stood still, a baby carrier in each hand. She had tears in her eyes. "Enjoy your visit."

I went back outside and took the ATV back to the barn. Towards the west, gray clouds swirled over the mountaintops below. It looked like a storm was brewing. I loaded up the fire rings on the porch, then carried enough wood to fill the ring by the hearth.

With nothing more to do, I headed back in with the wood. The dogs met me at the front door. "Behave you two, we have company." I pushed through the door. A sheet hung from the banister, Fiona stood below it, the twins at her feet in their carriers, Anya holding her hand, dancing in place. I looked up again, the white sheet had black writing on it. I read the words, 'Will you marry us?' There was an arrow pointed down where Fiona, the twins and Anya stood giggling. I turned to Mary, she nodded. Sophia and Lorraine stood in the kitchen watching, waiting.

I looked back at the sheet, the words echoed in my head. 'Will you marry us.'

"You better say yes, or you're gonna get hit with something real quick," Mary said.

"Yes." I said in her direction. Then I turned to Fiona. "Yes, always and forever, yes." I rushed over to her and pulled her into my arms. "I love you."

"I love you too."

Anya screamed in glee then ran to Mary. "They're my sisters now, right?"

"Yes, they are," Mary said.

Sisters

Anya ran to Sophia. "It worked, I asked Santa and it worked. I haft two sisters now." She ran to us and I picked her up. "You win, Munchkin, you get your sisters and a new mother."

Anya hesitated but a second. "I'll be Fiona's too?"

"If you want to be, yes. But you can still call me Fiona. I never want to take your Mama's place."

"Okay."

"I'd say this calls for a drink," Sophia said.

"Here, here," Mary added.

Chapter Fifty-Nine

May 13, 2009

MUCH, MUCH LATER that night, long after the Nanas left for home, after the twins had been put down for the night, and after Mary and Anya had gone to bed, Fiona came down the stairs.

Maddison was sitting in the chair staring into the fire.

"What are you thinking about."

She put her arm out and pulled Fiona onto her lap. "You."

"Good answer." Fiona leaned down and kissed Maddison.

"I love you."

"I love you too." Fiona kissed Maddison, a simple brush of the lips, then she took the kiss deeper. She sighed deep in her throat.

Maddison pulled back. "What's wrong?"

"Nothing, absolutely nothing. In fact everything is perfect. You're perfect, our children are perfect, and we're all going to be very happy." Fiona shook her head. "I never imagined when I got lost last fall that my life was about to change so drastically, that I was going to achieve all my dreams simply because of a wrong turn."

Maddison leaned closer and kissed her softly. "Don't forget your sister's part in all of this."

"How do you mean?"

"Well the little matchmaker was determined we would meet, even if you hadn't gotten lost."

Fiona nodded. "True, very true. She was emphatic that I give you a chance, that you deserved a woman who would love you and put you first." Fiona clasped Maddison's hand. "I'm going to do everything to make myself worthy of you."

"Worthy of me? Are you crazy. I never expected to find love. But I knew the day you walked into my life that nothing would ever be the same."

"We should go to bed."

"We should?"

"Definitely."

She led Maddison up the stairs and into the bedroom. "I love you Maddison Delanie and I'm going to spend the rest of my life showing you just how much."

Maddison visibly gulped. "I'm really nervous. I want you so badly, but I want it to be special."

Fiona pulled Maddison's T-shirt over her head. "Oh my. I've dreamt of this." She tilted her head down and started kissing Maddison's breasts.

282

"Me too," Maddison croaked.

Fiona avoided her nipples, though they hardened under their own power.

Maddison wanted to reciprocate, but Fiona was determined to maintain complete control of their love making. "No touching, I'm going to make love to you." She moved her mouth back up to Maddison's as her hands dropped to her jeans.

"Wowza." Fiona mumbled against Maddison's lips. She undid the button and slowly lowered the zipper, the pants fell down on their own accord. "I've fantasized of doing this for weeks." Fiona pushed Maddison back onto the bed and climbed up beside her. Fiona kissed her breasts as she pushed her thigh between Maddison's legs and thrust up against her center. "Tell me what you want?"

"You, just you." Maddison's whole body jerked. "Please get undressed. I need to feel your skin against me. You're driving me crazy."

"Good." Fiona stripped immediately, needing the touch of skin as much as Maddison. "I love you Maddison, let me show you how much." Fiona laved Maddison's breast, drawing it into her mouth, suckling greedily.

"Oh god."

Fiona's hand played with Maddison's other breast, squeezing it. Rolling the nipple between her fingers as it hardened even more. A moan escaped Fiona.

"Fiona, please," Maddison begged.

Fiona leaned up and kissed her. She rocked her thigh, adding pressure to Maddison's center and felt the warm stickiness against her skin. Maddison was soaking wet and arching to meet Fiona's thrusts. "You belong to me. Tonight and always."

"Yes. Oh god, Fiona, I'm gonna come."

She concentrated on Maddison's lips, kissing her, swallowing her moans as they moved together.

Maddison gripped Fiona's hips, pulling her tight against her center. Needing the contact, craving the release. "I'm gonna come. Inside . . . please, I can't take anymore."

Fiona moved her mouth to Maddison's breast, taking the nipple between her lips. She felt the jolt rush through Maddison's body as she slid her fingers through her neatly trimmed curls. She plunged two fingers into Maddison's warm, moist folds. Maddison groaned as Fiona pumped her fingers in and out in unison with the thrust of Maddison's hips.

"I'm on fire, please I can't take much more, I'm so close."

Fiona worked her way down Maddison's body. "Soon, love, soon." Maddison had her eyes closed. It was an intoxicating sensation for her to realize that Maddison was hers to do with as she wished tonight and all the nights to come.

Maddison thrashed about as Fiona pushed deeper inside.

She needed to taste Maddison. As Fiona lowered her mouth and took the hard clit between her lips, she felt Maddison shudder beneath her. She knew Maddison was on the precipice, she curled her fingers pushing rhythmically, feeling the first flourish of contractions as she took Maddison over the edge.

Maddison dug her hands into the sheets, her head was pushed back against the pillow, her teeth gritted, as Fiona sucked her clitoris between her lips.

"Oh, yes, there. I'm coming, I'm coming."

As the last of her climax spread through her, Fiona slid up her body. "I needed you."

After a while, Maddison stuttered. "Wow, just wow."

Fiona groaned and pulled Maddison over on top of her. "I want to hold you. I've missed holding you. I've missed you so much."

They made love twice more. Each time right after a baby feeding.

Fiona couldn't remember ever being so happy. Completely and utterly sated and content. "We're gonna kill each other if we keep this up."

"Yeah, but what a way to go."

WHEN I WOKE early the next morning, I turned to look out the window. "Oh boy!"

"Hmmmm, what's wrong?" Fiona's face was buried in my neck.

"The good news is, I have a large supply of brandy on hand."

"Huh?"

"Look outside."

Still naked, Fiona jumped up and walked to the balcony to look out the front doors. There was over six inches on snow on the landing outside and it was still falling heavily. She came back to bed and leaned over me.

"You still have to marry me when this clears. Being stranded with my mother, however long, will not release you from your promise."

"I'd marry you anywhere, anytime"—I captured her lips in long slow kiss, loving the taste—"but you're gonna break the news to your mother."

Fiona swatted my arm. "Chicken."

The End

About The Author

DeJay's short stories include "Who's In Charge" and "Silent Journey" in *Khimairal Ink* (Bedazzled Ink), October 2008; "Bareback" in *Lesbian Cowboys: Erotic Adventures* (Cleis), 2009; "Silent Journey" in *Year's Best Lesbian Fiction 2008* (Nuance/Bedazzled Ink), 2009; "Never Too Old" in *Lesbian Lust: Erotica Stories* (Cleis), 2010, and in *Best Lesbian Erotica* (Cleis), 2012.

DeJay's novels, *Redemption*, and *Strangers* are available through (Lesbian Fiction Press), 2013

DeJay and her lovely wife of 36 years live in their log cabin in the rural mountains of Pennsylvania with two year old Abby, their fur baby.

Elisabeth Glaser Pediatric AIDs Foundation

The Elizabeth Glaser Pediatric AIDS Foundation has reached **20 million women** with lifesaving services, such as HIV testing, counseling, and treatment, to prevent HIV-positive women from passing the virus to their babies – a significant milestone worth celebrating in the effort to achieve an AIDS-free generation.

Each day, 700 children worldwide become infected with HIV (UNAIDS 2013), 90 percent of whom will contract the virus through mother-to-child transmission. Without diagnosis and treatment, one-third of infected infants will die before the age of one, and almost one-half before their second birthday.

EGPAF's program implementation efforts seek to extend HIV prevention, care, and treatment services to at least 80 percent of children, women, and families affected by HIV in the countries where we work.

Key programmatic areas that EGPAF supports include:

- Preventing Mother-to-Child Transmission of HIV
- Care and Treatment for Children, Women, and Families Living With and Affected by HIV
- Health Systems Strengthening
- Community Engagement
- Strategic Information and Evaluation
- Research

Donate today -
https://secure.pedaids.org/page/contribute/donate-to-egpaf

A portion of the royalties from the sale of this book will be donated to the EGPA Foundation.

Another Book By DeJay

Redemption

Architect Mackenzie Taylor will tell you she's married, that love transcends eternity, and vows are meant to be honored. She builds homes through her business, helps to rebuild lives through her volunteer work at a women's crisis center and strives to build self-esteem in children with special needs as sponsor and coach of Team Bella. What she can't rebuild is her family. The deaths of her wife, Isabella, and their daughter, Bella, haunt her every breath. While she attended a business meeting they were kidnapped and senselessly murdered. The guilt is all encompassing.

Emily O'Brien, a widow, and straight, arrives in town to open KK's Book Emporium. She lives in the apartment above the store where she struggles to make a new life for herself and her orphaned grandchildren.

Renee McVee's partner, Emily's daughter, was killed by a drunk driver, on the way to pick up her children from school. Renee's response to her grief is to drown her sorrows.

Redemption takes a gritty look at domestic violence and how it influences the lives of these three women and how they learn to deal with the devastating fallout. It's also a story of love, old and new. It answers the questions, is it possible to love again? Is it possible to forgive yourself? Is it possible to find redemption?

Another Book By DeJay

Strangers

Justina Murphy has lived on the streets since the age of thirteen. Outed by her best friend, Justina was beaten extensively by her mother then thrown out of the house. She has spent the last thirty years building a life for herself, a place where she feels safe, has the amenities she was deprived of growing up and finally a certain sense of peace.

Victoria Cartwright works for DCS, Department of Child Services. Her job is to convince Murphy to make changes to her very minimalist life, to open her home and her meager bank account to two strangers. Victoria needs to do this while struggling with her own demons.

Jesse has very specific instructions from her mother. She's the eldest and responsible for her baby sister, Brianna. It's her job to look out for them and to help her aunt learn about love, trust and family. Jesse is also struggling with her sexual identity, even in 2003 this can pose a problem when attending Catholic High School.

The three women come together, the fights are explosive, the learning curve more like an insurmountable mountain, and the results provide answers to a suicide that has hung over Murphy's head these last thirty years.